P9-DCP-979

TIT FOR TAT

"I'd really like to hear the reason you look so . . . flustered."

"I don't think," Annie said, "that you could handle it."

"I'm a big boy. Try me."

"I was wondering what it would be like to go to bed with you." She turned and sashayed past him and out the door. "Coming?" she called over her shoulder. *This is somebody else in my body. This isn't me saying these wild things. I never said anything remotely like that to a man before . . .*

She turned to look. He had followed her.

"Sit!" he commanded. "I'll be right back."

Annie sat. She waited and waited. *I scared him off.* She stood up.

"I thought," he said, returning, "I told you to sit."

"I was sitting. Now I'm standing. What difference does it make? You tell dogs to sit, not people." Annie sat.

"Now close your eyes."

Annie closed her eyes.

It was the sweetest, the most demanding, the most wonderful kiss she'd ever received in her life . . .

Also by Fern Michaels

ANNIE'S RAINBOW

FERN MICHAELS

Zebra Books
Kensington Publishing Corp.

http://www.zebrabooks.com

For my friend Helen Kraushaar.

ZEBRA BOOKS are published by

Kensington Publishing Corp.
119 West 40th Street
New York, NY 10018

Copyright © 1999 by First Draft Inc.
Fern Michaels is a registered trademark of First Draft, Inc.

All rights reserved. No part of this book may be reproduced in any form or by any means without the prior written consent of the Publisher, excepting brief quotes used in reviews.

If you purchased this book without a cover you should be aware that this book is stolen property. It was reported as "unsold and destroyed" to the Publisher and neither the Author nor the Publisher has received any payment for this "stripped book."

Zebra and the Z logo Reg. U.S. Pat. & TM Off.

First Printing: April, 1999
20   19   18   17   16   15

Printed in the United States of America

CHAPTER ONE

Annie Clark opened the door to the old-fashioned drugstore. She loved the sound of the tinkling bell hanging from an ancient nail at the corner of the door. For one brief second she wondered if she could steal the little cluster of bells. No, better to tuck the sound into her memory bank.

How she loved this little store. She sniffed as she always did when she entered. The smell was always the same—Max Factor powder, Chantilly perfume, and the mouthwatering aroma of freshly brewed coffee from the counter tucked in between the displays of Dr. Scholl's foot products and the Nature's brand vitamins.

She'd worked here five days a week for the past six years. She knew every item on every shelf as well as the price. Thanks to Elmo Richardson's mother's recipe, she knew how to make and serve the best tuna salad in the world to the students of Boston University. On the days she served cinnamon coffee and the tuna on a croissant, the lines outside the store went around the block. Yes, she was going to miss this place.

As Annie made her way down the aisle, she cast a critical eye over the shelves. Who was going to take her place? Would they love Elmo and the store the way she had? She reached out to straighten a row of Colgate toothpaste boxes.

"Annie! What brings you here today?" the wizened pharmacist asked.

Annie smiled. "I guess I need my drugstore fix for the week. Did you find someone to take my place?"

"I found someone, but he can never take your place, Annie." The pharmacist twinkled. He looked down at the bottle of aspirin in her hand and clucked his tongue. "You won't be taking those tablets after tomorrow, will you?"

"I'll probably be taking more. Just because I'm getting my master's doesn't mean my troubles will be over. I have to find a job and get on with the business of earning a living. One of these days, though, I'm going to start up my own business. You just wait and see. I'm going to miss you, Elmo. You've been more than kind to me all these years."

"I don't understand why you have to leave immediately. Don't you think you've earned the right to sleep in for at least a week? What's the harm in delaying your trip for a few days?"

"The rent is up next week. When I get to Charleston and find a place to live, I'll sleep in for a few days. It's a beautiful day, isn't it, Elmo?"

"One of the prettiest I've seen in a long time. Good weather predicted for tomorrow, too. I'm closing the store to attend your graduation," Elmo said gruffly.

"Really! You're *closing* the store!"

"Yes, and the dean gave me a ticket for a seat in the first row."

Annie walked behind the counter to hug the old man. "I don't know what to say. My brother wrote to say he couldn't make it. Mom doesn't . . . what I mean is . . . oh, Elmo, thank you. I'll be sure to look for you."

"I'm taking you and Jane to dinner afterward. Won't take no for an answer. I might even have a little gift for the two of you." He twinkled again.

Annie laughed. "Don't forget, you promised to write to me. Oh, oh, what's that?" Annie asked, whirling around.

"Backfire. Dang bunch of kids racing their motors is what it is," Elmo grumbled.

Annie pocketed her change. "I'll see you tomorrow, Elmo."

"You bet your boots you'll be seeing me. Go on now. I know this is your sentimental walk before it all comes to an end. Walk slow and savor it all."

Tears welled in Annie's eyes. "I will, Elmo."

"Git now, before you have me blubbering all over this white coat of mine."

"Did I ever tell you that you've been like a father to me, Elmo?"

"A million times. Did I ever tell you you were like a daughter to me, Annie?"

"At least a million times," Annie said in a choked voice.

"Then git!"

Annie fled the store, tears rolling down her cheeks.

She rounded the corner, walked two blocks, sniffling as she went along, before she cut across the campus parking lot. She was aware suddenly of running students, shrill whistles, and wailing police cars. She moved to the side to get out of the way of a careening police car, whose siren was so shrill she had to cover her ears. "What's going on?" she gasped to a young girl standing next to her.

"The cops just shot someone. I think he's dead."

"Was it a student?" Annie crossed her fingers that it wasn't someone she knew.

"I don't know," the girl said in a jittery-sounding voice.

Annie advanced a few steps to stand next to a police officer. "What happened, Officer?"

"Two guys robbed the Boston National Bank. One of them got away, and the other one was shot."

"Oh."

"Move along, miss, and be careful. Until we catch the other guy, don't go anywhere alone and keep your doors locked."

"Yes, yes, I will."

Annie weaved her way among the rows of cars, passing her own Chevy Impala, the bucket of bolts that would hopefully get her to Charleston, South Carolina, the day after tomorrow. Parked right next to her car was Jane's ancient Mustang. She took a moment to realize the windows were open in both cars. Neither she nor Jane ever locked their cars, hoping someone would steal them so they could collect on the insurance. It never happened. She shrugged as she eyed the array of cars. Beemers, shiny Mercedes convertibles, Corvettes, and sleek Buicks. All out of her league. Any car thief worth his salt would go for the Mercedes or the Beemers. She shrugged again as she made her way to the small apartment she'd shared with Jane for the past six years.

Annie opened the door to the apartment and immediately locked it.

"Oh, Annie, you're home. Thank God, I was worried. I just heard on the radio that the bank was robbed. I have three hundred ninety-five dollars in that bank. What's it mean? Is that what all the ruckus is about out there?"

"Yes. I was talking to one of the cops, and he said not to go anywhere alone and to keep our doors locked. One of the gunmen got away. My two hundred eighty dollars is in that bank, too. They're covered by insurance, but I'm taking mine out first thing in the morning. How about you?"

"I think we should go now and do it."

"We can't. The bank is a crime scene now. Tomorrow it will be business as usual. I don't think we have anything to worry about."

Jane Abbott crunched her long, narrow face into a mask of worry as all the freckles on her face meshed together. Her curly red hair stood out like a flame bush as her paint-stained fingers frantically tried to control it. Annie handed her a rubber band. "I'd kill for curly hair," Annie muttered.

"Not this hair you wouldn't. I've been cursed. As soon as we get to Charleston, I'm getting it cut. We're doing the right thing, aren't we, Annie?"

"I think so. We promised ourselves a year to work part-time and to do whatever we wanted before we headed for the business world. It won't be like we aren't working. We proved we can live on practically nothing for the past six years. We can do it for one more year. You're going to paint, and I'm going to serve coffee and tuna sandwiches in a hole in the wall. It is entirely possible we'll become entrepreneurs. We agreed to do this, and we're not switching up now."

Always a worrier, Jane said, "What if our cars conk out?"

"That's why we decided to take both of them and follow each other, remember? If that happens, we ditch one car and transfer our stuff to the other. It's not like we have a lot of stuff, Jane. Clothes and books, that's it. We can do this, I know we can. Guess what, Elmo is coming to our graduation and taking us to dinner. I didn't tell him about the part-time thing or our hope to go into business. He'd just worry about us. He said he might even have a present for us. We'll be just like everyone else who has someone to kiss and hug them when it's all over. We'll be friends forever, won't we, Jane?"

"We lasted six years, so there's no reason we can't last sixty more. That will make us eighty-six, and at that point we probably won't care if we're friends or not."

Annie laughed. "What's for dinner, or are we going to grab a burger and fries?"

"I'm throwing everything in the fridge in one pot. Whatever it turns out to be is what we're having for dinner. Everything's ready for the new tenant. Sunday morning we'll get up, strip the beds, and roll out of here as soon as it gets light. Do you want to pack up our cars tonight or wait till tomorrow night? Bear in mind that we'll probably be drinking wine with Elmo tomorrow night. We'll have hangovers Sunday morning. It's your call, Annie.''

''We can do it after dinner. Instead of taking all our books, why don't we sell them to the exchange? We can pick up a few dollars, and it will be less of a load on our springs and shocks. It will give us more room for your paintings. There's no way you're leaving those behind. Someday you are going to be famous and these first paintings of yours are going to be worth a fortune.''

''I love you, Anna Daisy Clark. You always make me feel good. We're both going to be famous someday,'' Jane said, hugging her friend. ''I just hope it's sooner than later.''

''We've worked like Trojans for six years. We held down jobs, and we're graduating in the top ten percent of our class. I think that says something for both of us.''

''Don't forget you helped your brother with your mother's nursing-home bills. I'm sorry she can't be here, Annie.''

A lump formed in Annie's throat. ''She'll be here in spirit. I hope I make enough money someday so I can transfer her to one of those places that has rolling green lawns and lots and lots of flower beds. She still loves flowers and gardening. She has little pots of flowers on the windowsill of her room. Sometimes she forgets to take care of them. I'll be able to visit her more often so that's a plus.''

''We'll both visit her. If I make more money than you, and that's probably the joke of the year, I'll help you with her care. I never knew my parents, so that will make me happy. Is it a deal, Annie?''

''It's a deal,'' Annie said solemnly. ''You know what, Jane?

I know there's a pot of gold at the end of our rainbow. I just know it.''

"The eternal optimist!" Jane laughed. "Tell me, are there any red-blooded men at the end of that rainbow?''

"Of course. They're going to sweep us off our feet and make us live happily ever after. Of course I don't know exactly when that's going to happen, but it will happen." Annie caught the dish towel Jane threw at her as she made her way to the end of the hall and her bedroom.

In her room with the door closed, Annie allowed her eyes to fill with tears. Tomorrow would be the end of the long road she'd traveled these last six years. The optimism Jane saw was just a facade for her friend's benefit. So many times she'd wanted to give up, to just get a job that paid decent money, to live in a place that didn't crawl with bugs. She was tired of counting pennies, of eating mayonnaise sandwiches, macaroni and cheese, greasy hamburgers and drinking Kool-Aid because it was cheap. At times she resented the mind-boggling monthly sums of money she had to send for her mother's care. Tom had a good job, but he also had three small kids and a demanding wife. He paid what he could. Tom didn't have student loans the way she did. Tom ate steak and roast beef. She hadn't had a steak in two years. How, she wondered, had she managed to survive all these years sleeping just a few hours each night, studying and working? *If you persevere, you will prevail,* she told herself. She'd done just that. One more day, and it would be the first day of the rest of her life. An adventure. And she was ready for it.

God, I'm tired.

Annie woke two hours later when Jane banged on her door, shouting, "Annie Daisy Clark, dinner is now being served!"

"Be right there."

"This looks, uh . . . interesting," Annie said when she took her place at the table.

"Not only is it interesting, it's delicious. If you don't like the way it tastes, spread the rest of the grape jam over it. At least it will be sweet, and there isn't any dessert. Let's go get an ice-cream cone later. My treat."

"I'd love an ice-cream cone. Shhh, the news is on. Maybe they caught the other guy. I don't know why but that whole thing made me really nervous." Annie's eyes were glued to the small nine-inch television set perched on the kitchen counter.

"Wow! They caught him! Like he really doesn't know where the money is. Do you believe that, Annie?"

"I don't know. There were cops everywhere. They didn't say who was carrying the money, the one they caught or the one that got shot. The campus security team is helping the police so they have a lot of manpower. They'll find it. By tomorrow the money will be safely back in the bank vault. We'll go to the drive-through and close our accounts at eight o'clock when the bank opens. You did good, Jane, this was a decent dinner. I never want to eat macaroni and cheese again as long as I live. You cooked, I'll clean up."

"Do you want to pack up the cars before we go for ice cream or after?"

"Let's do it first. We'll get it out of the way, and we can take a last walk around the campus. It's a beautiful spring night."

"Then that's exactly what we'll do. What did we decide about the books?"

"I called the Book Exchange and someone is coming over to pick them up at nine-thirty. We'll get two hundred and ten dollars. We can stay in a cheap motel one night and not have to worry about making the trip all in one day. How does that sound?"

"Perfect."

"Okay, while you're doing the dishes, I'll go get my car. I can drive yours over, too, if you want me to?"

"That's okay. There are only a few dishes. It's going to take you longer to load your car since you have all those paintings. We'll both finish up at the same time."

An hour later, Annie carried her last suitcase down to the car. Her small carryall with her cosmetics, along with her laundry bag with the bed linens, would be the last thing to go in the car Sunday morning.

"I have some extra room in the backseat if you need it, Jane."

"Do you think you can fit my small easel in there? If you can take it, I'll be able to see out of the rearview mirror."

"Hand it over," Annie said.

"Okay, I'll meet you in the parking lot."

Annie opened the door to shove the easel between the front-passenger seat and the backseat. When the leg of the easel refused to budge, she shoved it with her shoulder. She looked down to see if her old running shoes were in the way. They were, but it was the canvas bag with the black lettering that made her light-headed. Boston National Bank. She swayed dizzily as she lifted the leg of the easel to move it behind the driver's seat. The moment her vision cleared, she rolled up the windows and slammed the car door shut. Another wave of dizziness overcame her as she held on to the door handle for support. When the second wave of dizziness passed, Annie raced into the apartment, where she ran for the bathroom and lost her dinner. She stayed there so long she knew Jane would come looking for her.

Five hundred thousand dollars, the news anchor had said. Two hundred thousand of the five in bearer bonds. Untraceable bearer bonds. In her car. *Call the police. Turn it in,* her brain shrieked over and over. The pot of gold at the end of the rainbow. If she didn't turn it in she could move her mother to a nursing home with rolling green hills and flower beds. She could help her brother Tom. She could set Jane up in a little studio. *Call the police. Turn in the money.*

Annie walked out of the apartment in slow motion, her brain whirling in circles as she contemplated the contents of her car. The bank robber must have thrown it through her open car window when he was running from the police. Surely they searched the area. Would they come back and do a more thorough search? Should she cover it up? Should she pretend she hadn't seen it? What should she do? The pot of gold at the end of the rainbow. Her pot of gold. The news anchor had said the money was in small bills. It wouldn't be traceable. Her battered gym bag found its way to her hands from the trunk of the car. She tossed it on top of the money bag. *No, no, that won't work. If the police do a second search, they might see it in my car and realize that I covered up the money bag. Better to move the gym bag and running shoes to the other side and just toss the easel on top of the money bag. It's dusk. I'll say I didn't look inside. I'll say I just put the easel in and didn't look. How many people look at the floor of the car? I never do. Most people don't. The pot of gold at the end of the rainbow. No one will ever know, not even Jane. I won't tell a soul. Call the police. Turn in the money. I can make Mom's days happier. Tom will be able to spend more time with his wife and kids. Jane needs a chance. Do it. Make a decision. Keep the money or give it back. Keep it or give it back. Yes. No. Call the police. Turn in the money. Decide now before it's too late. Decidedecidedecide. I'm keeping it. No, I'm not. I'm giving it back.*

"Annie. What's wrong? I waited and waited. Then I got scared and decided to come back," Jane said breathlessly. "You look funny. Is something wrong?"

"Kind of. I lost my dinner. I feel kind of wobbly." It was the truth.

"It could be the excitement. I didn't get sick, so it wasn't the food. Stress will do it every time. Do you want to forgo the ice cream and the walk around the campus?"

"No, let's do it. Maybe the ice cream will help. You're probably right, it's stress. I thought it was going to be so easy to walk away from here. We will miss this place." Good God, was this trembly voice hers?

"Any trouble with the easel?"

"No. Actually, there's room to spare. All I have left to put in the backseat is the bedding and my carryall. How about you?"

"I'm crammed to the ceiling but that's okay. Boy, the cops are everywhere. They're checking all the cars on campus. They even went through mine."

"No kidding." Annie thought her heart was going to leap right out of her chest.

"If you don't want them going through all your stuff, leave your car parked here on the street. Just lock it."

"Okay, that sounds good. I probably wouldn't be able to wedge everything in again the way I did the first time."

"Tell me about it. That's what took me so long getting back here. The cop was really nice, though. He said they think there was a third guy, and the one who got shot passed the money to him. Guess it makes sense."

"They didn't say anything about a third man on television."

"It's a theory. If the guy just tossed it, don't you think the cops would have found it by now?"

"Maybe someone found it and kept it," Annie said.

"Are you kidding, Annie? That's a federal rap. No one in their right mind would do something like that. You always get caught in the end."

"Not always. If there was a third person he could be out of

the state by now. If he took a plane, he could be in California. All he has to do is walk across the border. Think about it, Jane.''

''Better him than me. I wouldn't want to live the rest of my life looking over my shoulder.''

''I agree with you. Are they going to search through the night?''

''I got the impression they're just searching the routes the two guys took. They're probably done by now. I saw a bunch of cop cars leaving as I was coming back to get you. Are you feeling any better?''

''A little. I hope I'm not coming down with something.''

''If you are, Elmo can give you something. We could stop by after we do our walk.''

''I'll be fine. Tomorrow is our big day. I guess I just never thought it would get here,'' Annie said, her voice cracking with the strain.

''Okay, what flavor do you want?''

''Rocky Road. I'm going to sit out here on the bench, okay?''

''Sure. Listen, we can sit here and eat the cones. We don't have to do the walk if you aren't up to it.''

''I feel better. It's okay, Jane. Stop fussing.''

''If you say so.''

Annie almost jumped out of her skin when one of the campus police force sat down next to her. ''Evening, Annie.''

''How are you, Kevin?'' Annie asked quietly.

''Tired and hungry. I have to pull a second shift. You want my opinion, that money is long gone. The only thing that makes sense is the guy passed it to a third party. When you don't catch the perp in three hours, it's a lost cause. That's just my opinion, mind you. What do you think?''

''I think I agree with you. Don't they have *any* clues?''

''I shouldn't be telling you this but no, not a one. They got the one guy in jail and he says he was just an innocent bystander that got sucked into this, and he doesn't know anything about the first guy or the third guy. He's sticking to his story, too. They don't share much with us lowly campus police. There's going to be hell to pay because the kid that was shot didn't have any kind of weapon. His father is some Wall Street broker in New York. The other one's father is old money in Boston. Money or not, they'll make an example of the kid. Mark my word. They were best buddies from what I hear, so how could he not know what was going down? Why do rich kids rob banks? Guess I won't be seeing you or Jane after tomorrow, eh?''

"That's right. Sunday morning we're leaving bright and early. It was nice knowing you, Kevin. You take care now. Wait, here comes Jane. I'm sure she'll want to say good-bye.''

Annie listened as Jane made small talk with the campus officer. She licked at the dripping ice-cream cone, Kevin's words ringing in her ears.

"Jane, what do you think about leaving right after graduation tomorrow instead of waiting until Sunday morning?'' Annie asked.

"What about Elmo?''

"Elmo will understand. We could leave around one and drive for six or seven hours and stop somewhere for the night. We'll treat ourselves to a nice steak house and finish up the trip Sunday. Monday morning we'll start fresh on our new lives.''

"That's fine with me. Are you sure you're up to it?''

"I'm sure. Graduation will be over by twelve-thirty. Maybe we could do lunch with Elmo and still be on the road by two o'clock.''

"Whatever you want to do, Annie, is fine with me. We need to get back. The guy from the bookstore is supposed to come by at nine-thirty. We can walk some more after he leaves if you want.''

"Let's see how we feel," Annie said.

It was close to midnight when Annie closed her bedroom door. She thought about locking it, then wondered where that thought had come from. The word *witness* ricocheted around inside her head. There was always, somewhere, somehow, a witness to everything in life. How could this time be any different? Didn't the police take photographs of the crime scenes? Of course they did. But, was the campus parking lot part of a crime scene? Would her car show up in some photograph with the license plate showing clear as day? Of course it would. Sooner or later they would track down her car through DMV. It wouldn't matter what state she was in. If she could make it to South Carolina, as planned, trade in the car or junk it, hide the money, she would be okay. She was in the drugstore with Elmo when the robbery occurred. She was safe in that regard. She'd walked home. Kevin or one of his colleagues would be able to testify that her car was in the lot. Kevin checked the lot hourly to be sure every car parked had a university sticker on it. He constantly teased her about her bucket of bolts and all the rust on the chrome. Kevin would remember. Kevin knew she and Jane were leaving right after graduation. They'd even talked about it earlier in the week. Yes, lunch with Elmo was necessary. A quick lunch. She really wasn't deviating from her plan.

I guess that means you're planning on keeping the money, her conscience needled.

"I haven't decided," Annie muttered.

Sure you have. You already have it planned out. You need to think about what you'll do if you get caught. Jail time isn't pretty. You'd hate it. You can still call the police. You can turn the money in. Or, you could package it up and send it to them tomorrow morning. The post office is open half a day on Saturdays.

It's my answer to a long list of prayers. Do you have any

idea how much easier my life will be? I can pay it back at some point in time. It's for now. Just temporary to get me over this awful hurdle in my life. I swear to God I'll pay it back. With interest. I'm a business major. I know how that works. I can compute interest right down to the last penny. I've never lied, cheated, or stolen a thing in my life. I've worked harder than some men. I've always done what's right. I never begrudged Tom his free education while I had to work for mine. I pray every night that Mom will get better. She won't, but I pray anyway. I can make her life more bright, more cheerful. I can do so much with the money. I'm keeping it!

Someday you're going to regret it.

Someday isn't here. This is today and today I won't regret it. I won't regret it tomorrow or the day after tomorrow, so be quiet and leave me alone. I need to think.

What's Jane going to say when she finds out?

Jane isn't going to find out. Tom isn't going to find out and neither is my mother. Elmo will never know. Those four people are the only people in this whole world that are important to me. The only way they could ever find out is if I tell them. I didn't even open the damn bag. For all I know it could be stuffed with paper. The police and the media could be mistaken about the amount of money.

What about the boy's parents? They have money. They'll hire detectives and detectives sniff around and detectives are like dogs with bones. Their bonuses depend on results. They'll love someone like you. Give it back!

No!

Yes!

Annie bounded off the bed to drag the small slipper chair to the window. She withdrew her diary, one of many she had accumulated over the years. She never went to sleep without writing at least one line about what happened during the day. Someday, when she was old and gray and sitting in a rocker, she would show them to her children and grandchildren. For the *zillionth* time she wished her own mother had done the same thing.

Annie wrote carefully, composing the words in her mind first so she could fit them into the three lines afforded this date. *I saw my own personal rainbow today. It's so strange that I was the recipient of this rainbow and no one else. I view it as a personal message that life will be whatever Jane and I choose to make it as we prepare to start our new lives with all our schooling behind us.*

"If anyone reads this, they won't know what I'm talking about," Annie muttered.

She didn't bother to get ready for bed. She knew there would be no sleep for her this night and probably for many nights to come. Instead, she sat on the small tufted chair and watched her car all through the night.

"It was a wonderful lunch, Elmo. Thank you so much. I'm really going to miss you."

"Me too," Jane said in a choked voice. "Promise you'll come to visit."

The old man nodded solemnly. "Maybe in August when I close the store. Things are slow right before the new crop of students arrive. You can call me from time to time, and letters will be welcome. I do love to get letters."

"At least one a week," Annie promised.

"I have a little going-away present for both of you," Elmo said, withdrawing two white envelopes from his inside breast pocket. "Open them."

Both women opened the small envelopes and gasped. "Elmo, this is outrageous. I can't accept this. A thousand dollars is a fortune. No, no, you have to take this back."

"Annie's right, Elmo. This is beyond generous," Jane said.

"Can't. Won't. It's a gift. From my heart. It's going to be hard for the two of you at first. You need rent money, gas money, jobs. Utilities don't come free, you know. How long do you think those ancient vehicles are going to last you? All I want in return is for you to call and write. I don't want to worry about you. Not another word. I have to be getting back to the store now. Call me collect when you arrive. I want your promise."

Both women wrapped their arms around the pharmacist, hugging him until he cried for mercy. "You take care of yourself, Elmo. Remember now, if we ever get married, you promised to give us away."

"Won't forget. Consider it an honor," the old man snapped, his voice gruff and choked. "You git going now before traffic starts building up on the highway."

"My God, Annie, do you believe this?" Jane asked, waving the check in her hand under her friend's nose.

"I love that old man, Jane," Annie said tearfully. "Let's make the trip all in one day. I'm so wired I won't be able to sleep. We can drive through the night and arrive by morning. What do you say? Are you game?"

"Right now, Anna Daisy Clark, I feel like I could fly to South Carolina. Let's hit the road. We will stop for coffee along the way, won't we?"

"Yes. I guess we should just get in our cars and go," Annie said.

"That's a good plan, Annie. Let's do it."

Annie licked at her dry lips. "Yes, let's do it."

CHAPTER TWO

"Tell me again why you wanted to come to this wonderful, warm, sunny place," Jane said as she leaned back in the booth, at the same time pushing her luncheon plate to the middle of the table. "God, I'm tired. You look exhausted, Annie. Both of us need to sleep around the clock."

Annie sighed, a sound that could be heard clear across the room. She lit a stale cigarette, something she rarely did because she couldn't afford to smoke. "My parents used to bring Tom and me here every summer. I remember how happy I was when I got here. My steps were lighter, my face hurt from smiling so much. I clearly remember the early-evening smell of confederate jasmine and sweet olive. I swear, Jane, the scent used to stop me dead in my tracks. My mother always said she wanted to bottle the smell so she would have it nearby once we got back to Tennessee. They call this the low country, and I swear it has a way of creeping into your sleep until even your waking dreams are filled with its spirit and you find yourself in a longing state. I always said I was going to come here and live someday. Now, I'm here. I hope you're going to love it here as much as I do.''

"I love it already. I don't think I've ever seen such a glorious array of flowers. What did you say that purple hanging stuff is?''

"Wisteria. The big bushes are azaleas and the flowering trees are dogwood. The sweet olive trees are the ones with the little yellow buds. That was a good lunch, Jane.''

"We need to move, Annie, or I'm going to fall asleep. First stop, the bank, so we can open an account. It's going to take at least five days for Elmo's check to clear.''

"You're right. Thank God we have our apartment. I can't wait to see it. The landlady said she would have it all ready. All we have to do is put the sheets on the beds and buy some groceries. We have a roof over our heads for a month.''

Her eyelids drooping, Jane said, "Is our game plan the same? We get part-time jobs as waitresses while we look for a vacant shop to open our own business. In the meantime we send out résumés by the dozen in the hopes someone will snap us up to add to their payroll or are we going to forget about that for the time being?''

Annie crawled out of the booth. "I don't think I've ever been this tired. Let's use the Broad Street Bank for now. Later on we can change if we want to. For now it will fit our needs. All the other stuff we'll just play by ear. I'm too tired to think.''

It was two-thirty when Annie parked the Impala next to Jane's Mustang. "Here we are, one-thirty Logan Street. Apartment Seven. The key is under the flowerpot. I'm just carrying in my bedding. We can unpack the car later.''

"I'm with you,'' Jane said, hauling the canvas laundry bag from the backseat of her car. "Be sure to lock the doors,'' she called over her shoulder.

Annie drew in her breath when she opened the back door of the Impala. For one heart-stopping moment she wished the money bag would be gone. She felt faint when she saw it nestled next to one of her running shoes. Surely it was okay to cover it up now. No one had followed them, no one had seemed the least bit suspicious. Maybe she should just throw the bank bag into her laundry bag.

The moment you do that, you become a thief. A criminal. It's premeditated something or other, she told herself.

I have to move it sometime. The sooner the better. I'm keeping it.

"What are you doing, Annie? I want us both to see our new home at the same moment. Did you lose something?"

"I'm looking for my other running shoe. I found it!" she called as she stuffed the bank bag down deep into her laundry bag. She swore it weighed a thousand pounds as she made her way up the walkway that led to Apartment 7. Guilt was always heavy.

"Okay, open the door, Jane."

"It's not bad," Jane said, looking around. "Actually, it reminds me of the apartment in Boston. It's clean, too. Kitchen is small. Bedrooms are a good size. We can live here comfortably, Annie. I can spruce it up once we get settled."

"The rent is good, it's a quiet little street. I like it that we're close to King Street. That's where all the shops are. We might even be able to get around on foot if our cars give out. Which bedroom do you want?"

"I'll take the one without the wallpaper. Cabbage roses make me dizzy. I'm going to say good night, Annie."

"There's a grocery store on Rutledge. First one up buys the groceries. I expect we'll sleep until tomorrow. Night, Jane."

Annie closed the door. She felt a surge of panic when she saw there was no lock on it. Maybe that was good. The bank bag went under the bed in the blink of an eye. Sooner or later she was going to have to open it. "Later rather than sooner," she mumbled as she whipped out sheets and a light summer blanket. Ten minutes later she was sound asleep.

Annie woke thirteen hours later to the smell of coffee and frying bacon. She realized she was ravenous. "Guess you got up first, huh?" she said, shuffling into the kitchen.

"Sure did. The shower leaves a lot to be desired, but the water was hot. I got everything at this neat little store. We need to find a real grocery store. That one was expensive."

"What time is it?"

"It's eleven o'clock. If you don't dilly-dally, we can be out of here by one. By the way, the phone is hooked up. Do we have anyone to call?"

"Not a soul. This is so good, Jane. Why is it I eat three eggs every morning and you only eat one?"

"Because I am a one-egg person. Maybe someday I will eat three. There's a first time for everything."

Annie felt her heart thump in her chest. It was true, there was a first time for everything. Every criminal did something wrong for the first time. The word *criminal* drained the color from her face.

"You look kind of peaked, Annie. Are you sure you're feeling okay?"

"I'm fine. Maybe I got too much sleep. You know, everything is so new and yet not new if you know what I mean. It was a great breakfast. Do you mind cleaning up?"

"No. Take as long as you need."

Annie bolted for her room. On her hands and knees, she dragged the money bag out to the middle of the floor. Her hands trembling, she undid the metal clasp and dumped the contents on the floor. Loose bills of every denomination, slender packets of bills, and the crinkly bearer bonds littered the floor. She scooped it all into a pillowcase and stuffed it back into the laundry bag. At some point she was going to have to burn the bag and toss the clasp into the ocean just on the off chance that the clasps on the money bags were identical to the bank's logo or crest. At the last second, she pulled out two hundred dollars in twenty-dollar bills. She would need deposit monies at some point. Better not to keep going into the bag.

Anna Daisy Clark, you are now a bona fide criminal. A thief of the first order. If you get caught, you will go to jail. I'm not going to get caught. This is for now. I'm going to pay it back as soon as possible. I'm not just saying that. I will pay it back. I promise.

That's what every thief in the world says when they find themselves behind bars, her conscience needled.

Annie ignored the voice inside her head as she stepped into the shower. Glorious, hot, steaming water pelted her naked body. She washed her hair twice and lathered her body three times before she was ready to leave the little cubicle.

She towel-dried her hair, having no idea where her blow-dryer was. She thanked God again as she always did for her wash-and-wear hair. Dressed in wrinkled chinos, worn sandals, and a tank top, she stood back to survey herself in the blurry mirror. For today it would do.

The diary was in her hands almost before she knew it. She wrote quickly, wanting her small confession condensed in as few words as possible. *We arrived in Charleston yesterday and slept for thirteen hours. All is secure.*

Annie closed the diary with a loud snap. The two hundred dollars went into the pocket of her chinos.

"Where to?" Jane asked.

Annie rummaged in her purse for the small notebook she was never without. "I thought we would apply for jobs at Hyman's first. Then we can check out this list of available storefronts the Chamber of Commerce sent me. I don't have a clear memory of the places on the list. We stopped coming here when I was around fourteen or so, and I'm sure things have changed. There's a map, though, so we'll be able to get around easily.''

At three-thirty, both women had the promise of temporary part-time waitressing jobs. ''Eight hours a week if the tips are good is okay,'' Annie assured Jane. ''It will get us over the hurdle if we can't find a location to open a business. This one on George Street looks pretty good. It's smack-dab in the middle of the Charleston campus and will draw students. Bishop England High School is close, so that's a plus. Let's go there first and see what we can work up if anything. According to this map the building is between King and Phillips. Do you think we should call the broker first?''

Jane snorted. ''Do you know who the broker is?''

''No. Okay, let's go. It can't be far. If it looks promising, we can call the broker from a phone booth.''

It was almost five-thirty when Annie pressed her nose up against the grimy storefront window. ''It's a dump, that's for sure. Do you think it's *doable,* Jane?''

''Doable as in Annie and Jane doing all the work. I don't know, Annie. I need to see the inside. It's big. For some reason I thought it would be, you know, little, kind of like a big walk-in closet. I saw a phone booth down the street. I'll call. In the meantime, go into that store next to it and ask some questions. It looks like it's been empty for a long time.''

Annie's brain whirled as she moved along the wide front windows to rub at the grime. All things considered, it would be perfect for what she and Jane had in mind. There was even a counter.

''He's coming right over,'' Jane said. ''What did you find out?''

''Nothing. The man was locking up. I didn't want to bother him. If the rent is right, this might work, Jane. Look, there's a counter. My end would be here, yours to the right. Once these windows are cleaned you'd have really good light. Coffee

by Annie and paintings by Jane. I'm liking this more and more.
Cross your fingers that the rent is something we can handle.
Do you think that's a cash register?''

"It looks like one to me. I guess this is Mr. Peabody coming
toward us. He said his office was just a block away. He doesn't
look like a shark, does he?''

"All real-estate people are sharks. Stay alert. Go across the
street and ask the music people how long this place has been
empty.''

"Anna Clark, and you must be Mr. Peabody,'' Annie said,
holding out her hand. The Realtor's hand was moist and
clammy. Annie fought the urge to wipe her own hand on her
chinos. Instead she jammed both her hands into her pockets.

Peabody was round like a melon. Even his face was round,
with a goatee. He looked to Annie like a benevolent barracuda
listing to the left. He removed his Panama hat with a flourish,
revealing a shiny bald head that was wet with sweat. A massive
ring of keys appeared in his hands. She watched as he fit key
after key into the lock until finally he found the right one.

"Wonderful location. Right in the heart of things. You
couldn't want anything better. A little paint will work wonders.
The other shopkeepers are just wonderful people. Neighborly,
if you know what I mean. They help one another. You ladies
aren't from around here, are you?''

"You mean are we *Yankees?* Actually, Mr. Peabody, I am
Anna Clark, and my friend is Jane. That's who we are.''

"Lord love a duck. You young women today say the goldang-
est things.''

Jane returned to the shop holding up two fingers and then
whacked the first finger at the second knuckle, meaning the
store had been empty for two and a half years. Annie's brain
buzzed.

"How much is the rent, Mr. Peabody?'' she asked.

"Seven hundred and fifty dollars.''

Annie laughed. Jane joined in. Annie's brain continued to buzz as she tried to calculate rent for two and a half years. Somewhere in the neighborhood of $23,000.

Peabody's voice was unctuous sounding. "Does the amount offend you ladies?"

Annie squared her shoulders. She was a business major. She should be able to handle this in a mature, professional manner. "Let's cut the bullshit, Mr. Peabody. This store has been empty for two and a half years. At the price you quoted, you lost approximately twenty-three thousand dollars. My friend and I are willing to pay three hundred a month providing you do certain things. Mainly clean up this dump and take out all this trash. A paint job goes with the deal. We're willing to sign a three-year lease and a renewal at the end of three years with a fifty-dollar increase. It won't do to haggle. It's all we can afford, so it's a take-it-or-leave-it offer."

Peabody mopped at his glistening bald head. "I need to think about this."

"So think," Annie said smartly. "When we walk out of here the deal is off the table. Don't think about asking us for a security deposit because we can't afford it. However, we can possibly work out something where we could pay something every month toward a month's rent as security. Tell me, does the plumbing work in the bathroom and the sink behind the counter. If it doesn't, it will have to be fixed. What was in this store before?"

"Homemade candies, crafts, gifts, that sort of thing. The Hobart ladies were here for eighteen years before they closed up."

"Do you really expect me to believe the Hobart ladies paid you seven hundred and fifty dollars a month selling homemade candies, Mr. Peabody?" Annie asked, her voice ringing with disdain.

"My memory could be off a little. I'm not as young as I used to be," Peabody said. His handkerchief was soaking wet.

"Does that mean we have a deal?"

Peabody hedged. "When would you want to take possession?"

"The minute this dump passes inspection. Electric, plumbing, paint job, trash removal. The cash register stays, as does the counter and those two round tables and chairs."

"Now, I don't know about that, Miss Clark."

Annie was in the man's face a moment later. "What don't you know, Mr. Peabody? That has to be part of the deal. It's after six, Mr. Peabody, and we've had a very long day. I'd like a handshake agreement until we can have a lawyer draw up a lease we're all happy with. What's it going to be?"

"Well, all right. I know I'm going to regret this at some point, but it's a deal. There's a young lawyer in town, Robert Rose, who can handle the lease. I've never used his services so we'll be neutral in that respect. If we're both agreeable, I don't see the need to engage two attorneys."

"That's fine with us. I'll call for an appointment. We'll split the fee and tell him we don't consider it a conflict of interest for him to represent both of us. If we can, we can set it up for tomorrow or the day after. In the meantime, I'd like to leave a deposit of two hundred dollars. In cash. It shows our good faith."

"Certainly, certainly. What are you ladies going to be doing here? I guess I should have asked earlier."

"Coffee," Annie said, counting out the two hundred dollars from her pocket. She pretended not to see the surprise on Jane's face. She shot her a warning look that said I'll explain later.

"When do you think the repairs will be done, Mr. Peabody?"

"By the end of the week. You'll have the weekend to set things up the way you want them. I don't like that part about the extended lease after three years," Peabody fretted.

Annie snatched the money back from his hand. Peabody grabbed for it saying, "I just said I didn't like it. I didn't say I wouldn't go along with it."

"You need to write that down on the back of the receipt," Annie said coldly. "I don't want this coming back to slap me in the face later on."

"You certainly do drive a hard bargain. You've got to be a *Yankee.*"

"Mr. Peabody, I am Anna Clark. Let's put that to rest right now."

Peabody sucked in his fat cheeks. "It's resting."

Annie held out her hand. Peabody hesitated a moment before reaching for it. Annie squeezed hard. Jane did the same thing, smiling all the while.

"The key, Mr. Peabody. Jane and I want to walk around, take measurements, that kind of thing. I think two hundred dollars is sufficient for the key. We'll lock up when we leave. I'm sure you have an extra, don't you?"

"Yes, yes, of course. It's someplace back in the office. I'll say good night then, ladies."

Annie and Jane whooped their joy the moment the door closed and Peabody was across the street.

"Lord, girl, I didn't know you had it in you!" Jane said. "This dump is worth at least four hundred dollars."

"Time will tell. It's ours, and that's all that matters. I know you're dying to know where I got that two hundred dollars. You aren't going to believe this. It was in my gym bag. Remember when we were saving for that television we were going to put in the living room? We finally gave up on the idea. I guess both of us just forgot about it. Good thing I found it, huh?"

Not only are you a crook, a thief and a criminal but you're a liar as well. You just lied to your best friend. See how easy it is to go off the straight and narrow?

Annie gave herself a mental shrug, her breath exploding in

a hissing sound. *Yes, damn it, I am all those things but I'm not going to think about it now. I am going to pay it back, every single cent plus interest. Absolutely I am going to do that.* Her shoulders felt incredibly heavy as she followed Jane around the spacious shop. The word *felon* found its way into her head just as Jane said, "Take a good look at this counter. It's solid oak. Oak is such a beautiful wood. Why would someone paint it? Let's strip and refinish it, Jane."

"Sure, but we can't do that until all the dust settles. The floor has to be sanded. Damn, we didn't put that on the list for Peabody. Maybe for the time being we can just wash it real good and put some kind of wax on it. Or hire someone to clean it, buff it, and polish it with that shiny stuff they use today. It's heart of pine and durable as hell. The boards are even, no sagging anywhere. Let's not spend any money we don't have to spend. Do you think it's possible to rent a sewing machine around here, Annie?"

"That's why they have Yellow Pages. I would think so. Why?"

"Take a look at those windows. They're just crying for something cheerful. I could make them. If we can fit some material into our budget, I can buy some great fabric and some sailcloth to make an awning for over the front door. There's something quaint and homey about an awning. Don't ask me what it is, it just is. I could paint daisies and sunflowers all over it. White muslin for the curtains with the same hand-painted flowers. For some reason people just seem to home in on things like that. I can redo those two tables and cover the seats with the same muslin. I bet we could find a bench to put outside the door, too. Little things like that for eye appeal. We have to get them in the door."

"We're going to need a catchy name for this place," Annie said, her shoulders lightening imperceptibly. "Something we can both relate to. Something that takes in my coffee and your painting. You can make the sign, can't you?''

"Sure, and the chains are still hanging outside. I could make it in the form of a daisy or a sunflower, or how about a rainbow?''

Annie choked on her own saliva. Jane thumped her on the back. "You okay?''

"I just swallowed wrong. None of them sound professional. We need something with some zip to it. We'll think of something tonight.''

"I'm really psyched about this, Annie. I'm disappointed, though. I thought you'd be just as excited. It's not as though we haven't talked about this for years.''

"I guess it's the financial end of things that's spooking me.''

"You!'' Jane scoffed. "You're the girl who makes things happen, the girl who knows how to squeeze a nickel eight different ways, the girl who can make a six-course dinner out of nothing and have it taste good. You!''

Annie laughed. "We're going in three different directions. We agreed to waitress part-time. We're sending out résumés for full-time jobs. Now this. I know it was part of our grand plan, but how are we going to do it all now? What if we don't make a profit? Think about the bills.''

Jane planted her hands on her bony hips. "You're starting to scare me, Annie. Look, we don't have to waitress. We don't have to send out résumés. We can tackle this and hope for the best. I'm for whatever will take that awful look off your face. This is supposed to be a happy time for us.''

"You know what, Jane, you are absolutely right. Let's go home, unpack the cars, go out to dinner to that big steak we promised ourselves, and really talk this through. Look, if things start to get sticky, I can always ask Elmo for a loan. I'm sure he'd give it to us. I think it's not having a cushion to fall back on in case things are lean for a while,'' Annie said.

"We aren't going to think about that. I like it when you're being the eternal optimist and I'm the pessimist."

Annie shivered. "Then that's the way it's going to be," she said, linking her arm through Jane's. "Come on, let's lock up *our* shop and head home. We have a home now, you know."

"Good idea," Jane said.

On Monday, June 6, 1980, the Daisy Shop opened for business. There was no advance notice, no fanfare, and no publicity because the owners couldn't afford it. No one was more surprised than the owners at the steady stream of customers. Jane said it was because of the daisy-patterned awning. Annie said it was Elmo's mother's tuna fish sandwiches that were served from twelve to one.

By four o'clock, they had gone through ten pounds of coffee and 150 tuna sandwiches. By four-thirty they had to tell disappointed customers they had to close to restock. The groans and moans were music to their ears.

In the small storage room at the back of the shop, the two women danced and twirled in glee. "Do you think it will be like this every day, Jane?"

"God, I hope so. I sold, are you ready for this, eighty-five hand-painted postcards of this shop at three bucks a pop. Annie, that is two hundred forty-nine dollars. I know that isn't going to happen every day, but tourists will still come in. If I sell twenty or twenty-five a day it will keep me in paints and cards. I sold two eight-by-tens for forty dollars each. We covered half the rent with just that alone. God, you were so right. This is going to work. The students loved it. How many requests did you have for espresso and latte?"

"I lost track. I never thought the tuna would go over like it did. We have to call Elmo tonight and tell him. He'll be so tickled. It's all so wonderful, Jane. Everything is so fresh, so clean and pretty. You want to bet tomorrow *jams.*''

''Does that mean we're going to be making tuna all night?''

''It means we have to go to Harris Teeter for coffee—vanilla, hazelnut, and cinnamon. Twenty pounds, Jane! Say it out loud!''

''Twenty pounds!'' Jane giggled. ''I can't wait to count the money.''

''We're going to need a supplier. We can't keep running to the supermarket and paying full price. That eats into our profits. Elmo can tell us how to go about all that. We need to buy wholesale. You should think about that for your supplies, too, Jane.''

''Oh, I will. I think God smiled on us today, Annie.''

Annie's exuberance died at Jane's words. She turned away so Jane wouldn't see her miserable face.

''Phone's ringing, Annie. You're the closest.''

Annie picked up the phone. ''Tom! Oh, Tom, wait till I tell you! We sold out. We actually had to close up shop. You did call to congratulate me, didn't you? What's wrong?'' Annie listened, her eyes filling with tears. ''That can't be, Tom. The place was clean. We both checked it out. There was ample help. Mom wouldn't . . . there are no animals there. Is the doctor sure? Oh, God! Tom, I'm living in a tiny two-bedroom apartment. I can't take care of her. I would if I could. Couldn't you convert your garage until I have this place up and running? You could make two nice rooms for Mom and Social Services would send someone to watch her. I can't do it all, Tom. I just can't. Look, I worked three part-time jobs, put myself through school, while all that was handed to you. Maybe you need to think about *that.* I, personally, don't give a good rat's ass what Mona wants, Tom. It's just for a little while until I can get things together. I'll take care of Mom then. Can't you at least meet me halfway?'' Annie blinked when she heard the sound of the dial tone. She felt sick to her stomach at what she was about to do. With her finger on the bar so Jane couldn't hear the dial tone she said, "How much money and how soon can you send it? That much? Fine, Tom. Okay, I'll call the nursing home and the doctor. I'll find a nice place for Mom here. Of course I'll pay my share. So I'll have to moonlight if I need to. I've done it before. Fine, fine, I'll let you know."

"What is it, Annie? What happened?" Jane asked, putting her arms around her friend. Just then, the shop bell rang, but neither woman noticed.

"Tom said . . . what he said was . . . what the doctor told him was Mom got bitten. On both her legs. The doctor said it was from a . . . raccoon. She wasn't the only one either. Mom said it was a kitten. She would think that in her condition. They're going to keep her in the hospital for a few days, then send her back to the nursing home. I just don't understand. It was clean, well maintained, a good staff. The food looked appetizing. Mom seemed to like it. It wasn't the prettiest place in the world, but it was the best we could do at the time. Tom wants me to bring Mom here. He even gave me the name of a place that sounds wonderful. He's going to send some money. He didn't say how much, though." Annie burst into tears.

"Now what am I supposed to do?" Annie wailed.

"I'll tell you what you're going to do, young lady. You're going to pull up your socks and do what you're supposed to do. Go get your mother and bring her here."

"Elmo! What are you doing here?" Annie and Jane squealed in unison.

"Came for the grand opening! Damn plane got stuck in Roanoke and had to wait for six hours. Could have walked here in that time. Blow your nose. I hate a sniffling woman."

"Did you close the store?"

"Hell no, I didn't close the store. I sold the damn thing."

"You sold the drugstore?" Jane and Annie said in amazement. "You love that store. You said you would never sell it."

"I did say that. I happen to love you girls more. I missed you. Got twice as much as the store was worth, too. I'm moving here to keep my eye on you two. Seems like I arrived at just the right moment."

"We were going to call you tonight, Elmo. Everyone liked your mother's sandwiches. We sold out."

"Knew you would. Let's sit down here and palaver. My daddy used to say that. Never had the occasion to use that word until now. The way I see it is we're faced with a crisis. I'm good in a crisis. Real good. I worked behind the counter at the store for years. Filled prescriptions, sold toothpaste, cleaned the place at the end of the day. I think I can serve coffee and sandwiches while you go for your mama. You look into that place your brother mentioned. If she don't care for it, she can move in with me when I get my place. I'm just itching to spend that money I got from the sale of the store. Is this all getting through to you, Annie?"

"Yes. Elmo, Mom doesn't know any of us. She lives in her own little world. She wanders off and can't remember her name or where she belongs. She needs constant care. This is all so wonderful of you, but I can't let you do it."

"Don't have much else to do now, do I?"

"Well . . . are you sure, Elmo?"

"Child, I am sure. I wouldn't be here otherwise. I missed you two girls so much I couldn't wait to make my plane reservation. I'm here. That says it all. I'm sleeping on your couch tonight until I can find my own place."

Annie blew her nose again. "You're right, Elmo, that says it all."

"This is a classy little store. Not the best neighborhood, but maybe the rest of the shopkeepers will update a little. Good crowd today, eh?"

"Jane sold eighty-five hand-painted postcards and two eight-by-tens. She sat right there and painted them for the customers. They loved it. How are things back in Boston? Did they ever find the money those guys took off with?"

"No. They must have been in my store six or seven times. Insurance people, cops, detectives, lawyers, and even a private detective. Did they ever call you? When I told them you were talking to me and buying aspirin they asked for your address and phone number. Jane's, too. Don't know why. Told them all we heard was a backfire that turned out to be a gunshot. The trail is stone cold. They're never going to find that money. The third guy is probably sunning himself on some South Sea island. Newspapers are saying the boy in jail is going to get twenty years. Pity."

"Yes it is. You were right, Elmo, when you said open near a campus, and you won't go wrong."

"Maybe we need to think about expanding. This is a big state."

"Elmo, I just opened. Today could be a fluke. Business will taper off in the summer when the students leave."

"Summer school, tourists, regulars. Might see a slight dip, but it's only two and a half months out of the year. My store was always down in summer but it evened out in the fall. You take the good with the bad and work with it. You don't stock heavy during that time. We'll work it out. You girls did real well. What'd it cost you?"

"Rent's three hundred. It cost us seventy-five to get the floor in shape. It's heart of pine. If we keep up with it, we should be able to save it, heavy traffic and all. Jane rented a sewing machine and made the awning and the curtains. She did the murals and painted the tables and chairs. That all came to a hundred. Ten bucks to rent the sewing machine. We stripped and varnished the counter ourselves. That was another twenty dollars. We're leasing a refrigerator. We can't cook here, so we're just going to serve sandwiches and maybe brownies one day a week. It's all we can handle. We do need to buy wholesale, though.''

''You certainly do. Do you think we could go out to dinner, ladies? I haven't eaten all day, and my mouth is watering for some of those fat Southern shrimp I hear so much about. It will be my treat. We can talk about your mother and business over a nice glass of wine.''

''We accept, don't we, Jane?''

''I love you, Elmo Richardson,'' Jane said, wrapping her arms around the old man.

''Me too,'' Annie said.

Everything was going to be just fine now. Or was it just wishful thinking on her part? A chill ran up Annie's spine when she recalled Elmo's words about all the people who had questioned him. Would those same people think it suspicious that he sold out right after the robbery and moved here to be with Jane and her? Probably. Elmo would put them in their place lickety-split. Thank you, God, for sending Elmo. I wish I knew why You're being so good to me after what I did.

''Lock the door, Annie.''

''Okay. It does look pretty, doesn't it?''

''Just like my postcards,'' Jane laughed.

''And I have the two prettiest girls in town going out to dinner with me. Who could want more?'' Elmo said.

Who indeed? Annie thought.

CHAPTER THREE

"Dr. Mitchum, are you sure Mom is up to the trip?"

"Annie, your mother is right as rain. The bites have healed nicely. She had no adverse effects from the drugs. The raccoon was tested, and it wasn't rabid. She was lucky. Tall Pines is a wonderful nursing home. I don't think your mother will be taking any more naps in a woodshed anytime soon. It was a freak accident."

"That's just the point. Mom shouldn't have been allowed to wander off. However, I understand what you're saying. She used to do a lot of gardening, and we did have a toolshed where she kept all her potting tools and such. Maybe she thought she was back home. This is just a guess on my part, but she might have thought the raccoon was our old cat Flossie."

"Sometimes there's a little spark, Annie. Not often. Your mother can be quite vibrant at times. I've taken care of everything with Tall Pines. Norma is free to go whenever you're ready. I'm truly sorry this happened."

"Me too, Dr. Mitchum. In a way it is probably a good thing.

I'll be able to visit more often and take her on outings. Guess I'll say good-bye. Thanks for taking such good care of Mom.''

Annie was almost to the door when the kindly doctor called her name. ''Annie, always be kind to your mother. Even though she's in her own little world, she has feelings and anxiousness. Lately she's been crying a lot. We don't know why. I just wanted you to know that.'' Annie nodded.

Annie pasted a tired smile on her face when she rounded the corner to enter the visitor's lounge. Her mother was pacing, a nurse's aide alongside her.

''Ready, Mom?''

Norma Clark looked around, a confused look on her face. ''Are you speaking to me, child?''

''Yes. I'm Annie. We're going to go for a ride.''

''I don't think so. Not today. I'd just like to go home.''

''Okay, then let's go home.''

''That's very kind of you. What did you say your name was?''

''Anna Daisy Clark,'' Annie said with a catch in her voice.

''That's a very pretty name. Were you named after a flower? I used to have daisies in my garden. I planted them myself.''

''I know. I used to pick them for you.''

''My goodness, I don't remember that.''

''Careful now. The car is right over there. Do you want to sit in the front or the back?''

''It's a short ride, so it doesn't matter.''

''Mom, it's a long ride. Six hours or so. Front or back? There's a pillow in the back.''

''That's just like your father. He always thought I needed a pillow. How did you get here, Annie?''

''Mom, you know me?'' Annie asked incredulously.

''Of course I know you. Anna Daisy Clark. Sometimes I used to call you Lazy Daisy when you didn't clean your room.''

''Oh, Mom,'' Annie said tearfully. ''This is the best thing

that's happened to me in a long time. Tom is going to be so happy when I tell him.''

''Who's Tom?'' Norma asked as she climbed into the backseat.

Annie's clenched fist hit the side of the door with such force, pain ricocheted up and down her arm. *This must be one of the little sparks Dr. Mitchum was talking about,* she thought as she settled herself behind the wheel. *A spark is good. I'll settle for a spark once in a while. Thank you, God, for that one. I promise not to be greedy.*

Annie chattered nonstop for the first half of the trip. It wasn't until they stopped for coffee and gas that she withdrew the last piece of the metal lock from the money bag in her purse while her mother was using the rest room. She'd hacked it to pieces back in Charleston and now she was leaving a piece of it wherever she stopped. This last piece she planned on throwing out the window in the first rural area she came to. She'd burned the canvas bag the night she'd left. In the middle of the night she'd scattered the ashes all along Rutledge Street.

Norma Clark tapped Annie's arm. ''Young lady, we're never going to get home if you stand there staring off into space. What is it you do besides driving ladies home?''

Annie felt her throat tighten up. ''I have a coffee shop. I sort of, kind of, robbed a bank, Mom.''

''Mercy, child. Whatever did you do that for? Are you poor?''

''Dirt-poor. I thought I did it for you. That's probably a lie because I used two hundred dollars of it for a rent deposit. I'm going to put that back, though. You know what, Mom, it all just closed in on me. There it was, right in front of me. I took it. It's a really long story. I have all this money now and I'm not sure what I should do. Then the call came about you from Tom. It was almost like it was meant to be. I know it wasn't, but that's how it felt,'' Annie babbled. ''Then Elmo came, and he offered to help. He sold his store to come here with Jane and me. He needs someone, too. Everyone needs someone, Mom.''

''Young lady, why do you keep calling me Mom. Do I remind you of your mother?''

The knot in Annie's throat grew in size as she struggled with the words. ''You . . . you look just like her. She was always so pretty, just like you. She made the best peanut butter cookies. Her tulips were the prettiest ones on the street. Especially the purple ones.''

''I remember those. I ordered the bulbs from Holland. They were so beautiful. Your father wouldn't let me pick them. He used to count them when he came up the walkway. Why isn't your father here? Is his arthritis bothering him again?''

Another little spark. ''I love you, Mom. God, how did this happen?''

''Goodness, Annie, watch where you're driving before you kill us both. Are we about home now?''

''Soon,'' Annie said tearfully. ''Do you love me, Mom?''

''Goodness sakes, child, I don't even know you. I'm sure when I get to know you better I'll love you.''

Annie drove in silence, tears rolling down her cheeks.

Annie felt soft pats on her shoulder. ''Now, now, it will all work out. Don't cry. If I could just remember what it was I said to make you cry, I would apologize.''

''Don't worry about it. I'm not crying anymore. Now I'm mad. Your son Tom is a shit. And you know what else? His wife Mona is an even bigger shit. Right now I don't like either one of them. You know, Mom, I never complained. Not once. I worked my ass off, I really did. Tom got everything handed to him. You'd think he'd want to help or at least offer. Is it because I'm a daughter, and he's a son? That's why I did what I did. I'm not a thief. Well, I am, but I wasn't before. I turned into a liar, too. Are you ashamed of me, Mom?''

Norma Clark clamped her lips shut, then opened them. "I won't tell a soul about your secrets."

Annie took her eyes off the road long enough to turn around and say, "If you do, I'll go to jail. They'll lock me up and throw away the key."

Norma Clark's shoulders stiffened. "That's what they do to me. They lock me in my room. It's the same thing as jail. People steal my clothes and my shoes. I never tell. I don't want to get punished."

Annie's foot hit the brake as she steered the car to the side of the road. There was outrage in her voice when she said, "Did they punish you?"

"Yes. They didn't let me go out among the flowers. They even tied Grace in her chair. I untied her," Norma said defiantly. "We didn't get any dinner. They always slapped Grace because she wouldn't listen."

"Oh, God," Annie said.

"I used to pray that my daughter would come and get me. She never did."

Annie let the tears flow. "When we get home you can write to Grace," she managed to say.

"Grace is dead," Norma said flatly.

Was this real? Did her mother know what she was talking about? Was this all some figment of her imagination? "Oh, God, oh, God," Annie wailed.

"It's too late to cry," Norma said.

"When did Grace die, Mom?"

"A long time ago. Maybe it was yesterday. Sometimes I can't remember. Don't tell anyone."

Annie felt light-headed. "I won't tell anyone about Grace if you don't tell anyone I took the money."

Norma's head bobbed up and down. "That sounds fine to me. Should we shake hands?"

"Why the hell not," Annie muttered as she extended her

hand. Norma pumped it vigorously. "How did Grace die, Mom?"

"They punished her and she died. Billie said we have to mind our p's and q's or the same thing will happen to us. I mind my p's and q's," Norma said primly.

Annie turned around and took a deep breath. "I don't think we should talk about this anymore. Let's talk about something nice." She made a mental note to find out who Billie was.

"This certainly is the long way home. Did you take a wrong turn, young lady?"

"More than one. Why don't you take a nap on that nice pillow. I'll wake you when we get home. Mom, do you remember that frilly flowered dress, the one with the purple and pink flowers? You had a sun hat with a big purple ribbon on it that you used to wear in the garden."

"I told you, young woman, they steal all my things."

"I'm going to buy you one just like it," Annie said. "No one is ever going to steal your things again. I promise."

When Annie looked in the rearview mirror she saw that her mother was sound asleep. "Goddamn it, I will not cry. I absolutely will not cry. I am so sorry, Mom. I did the best I could. Even Tom did the best he could at the time. I thought we were on top of things. I really did. From now on you are going to be safe and happy. I don't care what that makes me." To make her point, Annie leaned her head out the window and shouted at the top of her lungs, "Do you hear me? I don't give a good goddamn what that makes me. I don't care if I go to jail. I don't care if I fry in hell. So there, damn it!"

Norma Clark slept deeply and soundly during her daughter's tirade.

Annie woke while it was still dark outside. It was her day to open the shop for the early-morning coffee trade. She was bone tired, but, as she put it, it was a good kind of tired. Elmo had arranged for Norma to be looked after by two women until there was an opening at the Westbury Center. He had been delighted when he described the facility, saying each resident had his or her own apartment with a small walled garden. Security, he went on to say, was high-tech with a twenty-four-hour monitoring system. The part he liked best, he said, was that patients with Norma's condition wore a decorative bracelet that allowed the orderlies to know where they were at all times. The grounds contained a pool, a hot tub, a small petting zoo, a tennis court, as well as a basketball court. A community room with a fully stocked library, a sixty-inch television, and a stereo system rounded out the amenities. The bottom line, Elmo said, was, "It's not as expensive as you might think. With Norma's social security and the part of your father's pension that reverted to her, you and Tom only have to pay two thousand dollars a month. That's just six hundred more than what you were paying in Raleigh. With things going the way they are, I think you can handle it, Annie."

"I can't count on Tom, Elmo. Tom said Mona refuses to pay another nickel. He's got three kids, and he's already holding down a part-time job at night. For now, I have to pay the whole thing."

"You've made a pretty penny since opening day. This is just a guess on my part, but I think you're going to have to hire a few part-timers. The two nights we stayed open till nine were very profitable. However, I'm the first to admit that five in the morning till ten at night isn't a pace anybody can keep up with. When you own your own business, you're married to it. I'm the living proof. When you're dealing with a cash business, you need honest people working for you. Like you and Jane when you worked for me. I lost money over the years with help that thought my money was theirs. Among the three of us, we'll work something out."

"I hope so, Elmo, because I'm starting to get nervous. I never expected anything even half as successful as this. This is just short of phenomenal."

"I know, Annie. If you opened other stores on other campuses like this one, they'd be just as successful. When this one is truly off the ground, you might want to think about it. You started this one on a shoestring, and look what happened. If you need an investor, I'm yours for the taking."

"Elmo, I can't even think about that yet."

"You have to think about it, Annie. We've sold out every single day we've been open. Would you listen to me. I sound like I'm part of this."

"You are!" Jane and Annie said in unison.

"You get up when we do," Annie went on. "You make coffee, boil milk, make sandwiches just like we do. That makes you a one-third partner."

"I don't want to be a partner. My business days are over. I only want to help. I get a kick out of talking to the kids. They call me Pops, can you beat that?"

Annie laughed. "They called you Pops back in Boston, too."

"Speaking of Boston, I got a form letter today that was forwarded from that same insurance company asking me to make a list of all the people I knew who frequented my store that day and any personal information I might have. I tore it up. They're getting to be a pain in my behind. I think they're desperate is what I think."

"I think I hate insurance companies as much as I hate used-car salesmen. They want their premiums, and when it's time to pay out they fight you every step of the way. On top of that they then raise your rates. If I get one, I'm tearing up mine, too," Jane said.

"Yeah, me too," Annie said quietly.

"I did a watercolor the other day of a Charleston garden,

Annie. Do you want to take it to your mother? I know she loves flowers. I just put a plain white frame on it.''

"She'll love it," Annie said.

"You sound funny. Are you okay?''

"I'm getting a headache. I used to get headaches when I didn't know if I could make the rent and buy food. Now, when things are going well, I'm worried it won't last. I guess I'm going to have to go back on my aspirin kick again. By the way, Jane, did we leave a forwarding address?''

Jane slapped at her forehead. "Damn, I forgot. I was going to do it the day of the bank robbery, then you came home and I forgot. I can send one of those forms to the post office tomorrow. I'm sorry, Annie.''

"Don't do it for me. All our bills were paid. Tom has this address. Mom isn't in that nursing home anymore, so who would write me? Forget it.''

"Okay, I will. Well, I'm going to pack up my gear and head home. It's my turn to cook. How about stuffed pork chops?''

"Make me two," Elmo said smartly.

"Me too," Annie said just as smartly. No forwarding address meant the insurance company couldn't locate her or Jane. *Thank you, God.*

"Annie, I forgot to tell you something. Your mother can use her own furniture when she moves into Westbury Center. Didn't you tell me you put your family things in storage in Raleigh?''

"That's wonderful. She'll love having her own things even if she only remembers them once in a while." This was all just too damn coincidental or she was becoming paranoid. On the way to North Carolina to pick up her mother, she'd stopped at the storage unit she'd paid rent on all these years and hid the pillowcase with the bank money in one of the dresser drawers, keeping ten thousand dollars in case of an emergency. She'd replaced the two hundred dollars from her own account and then taken ten thousand. What kind of pretzel logic was that? A criminal mentality was taking over her mind, and there wasn't anything she could do about it.

"Mom really likes those ladies that are staying with her, doesn't she?" Annie said to have something to say.

"She calls them both Grace. They don't mind, though. They understand. Helen likes me. A lot," Elmo said slyly.

Annie and Jane whooped with glee. Elmo's face turned fire red. "When is your house going to be ready?"

"Three weeks, and, no, she isn't moving in. Helen, not your mother. I like to play chess, and so does she. She doesn't like tuna and she hates coffee. Drinks tea all day long. Sweet tea, they call it down here. That's all there is to it. Don't you two be badgering me now."

"A nifty bachelor like yourself is going to find himself in big demand around here. Before you know it you'll be beating off all those rich widows with a stick. They're going to try and tempt you with their shrimp and grits and their she crab stew," Annie teased.

"Hrumph. Don't like grits and never did care for stew. I'll be seeing you in a bit. Be sure to lock up tight."

"We will. Dinner's at eight."

"I'll be there."

"If you don't need me, then I'm off, too," Jane said.

"Go ahead. I have to do the books. I'll be home by eight."

"Annie, we're doing so well, it's scary. If we wanted to, we could buy ourselves a new outfit. When was the last time we did that?"

"At least a hundred years ago. We need a fella before we get duded up."

"I'm looking." Jane laughed as she scooted for the front door.

* * *

Annie brushed at a swarm of gnats as she made her way down the street. The humidity made it hard to breathe. Her mind wandered as she passed tourists and summer-school students. Where had the time gone? It seemed like yesterday that they opened the Daisy Shop, and here it was mid August. In another week the fall-term students would be swarming back onto the campus and they'd be run ragged again. Still, it was always better to be busy. When you were busy you didn't have time to think. Some days she almost forgot about her big, dark secret. As Jane said a while back, things were going so well it was downright scary.

Her mother loved the Westbury Center, where she now lived. She worked in her garden every day, played the piano on occasion, and actually seemed to have a routine of sorts. She cooked simple things, and if she forgot to wash the dishes, there was someone to do it for her. She had adopted a kitten from the petting zoo and walked it on a bright blue leash several times a week. Visitor days were happy occasions. Jane and Elmo always went with Annie, and, weather permitting, they picnicked in the small walled garden.

Norma Jean Clark was happy. Annie was grateful.

"Oh, I'm terribly sorry. I wasn't watching where I was going. I guess I was woolgathering."

"Now that's an expression I haven't heard in years. My grandmother used to say that. It wasn't your fault, it was mine. Daniel Matthew Evans," the man said by way of introduction.

Annie laughed. "Anna Daisy Clark," she said, holding out her hand.

"I don't think I ever met anyone named Daisy. You wouldn't by any chance be the Daisy from the Daisy Shop, would you?"

"I am indeed."

"Best coffee I ever drank. I like those tuna sandwiches, too."

"I don't think I ever saw you in the shop," Annie said.

"Usually I have one of my students pick it up for me. I'll have to make it a point to come by more often."

Annie laughed again. *My God, I'm flirting.* "We have a pretty good brownie on Mondays. Goes with the sandwich, no extra charge. Mondays are downers as a rule. Does that make sense?"

"In a cockamamie kind of way."

"You don't look like a professor," Annie blurted. She felt her neck grow warm. "I'm sorry, I didn't mean to say that."

"Of course you did. Don't apologize. My mother doesn't think I look like a professor, either. It's these shorts and running sneakers. Now you, on the other hand, look like both a Daisy and an Annie."

"I'll take that as a compliment."

"It was meant as one. See you around. I have three more miles to go. It was nice meeting you, Anna Daisy Clark."

"Likewise," Annie called over her shoulder. Wait until she told Jane about this encounter. She practically danced the rest of the way home.

Ten minutes later, Annie bounded up the steps and into the apartment, yelling at the top of her lungs. "Jane, you aren't going to believe this. I just met this man. I think he's a professor. Jane, where the hell are you? I think he was gorgeous, but I can't be sure. It was dark. I bumped into him. Talk about chance happenings. He had great legs and nice buns. Do we have any wine. It's in our budget this week, isn't it? Oh, I didn't know you had company. I'm sorry. I could go back out and come back in like a lady instead of a hooligan." Her eyes full of questions, Annie waited for an introduction.

"Annie, this is Peter Newman. He's investigating the bank robbery in Boston."

"Really. How can we help you, Mr. Newman?" Annie said, sitting down across the table from him. "You came all the way to South Carolina to talk to us. No wonder insurance rates are so high. Do we have wine, Jane? Maybe Mr. Newman would like some.'' *I can pull this off. I know I can do this. Stay calm and cool. There's no evidence. Take it slow and easy. The ten thousand dollars is safe in your dehumidifier. He'd never look there. Besides, he needs a warrant before he can search the house. Cool and calm. I can do this.*

''Mr. Newman said he ran our license plates,'' Jane said coolly.

''Why?'' Annie asked as she sipped the wine Jane handed her. *He looks like a skinny bulldog,* she thought.

''It wasn't just your cars. We ran the plates from all the cars parked in the campus parking lot. Those that we could make out. The rest we got from the campus parking authority. We're talking to everyone.''

''What do you want to know?''

''Where were you when the robbery occurred?''

''I was in the drugstore buying aspirin. I walked because it was such a beautiful day. I was talking to Mr. Richardson, or maybe I was paying him. I'm not sure. We both heard the shot at the same time. When I was walking home, I crossed the lot and saw what happened. That's all I know.''

''I was in our apartment,'' Jane said. ''Actually, I was getting ready to go to the post office to drop off our change of address when Annie came in. In the excitement of worrying about my money in the bank, I forgot to go. I never did leave an address.''

''Did either one of you see or hear anything else?''

Both women shook their heads.

''Do you always leave your car windows open?''

''The backseat windows of my car really stick. If it's nice out, I let them down. If it's raining, I struggle with them. But, to answer your question, most of the time in nice weather they're down,'' Annie said

''Mine too. I'm just too lazy to roll them up,'' Jane said. ''Why?''

"We think there's a possibility the robber tossed the money bag into one of the cars on the campus lot."

"But I thought the robber gave the money to a third person," Annie said, her eyes wide and innocent.

"We haven't ruled out that possibility."

"Almost all the cars on campus have their windows open in the spring," Jane said. "There was a picture in the morning paper on graduation day. I saw the picture on the front page and almost all of them had the windows open. Are you saying you suspect *us?*"

"I'm not saying that at all."

"Then what are you saying?" Annie asked bluntly.

"I'm saying we're at the asking-questions stage."

"Maybe you should post a reward," Jane said. "They do that on television shows all the time."

Annie held her glass out for a refill. Jane poured for Annie and herself, a worried look on her face. "Is there anything else you want to ask us?"

"Not at this time. I might have questions later on."

"Then it might be a good idea to call ahead," Annie said.

"Why is that?"

"Because you're eating into our dinner hour. As you can see it's almost eight o'clock. We get up at five. It's been a long, hard day, and I want to relax before I go to bed and have to get up and do it all over again. In short, Mr. Newman, I'm dog-ass tired. If there's nothing else, I'd like to eat my dinner."

"Then I'll be on my way. I'm sorry for the inconvenience. I'm just doing my job. If you give me your phone number, I will call ahead."

It's just a formality. It doesn't mean anything. Be cool. Look him in the eye. Annie got up from the table and reached into the cabinet for the dinner plates as Jane handed over a slip of paper with their phone number on it.

"The number on the bottom is the Daisy Shop. We're there all day long and don't have an answering machine," Jane said.

"Nice little shop. I saw it earlier."

"We started it with less than five hundred dollars and a lot of hard work," Annie snapped irritably.

"That's what Mr. Peabody said. Good night, ladies."

I'm going to faint or throw up or both and choke at the same time, Annie thought. She swigged from the wineglass until her eyes started to water.

"Do you think he suspects *us?*" Jane asked nervously. "By the way, Elmo canceled. The lovely Helen is preparing something for him."

"Us? Nah. He was just being obnoxious. Was he a detective or an insurance person?"

"Both I think. Investigative insurance adjuster. Something like that. He reminded me of a bulldog. Smart-ass."

Annie forced a laugh. "Hey, he can go through my car anytime he wants."

"I think he did. Mine too."

"He needs a warrant," Annie said.

"Maybe he just stood outside and looked in or something. Guess what, my windows are down."

Annie's laugh was genuine this time. "So are mine. So are half the car windows in this city. So, what's for dinner? Boy, I can't wait to tell you about this guy I bumped into. We are talking hand-some!"

"Since Elmo canceled, I decided on filled peppers, and tell me more."

"There he was in those cute running shorts . . ."

It was close to midnight when Annie pulled her diary out of her knitting bag. *I met two men today. My heart feels like it's too big for my chest and will explode any minute. I feel frightened and yet I feel elated. A lady from Texas bought three of Jane's paintings today. Business has quadrupled.*

*　*　*

Annie looked at the calendar on the small makeshift desk in the back room. Time to pay the quarterly taxes. Her eyes crossed when she stared at the neat rows of numbers in the ledger. "We need an accountant. All this stuff is eating into my time," she grumbled to Jane. "Elmo is like a caged cat. He says we need to open another shop over by the Baptist College in North Charleston. How are we going to do it, Jane, and keep up with all this?"

"We have to delegate. One of us needs to be here all the time. So far we've been lucky with the two part-timers we hired. I guess we do need to hire more help. Elmo has a very good business head, but he's running us ragged."

"I know," Annie said. "He's right, though. It is time to open another shop. We can afford it as long as we don't go overboard. God, Jane, do you remember how we had those ten coffeepots from Super Mart when we first opened? Twelve cups to a pot and all ten of them were going all day long. That fancy-dancy Bunn coffeemaker is a godsend. I can't wait till we have enough money to buy the cappuccino machine. This is just so fantastic."

"See, Annie, our gut instincts were right. We're making more money serving coffee than we would make working in the business world. I get to paint, drink all the coffee I want, and know I'm a half owner in a business that is thriving. What more could anyone want?"

"More hours in the day. A day off just to sleep once in a while. A couple of really nice men in our lives. I'd settle for all of the above." Annie laughed.

"Speaking of men. What's with the professor?"

"He's called for dates three times and three times he canceled. I gave up on him. Now, are you in favor of hiring an accounting firm to handle all of this?"

"Absolutely. I'll check it out today. I'm ahead on my post-cards. I can paint them now with my eyes closed. Some man came in here last week and said he would hang some of my pictures in his gallery on Charlotte Street. He said I just might be the next Josie Edell. I don't know who she is, but he sounded impressed."

"Oh, Jane, that's wonderful. Then it's settled. You're going to find us an accounting firm. I'm going to go over to the college and post a notice for more part-time help, then I'm going to head out to the Baptist College and check out the situation."

"As long as you're going over to the college, why don't you take the professor some coffee and brownies?" Jane asked slyly.

"Why don't you mind your own business." Annie grinned.

"Phone's ringing," Jane said.

"The phone's always ringing. You get it."

"You're closer," Jane shot back.

"Daisy Shop," Annie said, a smile in her voice.

"Miss Clark, or is it Miss Abbott?"

"This is Annie Clark. How can I help you?"

"This is Peter Newman."

Annie's voice soured immediately. "What can I do for you, Mr. Newman?"

"You can give me permission to run a forensics test on yours and Miss Abbott's automobiles. We're checking all the cars. There's a possibility fibers from the canvas money bag might show up. We're now working on a theory that the money bag was tossed into one of the cars with open windows and then a third party retrieved it later on."

"That's going to be difficult, Mr. Newman. My car gave out on me about three weeks ago, so I junked it. I can give you the name of the scrap dealer. Jane's car is still here if you want to check it."

"When would be a convenient time?"

"I'll put Jane on the phone. You'll have to work out 'a time with her. The junk dealer is Casey and Sons in Jedburg."

Annie made a face as she handed the phone to Jane. She turned away to gather up the papers on her desk, her heart pounding so loud she thought for sure Jane would hear it.

Jane slammed down the phone so hard it bounced out of the cradle. "That damn guy just doesn't give up. Fibers my foot! Do you think he's harassing us? He's coming by at six on Wednesday. My, God, Annie, what if it was my car? What if there are fibers in it?"

"Jane, you didn't do anything wrong. If somebody dumped something in your car and took it out later, you are not responsible."

"Tell that to some cop when he comes to arrest us. I could tell by the look on his face that night he came to the apartment that he didn't believe one thing we told him. He thinks there's something fishy about us. The suspicion just oozed out of his pores."

"He's doing his job. He's leaving no stone unturned. Isn't that what they say on those cop shows on television?"

"Yeah. What'd that junk guy say he was going to do with your old bus?"

"Sell it for parts and compact the frame. It's probably in some landfill by now."

"That guy will buy hip boots and go digging around. Trust me."

"Do you think so?"

"Yeah, I think so. He's probably thinking you did it on purpose to get rid of the evidence. I bet the rat is calling the scrap dealer as we speak."

Annie's heart skipped a beat. "So let him." Her voice was so defiant-sounding, Jane raised her eyebrows. "I think the guy is a weasel, and I didn't like him the first time I met him. He's slick. If he bothers us again, I think we need to report him to his agency.''

"I'll be glad to do it.''

"Ha! You'll have to fight me for the phone. Nothing would give me greater pleasure.''

"I'm going to try and find a female CPA. I'll be back in a little while. Are you sure this is all I need to give him or her.''

"It better be. It's all I have. Good luck, Jane.''

Annie sat for a long time, one hand on top of the phone. Should she call Casey and Sons or leave well enough alone? Leave well enough alone. If a car was compacted, would it be possible to pry it open? Could the old mats and seats be taken out? Did Casey and Sons sell the seats or the mats? Was the insurance investigator trying to scare them? If he was, he was doing a good job.

She was scared out of her wits.

CHAPTER FOUR

Annie sat alone in the living room of her new house staring at the twinkling Christmas tree lights. With the two Daisy Shops closed for holiday break, she felt at loose ends. Two days of sleeping around the clock had left her rested . . . and bored. These days Elmo was busy with his two lady friends, Jane was dating the accountant who was managing their financial records, and her mother was so busy at Westbury Center she didn't want to be bothered with visits from her daughter.

She toyed with the idea of calling Daniel Matthew Evans but realized at the last moment that he, too, like his students, probably went home for the holidays. One luncheon date and one concert hardly made for a relationship or gave her the right to call and ask him to come over for a glass of wine.

She felt tense and didn't like the feeling. Was something going to happen? All manner of horrible thoughts whirled through her head. Was the bulldog going to show up and ruin their holidays? Was Elmo going to get sick? She worried about him. Would Jane get serious with Bob Granger? Three dates a week and all-day weekends led her to believe so. She was happy for Jane, but just a tad jealous.

Damn! What is wrong with me? Maybe I should call Tom. She hadn't spoken to him since early summer. The holidays were a time for forgiveness and family. It wouldn't hurt her to call him just to wish him and the kids a happy holiday. She'd sent gifts and even included one for Mona. It wouldn't have hurt him to call and say thank you. Maybe he was embarrassed. Maybe a lot of things.

Annie bounded up from the couch and started to pace. She liked this new house of hers. It was old, ancient really, but it had character and great old fireplaces and wonderful heart-of-pine floors. The furniture was sparse but sufficient for now. Later, when she had more time, she would pick and choose furniture that would go with the old antebellum house. It still boggled her mind that she owned a house at all. Like Elmo said, ''You need the tax deduction now.''

Annie poured herself a glass of wine as she continued to pace. Without realizing it, she was on the second floor, her hand on the closet doorknob. The dehumidifier box with the ten thousand dollars was still there, pushed to the end of the long shelf. The same money she'd used to set her mother up at Westbury. She should have given it back a long time ago. The ideal time would have been when Newman tried to track down her old car with no results. Why was she keeping it? Was she afraid to give it back? Was it some kind of security? What did she hope to gain from keeping it? Nothing. Absolutely nothing.

Annie closed the louvered doors to the closet. Her head was above water. She was able to pay for her mother's care, she'd bought this house and a secondhand car that looked good and ran like a dream. Nothing extravagant, just a good, serviceable car. The interest payments were deductible along with her mortgage interest as well as the monies she paid out for her mother's

care. All her bills were paid, and she had money in the bank—
not a lot but enough of a cushion to make her feel comfortable.
Right now she and Jane could sell the Daisy Shops for a
handsome profit if she wanted to. Her heartbeat quickened
when she thought of the two new shops that were going to
open up after the first of the year, both of them at Clemson
University. "A veritable gold mine," Elmo had chortled. And
he was right. Elmo was always right. He was probably right
about the business plan he'd hired someone to draft up, too.
She wasn't sure about the plan to hire a business manager,
though. Someone to handle the accounting was different. No
one was going to handle her money but Jane and herself.

The phone rang just as Annie poured herself a second glass
of wine—or was it her third? She looked at the small clock
on the mantel: 10:15. An hour and fifteen minutes past her
normal bedtime. Her greeting was cautious. It might be Newman, with some new trick up his sleeve.

"Annie, it's Tom. The kids told me you sent them some
Christmas presents. I'm calling to thank you and to ask you
how Mom is. Look, Annie, if you don't want to talk to me,
it's okay."

"I have mixed feelings, Tom. I sent a gift for you, too."

"I was sure you did. I guess Mona didn't see fit to give it
to me. I haven't been to the house in quite a while."

"What does that mean, Tom?"

"It means Mona and I separated in September. I'm living
in a small apartment. It's hard as hell paying support and trying
to maintain a life for myself. She's going to clean me out.
That's not really why I called. I wanted to ask about Mom and
to tell you some guy was here asking questions about you and
Jane. I told him off, then booted his ass out the door. I'd had
a couple of beers, but he gave me the impression he thinks
you, Jane, and that guy you worked for are somehow involved
in some bank heist. I could be wrong about this, but Mandy

said he came to the house and talked to Mona. Christ alone knows what the hell she would say. I just thought you should know. I'm not even going to ask you about that because I know what kind of sterling character you are and the guy was so full of it his eyes were turning brown. How's Mom?''

Annie's heart hammered in her chest. ''Mom's doing great, Tom. She really seems happy. Most times when I go to see her she doesn't want to visit. She has friends and she gardens. The little villa she has is just perfect for her. She doesn't wander off, and the security is great. She's coming for Christmas. I have a real tree and everything. We closed up shop, since the college is closed. So is Bishop England. What are you doing for Christmas, Tom?''

''I'll probably sleep all day. Mona took the kids kicking and screaming to her parents' house.''

''Why don't you come here? I have an extra bedroom, and I know Mom would love to see you. It's been a long time since you've seen her.''

''I can't afford it, Annie. I don't have two extra nickels to rub together. It's kind of you to ask since I . . .''

''Will you come if I get you a ticket?''

''You don't have to do that, Annie. Drink a toast to me. I don't want you feeling sorry for me.''

''I don't feel sorry for you. You're my brother. I'd love it if we could all spend Christmas together. Say yes, Tom. I'll call the airline and make the reservation now and you can take the next flight. I'll pick you up at the airport. It will be like old times.''

''Okay, it's a deal. Listen, Annie, you and Jane aren't in any kind of trouble, are you?''

''No, of course not. That guy has been dogging us for months now. Sooner or later, he'll give up. If he doesn't stop soon, though, I'm going to call his home office and tell them he's harassing us. Elmo is getting real feisty about all of this. I think because he sold his drugstore and moved here when we did, the investigator thinks we had something to do with it. The shops are doing extremely well. He's probably running bank checks on us and all that other stuff they manage to do. Whoever would have thought he would track you down in California? Hang up, Tom, and I'll call the airline and then call you back."

"I'll pack in the meantime. Jeez, Annie, this is so nice of you."

"If you could, would you do it for me?"

"Yeah, Annie, I would. I want you to believe that."

"Okay, then. Hang up."

The moment Annie hung up the phone, she dropped her head to rest between her legs to ward off the dizziness engulfing her. *I have to give it back. I have to give it back. I'm sending it back. I'm sending it back as soon as I can figure out a way to do it without it coming back to haunt me. I'm going to do it. I swear I am. I can't take this anymore. Get a grip, Annie. It's all part of the investigative process. If he does suspect, this is his way of trying to wear you down. If you send it back now, he'll know it was you. You replaced all the money you borrowed. You're just holding it for the right time to mail it back.*

Annie gave her head a shake to clear her thoughts before she dialed the airline. Within minutes she had a reservation for her brother on the red-eye. She whipped her credit card out of the desk drawer and rattled off the numbers. It was the first time she'd used the card since coming to South Carolina. It gave her a good feeling to know she could afford to charge the ticket and pay it off when the bill came in. A very good feeling. "Do what you want with this, Mr. Snoop," she muttered. There was no doubt in her mind that the insurance investigator had her account as well as Jane's flagged for any charges that might appear. "Tough, Mr. Snoop. Just plain old tough.

"You know something else, Mr. Snoop?" Annie said, sloshing more wine into her glass. "I'm going to be so successful you aren't going to believe it. I'm going to do it on my own, too. By the time I'm thirty I'm going to be a millionaire.''

As she guzzled the wine, her head spinning, Annie placed the call to her brother. ''It's all set. Just go to the airport and take the United red-eye. I'll pick you up in the morning. I'm glad you're coming, Tom.''

''Are you okay, Annie? You sound like you've been crying.''

''Actually, Tom, I'm probably drunk. I'm not sure why that is. Then again, maybe I do know, and I just don't want to deal with it.''

''Are you by yourself, Annie?''

''Yes. I bought this beautiful old house, but I don't have much furniture. I do have a Christmas tree. Jane is seeing someone. We don't see too much of each other after work anymore. Elmo is fending off two ladies who are hot on his tail, and he loves every minute of it.''

''Guess you're feeling kind of shortchanged, huh?''

''Kind of. All I do is work. I did meet a professor, but he canceled out on three different dates, so yeah, I'm alone. I might get some goldfish. Remember when we had gerbils, Tom?''

''Yeah, one day we had one and the next day we had twenty-three or was that hamsters?''

''Who cares. We had them. Ya know, Tom, sometimes Mom has a spark and she remembers me. Then I cry and blow the whole moment. I hope she remembers you.''

Tom's voice was husky. ''Yeah, let's hope so. Can I bring you anything from sunny California?''

''I thought you said you didn't have any money.''

''I don't, but I still have a charge card. Name it.''

''Just yourself, Tom. We can go shopping when you get here and buy Mom some stuff for Christmas. Remember how she always loved the wrappings better than the presents. What'd you do with the money from the sale of the house, Tom?''

"Paid Dad's medical bills. There were two mortgages. I paid those off. Mom's condition hit around then. More medical bills. I have all the records, Annie. I would never snow you on that."

"I never liked your shitty wife," Annie said, uncorking a second bottle of wine. "You were too good for her. I like your kids, though. Do you think I'll ever have kids, Tom?"

"Not at the rate you're going. We'll have to do something about that."

"Yes, let's do something about that. Somebody without any deep, dark secrets. I hate people who have secrets."

"Are you trying in your own inimitable way to tell me *you* have a deep, dark secret?"

"Me? Sorry. No secrets here. Do you have any?"

"I was going to keep my divorce from you, so I guess I don't, now that I told you. You probably should go to bed, Annie."

"Why is that, Tom?"

"So you're bright-eyed and bushy-tailed when it's time to pick me up instead of being hungover. Is that a good enough reason?"

"The best," Annie hiccuped. "What's it like to be really happy, Tom?"

"How about if I tell you tomorrow when you pick me up. Unplug your tree lights and go to bed. Will you promise me to do that?"

"Sure, Tom."

"Good girl. I'll say good night then."

Annie corked the wine bottle and dutifully turned off the Christmas tree lights. She thought about her old cat Flossie as she made her way up the stairs to her bedroom. It had always been her job to let the cat out before going to bed.

Tomorrow she was definitely going to get some goldfish.

*   *   *

Annie waited impatiently, her head throbbing, for her brother to walk through the gate. When she saw him she ran, her arms outstretched. "I'm so glad you came, Tom. This is going to be such a good Christmas. I'm going to cook a big turkey with all the trimmings. Do you have baggage?"

"A ton of it and something special for you. I took vacation time."

"That's great. How long?"

"Do you think you can put up with me for a whole month? I thought maybe I could help out a little. I owe you, Annie."

"I can use all the help I can get if you're serious. I can even offer you a job if you want one. We're going to open two shops near the Clemson campus. I'd love to turn one over to you. Both actually. You won't be making what you made in California, but the cost of living here is less. We're going big-time here. That means health benefits, a profit-sharing plan, all the coffee and tuna you want."

"I'll take it."

"Really, Tom?"

"Really, Annie."

"What about the kids?"

"Mona is playing hardball. She wants alimony and astronomical child support. I might as well tell you, she has a boyfriend. That's what started the whole thing. But, to answer your question about the kids, you'll have to give me time off to visit them or to fly them here. My lawyer says I can get them summers, weekends, and some holidays. Once every six weeks sounds good to me with the holidays and summers."

"That would be so nice, Tom. Which bags are yours?"

"The two big gray ones. They have wheels. We can't go yet. I have to wait for your present to come up. Stay here with the bags. I think I see it now."

Annie craned her neck to see where her brother was going, but the heavy holiday traffic pushed and jostled her until she finally gave up. It would be like Tom to bring her an orange tree loaded with oranges. She sat down on top of the largest traveling bag to wait. When she felt a tap on her shoulder she turned.

"Merry Christmas, Annie," Tom said, handing her a bright blue dog kennel.

"A dog! You got me a dog! Oh, Tom, how wonderful! Can I take him out? What's his name?"

"Of course you can take him out. He's yours. Rosie is her name. She's the best of the best, Annie. Championship lines all the way. Now that you're living alone, you need someone like Rosie here."

"A German shepherd! Oh, she's just gorgeous. I love her. I will love her forever and ever. Oh, Tom, this is just so wonderful of you." Annie buried her face in the dog's soft fur. She thought she could hear the dog purr her approval.

"You have to bond with her. That means you hold her close to your heart and snuggle with her. I didn't handle her at all because I didn't want to confuse her. Tell me where the car is, and I'll get it. You stay here with the baggage and Princess Rosie. She's six weeks and two days old. Do you really like her, Annie? You know, really like her?"

"How could I not, Tom. She's adorable."

"You can do anything you want. She's your dog. Now, where's the car?"

"It's a Volvo station wagon. Dark green and parked in Row C, third one from the end. Here's the key. Drag the bags outside, and I'll carry the kennel. We'll wait on the curb for you. Oh, look, she's asleep."

"She can feel your heart beat so she feels safe with you," Tom said.

"How'd you learn so much about dogs? We always had cats."

"I got a crash course last night. I found this dog in a little less than three hours and still made it to the airport. I have _books_ in my baggage on what to do and not do. The breeder said you need to read them. All of them," he said ominously.

"Okay," Annie said, nuzzling the dog. This time she thought she heard the puppy sigh. Suddenly her world felt right side up. Tom was here and bygones would now be bygones. She wouldn't be alone anymore, and now she would have someone to love. Someone to love her back. "You can't take Mom's place but you'll do," she whispered into the puppy's ear. "This is going to be the best Christmas ever."

Annie set the table as the new pup tweaked her ankles and shoes. She was everywhere, but always within sight, curious and devilish as she explored every inch of the old house.

"Okay, big gal, let's go for a stroll in the garden. We don't want any messes when company gets here. Go get your leash. That's a good girl," Annie praised, as Rosie brought her a frayed and tattered string that had once been a leash. "Guess it's a chain from now on. We do not chew our leashes. Is that understood?"

The shepherd sat up on her haunches, her ears straight as arrows as she stared at her mistress. Her bark was deep and joyful at the prospect of an outing.

Annie walked the dog through the garden. "You know, Rosie, I bought this house because of the garden. I saw myself sitting out here on one of those old Charleston rockers, reading and sipping lemonade. I bet that angel oak is at least three hundred years old if it's a day. When you get a little bigger you're going to love lying under it. It stays green all year long, so on sunny days we can come out here to contemplate the conditions of the world and my deep, dark secret that suddenly doesn't seem so deep and dark. Of course that just means I'm in denial.''

Annie eyed the ancient wooden gate with the stout padlock. No one could get in from the outside. If she wanted to, she could hide out here for days, and no one would know the difference. She watched indulgently as Rosie dug at the luscious green moss growing between the cobbled stones. She didn't stop her. It was, after all, her garden, too. She'd outgrow her curiosity soon enough. She stopped her frantic pawing, her puppy eyes alert, her head tilted to the side. ''Company, huh? Yes, I hear the car. Okay, let's go in and welcome our guests.''

The little dog bounded across the small courtyard to struggle up the two steps that led to the kitchen. Annie had to boost her fat little bottom over the second hurdle. She woofed her pleasure when Tom walked into the kitchen, Norma behind him. The pup sniffed his shoes and growled as she pawed at Norma's leg. Tom scooped her up into his arms, and said, ''You should have warned me, Annie. You did, but I still wasn't prepared. There hasn't been one sign of recognition.''

''I know. It's like that sometimes, then bingo, she'll say something that makes perfect sense.''

''Mom, I'm so glad you could come. Isn't it wonderful that we're all going to spend Christmas together?''

''Did we get a tree? I don't seem to remember that. What's your name again? This nice gentleman didn't introduce us.''

''Anna Daisy Clark, Mom. Are you hungry? I made a turkey and all the stuff you used to make on holidays. I can give you some to take back when you leave.''

''That would be nice. This isn't my house. My kitchen cabinets are white with those little crisscross panes. Who lives here?''

''Me and Tom. Would you like a glass of wine, Mom?''

''If this is Christmas, then I'd like a good slug of bourbon.

Did anyone see my husband? We always had bourbon on Christmas. Never mind, he's probably shoveling the snow. We'll have it later. I keep forgetting I need to mind my p's and q's. I didn't say anything wrong, did I?''

"No, Mom." Annie met her brother's gaze and muttered, "I'll explain it all later."

"More company," Tom said. "I'll get it." Still carrying the dog, he pushed his way through the swinging door.

"He's such a nice man. He reminds me of someone," Norma said vaguely.

"Tom's your son, Mom. I'm Annie, your daughter. Don't you remember?"

"I remember your secret. I didn't tell anyone. I really didn't."

Annie stared into her mother's eyes and swore later that she felt her blood run cold. "We promised not to mention it, Mom. I didn't tell anyone about your secret. Please don't mention it again."

"All right, my dear. I like your name."

"Lazy Daisy. That's what you used to call me."

"Yes. I forget sometimes. It smells wonderful. The owner must be a good cook."

"She is. She had the best teacher in the world," Annie said, biting down on her lower lip. "Let's go into the living room. We have company. We need to be sociable."

"That's what Joe always says. Where in the dickens is that man? Did it snow that much?"

"I guess so. Mom, do you remember Jane and Elmo?"

"No. Maybe Joe remembers who they are. I haven't seen Flossie for a while. Did she get out?"

"I think she's upstairs," Tom said.

"Oh."

"Listen up everyone," Jane said, her face flushed. "Bob and I have an announcement to make."

I knew it. I knew it, Annie thought as her stomach started to churn.

"Bob asked me to marry him. Look," she said, flashing her new engagement ring.

"Oh, Jane, I'm so happy for you both. When's the big day?"

"Valentine's Day. Isn't that romantic? Annie, Bob wants to move to San Francisco. A friend offered him a partnership in a four-man firm. I'll be able to paint all day long. I know you're upset. Please don't be. Bob can still do your accounting. It won't be a problem."

"Jane, I can't buy you out."

"Oh, Annie, I'm not asking you to buy me out. I'm giving the shops to you. You really did all the work. It was your idea. I just helped. You don't owe me anything."

"No, no, that's not fair. You worked as hard as I did to get them up and running. I could never do that, and you know it."

"Okay, how about this then? Someday when you're a multi-millionaire, you give me one of the shops. If you don't like that idea, it's okay with me. Honestly, Annie, I don't want anything. I feel terrible leaving you like this. But, now that your brother is here, I don't feel so bad."

"It sounds like a good deal to me," Norma chirped.

"Do you think so, Mom?"

"Your brother is so handsome, isn't he, Annie?"

"The handsomest guy I know," Annie said in a choked voice. She watched as Tom wrapped his mother in his arms, his eyes glistening with unshed tears.

"That's because I get my looks from you," he said gruffly.

Rosie growled playfully as one paw snaked out to play with the string of pearls around Norma's neck. Annie smiled when her mother giggled at the dog's antics. "Tom and I will take anything we can get," she murmured. Only Tom heard her and nodded his agreement.

"Annie, are you okay with this?" Jane asked.

"Of course I am. I would never stand in your way. I don't want you to give it all up, though. If you're sure one shop for you is okay, then it's okay with me. Consider it a nest egg for the future. It's expensive to put kids through college even on a partner's pay. I'll find a lawyer after the first of the year to draw up the papers. We want to do this all legal. I'm happy for you, Jane, I really am. This is turning out to be a wonderful Christmas. I wonder where Elmo is?"

"There's the doorbell. Right on time. Is he bringing either one of his lady friends?" Jane asked.

"Nope. He said he wanted to enjoy Christmas Eve with his family. Is he going to give you away at your wedding?"

"You bet!" Jane said. "I want you to be my maid of honor. We're just going to do the JP thing. We'll do dinner, then be on our way to San Francisco."

"I'm so jealous," Annie said.

"It's not your time yet, child. The right man will find you when it's time."

"Is that a promise, Mom?"

"Lazy Daisy, of course it's a promise. I never broke a promise to you or Tom, did I?"

"No, Mom. Never ever."

Tom beamed.

"Merry Christmas. Merry Christmas," Elmo called out.

"Tell Elmo the news, Jane," Annie said, her eyes star-bright as she put an arm around her mother's shoulders.

"I'm getting married and moving to San Francisco. I want you to give me away. Will you do it, Elmo?"

The wizened little man twinkled. "I'm honored that you would consider me for such an important role. Of course I'll give you away."

"Norma, you're looking particularly pretty this Christmas Eve. And you must be Tom," Elmo said, holding out his hand.

"Seems we're going to have our work cut out for us with Jane leaving us. You up to it, boy?"

"I'm up to it, sir," Tom said, tongue in cheek.

"Then we're in business. It's our job to make Miss Anna Daisy Clark into one of the richest women in the country. I think we can do it. What's your opinion, son?"

"I think we can do it, sir," Tom said, winking at Annie.

"Call me Elmo."

"Where's the bourbon?" Norma queried.

"I'll get it, Mom," Tom said.

When Annie closed and locked the door hours later, she turned to her brother. "All things considered, it was a wonderful Christmas Eve. Mom knew us for a little while. Jane is delirious with happiness. We called your kids, and everyone said 'Merry Christmas.' Elmo is in his glory plotting our next business steps. You're here. I'm here. And I have Rosie. I don't think I could ask for more. Tomorrow we'll go to church, then we'll start working on the new year. Merry Christmas, Tom."

"Merry Christmas, sis," Tom said, wrapping his arms around Annie to hug her until she squealed. Rosie came on the run and skidded to a stop when she saw that it was Tom making her mistress squeal with delight. She backed up a step, squatted, and peed in the middle of the floor, then ran to her kennel, where she went when she made mistakes.

"It's okay, Rosie. My fault. I lost track of time. C'mon, you can come out." The pup waddled her way over to Annie, her tail swishing furiously. Annie scooped her into her arms. "Tomorrow's another day. Let's go to bed, Tom. We can clean up in the morning."

"Sounds good to me. Were you serious about me living here with you, Annie?"

"Yes. I told you, the cost of living here is cheaper. Think of all that extra money you'll have, not having to pay rent in California."

"Elmo has such big plans. Are we up to this, Annie?"

"We're up to it, Tom. Trust me on this. I am going to miss Jane, though."

"You can hire someone to sit at an easel and paint postcards. A young art student will jump at the chance."

Arm in arm, brother and sister walked up the steps.

"I'm glad you're here, Tom."

"Me too, Annie. Thanks for giving me the chance."

"My pleasure. Thanks for giving me this dog. Did I thank you before?"

"At least five hundred times. *That* was my pleasure."

"Night, Tom."

"Night, Annie."

In her room, with Rosie settled on her own little blanket, Annie withdrew the note Jane had passed her early in the evening. Her heart pounded inside her chest when she thought about why her friend hadn't taken her aside to tell her whatever was in the note. Why would Jane write her a note? *She knows.*

Annie sat down on the bed and unfolded the note.

Dear Annie,

I knew tonight would be hectic, and I wouldn't be able to get you alone. Also, I didn't want to spoil the evening. Hence the note. I am so worried about Peter Newman. He's been dogging Bob at the office. I know in my heart of hearts he thinks my car was the one where the money bag was tossed. Maybe by moving to San Francisco, I can get him out of my hair. I don't know why he's homed in on me like he has. He's scaring me and Bob as well. I'm just sorry I don't have your guts when it comes to dealing with that creep. He actually came right out and said I might have had a blanket or something on the floor and then thrown it away. This man is not going to go away. Not ever. I'm just so happy I can't stand the thought of that jerk spoiling my happiness. I haven't had a really good day since that creep invaded our lives, and I know you haven't either, for all your bravado.

Annie, you will always have a special place in my heart, and I want you to be the godmother to my first child. I want us to promise each other we will never let our friendship dwindle away to the point where we just send Christmas cards. You are the sister I never had. The best friend in the whole world. I hope your life turns out to be as wonderful as I hope mine will be.

Much love and affection.

Jane

Annie folded the note and placed it in her night-table drawer. *That does it. The day after Christmas, I'm mailing back the money.* She felt so dizzy and light-headed, she ran to the bathroom and stuck her head under the cold-water faucet. Then she started to cry. *She knows. The note is Jane's way of telling me she knows and would keep the secret. She couldn't face me. She doesn't want to be around me for fear she'll slip and say something or that something will show on her face. I know it as sure as I'm sitting here on this bed.*

If Jane thinks it's me, and Newman thinks it's her, where does that leave me? If I send the money back and Jane moves to San Francisco, will he pursue her? What can he do? He needs proof. He doesn't have proof. The bag went up in flames. The clasp was hacked to pieces and tossed all over the state of North Carolina. He has no proof. Money has fingerprints on it. Well, I can put it in a pillowcase and run it through the wash cycle in the washing machine. I never touched the bearer bonds. I'll wear gloves to pack it up. I can drive to Atlanta and mail it from there. If not Atlanta, then Alabama. Or, I could drive all the way to Virginia or Washington, DC. I'll tell Tom and Elmo I want to scout an area for some new locations.

Then I'll go in the opposite direction. I can do it all in one day. I know I can do it.

If I mail it back and Jane finds out, she'll know for certain her note worked, and it was me all along. Can I live with that?

Maybe I should tell Tom. Tom would know what to do. No, better not to involve anyone. Elmo. God, no.

Annie curled up next to the little dog and hugged her. ''We'll think about this tomorrow, Rosie. I'll do the right thing. I really will.''

CHAPTER FIVE

Annie waited until she was sure Tom was sound asleep before she crept downstairs with the pillowcase full of money, which she'd been forced to bring home when her mother's furniture was readied for shipment to Westbury Center. Her whole body trembled as she stuffed it into the washing machine in the laundry room. How much soap was required to launder money? Should she use bleach? If she did, would it take the color out of the money? Dear God, what if she ruined it. Maybe she should use vinegar and baking soda. Her mother always said the combination would kill anything in its path. If it could kill an ant pile it should clean the money and destroy any and all of her fingerprints. Which cycle? she dithered. Gentle, normal, heavy-duty, or fine washables? Hot or cold? She started to shake all over again as she turned dials. Hot water and heavy-duty? She set the timer for a fifteen-minute wash cycle. With the soft water here in Charleston, what would she do if the money came out fluffy and hard to manage? "This is insane," she muttered just as the doorbell rang. Who in the world would be ringing her doorbell at ten o'clock on Christmas night?

Annie ran to the door, tripping over her own feet as she went along. She squinted through the peephole and gasped. Daniel.

"Merry Christmas," the professor said, holding out a luscious-looking poinsettia plant and a small gaily wrapped package.

"Daniel! How nice to see you."

Daniel laughed. "Guess I'm a little late. I went to Georgia to see my dad and just got back. I've been gone for the last two weeks."

"Oh."

"A drink would be nice. It is rather cold standing here. If this isn't a good time, I can come back."

"No, no. I'm sorry. My mind has been somewhere else all day. Come in. What would you like to drink?"

"What are you having?"

"Wine."

"Then wine it is. Nice tree. I always chop one down for my dad. We try to pretend it's like past Christmases when Mom was still here and my brothers were around. It never works, but we keep trying. How's your mother?"

"She was here last night. We do that Christmas Eve thing instead of Christmas Day. Mom started it when we gave up on Santa. My brother's here, and she had a few good moments where she knew us."

"Good God, what's that racket?" Daniel asked, whirling around.

"Well . . . it's probably . . . the washing machine probably went off center. I'll just turn it off."

"Let me help you. I'm an old hand where washing machines are concerned. I have this relic in my apartment that goes off center every time I wash a load of clothes. It's really a simple matter of redistributing the load and using your backside to slide the machine back to its original position."

"Really, it isn't a problem. Tom can . . . Tom can adjust it in the morning." She should have given more thought to the contents and going off center. *Damn, why didn't I think of that?*

"It's no problem. For you to be washing on Christmas, the clothing must be important."

"I was bored," Annie said lamely. "See, it stopped all by itself." With all the bouncing around the machine was doing, the money might be shredded by now. *You are one stupid woman, Annie Clark.*

"Tell me, how can you be bored? What are you doing alone on Christmas? Where are all your friends?"

"They're all busy. Elmo is with his two lady friends. Jane is with Bob. They got engaged and are going to move to San Francisco. Tom's here, but he's beat, so he went to bed early. He's going to move here and help with the business. He's going through a divorce."

"Don't tell me any more. Been there, done that. It wasn't a good time in my life. It still isn't. I wanted to tell you, Annie. It's just that I hate talking about it. Right now I can't handle anything more than friendship."

"Friendship is fine. I'm not in a hurry to . . . what I mean is, I'm not ready . . . this isn't coming out right. Friendship is fine. More wine?"

"Sure. That's a pretty tree. Did you have it cut down?"

Annie laughed. "Nineteen ninety-five from the Shell station."

"At least you have a tree. I didn't get one for the apartment. I put up a wreath on the door before I left, and when I got back it was gone. Some kids probably swiped it. I bought mine at the Piggly Wiggly. You know what I always say, if it works, then do it."

"Yeah, I say that a lot myself." Annie giggled. "Listen, if you're hungry, I can make you a turkey sandwich."

"I am, and I'll take it. How about some of that good coffee

of yours? Which brings me to the real reason I came by. When I got to my dad's house a Christmas card was waiting for me from an old college buddy. He owns a coffee plantation in Hawaii. Primo stuff. I called him just for the heck of it and he said you should order your coffee beans direct from him instead of buying through a middleman. Real nice guy. Single, no baggage. Women fall all over him. He's part Hawaiian, part Irish. Great athlete. He whipped my ass at every sport we ever played. He's competitive, rich as sin, and the best friend a guy could have. He was my best man when I got married. Anyway, he'll give you the best deal going. You need to go there and check it out. He said you could stay at the plantation. Trust me when I tell you there's nothing this guy doesn't know about coffee. I think he was weaned on the stuff instead of milk.''

"Really," was all Annie could think of to say.

"Mayo and mustard. Do you have any pickles?"

"I have a whole jar full."

"You shouldn't have said that. Pickles are my downfall."

"The only reason I have them is I forgot to put them on the table last night."

"So you and your brother are going to run the shops, eh?"

"Yes, but we're going to have to hire more help. Do you know any art students who might be interested in sitting in the shop doing the postcards?"

"As a matter of fact, I do. Great kid, hard worker. Gives a hundred percent to anything she does. She paints scenes on sand dollars. That's what's in the present I brought you. I had her come by while I was gone to paint your shop and this house."

Annie ran into the living room for the small gift box. She oohed and aahed when she saw the sand dollars. "These are beautiful. If she wants the job, tell her it's hers. What about her classes?"

"She clerks at Bob Ellis during the day. Takes classes at

night. She's in the master's program. I'm sure you can work something out.''

''Full-time. Health benefits. We're working on a profit-sharing program. It won't be up and running for a while yet. She helps out behind the counter when it's busy. Base salary, half of whatever the sand dollars go for. We pay for the paints and the sand dollars. Sound good?''

''Better than good. She'll take it.''

''How do you know?'' Annie asked curiously.

''Because it beats selling shoes, that's why.'' Daniel laughed. ''If you had a choice, would you like to deal with smelly feet all day or would you rather sit like a lady and paint sand dollars?''

''Point well taken. Would you like some pie?''

''I think I'll pass on the pie. I have to pick up my cat Radar from a friend, and I need some sleep. So, are you going to take Parker up on his offer?''

''Parker?''

''Parker Grayson. The coffee king.''

''I'll talk to Tom about it in the morning. I'm for anything that will save me money. We're going to open two shops near Clemson University. Five hundred pounds of coffee a week is a lot of coffee.''

''Okay, here's his phone number and address. He said he'd send someone to the airport to pick you up. All he needs is two days' notice. I'm outta here, Annie. My eyes are starting to cross. You're sure now that you don't want me to move your washer?''

The smile died on Annie's lips. ''I'm sure, Daniel. Thanks for the lovely plant and the sand dollars. What's the girl's name?''

''Dottie Frances Benton.''

''Tell her to come by and we'll talk.''

At the door, Daniel leaned over and kissed her on the cheek. "Merry Christmas, Annie."

"The same to you, Daniel."

Annie raced out to the laundry room the moment she was certain Daniel was off the porch and headed home. Thank God the laundry room had no windows. In a frenzy, she propped open the top of the washer, to be greeted by a sloppy mess. She tried to lift the pillowcase out of the water, but it was too heavy. Wet money was heavy. In desperation, she tried using two wooden spatulas from the kitchen drawer to try and slide the soggy pillowcase to the center of the washer. Perspiration dripping down her face, she finally managed to push the heavy case full of money to where she thought it would spin more effectively. Her breathing ragged, she turned the dial to the spin cycle. She jumped back when the machine bounded forward but continued to spin. Hardly daring to breathe, Annie waited out the cycle.

"Annie, do you mind telling me what the hell you're doing washing clothes in the middle of the night? What's the machine doing in the middle of the floor?"

"It's okay, Tom. Go back to bed. Rosie threw up on Mom's old quilt, and I decided to wash it. It lumped to the side and made the machine go off center. It's okay, I can handle it." *I'm really getting good at this lying business,* she thought miserably.

"I'm up now, so I might as well help you."

Annie almost choked. "Let's let it go till morning. How about a sandwich?"

"Sure. Do we have any cold beer?"

"Sure we do. I have something to tell you, Tom," she said as she ushered him toward the kitchen. She talked as she sliced turkey onto a plate. "Daniel Evans, that professor I told you about stopped by and brought me these. What do you think?"

"They're pretty."

"They're sand dollars, and one of the students at the college painted them. It's the Daisy Shop and this house. She can take Jane's place if I like her and she wants the job. Basically it would be the same deal I had with Jane."

Tom chewed with enthusiasm. "This stuff just falls in your lap, doesn't it, sis?"

"Seems that way sometimes. Jane's postcards and her paintings are part of the shop. Kind of like salt and pepper going together. This girl works full-time and goes to school at night. Don't ask me when she studies. Maybe she's a quick learner. Daniel said she sells shoes at Bob Ellis. I'm going to hire her. Do you agree?"

"Of course."

"He also thinks I should go to Hawaii to talk to his friend Parker Grayson, who has a coffee plantation. He seems to think we can get a better deal on the coffee from him and he might roast it for us, too. Eliminates the middleman. If both shops are successful at Clemson we'll be ordering about five hundred pounds of coffee a week. We need to get the best deal possible."

"I agree."

"There's something else, Tom. With Jane and Bob moving to San Francisco, I don't think I want him doing our accounting. I just don't know how to bring it up tactfully without causing hard feelings with Jane. I don't want to have to rely on the mail and worry about will it get there on time. He's been picking up the stuff on a weekly basis. I'm more comfortable with a local firm. What's your feeling?"

"I agree with you on that, too. I can talk to Bob. If it looks like it's getting dicey, I'll say I'm taking it over. Business is business, Annie. When friendship gets involved there's always trouble. I'll be the bad guy and take the hit so your friendship with Jane stays intact. Boy, that was a good sandwich. How about a chunk of that stuffing? Do you remember, Annie, how

Mom always made extra because we liked to eat it cold between two slices of bread? We ate that stuff for weeks.''

"I remember."

"Do you still write in that diary I gave you on your sixteenth birthday?"

"Every day of my life. All my memories are in there, or as many of them as three lines can hold. Someday when we're both home with the flu or a bad cold, I'll read some of it to you. How come you went to bed so early?"

"I was kind of down. I miss the kids. Seeing Mom and knowing it isn't going to get any better, realizing what a jerk I was where you were concerned. It all kind of piled up on me."

"There's more, isn't there?"

Tom's face closed up tight. "Yes, but I don't want to talk about it."

"That's why you should talk about it. Let's have another beer and sit by the tree and talk it out. We used to do that in high school. Then when we went to bed it all seemed bearable."

"That was a long time ago, Annie. We aren't kids anymore."

"That's exactly my point, Tom. We're adults now, and we think and act like adults. Now tell me what it is you don't want to talk about."

"Ah, it's Mona. I don't want my kids having a stepfather. Guys never treat other guy's kids the way they'd treat their own. Ben's immature, and he's sensitive. Jack is mouthy and going through a phase. Mandy is growing up so fast. She wants to be like Mona. Mona is too permissive. I was the disciplinarian. If Mona and the guy she's seeing decide to get married, where does that leave my kids? Even if I lived in California in a house two doors away, Mona would only let me see them on the days the court agreed on. She says I can have them. That's just the way she said it—you can have them if you give me a hundred thousand dollars. Do you believe that! She'd sell her own kids for a hundred grand. I must have been deaf, dumb, *and* stupid when I married her. Even if I had the money, I wouldn't be a part of that. I know Ben heard her that day on the phone when she said it, because he asked me to buy him. I had to do some fast talking to convince the kid he heard wrong.''

''That's terrible, Tom.''

''Tell me about it. Right isn't always might as they say. If it's meant to work out, it will. If it isn't, it won't. That's the way I have to look at it. You know, Annie, that's a damn good-looking Christmas tree. What's on our agenda for tomorrow?''

''I think I'm going to go clothes shopping in case I decide to go to Hawaii. You need to meet with Elmo and, if you have the time, take a ride up to Clemson and look it over. Elmo knows the area and will be glad to go with you. Tops, it's a two-hour ride.''

''Sounds good. I guess I'll say good night again. I love you, Annie. I really do. If there were times when it didn't seem like I did, I'm sorry. I just had too much on my plate back then.''

''I know that, Tom. Sleep tight.''

''Where's Rosie?''

''Sleeping on my bed. That long walk before dinner knocked her out. She slept through Daniel's visit.''

''That will never happen when she's full-grown. See you in the morning.''

''Okay, it's your turn to make breakfast.''

''Not a problem.''

Annie waited, hardly daring to breathe until she heard Tom's door close, before she beelined to the laundry room. She stared down at the bulging soggy pillowcase full of money. She could buy her niece and nephews from Mona if she wanted to. All she had to do was count out one hundred thousand dollars and hand it over to Tom's soon-to-be-ex-wife, and the kids would be his. There was something so barbaric about the thought she slammed the top of the machine so loud she winced. Then she crossed her fingers that Tom didn't hear the sound. She took a deep breath and held it. When she was satisfied Tom would stay upstairs, she expelled the air in her lungs in a loud *swoosh*.

Using every muscle in her body, Annie struggled with the wet pillowcase until she had it on top of the machine. Her heart pounding with the effort, she managed to get it into the dryer with a loud thump. Huffing and puffing, she turned the knob to high heat and waited to see if the drum would turn. She sighed her relief as the dryer tumbled and turned.

With nothing to occupy her, Annie cleaned the kitchen while she waited for the money to dry. Maybe she should have tried to dry smaller amounts in the microwave. But, to do that, she would have had to handle the money. This way all she had to do was dump the money in a box along with the bearer bonds and mail it back to the bank.

An hour later she cried her frustration when she opened the dryer to find the money almost as wet as when she put it in. She opened the pillowcase to see clumps of bills stuck together. It was obvious that she needed a bigger pillowcase. She turned the dryer back on and sat down on the floor, Indian fashion, to wait, tears dripping down her cheeks. Being a thief wasn't easy.

Three hours later the money was finally dry.

Annie slung the pillowcase over her shoulder and made her way to the second floor, where she tossed it into the closet. She fell into bed and was asleep in minutes, the tears still on her cheeks.

Annie woke slowly, aware of a strange noise in her room. She reached out to touch Rosie, but she was gone. She squinted at the bedside clock: 5:10. It was still dark outside. She switched on the lamp. Rosie bounded onto the bed, a twenty-dollar bill clutched in her teeth. Annie's head felt like it was going to explode right off her neck when she saw the littered money on

the floor of the bedroom. Bits and piece of different denomina-
tions were everywhere. Her flowered carpet was now a sea of
green.

Rosie barked once as she leaned over the side of the bed to
inspect her handiwork. Annie gave her a swat as she struggled
with the twenty-dollar bill she was planning to chew. It ripped
in two. She cursed, using every swear word she'd ever heard
her brother Tom use in his hellion days. Any minute now she
was going to lose it and have a nervous breakdown.

Annie slid from the bed, her eyes wild with panic. How
could she send shredded money back to the bank? On her knees,
she tried to gather up the bits and pieces of money to try and
determine how much the pup had chewed up. At eight o'clock,
with socks on her hands, she counted the money in the pillowcase, finally deciding Rosie had chewed up $23,420. She could
send it all back with a note saying . . . what? Did she dare wash
the bits and pieces again.

A headache, the likes of which she'd never experienced,
thundered inside her head. Rosie bellied over to where she was
sitting and crept onto her lap and started to lick her face. She
hugged her. The murderous headache subsided almost immediately. "This is a setback. A big one. I'm going to work this
out. I know I can work this out. I will work this out."

Rosie leaped off her lap and ran to the door when Tom
knocked, and shouted, "Breakfast in ten minutes!"

"Okay. Be right there," Annie responded, her eyes wild.
She was a lightning bolt then as she ripped the pillowcase from
her pillow. On her hands and knees, she crawled about the
room picking up the tattered money. "I know you ate some of
this money. I know it. You're going to be pooping twenty-
dollar bills all day. If this wasn't so serious, it would be damn
funny."

This time, Annie closed the closet door before she bent down
to pick up the pup. "Bad dog, Rosie. Now I'm in hock to the

bank for more than twenty-three thousand dollars. Oh, well, life is going to go on no matter what I do. I'll find a way to pay it back. I wonder if they'll let Tom bring you to jail when he visits me,'' she muttered. The pup yipped her pleasure at being carried down the long staircase.

''Oh, it smells good, Tom. What are we having?''

''The works. Pancakes, scrambled eggs, bacon, fresh brewed coffee, and I squeezed the orange juice myself. I know my way around the kitchen. How'd you sleep?''

''I didn't. I had a terrible dream.''

''Couldn't be worse than mine. Share.'' Tom grinned as he filled his sister's plate.

''I dreamed Rosie chewed up twenty thousand dollars I was going to put in the bank,'' Annie blurted. The moment the words were out of her mouth she wanted to take them back.

''That's not a dream, that's a nightmare. I had this dream that Ben put an ad in a yuppie magazine offering to sell himself to the highest bidder.''

''It was the turkey sandwiches and all those pickles we ate before we went to bed,'' Annie said. ''I'm not doing that again.''

''Twenty thousand, huh? In your dream did Rosie eat the money or chew it up?''

''Both,'' Annie said, guilt riding her shoulders like a yoke.

''What'd you do in the dream?''

''I woke up. I don't want to talk about it, Tom. It was a stupid dream. Rosie had been chewing on the newspaper in my room the other day. I guess that's what triggered the whole thing. Great breakfast,'' she said, pushing her plate away.

''I cooked, so that means you clean up. Get rid of that turkey. I hate eating it for a week after a holiday.''

''Bossy, aren't we,'' Annie said as she got up from the table.

''Just playing big brother, Annie. Twenty thousand? Wow.

Wonder what it means. I'll be in the living room studying Elmo's business plan if you need me.''

Annie wondered why her legs were so shaky. She'd never quite heard that tone in Tom's voice before. Was it her imagination or guilt? She needed a quiet place to think and plan. Maybe she would walk Rosie down to the Daisy Shop, open it up, and sit in the back room and ponder her immediate problem. Yes, that's exactly what she would do.

"I'm taking Rosie for a walk, Tom," Annie called from the kitchen.

"Want some company?" Tom called back.

The last thing she wanted was company. "Nope. It's just me and Rosie."

"Okay, see you later."

"Yeah, much later," Annie muttered as she hooked the leash onto the frisky pup's bright red harness.

CHAPTER SIX

Annie was tired and cranky. It seemed like she'd been traveling for days. Her eyes felt like they were full of grit, and she knew all the moisture had been sucked out of her face. Her hair seemed to have a mind of its own, and her smart linen dress was limp and wrinkled. Her feet and ankles were swollen, and she was getting a headache. If she could have any thing on earth, she would opt for a hot shower and clean hair.

Annie tipped the skycap and looked around for someone who appeared to be looking for her. All she could see were busy travelers in bright-colored garb wearing leis. She felt cheated as well as annoyed that she didn't have one. She'd heard the scent of plumeria was exquisite.

It was hot. Hotter than it was in Charleston when she left. Still, it was the middle of July. Even so, where were the warm, gentle island breezes the brochures touted? Island breezes scented with flowers. All she could smell was diesel fuel and exhaust fumes. "This is not going to endear me to you, Parker Grayson." On the phone, the coffee king had said someone would be waiting for her the moment she got off the plane. "Ha!" she snorted. Two hours later she mumbled, "I'm giving you five more minutes of my time, Mr. Coffee, then I'm outta here. I'll get my coffee from Sumatra. I always wanted to go there anyway."

"Five minutes are up," Annie muttered to no one in particular. Her hand in the air, she hailed a cab. It always paid to have Plan B at one's disposal. "Take me to the nearest hotel, please," she said to the cab driver.

An open-air jeep sailed to the curb the moment the taxi pulled away to enter the steady stream of traffic leaving the Maui Airport. *So much for island hospitality,* she thought sourly as she leaned back in the seat of the cab.

It wasn't just hot, it was sultry hot. The linen dress now felt like a damp dishrag. She winced when she remembered how much she'd paid for it.

"Are you visiting our wonderful island for the first time, miss?" the driver inquired.

"Yes, and it's probably my last."

"Long flight?"

"Very long. I had a four-hour layover in San Francisco. I started out in Charleston, then flew to Atlanta, and from there to St. Louis to San Francisco and from there to your Big Island and then the puddle jumper to here. Someone from the Grayson Plantation was supposed to meet me."

"Their jeep pulled into my parking space when we left. Everyone knows the Grayson jeep. I can turn around and go back if you want me to. I went to school with Roy Alabado. He's the driver. Maybe the jeep broke down or maybe he had a flat. Mr. Grayson is mighty particular about his guests being picked up on time. He treats his guests like royalty."

"The royalty theme doesn't seem to be working today," Annie snapped. "And, no, I don't want to go back."

"I can call Mr. Grayson for you, miss."

"Don't bother. I'll call him myself when I get to the hotel."

"Mr. Grayson usually isn't on Maui at this time of year. He spends most of the year in the Kona district of the Big Island. This is a small island where all the locals know everyone else's business." The driver laughed. "You must be an important guest for Mr. Grayson to come here now."

Annie wasn't impressed or amused. "Do you know Mr. Grayson?"

"We say aloha when we meet. Everyone says aloha to everyone else. It is a custom here in the islands. Mr. Grayson has a fine reputation, and his coffees are sold all over the world. He treats his workers well and all the ladies like him. He's a bachelor with many nieces and nephews on the mainland. He is going to be very upset that you didn't wait for his people to pick you up."

"*He's* going to be upset! Is that what you said? No, no, that's all wrong. I'm the one who is upset. What I should do is buy my damn coffee from the Piggly Wiggly. Oh, we're here. How much is the fare?" Annie counted out money and added a generous tip to offset her surliness, after which she trudged wearily into the hotel, registered, and headed for her room. She showered, washed her hair, turned the air conditioner as high as it would go before she crawled between the crisp, cool sheets. She was almost asleep when she bolted upright to ring the front desk. "Don't put any calls through to my room until I tell you otherwise." A minute later she was sound asleep.

On the ride back to the airport to pick up another fare, the driver stopped to call the airport and have his boyhood friend paged. "This is Miki, Roy. I think I just took your guest to the Royal Hawaiian. That was one pissed off lady. How long you been waiting? Dump the leis and let's catch a beer. Okay, your loss. What do you mean, what should you do? Tell Mr. Grayson you had *two* flat tires. On the other hand, the truth is always an option. Yeah, see you around."

*   *   *

Golden sunshine found its way into Annie's room just as she opened her eyes. She reached for the small travel clock on the nightstand. Ten minutes past six. She closed her eyes to see if she needed more sleep. When her lids snapped open she dialed room service and ordered breakfast and a newspaper. ''No, I do not want to know about my messages. No, I am not interested in any guests sitting in your lobby who are waiting for me. Leave the tray outside the door please.'' Annie stomped her way to the shower.

Thirty minutes later, Annie opened the door for her breakfast tray. She peeped under the lids. Just as ordered. The paper was folded neatly, there were fresh flowers on the tray, and the coffee smelled heavenly. As she munched and crunched the crisp bacon, she placed a person-to-person call to her brother.

''This was a mistake, Tom,'' she said the moment she heard her brother's voice. ''He left me cooling my heels at the airport for over two hours. He could have paged me. Why is it you guys always stick together? This is not acceptable business behavior. I am calm. I'm eating my breakfast on the balcony and staring at the incredible blue Pacific Ocean. Now I know why they call it a jewel. You want *me* to call *him?* Not in this lifetime, big brother. I'm going to go shopping. Maybe I'll go to the beach and get a sunburn. That's what you're supposed to do when you come to Hawaii. Does Rosie miss me? No kidding. Your whole shoe or part of it? The whole thing? That dog has great teeth. How's business? Ohhh, I like the way that sounds. I have to get dressed. I'll call you tonight. Remember now, there's a five-hour time difference. Don't lecture me, Tom. I think the way I do business has been satisfactory so far. Too bad more people don't operate the way I do. Goodbye, Tom.''

At ten minutes past ten, dressed in sandals and a pale blue

sundress, her hair piled high on her head, Annie sashayed down the hall to the elevator. When the door swished open on the ground floor she found herself staring straight into the most incredible blue eyes she'd ever seen in her life. The owner of the blue eyes was also the most handsome man she'd ever seen. She knew exactly who he was.

In the blink of an eye, Anna Daisy Clark fell in love with Parker Grayson. She walked toward him, her eyes appraising him. "Daniel was right. You really do have incredible blue eyes."

He was at her side in an instant, his hand outstretched. Annie clasped it and crunched his hand.

"That's no mean handshake, Miss Clark." Grayson grinned, showing perfectly aligned white teeth that had never seen a set of braces.

"My brother taught me to do it that way. We used to arm wrestle. I always won. You look, Mr. Grayson, like I felt yesterday while I waited for two hours in this blistering heat for a driver who never showed up."

"I apologize. My driver had *two* flat tires. Not just one but two. I've been sitting in this damn lobby since six-thirty last night. That's why I look like this. No matter how you look at it, I'm twelve hours up on you." Annie smiled sweetly. "Is this one of those tit-for-tat things my sisters always talk about? If so, I need to know, so I'll know how to proceed."

In spite of herself, Annie laughed. "I think we're starting out even now." She waited. He was more than handsome, he was—she searched her mind for just the right word—exquisite. Tall, six-three or -four, muscular, perfect tan, amazing dark hair with just a touch of wave or curl. Khaki shorts, deck shoes, and a pristine white shirt. She wondered what their children would look like. "Why are you looking at me like that?"

"Daniel said you were my destiny. I think he might be right. What's your feeling on the subject?" Parker teased lightly.

Her face flushed, Annie said, "I was wondering what our children would look like?"

Grayson's tan turned pink, then red. "If you get your baggage, we should be on our way."

"Then I guess you're going to have to wait a while longer."

"My time is your time, Miss Clark."

"Call me Annie."

"Okay. Annie it is. My mother's name was Anna."

"It's an old-fashioned name. When I was younger I wanted a name like Tiffany or Angelique. When I was sixteen I wanted to change it to Barbarella." Parker laughed as he motioned her to head for the elevator. "Is this where you tell me time is money?"

"Exactly."

Annie jabbed the elevator button. "*Two* flat tires defies belief."

"I knew you would say that. I saw them with my own eyes. The flat tires I mean."

"Really." The elevator swished shut. Annie's closed fist shot in the air. "Yesssss."

"What do you think of my home, Annie?"

Annie looked around, her eyes wide. "It's breathtaking. I don't think I've ever seen anything quite so beautiful. Did you grow up here?"

"Yes. I live on the Big Island most of the year, but I come back for a day or so at a time. I get homesick. My father built the house himself, brick by brick. My mother planted the gardens. The banyan tree that stands sentinel there at the front was the first thing my mother planted after I was born. My mother said my father took one look at the land and knew exactly where to build. It sits on the broad crest of a sloping meadow. If you look you can see the Haleakala Volcano, and if you look down you have a vast view of the North Shore. I surfed there as a youngster. Still do at times with my nephews. They like to take on this old man but invariably they wipe out. I'm still the Big Kahuna as far as they're concerned.''

"I never learned to surf," Annie said. "Who tends to the house and all these gorgeous flowers? What is that gorgeous tree?''

"I'll teach you. A couple takes care of it while I'm away. Mattie cooks and cleans while George gardens. That tree is a monkeypod tree. I used to play under it when I was little. My mother read me island stories in the afternoons. I didn't know any other life but this until I was eighteen and went to the mainland to college. I hated being away. I used to count the days until it was time to come home for a holiday or summers, then I fought like a tiger not to go back. To me this is paradise. I don't think there's a prettier place anywhere on earth. I don't know that for a fact. That's what my parents said, and they were world travelers.

"We're within walking distance of freshwater pools and waterfalls. Every afternoon around three o'clock, we have rainbows. Brilliant, perfect rainbows that can be seen for miles. If you like to windsurf, Hookipa Beach is just fifteen minutes away. Five minutes from there is Paia, the Aspen of Hawaii. It's commercial, shopping, excellent restaurants, and a great white-sand beach. Paradise just twenty minutes from the airport. Do you like to wish on the rainbow?''

Annie's heart started to flutter. Just fourteen months ago she'd sat on the floor in her bedroom congratulating herself on the pot of gold at the end of her own personal rainbows. "No. No, I don't. Sometimes you get what you wish for," she said flatly.

Parker laughed. "I know that statement has some deep, dark meaning known only to you. Perhaps you'll share it with me someday." Annie knew the smile on her face looked sickly at best. "Tell you what. I'll have Mattie fix you a nice cool drink. You can walk in the gardens or check out the house. It's much cooler inside. I need to take a shower and change my clothes. Would you like to freshen up? Mattie will show you to your room."

"Yes, I think I would."

"Good, I'll see you in a bit then. Mattie, our guest is here," he bellowed.

She was incredibly tall and graceful. Ageless with her coronet of braids and high cheekbones. Her island attire was as regal-looking as she was. Annie felt like she was in the presence of royalty. She smiled, and Mattie returned her universal greeting. "Come, I will show you to your room." Annie followed like a puppy and then giggled when she saw the woman's bare feet peeking out from the colorful muu-muu she was wearing.

"Your dress is beautiful," Annie said.

"If you like it, I will make you one. Which color would you prefer?"

"Oh, no, I didn't mean for you . . ."

"It will be my pleasure. There is not much to do when Parker isn't here. I sew for his nieces all the time. If you do not have a color preference, I can make you one that will look like our daily rainbow. I have many bolts of rainbow silk. You are a size ten, no?"

"Yes. Size ten." It was an omen of some kind. She was sure of it. She was jittery now with all the talk of rainbows. *Shift into neutral,* she cautioned herself. *It's all just a coincidence.*

"I will have your island dress ready when it is time for you to leave. Freshen up, Miss Clark, and I will have lemonade ready for you on the lanai."

Annie waited until the door closed before she looked around at the room that would be hers for the next few days. For some reason she'd expected white-wicker furniture. Instead she had wonderful mahogany polished to a high sheen. The floors were a burnished teakwood. She smiled at the high four-poster, with its colorful spread. A paddle fan circled lazily overhead, while the crisp organdy curtains billowed into the room from the open French doors. She felt almost light-headed with the heady scent of the plumeria wafting into the room.

Annie sat down on the small bench that matched the vanity. For a little while she'd almost forgotten her ugly secret, then it was in her face again with all the talk about rainbows. She tried to push the thought away by concentrating on what she was going to do when she returned home. If she was lucky, July's profits would allow her to finally make up the money Rosie had chewed to pieces and then she would be able to package it up and return it to the bank. Fourteen months' worth of interest would bankrupt her. She'd have to figure out a way to send an IOU of some kind that couldn't be traced. *Don't think about that now. Think about these beautiful islands and this mini vacation. Think about Parker Grayson. Think about how attracted you are to him. Think about what it would be like to go to bed with him. Right here in this big old four-poster with the gentle trade winds blowing over your slick naked body. Think about* that. A ring of scorching heat circled her neck and crept up to her face just as a knock sounded on her door.

Annie opened the door, her face flaming. She'd never felt so flustered in her life.

"What's wrong?" Parker asked, his voice full of concern.

"Wrong?"

"Yes, you're all flushed."

"Oh. You probably won't believe this but I saw a cobweb up near the molding and I was jumping up and down to swat at it with a towel. Your housekeeper is too old to be jumping up and down."

"You're right, I don't believe you." Parker grinned. "I'd really like to hear the real reason you look so flustered."

The rosy hue on Annie's face darkened. "I don't think you could handle it."

"I'm a big boy. Try me."

"I was wondering what it would be like to go to bed with you," Annie said coolly as she sashayed past him and out through the door. She turned once and called over her shoulder, "Coming?" *Guess you left him speechless, Anna Daisy Clark. He looks absolutely dumbfounded.*

"You were saying," Annie prodded.

"Ah, what I was . . . ah thinking . . ."

"Yes, yes. What were you thinking?" She was enjoying this.

"I'm easy, but I'm not *that* easy."

"Easy is good. Did you ever make love in a bed filled with those wonderful flowers they make the leis with? By the way, all island visitors are supposed to get a lei. I did not get one." She wagged a finger under Parker's nose. Then she smiled wickedly. *This is somebody else in my body. This isn't me saying all these wild things. I never said anything even remotely like what I just said to this man. Never in my whole life.*

"No." The single word exploded from Parker's mouth like a gunshot.

"That's a shame," Annie said. "Which way is the lanai?"

"You're standing in it. Sit!"

"Why?" Annie asked.

"Because I told you to. I'll be right back."

Annie sat. She waited and waited. When her lemonade glass was empty she got up. *Some host. You probably scared him off, Annie Clark.*

"I thought I told you to sit."

"I was sitting. Now I'm standing. What difference does it make? You tell dogs to sit, not people."

"Go ahead, spoil our island traditions. It won't work unless you're sitting. Now sit!"

Annie sat.

"There. Now you have been officially greeted by a native of Hawaii," Parker said, placing not one but two fragrant leis around her neck. "I made them myself. That's what took me so long. Turn around. There's more to the custom." Annie turned around. "Now, close your eyes."

Annie closed her eyes. It was the sweetest, the most demanding, the most wonderful kiss she'd ever received in her life. She never wanted it to end.

Annie licked at her kissed lips. "I liked that."

"And well you should. It was one of my better efforts."

"Effort?"

"You know what I mean. You always save the best till . . . just the right time."

"Which would be . . . when?" *How had an alien being invaded her body? Who was this person saying all these things?*

"Do you want to set a date, or do you think we should get to know one another a little better?"

"I'm a what you see is what you get kind of person, Mr. Grayson. How about you?"

"Does that mean you don't have any deep, dark secrets? Everyone has secrets. People always say they're a what you see is what you get kind of person, then you find out they have all these problems, secrets, baggage, whatever."

Annie could feel her stomach muscles start to tighten up. She tried for a light tone. "Are you saying you're one of those people who is an open book with absolutely no secrets or skeletons in your closet?"

"That's what I'm saying. How about you? By the way, how old are you?"

"How old are *you?*" Annie demanded.

"I asked you first," Parker said.

"Old enough to know better. You're not supposed to ask a woman her age."

"Who said that?"

"My mother said it," Annie shot back. "I'm twenty-five."

"That's a good age," Parker said.

"A good age for what?"

"Starting a business, making love, getting married, having babies. So, are we setting a date or what? We should get it settled before we sit down to business."

"You're making it sound like a business deal," Annie said sourly. "I'm a sharp, intelligent businesswoman, so don't think you can put anything over on me. I can always get my coffee in Sumatra." *Good, the alien being had left her body, and she was now in control again.*

"How does four o'clock tomorrow afternoon sound? My own private beach. We'll go skinny-dipping. Then if it looks like something might come of it, we'll be ready. It will be like *From Here to Eternity.*" He was laughing at her. *The alien being swished through her body again.*

Annie smiled. Ever so sweetly. A wicked gleam in her eye, she said, "I hope you're *up* to it." She dusted her hands dramatically. "That's a really *big* beach down there. I bet it would take a *ton* of these petals to cover it. If there's one thing I hate, it's getting sand up my butt."

Parker choked on the lemonade he was about to swallow. Annie was off her chair in a heartbeat to pound him on his back. "Was it something I said? I love these leis. They make me feel . . . like I should be doing sinful things." *I've lost what's left of my mind. Think about the bank money. That will get you back on track.*

Parker cleared his throat. "I thought I'd give you a rundown on the coffee business before we fly out to Kona tomorrow."

"I'm all ears," Annie said as she propped her elbows on the table. "I hope you're going to tell me something I don't know."

"Daniel didn't say you were a smart-ass."

"Daniel doesn't know me. He's got great buns. Good, sturdy legs, too. He's a nice guy. Not my type, though." *You need to think about Peter Newman and the bank money. He's going to nail you when you get back.*

"Parker, I've been teasing you. I don't know what in the world got into me. I've never behaved this way in my life. I've always been a very boring, bookish person. I take my responsibilities very seriously. Something must have happened to my hormones when I set foot on this island. I apologize for my . . . tacky behavior. I did enjoy the kiss, though. Could we just forget everything that came before and after and concentrate on the reason I'm here."

"How's that going to work? Daniel said you were my destiny. He never lies."

"He does so lie. Everyone lies at some point or another."

"I don't," Parker said virtuously.

"We were going to talk about coffee."

"Fine, let's talk about coffee. For starters, the coffee grown here in Maui is not Kona coffee. The only place in the world that grows Kona coffee is the Kona district of the Big Island. We've been growing it in the rich volcanic soil on the slopes of Mauna Loa and Hualaalai for more than a hundred and fifty years. We tend our trees by hand and we're very selective about the ripe red cherries we pick. After we pick the cherries, the outer skins and pulp are removed in the pulping mill and the beans are put out to dry. When the beans dry completely the outer parchment skin and the inner silverskin are removed. We grade by size and density before we sew them in the burlap bags that carry our certificate. We ship to roasters around the world. We have our own roaster also. It's up to the clients if they want us to roast it or not. If you buy our coffee, do you want us to roast it or will you have it shipped to a roaster on the mainland? That's my spiel. My father made me memorize it when I was a kid. Did it sound rehearsed and flat?"

"Yes, but that's okay. Depends on the price," Annie said.

"Kona coffee is expensive. We sell it for twenty-two dollars a pound. I'll sell it to you for sixteen and we roast. Providing you buy in thousand-pound increments. I'll drop an additional two dollars a pound for every additional thousand pounds you buy. How many shops do you have now?"

"Four. Elmo wants to blitz the South. Start-up costs are nil. It's finding the right, trustworthy people. Tom and I can only do so much. Elmo is in his late sixties. So far we have good people. The fact that we open the shops near college campuses helps because kids are always looking for part-time jobs. The downside is it's strictly a cash business. Money is tempting when you're on a short leash."

"What's your control?"

"The cups and the croissants. In the beginning we just served coffee and tuna sandwiches, using Elmo's mother's secret recipe. The control was really tight. Then we included brownies on Mondays and went on to espresso, lattes, and cappuccino. You need more of some coffees and less of others. If I follow Elmo's business plan, and Tom agrees to work his tail off, we could open five more shops by the end of the year. I'll be spending all my time on the road checking on the shops. You should know what I'm talking about. When you own a business, you're married to it. There's no time for anything else. There's no time for a private life. All I've ever done in my life is work. I don't know if I want to go after all this on such a grand scale."

"There's an alternative," Parker said seriously.

"What's that? Move to the islands and drink coconut milk?"

"You could open shops all across the country. Get them started, keep good books, and in a year, sell the franchise. There's big money in that. Go to a good headhunter for managerial positions. That's what I would do if I were in your position.

However, that doesn't mean you have to do it just because I suggested it.''

"It makes sense. In the beginning it was kind of a lark. You know, starting your own business with very little money and then, bam, it just took off. I wasn't prepared for it, and neither was Jane. In the end it was too much for her. My brother came back at just the right moment. It's certainly something to think about. I'm going to have to call my brother to talk to him about the prices you offered.''

"Take all the time you need. My coffee beans and I aren't going anywhere. There was a time when more than ten million pounds of Kona coffee was produced each year. Today there are less than two million pounds being produced. It's the rarest of the rare. We want to keep it that way. That concludes our business for the day. Let's have some fun.''

Annie grew still. "What do you mean by fun?''

"Explore the island. Run under the falls. Jump in the water. Climb the monkeypod tree, come back, take a nap. Separately, of course. Get dressed up, go out to dinner and then come home and go to bed. Separately, of course. Rise and shine in the morning, eat a wonderful breakfast, after which I will fly us to Kona and give you a tour of my coffee plantation. How does that sound?''

"Should I change? Do you treat all your prospective customers like this?''

"Sneakers and shorts would be good. No. Most of them are stuffy old ducks who want everything for nothing. You're my first beautiful female customer. Plus, Daniel said you were my destiny, so I have to find out if he's right.''

"Okay. Give me ten minutes. Daniel needs to mind his own business.''

"Five.''

"You got it.'' Annie giggled.

* * *

"It s been a wonderful afternoon, Parker. I had fun, I feel rested, and I learned a lot. You're a very good tour guide. I never hid behind a waterfall before. I feel invisible."

"I used to hide here from my father when I was little. At least I thought I was hiding until he told me he used to do the same thing. This big old stone we're resting in is like a chair. That leads me to believe hundreds of children over the years did the same thing we're doing. How is it you never had time for fun, Annie? Look! Now, I'd say that's something special! Just for you, Annie. We should call it Annie's Rainbow. I've been coming here since I was three years old, and I never saw a prettier one. It's bigger, more vibrant and can be seen for miles. I guess it's your special welcome to Maui."

Annie stared at the rainbow, a chill running up and down her arms. She squinted to see through the shimmering waterfall. Where did it end and what was in the pot of gold here in this beautiful paradise? She shivered again. Parker put his arm around her shoulders. "I never had a rainbow named after me. To answer your question about fun, first my dad got sick, then my mom got . . . she has Alzheimer's disease. We didn't know what it was at first. Tom was in college, so I had to take care of Mom while I was in high school. I had to rush home after school. Baby-sitters for older people are expensive. Mom got worse, and we had to put her in a nursing home, and that was expensive. We sold the house to pay off Dad's sky-high medical bills and our share for Mom's care. Their savings went to pay for Tom's college tuition. There wasn't any left for me, so I had to work my way through. Thank God for Elmo. If you ever want to know anything about the drugstore business, just ask me. I had a mountain of student loans. It all turned around when we opened the first shop. If there were more hours in the day, I could have tripled my money. I went to bed tired and woke up tired. This is the first vacation I've had in seven years. Not only that, it's tax deductible. At least the airfare is. If your next question is, did I ever have boyfriends or relationships, the answer is yes but time ruined all of them.

"Having my own business where I didn't have to answer to anyone was always a dream of mine. I did the college thing because both Mom and Dad wanted Tom and me to have degrees since they didn't have the opportunity to go to college. The business helped move Mom closer to me, and the facility is really great. I get to see her weekends. I told myself I was giving it three years, and if I didn't make it by then, I would look for a nine-to-five job. Sitting behind a desk is not what I'm all about. Jane felt the same way. All she wants to do is paint. She's looking forward to having kids. She was a foster-home child, so having her own family is very important to her. Do you have any idea how lucky you are, Parker?"

"Yes. Sometimes it seems a little hollow. Life should be shared."

"How is it you aren't married?"

Parker laughed. "I came close several times. It didn't feel right, so each time I broke it off."

"Do you run everything? Why do your sisters live on the mainland? Don't you miss them?"

"Of course I miss them. I inherited because I'm the oldest male child. It's tradition."

Annie's eyes snapped open and she sat up. "Wait right there. Are you saying all of this belongs to you and not your sisters? Do you share the profits with them?"

"Our traditions here are different from what you're used to. It's our way."

"That's incredible, and it certainly isn't fair. You get everything, and they get nothing?" Something in Annie snapped. There was such outrage in her voice, Parker reared back. "Aren't they bitter?"

"Bitter? I don't think so. They're all very well off. They moved by choice."

"Well, hell, I'd move, too," Annie exploded. "That's exactly what happened to me through no fault of my parents. Tom got it all. I had to bust my ass. I don't want to hear any crap about it building character, either. You can't take character to the bank. I used to eat mayonnaise sandwiches and drink Kool-Aid. That sure as hell didn't build my character. I was always hungry."

"Wait just a damn minute. You're making it sound like I cheated my sisters. I didn't. It was all laid out. I told you, it's our tradition."

"Your tradition stinks. What that says to me is women don't count. If they counted, you would have shared. You live like a king in this beautiful paradise. They grew up here, too. Another thing, *Mr. Coffee,* remember that it was a *woman* who gave birth to you. I've just decided I don't think I like you. And I sure as hell don't like all these traditions you're steeped in. I made the mistake of letting this stray off the business path. I can't respect you now. I'm sorry."

Parker Grayson stared at his destiny with disbelieving eyes. "Just hold on here, Miss Clark. What you don't seem to understand is no one is complaining. Furthermore, it's none of your business."

"You're right, it is none of my business. Why would your sisters complain? What good would it do? They have to accept it since they have no other choice. What do you do for them?"

"Do?"

"When you inherited all of this, what did you do for them?"

"I didn't do anything. They didn't want me to do anything. They got married and had babies. That was what they wanted to do."

"Scrooge! Don't deny it. That's exactly what you are. Would it hurt you to share your good fortune with them? You know what, I hated my brother for a long time. Deep-down, gut hatred. It started to consume me. I had to let it go for my own survival.''

''My sisters aren't like you. I don't mean that the way it sounds,'' Parker said, a helpless look on his face.

''How do you know? Did you ever ask? How many sisters do you have?''

''No, I never asked. I have six sisters. They all have well-to-do husbands.''

''One seventh of something is a lot less than the whole of something. And, they probably don't have a dime in their own names.''

''Where is this coming from? We were having such a good time. Why do my sisters need to have money in their own names?''

''For the same reason I do. Parents have no right to do that to their children. You are no better than your parents. One of your sisters, given the chance, might have been a whiz at running your coffee company. Maybe you're right, and maybe they don't care. I care, and that's all that's important. Women are not second-class citizens. I can't believe you went to school on the mainland. This is the eighties, Mr. Grayson. Women no longer take a backseat to men. I want to go home, and I want to go home *now!*''

''Fine,'' Parker snapped. ''Watch your footing, or you'll go into the falls.''

''God, I just hate it when people disappoint me,'' Annie seethed.

''What?''

''Shut up. I wasn't talking to you,'' Annie continued to fume.

The trip to the plantation house was made in silence. When Parker held the door open for her, Annie marched inside and down the long hall to her room. ''Damn!'' Her bags had been unpacked. Now she had to pack them again. She did it any old way. The sound of the zipper closing was so loud in the room, Annie found herself wincing. "Just when I thought I found the perfect man he turns out to be a dud. Damn, damn, damn!"

"This is stupid, Annie," Parker said.

"Yes, I could see how it would seem stupid to you," Annie said. "Who's taking me to the airport?"

"It looks like I'm the lucky winner."

The housekeeper looked from one angry face to the other. Hesitantly, she held out a rainbow-colored gown. Tears welled in Annie's eyes as she reached for it. "Thank you so much for . . . for this." She slung the dress over her shoulder as she made her way to the front door.

"She doesn't understand our ways. She's upset because I inherited the plantation and my sisters didn't," Parker whispered to the old woman.

"Miss Clark is right, Parker. It was a terrible thing your parents did to your sisters. The old ways no longer work, as my children point out to George and me on a daily basis. It is a new time we live in, Parker. If we are to grow with the times, then we must embrace that same time. Why do you close your eyes to this? You were educated on the mainland at great expense. I can speak like this, Parker, because I raised you along with your mother, and when she was no longer here, I raised you alone. Now, go to the young lady and make peace. She looked very angry to me. She is the best one yet. As George says, you snooze, you lose. Go now, Parker."

"We'll discuss this later in *greater* detail, Mattie," Parker hissed in the old housekeeper's ear.

Mattie drew herself tall until she was eyeball-to-eyeball with Parker. "No. I have said all I intend to say. If you wish to discuss the matter, it should be with your sisters."

"I'll be damned. When did you go modern on me, Mattie?"

"When I learned about social security, pension plans, and

estate planning. Sometimes I think you have coffee beans for brains. I told you to go, Parker!"

"Yes, ma'am," Parker said, turning on his heel. It didn't pay to argue with either Mattie or George.

In the car, Parker reached up to the visor for his aviator glasses. Behind the dark shades he felt more confident. Out of the corner of his eye he could see how straight Annie was sitting, how prim and proper she looked. He slammed the car into gear. "Listen, you can't just barge into my life, tell me what to do, then barge back out because you don't like my culture. I wouldn't even think about doing something like that to you. What the hell kind of destiny is this?"

"I don't have any trouble with your culture. It's your attitude about women. Let's just say for the sake of argument that you and I got married. I have a successful business. You have a successful business. We have one boy and two girls. Who gets our estate when we die?"

"I got the point back at the falls."

"Who gets the estate, Parker?"

"The oldest son."

"My business, too?"

"Yours becomes mine at marriage."

"Stop this fucking car right now. I'll walk the rest of the way, thank you."

Parker's foot slammed on the brake. "You can send me my bags." Hands on hips, Annie glared at the man behind the sunglasses. "Do not ever, even for one second, think I would bust my ass working sixteen or eighteen hours a day so *your* son could inherit over *my* daughters."

"We aren't married," Parker bellowed.

"Damn right we aren't, and we aren't going to get married, either. I wouldn't marry you with your archaic ideas if you were the last man on earth!"

"Get in this damn car before I pick you up and throw you in it," Parker bellowed again.

"Kiss my ass, Parker Grayson."

"Where did you learn to talk like that? You should be ashamed of yourself."

"From my brother and his friends. I am not ashamed of myself. Now, get the hell out of my way before I push that car you're sitting in over the edge."

From the set of her jaw and the murderous look in her eye, Parker knew she meant business. A sick feeling settled in the pit of his stomach. In the few hours they'd spent together, he'd realized he really liked the feisty young woman. There was no doubt in his mind that Daniel was right. He could see the two of them watching their children growing up, traveling together, growing old together. *Is she right? If she is, what does that make me? Mattie would say a horse's patoot.*

"Fine, do it your way, Miss Smart-Ass."

"I'd rather be a smart-ass than a jackass," Annie shot back. *Shit, shit, shit. How could something so perfect suddenly turn so ugly and hateful?* Was she overreacting? Of course she was, but she wasn't backing down. She'd had it with people, men in particular, who thought of women as second-class citizens.

What seemed like an eternity later, Annie limped into the airport parking lot, Parker gliding along behind her in the plantation car. "Just put my bags on the curb."

Parker stood facing her. He removed his sunglasses. "If my father were alive, he'd take a switch to me for allowing you to walk to the airport."

"Is that the same father who cut his daughters out of his will? If so, forget it. I've walked longer distances in my life."

"Annie, I'm sorry. I'm not sure what it is I'm sorry about. If it's a word, I've said it. You don't understand."

A second later Annie was in his face. "You see, you're wrong. I do understand. What I understand is you are a greedy son of a bitch like my brother Tom was. I forgave him because he's my brother. You, on the other hand, have no excuses. You probably have more money than I could ever dream about. I'll just bet you a thousand pounds of coffee if we planned on getting married the first two words out of your mouth would be prenuptial agreement. Ah, I see by the stricken look on your face I'm right. Now, that's a modern, eighties legal agreement. Why would that be good enough for you and yet the old way of disinheriting your sisters is still good. I rest my case. If I decide to buy your coffee, I'll be in touch.''

''Annie, we're both adults. Can't we go into the bar, sit down, and talk? I'd like to try and explain the way it is.''

She was in his face again, their noses almost touching. ''I'll tell you what, Parker Grayson. You go talk to your sisters. Be an honest, open, big brother and ask them what they think and feel and how they felt when they knew they were cut off because they were *just women.* If they tell you it's fine with them, call me and I'll come back here. I'd like to meet six women who feel like you *think* they do. If I prove right, you supply my coffee for a full year. *Free.* Here,'' she said, throwing the leis he'd made for her, at him.

Annie stalked off. Parker watched her until she was out of sight. Suddenly the sun dimmed and the sick feeling returned to the pit of his stomach. He wished he was a little boy again so he could cry.

CHAPTER SEVEN

"You don't seem very happy, Parker. Is something wrong?"
Mattie asked. "The house is in readiness. I cooked everything
you asked me to cook. The presents for your sisters are all
under the tree. It is a joyful time. You always loved Christmas,
so why don't we sit down and talk about it? I would have to
be blind as well as deaf not to know you haven't been the same
since Miss Clark left, back in July. Five months is a very long
time, Parker. I've never asked what went wrong. Sometimes
talking about things helps."

"There isn't all that much to talk about, Mattie. Nothing
much has changed. Miss Clark's visit was for business purposes.
She chastised me for the way I do . . . did things. The truth is,
my culture is none of her business. She's one of those modern
eighties women everyone talks about. I did like her tremen-
dously until she started . . . It's not important. I don't think I
could ever feel the same about her. She was so . . . I don't
know, brash, uncouth, so . . . mainland."

"Do not tell me a lie, Parker. Your eyes tell me something different. You never did talk to your sisters, did you?"

"No. I was going to do that today. They didn't want to come, Mattie. I guess that bothers me."

"This is the first time you invited your sisters to their old home in many years. Why would you think they should be overjoyed to visit you now?"

"They have husbands and children. I thought, old times, memories, that sort of thing might appeal to them. They wouldn't come for dinner, so I settled for lunch. They want to leave right afterward, which tells me I should have scuttled the whole idea the moment it entered my mind."

"And that surprises you?"

"Doesn't it surprise you, Mattie?"

"No. One always wants to know they can go home. This was your sisters' home as well as yours. When you returned from the mainland it became *your* home. There is a piece of paper in the courthouse that says this is so. Your sisters have never come here uninvited. Your nieces and nephews know nothing of this beautiful place. Once you went surfing with them, Parker. Once."

"There aren't enough hours in the day for me to keep going back and forth to the Big Island. They have fathers. They have each other."

"And you wonder why they don't wish to join you for this little luncheon. I think you just answered your own question."

"I guess what you're trying to tell me is my sisters don't like me very much."

"That is an accurate assessment, Parker."

"Do they resent me, Mattie?"

"Yes, Parker, they do."

"Then why didn't they say something? Why didn't *you* say something?"

"It wasn't my place."

"The hell it wasn't. You don't have the least bit of trouble telling me anything else. Why couldn't you tell me that?"

"That is family business. It is not *my* business. When was the last time you called any of your sisters just to say hello, how are you? I see. The answer is never."

"I have to leave now to pick them up at the airport."

"Where are the leis?"

"Leis?" Parker said, a stupid look on his face.

Exasperated, Mattie said, "Yes, leis for your sisters. It would be the nice thing to do. It is, after all, our custom."

"They live here, Mattie. They aren't coming from the mainland."

Mattie's shoulders stiffened. "You will wait right here, Parker, and you will not move," she said sternly. She was back almost instantly with six breathtaking leis. "I made them a short while ago. You will place one around each sister's neck and kiss her cheek. Do you understand me, Parker?"

"Yes, ma'am."

"Be sure to tell them how pretty they are. They are, you know."

"I know that," Parker said, shuffling his feet. "Is there anything else, Mattie, that's lacking in the manners department?"

"Ask George."

They weren't just pretty, they were beautiful. And they were his sisters. For a moment, Parker felt overwhelmed when they walked toward him. They waited expectantly as he draped a lei around each of them and then kissed them. "I'm glad you came," he said sincerely. He waited for them to respond and when they didn't, he ushered them through the airport and out to his waiting car.

They sat stiffly and primly, much the way Annie had sat

back in the summer, when he'd driven her to the airport. This was not going to be an easy visit. The six of them responded when he spoke to them but volunteered nothing to the conversation. He was relieved when they reached the house. He stepped back when all six of them ran to Mattie and George, who welcomed them with open arms. There was nothing shy about them now. They chattered and giggled like little girls, the little sisters he remembered. He suddenly felt like an outsider when he heard Lela, the oldest, say, "My God, this banyan tree is bigger than the house. I remember the day Mama planted it. She said it would grow big and strong like . . . Parker."

"Guess she was right about that," Teke, the second oldest said. "What's with this command performance, Mattie? I wanted to tell him to stuff his invitation, but Lela said we had to come." A deep frown etched itself on Parker's forehead at his sister's biting words.

"I don't want any fruit punch, Mattie. However, I'll take a double shot of Jack Daniel's on the rocks," Cassie said.

"I'll have a beer," Mahala said boisterously.

"Me too," Jana said.

"Scotch on the rocks for me," Kiki, the youngest said. "Smells good in here. Whatcha making, Mattie?"

"All your favorites," Mattie replied.

"Why?" the six sisters asked in unison.

"Your brother asked me to," Mattie said flatly.

Kiki whirled around. "Okay, big brother, now that you have us here, what's the drill? What do you want from us? You already have everything. In case you need a transfusion, count me out." Parker listened in horror as the rest of his sisters muttered the same words.

"Why don't we go into the library and have a little talk before lunch. Bring your drinks."

"Nice tree," Lela said, walking past the Christmas tree. "It's bigger than my whole living room."

"You must have a lot of friends or are all those presents for Mattie and George?" Teke said.

This was not going the way he'd planned. "Actually, they're for all of you."

"Really," Kiki drawled. "We didn't bring one for you. That means we can't accept yours. Money is always tight around this time of year. 'Course you wouldn't know anything about that, would you, Parker?"

Money was tight around this time of year. That didn't make any sense. "I didn't expect you to bring me a present."

"Let's cut the bullshit, Parker, and get to the chase. Why are we here?" Kiki said, gulping at her drink.

"What happened to you? What happened to all of you? You were never like this. You're Hawaiian women. You talk like . . ." For one split second he was going to say, like Annie. "It's not nice," he said lamely.

"We grew up. Guess you didn't notice. You being so busy here running things and all," Jana said tightly.

Parker stared at his sisters. He thought he saw disgust on all their faces. Disgust with him. It was all a bad dream. Annie Clark was preying on his mind and taking her revenge on him through his dreams. He shook his head to try to clear his thoughts. "Let's all sit down. I want to talk to you about something that concerns all of us."

"You know what, Parker, you're about ten years too late. None of us gives a shit what you want or don't want. Ah, I see my language offends you. That's just tough. Spit it out. What do you want from us? Wait a minute, I know what he wants," Lela said as she whirled around to face her sisters. "He wants absolution. Guess what, big brother, we're fresh out. That about sums up our contribution to this little visit. You called, we came, and now we're going. We can get a burger in town. George can drive us back to the airport."

Parker's jaw dropped when all six sisters set their glasses down on cue and turned to follow Lela to the door.

"Goddamn it! Get back here and sit down. I told you I want to talk to you. You're going to sit and listen whether you like it or not."

Teke whirled around at the speed of light. With her index finger she jabbed at the center of her brother's neck. "You see, that's where you're wrong. You gave up the right to tell any of us what to do. What do you say, girls, should we let him have it?"

They converged on him as one, backing him up to the sofa and pushing him down. Teke walked around to the back and held his shoulders to prevent him from getting up. Her grip was like a vise.

It wasn't a dream, it was a black, ugly nightmare. And from the looks of things he wasn't going to wake up anytime soon.

"I think I'll go first since I'm the oldest," Lela said.

The others nodded as they picked up their drinks. They were smiling now at his discomfort. The funny thing was, in his dream each one of his sisters looked like Annie Clark. Only it wasn't a dream.

"When you were born, Parker, this house was full of joy and happiness. It was like Christmas. Mama's miracle son. We were just little girls then, but we remember. Five days after your birth, Mama planted the banyan tree. I was holding you in my arms as we watched her dig out the dirt. It was something she had to do. Of course we didn't understand what it all meant to her. By planting the tree she thought you would live forever. She had become very frail and was too old to have a child at that time. Like most women, she wanted to give her husband a son.

"*We* raised you, Parker, not Mama, not Mattie. We did it because we loved you. We pulled you around in the wagon, we taught you to swim, to jump in the pools, hide behind the falls. We taught you to climb the monkeypod tree and taught you how to ride your first bicycle and when you fell off you had six nurses in attendance. We made sure you brushed your teeth and took your bath. We even followed you on your first dates and hid in the bushes so you wouldn't see us. We begged and pleaded with Papa until he couldn't stand our pestering, to get you your first car. We combed your hair and took you to church. We showered you with love and shared everything in our lives with you.

"And then, one day, you didn't need us anymore. Papa decided it was time for *you* to learn the coffee business because one day it would be all *yours*. Mama died, and Papa decided it was time to marry us all off. We didn't have anything to say about it. I wanted to be a schoolteacher. Teke wanted to study music. Jana wanted to be an artist. Cassie had dreams of being an entertainer. Mahala wanted to study law. Kiki was the one who wanted to learn the coffee business. None of our dreams came true.

"We mistakenly thought when Papa died that you would share your life and your fortune with us. Did I leave anything out?"

"Only that we hate his guts," Kiki said, finishing her drink.

Parker flinched. "I thought you were all married and happy. You never came here. I thought . . ."

"It's the same old bullshit," Teke said.

"Why are we bothering with this? Let's go back to town," Cassie said.

Teke yanked at her brother's head pulling it backward. She leaned down, her eyes boring into his. "You're never going to be happy, Parker. In your heart, tradition and culture be damned. You know you were wrong. We were part of this family long before you came along. You think about that while we go back to town."

"Okay, enough is enough!" Parker roared. "I don't need

to think about it. That's all I've done for the past five months. All of you are right. Yes, I was deaf, dumb, blind, and stupid. When you didn't say anything, I accepted the fact that you accepted the conditions of Papa's will. I never knew you had hopes and dreams. That in itself was incredibly stupid on my part. I thought all you wanted was to get married and have families. Again, that was stupid on my part. I want to make it right. I will make it right. It's not too late. I want us to share equally and evenly. I want you to know you can come here to this house anytime you want. You do not need an invitation. Your rooms are just like they were when you left. Mattie kept them that way for you. I'd like all your children to come here and enjoy the same life you had when you lived here. I'm just sorry it's taken me so long to do this. The business will now have seven equal partners. Kiki, if you want, I could really use an assistant. If you don't like that word, how would you like to be working partner.''

''What's the catch? Why are you being so generous all of a sudden?'' Jana asked.

''What do we have to do in return for this generosity?'' Mahala asked suspiciously.

''Just be my sisters and give me the chance to be your brother. There's room on this estate to build a dozen houses. Pick your spot. I'll have the houses built to your specifications.''

''Of course this will all be done legally,'' Mahala said.

''Of course. It's not too late for any of you to follow your dreams.''

''Yes, Parker, it's too late. We're willing to forgo our dreams so that our children can follow theirs. My son wants to be a lawyer. It takes a great deal of money to go to law school on the mainland,'' Mahala said.

''I should have known that,'' Parker muttered.

''Yes, you should have,'' Lela said.

''Will you stay?'' Parker asked.

"Yes, Parker, we'll stay," Kiki said. "I'm going to take you up on your offer to work at the plantation. I have some great ideas."

"I'd like to hear them. First, though, I have something I have to do. If you like, you can watch. Meet me outside by the front door."

The sisters looked at one another and shrugged as they trekked through the house to the front foyer and then out the door. They squealed in horror when they saw Parker swing the ax at the base of the old banyan tree. "Why are you doing this?" they shouted.

"Because it's a symbol of everything that went wrong with us. No one lives forever. If there were seven right in a row, I'd leave them be. One is no good. George can grind out the stump, and we'll decide what kind of welcoming plant we want by our front door."

When the giant tree toppled to the ground there were shouts of approval. George and Mattie clapped their hands. "One more thing," Parker said. "Last one up the monkeypod tree is a horse's patoot!"

High-heeled shoes sailed through the air as the Grayson siblings ran around the house to the side yard. "You remembered!" they shouted in glee.

They were slick and they were fast as they shinnied up the old knurled tree. Parker was the last to straddle the long, twisted branch.

"Merry Christmas!" Parker gasped.

"Merry Christmas!" his sisters shouted.

Annie tore the cellophane from the new calendar. She crossed her fingers that 1982 would be as good a year as the previous one. She sipped at the wine in her glass, her right hand tickling Rosie behind her ears. The shepherd stared at her with adoring eyes. "It's just you and me, girl. I thought he would at least send a Christmas card. I think the hardest thing was going to lunch with Daniel before Christmas and not asking about Parker. I wanted him to say something so bad, and he didn't. So much for destiny and love and all that garbage. When you're right, you're right. When you're wrong, you're wrong. I'm not some dumb female that needs a man in her life. It would be nice, but it's not necessary. I really liked him, Rosie. He's a great kisser, too. The best so far," she clarified. "He even named a rainbow after me. Then, bam, it was all over. Come on, get your leash and let's go for a long walk along the battery. I'm going to buy a house there someday. I'm going to get us one of those big old houses with a walled-in courtyard where you can romp and play to your heart's content. I'm going to get you a playmate, too."

The shepherd pranced over to the coatrack and daintily removed her leash.

"You're so beautiful you belong on a calendar. Maybe I'll look into that. After I open the next six stores. That's going to make sixteen stores in total. When we come back after our walk, you and I are going to talk about *that money* because Mr. Peter Newman is still sniffing around. I've reconciled myself to the fact the man is never going to go away." Annie snapped the leash onto Rosie's harness and left by the back door.

When they turned the corner leading to their street at three o'clock, Rosie strained at her leash. She growled and bared her teeth when she saw the man sitting on the stoop waiting for them. "Easy girl. We can deal with him."

"I thought I told you to call before you came here. I'm much too busy to talk to you today, and I have nothing new to say to you. What that means is, get off my property or I'm calling the police. I'll get a restraining order if I have to."

"I have something new to report to you. We finished up our investigation before Christmas. We have successfully eliminated every car owner but you, Miss Abbott, and Elmo Richard-son. We're satisfied that there was no third party. We became satisfied when we offered a deal to the young man in jail. He couldn't take advantage of it to cut down on his prison time, because there was no third party. That brought us back to the cars on the street and the campus parking lot. It is my personal belief that the money was tossed into Jane Abbott's car, you covered up for her, and Elmo Richardson took care of the money. Sooner or later, I'll be able to prove it.''

Annie fought the urge to put her fist through Peter Newman's face.

Rosie sensed her owner's fear and lunged at the investigator. It was all Annie could do to hold the huge dog in check. ''Get off my property. If you think I'm guilty of something besides leaving my car windows open, charge me or get the hell off my property and don't come back. I don't have anything else to say to you, not now, not ever. Are we clear on that matter?''

Her insides shaking like Jell-O, Annie led Rosie up the steps and into the house. She unhooked the leash, locked and double-bolted the front door. She ran to the back door and did the same thing before she took the steps two at a time to the second floor, where she fell onto the bed gasping for breath. She needed to calm down and call Jane. And Elmo. And Tom. And the police. Another call to the insurance company and one to her lawyer would not be out of order either. When you were guilty you had to act like you were innocent. No, she couldn't call Tom. Tom would suspect immediately. He'd been as good as his word when she came up with the hundred thousand dollars to pay off his ex-wife for the kids.

The scheme had been elaborate, and it had worked. Mona, so greedy for the money, would have done anything to get it. Tom had told her he borrowed it. There was nothing in writing; the payment had been in cash. Mona had promised never to interfere in the children's lives. A month after she sold the house, keeping all the equity, Mona had disappeared off the face of the earth. The children now lived with Tom and a part-time housekeeper in North Carolina. Everyone was healthy and happy.

Except for the Boston National Bank, who still hadn't gotten their money back. As soon as the accounting firm gave her a date to take the last quarter's profits, Annie would pay back the bank. Everything was ready to go. The moment she had the remaining money from the hundred thousand dollars, which amounted to thirty-three thousand, she would ship the money back. This time there would be no more delays. Tom was already paying her back and didn't take a year-end bonus even though there was more than enough in their business account.

Annie sighed. Life was never dull.

Rosie watched her mistress until she was certain her breathing was under control. Only then did she lie down, her head between her paws, her eyes bright and alert.

Suddenly, Annie wanted to cry, as her thoughts carried her to a faraway place behind a silvery, shimmering waterfall. She wondered then, as she had a thousand times before, if she'd overreacted. She'd picked up the phone to call Parker at least a hundred times only to replace it at the last second. There was something wrong there. She just didn't know exactly what it was. Then, of course, there was her pride. Pride was a terrible thing.

Time to call Jane and ruin her day. "Hey, Jane," she said a moment later, "how's my best friend? Wonderful. Happy New Year, Jane! I love this time of year, when the shops are closed for the school breaks. Oh, I'm not doing much. I hang out with Rosie. We just came in from our walk, and guess who was sitting on my front steps. I have bad news, Jane. Mr. Newman has decided through the process of elimination that the money went into your car, I covered up for you, and Elmo kept the money bag. He didn't say so, but I think he thinks we split it among ourselves. He said something new this time around. He said they offered to cut a deal with the kid in prison to lighten his sentence if he would tell who the third person was. The kid said there was no third person. That brought them back to the cars that had open windows. If there was a third person, the boy would have gone for the deal. This is what we're looking at, Jane. I'm calling the police to get a restraining order on him, and I think you should do the same thing. I'm also going to call the insurance company again or have my lawyer do it. I just wanted you to be prepared. They have no proof, Jane. Any lawyer would have us out on bail in five minutes. No prosecutor would take this case. It's now a cat-and-mouse, wait-and-see game he's playing with us. My books are in order. Every shop we opened was opened the same way as the first one. I pay my taxes, salaries, and the rest is mine. You can't argue with the numbers and numbers are proof. I suppose he thinks we stashed the money somewhere and will spend it sooner or later. He isn't going to give up. I want you to know that. Statute of limitations? I don't know anything about stuff like that. I'll ask the lawyer when I speak to him.

''Mom's fine. Tom is fine, too. The kids are getting big. Mona found herself some young hunk who wants to party like she does. Tom hasn't heard from her. Tom's a great father. I don't want to talk about Parker Grayson, Jane. There's nothing to tell. I hoped he would send a Christmas card, but he didn't. I didn't send one, either. I had lunch with Daniel Christmas week and he didn't bring up Parker's name. I didn't either. We buy our coffee from him, though. Tom handles that end of it. He says I'm too emotional when it comes to Parker. I almost thought he was the one, Jane. I really did. Something didn't, I don't know, jell, I guess for want of a better word. Then I blew it out of the water, and now I'm going to be an old maid. I hear the baby. I have to hang up anyway. Take care, say hello to Bob for me. Bye, Jane.''

* * *

On March 1, the day after four bombs rocked Wall Street in New York City, Annie walked downstairs to the basement, where she'd secured the Boston National Bank's money, dressed in her plastic raincoat that zipped up the front, her hair wrapped in Saran wrap and her hands in latex gloves. No hairs or fibers were going to get anywhere near the money she was about to package up and return to the bank. All the money had gone through the washing machine not once, not twice, but three times. She now sported a brand new General Electric washer and dryer and had switched her brand of soap just in case there was some residue left over in the machine from the money.

The box was huge, but then so was the pile of money in the three dark green trash bags. She'd worked diligently with her calculator trying to figure out, to the penny, the interest the bank lost while the money was in her possession. The biggest problem facing her now was how and where to mail the box of money once she packaged it up. If she was smart, which she wasn't, she would drive to Boston and leave the box on the bank's doorstep. She could leave now and drive through the night, turn around, and drive back. If she swilled coffee all day and night she could probably pull it off. Or she could drive to a distant city and take the box to the nearest post office or UPS with money taped to the box for shipping costs.

Postal authorities would probably think it was a bomb. That would call in the FBI. Damn, why was it so hard to return money? Maybe what she needed to do was make smaller boxes, boxes similar to shirt boxes that would fit into a mailbox on any street corner. If she had the right postage on each package, it would work.

Annie headed for the attic and the empty boxes she'd saved from Christmas. She panicked then. Everyone's fingerprints were on the boxes. Tom's, hers, the kids', Elmo's, her mother's. Rosie's pawprints were sure to be on some of them as she'd trampled through the papers and empty boxes. She was back to square one.

At ten-thirty, Annie loaded three green double-bagged lawn bags containing half of the bank's money into the trunk of her car. She wanted to return all of it, but something perverse inside her warned her to keep the other half. For the time being. Her destination—Atlanta, Georgia. On a plain white envelope tied to the string on each bag was the message: PLEASE RETURN TO BOSTON NATIONAL BANK AS SOON AS POSSIBLE. In smaller letters, she pasted the address of the bank.

It was a five-and-a-half-hour drive to Atlanta. She'd wait around, leave the money at the first bank she came to, then drive back home. She'd be back by noon the following day. Back in September, when she'd planned on returning the money, she'd thought ahead and purchased two cans of gasoline. That would see her to Atlanta and back. No one would even know she was gone. If anyone did come by or call and found her gone, she could say she had taken to her bed with an excruciating headache.

"Okay, Rosie, you have to stay here. I'll put down some papers for you. There's enough food and water to last you till I get back. I'd take you, but someone might remember seeing us together. You stay here and keep your eye on things." The big dog stared at her with unblinking eyes. At one point, Annie thought the dog nodded.

A baseball cap jammed on her head, and wearing an old windbreaker, Annie loaded up the car. At the last moment she stuck her wallet with her license and registration in the hip pocket of her jeans.

Ten minutes later she was headed south on the interstate.

Five hours later Annie cruised past the Georgia National Bank. She drove up and down the street twice to get a feel for car traffic as well as any pedestrian traffic on their way to an early-morning job. On her third cruise-by, with no traffic behind her, she pulled into the parking lot and around to the back of the bank. She turned off her lights, waited five minutes to see if anyone had noticed her. Satisfied that she wasn't the object of anyone's attention, she moved like lightning, wedging the bags as close to the door as possible. Janitors always reported early for work. She crossed her fingers that the janitor assigned to this bank was an honest man.

At 6:35 she was back on the interstate, headed north.

Annie walked in the door of her house at 11:10 to be greeted boisterously by Rosie. She tussled with her for a few moments before she hooked the leash onto her harness and led her outside. "A quick one, girl. I can't believe you held it in this long. That's what the paper was for. God, I wish you could talk. Did anyone call or stop by? Good girl. Okay, time to go in."

The phone rang just as Annie pulled some eggs and bacon from the refrigerator. It was Jane. Annie made her voice as cheerful as she could. "Hi, how's it going? Did I hear what? I didn't have the television on this morning. Why? Wow! No kidding! Are you sure? Wait, I'll turn it on. What station? Wait a minute, you're three hours behind me. I'll catch the next newscast. I can't believe it! Somebody just left three bags of money at a bank in Georgia. Only half but with interest, too? That's amazing. Oh, well, it's not our problem. So, how's the weather out there? You lucky dog. It's thirty-six degrees here. I'm going to light the fireplace. I'm working one to nine today. Do you ever miss the shop, Jane? No, no word from Parker Grayson. I haven't seen Daniel either. I can't worry about that now. Those six new shops we're opening are taking up all my time. Oh, Jane, listen to this. Tom had a brilliant idea, and he had these little cards made up asking customers what they liked about the shop and what drew them to it. Guess what they said! The daisy awnings over the doors and the daisies we painted on the walls. The coffee, of course. Since it was your idea, I thought you'd like to know. Okay, I'll let you go. I have to get ready for work. I'll turn on the news tonight when I get home. It's good news, Jane. I know you were worried. Rest easy now. Talk to you soon.''

Annie literally tripped up the steps to the shower where she sang at the top of her lungs. Rosie howled her distress at her off-key singing. ''Can't help it, Rosie. I feel like the weight of the world has been taken off my shoulders. We are almost home free, my friend. Now we can concentrate on living our lives instead of a lie. The best part of this whole deal is I never spent one penny of that money on myself. Yes, yes, I used two hundred dollars of it that first week, but I paid it back in a few days. It wasn't for me personally. I didn't let greed take over. I suppose they could hang me for the money I gave Tom to give Mona or the money I used to get Mom situated. So, I used a little of it for a few of the shops. I put it back within a month. I'll have to live with that one. The end justifies the means in that case. The kids are happy with Tom. Tom's happy. Our bills are paid, and I can sing again.

''Life is lookin' good, Rosie. Real good!''

Dressed in a woolly robe, her feet tucked under her, Rosie at her side, Annie stared into the flames as she waited for the eleven o'clock news. She was breathing hard and felt jittery. She knew Tom and Elmo were also glued to the television screen.

The segment was so short, Annie felt cheated. A few seconds of the bank president saying how delighted he was that half the money had come back. Then a short clip of Peter Newman taking credit for putting the fear of God into people his insurance company felt were suspects. His bulldog countenance intensified when the reporter asked him to comment on the fact that interest was paid on the money. He offered a curt "no comment."

Just as Annie was about to turn off the television, a clip came on of an interview with the young man sitting in jail for the crime. He looked more fierce than Peter Newman. She found herself starting to shake when she heard the man say he had his own suspicions and would follow them up when he was released. He also said he had cooperated fully and completely with Peter Newman the insurance investigator. "This is not over," he said belligerently. Annie turned off the set and threw the remote control clear across the room. She was still shaking when Rosie wiggled and squirmed until she was half on her lap and half off. Annie hugged her tightly. She should have returned all the money. Why in the name of God was she keeping it?

"It is so over. I gave half of it back. It's done."

Rosie growled deep in her throat.

"Yeah, girl, that's how I feel."

CHAPTER EIGHT

Eleven years later

Annie hated hospitals. She hated the crisp white uniforms worn by everyone, hated the antiseptic smell that made her want to gag. Worst of all was the knowledge that people died in hospitals. She thought about the endless hours she'd spent in the hospital when her father was so sick and the five-minute rush down the hall just three short months ago when her mother was rushed to the emergency room only to die a few minutes later. Now it was Tom in the hospital. People recovered from ruptured appendices. People didn't die from a little gut incision. Tom was too young. Tom had three kids who loved him with all their hearts. Surely God would be kind and compassionate. What would she do without Tom? The kids and Tom were all that was left to her family.

"I know you're out there, so you might as well come in," Tom called hoarsely.

"How'd you know I was out here?" Annie asked.

"I smelled your perfume."

"I got here as soon as I could. How are you, Tom?"

"My throat is sore from the tube they had down it. My gut hurts. The good news is I'm going to live to walk out of here. For God's sake wipe that awful look off your face, Annie."

"I'm sorry. I was . . . You know, remembering."

"Yeah, I know. I was thinking the same thing myself when I came in. I'm going to be all right, Annie. How's things going?"

"Believe it or not, things are running smoothly. You said you needed to talk to me about something important. Are you up to talking about it now?"

"Mandy brought my briefcase last night. Open it up and spread it out."

"Tom, you are a pack rat. What is all this stuff?"

"Look, kiddo, we have to make some decisions. Time has just galloped by. You opened your first shop in 1980. It's now 1993, thirteen years later. You own eighty-four Daisy Shops. It's time to discuss the franchising of those shops. Every single one of them is profitable to the point of being obscene. You're a multimillionaire. So am I, thanks to your generosity. My kids' futures are secure, again thanks to you. You have one of those old mansions on the battery filled with priceless antiques, you drive a pricey sports car, you set up a trust fund for your godchild. You were named Woman of the Year, three years running. You set up a scholarship fund on every campus where we have shops. You, little sister, have done it all. I guess my question is, how much more money do you need or want. What you have now will last you several lifetimes even if you go decadent on me. God, I forgot the animal shelters you built and fund along with the pediatric wings you've built onto four different hospitals. What's left to do, Annie?"

"The homeless, more food for them, better conditions."

"Annie, we took care of that last year."

"Summer camps for inner-city kids."

"We set that up two years ago. The funding is secure."

"A memorial for Mom and Dad. Something in good taste."

"It's under way, Annie. Sometimes it's hard to give money away."

Annie felt the blood drain from her face. She sat down. "Yes, sometimes it is."

"You look . . . ghostly. What's wrong?"

"I forgot to eat in my haste to get here. I'll grab something in the cafeteria when I leave. You know me, eat, eat, eat."

"So, do we go for it or not?"

"How many do you want to franchise?"

"All but four."

"Which four, Tom?"

"Well, I thought we'd keep the two in Charleston, your first one and Jane's at the Baptist College. I'd like to keep the two here in Clemson. My kids can work summers and holidays. I don't want life made that easy for them. We can handle two. I know you won't want to part with the first one. Check with Jane. She might want to put hers on the block."

"What kind of money are we talking about, Tom? Have you really thought this through?"

"I really have, Annie. Look, it's time you got a life, and I sure would like more time with my kids. Mandy's going off to college next year. But, to answer your question, I thought two hundred fifty thousand dollars was good per store. That would gross twenty-one million. That's not the end of it. You'll get a percentage every year. If the new owner fails, the store reverts back to you. It's more involved than that, but you have the gist of it. Each owner buys from our supplier, they adhere to our promotions. There will be more than enough money coming in to fund all your charitable works. You would, of course, retain the right to open more stores anytime you saw fit. The lawyers have to work that out. Taxes have to be paid, that kind of thing. What do you think?''

"It's going to be difficult to let go of thirteen years of hard work, Tom. What will I do?''

"You're going to take a vacation, and you're going to smell the roses. That's what you're going to do. You've done it all. Kick back before it kicks you.''

"Okay.''

"You're sure, Annie?''

"I'm sure. When do you want to get this under way?''

"When I get out of here. I can make phone calls sitting on the couch with my feet up. I can get it all started. But, and here's the big but. There's a clunker in everything. Since coffee is the main ingredient in this operation, it is of major concern when the price goes up. Take a look at the coffee figures.''

"We use, give or take a few pounds, around twenty pounds of coffee a day. If you multiply that times six it comes to one hundred twenty pounds a week multiplied by twenty-four days a month is two thousand eight hundred eighty pounds a month. Times eighty-four stores it's roughly two hundred forty-two thousand pounds a year. Your old friend gave us a good deal twelve years ago. That deal is no longer working. There's someone new in charge now, Kiki Aellia. Decaf is suddenly off the charts. We have to step up to the plate on that one. I want you to go to Hawaii and work some magic. If the Grayson Coffee Company raises its prices, we're going to have to look elsewhere. That's if we want the franchises to work. I can't go, Annie. I'll be laid up for at least six weeks. This operation was not a piece of cake. We can get things under way, but we need a better coffee deal. Can you do it? No, that's wrong, will you do it?''

Annie sucked in her breath. "Do you think I could take Rosie and Harry with me?''

"Why not. Buy them seats on the plane. Better yet, charter

a flight and they can have the whole damn plane to romp in. Charge it to the business. This is business of the highest order. Stay as long as you like. Call me, fax me, send up a smoke signal. Whatever. Go swimming, snorkeling, sun yourself, get a gorgeous tan. Go naked dressed in a lei. Do what you want to do, Annie. If you don't want to stay in Hawaii, go somewhere else. You followed your dream, now it's time to live it.''

Annie laughed. ''You should have been a used-car salesman, Tom. Okay, okay, I'll do it. When do you want me to leave?''

''As soon as possible.''

''How does the end of the week sound? I need to shop, charter the plane, take the dogs to the vet, get them traveling shots. I'll leave Sunday. Are you sure you're going to be all right with me gone?''

''For God's sake, Annie, of course I am. Talk to the doctor if you don't believe me. Go home now. I'm expecting a visitor.''

''Who?''

''None of your business.''

''Is this a serious lady, Tom? Who is she? What's her name? Do the kids like her?''

''Yes, it's serious. Her name is Lillian and she's a school-teacher. One of Ben's teachers, in fact. The kids love her, and she loves them.''

''And you didn't tell me! How could you keep something like that from me? I'm your sister!''

''The same way you wouldn't tell me where you got the hundred grand to buy off Mona. Jeez, I'm sorry, Annie. I didn't mean to say that. I know we agreed never to mention it. I didn't tell you because I wasn't sure. You know, if you talk about it, something will go wrong. I didn't want anything to go wrong. When you get back, I'd like to drive down to Charleston and have you meet her. She reminds me of Mom when Mom was young, and we were kids. She kind of smells like her, too.''

Annie leaned over the bed. ''I'm glad you found someone,

Tom. Okay, I'm on my way. I'll call you before I leave for any last-minute instructions. Do we set up an appointment or what?''

''Nope, cold turkey. Catch Kiki off guard. They aren't expecting us to complain. Be that hard-nosed businesswoman I know you can be. If you don't like their deal, leave. Don't be afraid to pull out your ace in the hole even if we aren't one hundred percent committed to it. Selling coffee by the pound or half pound in the shops will increase revenues greatly. An additional three to four hundred thousand pounds of coffee a year should make anyone sit up and take notice. We'll start small, and I'll work on the remodeling aspect while I'm home recuperating. Kiki doesn't have to know we aren't set to go on it. I merely alluded to it, and I heard the old salivary glands watering. All the way from Hawaii. If that doesn't work, we'll switch to Plan B. Whatever you decide is okay with me. Let's be clear on that, okay?''

''We're clear. Charter a plane? That's definitely decadent, Tom. I'm gonna do it.''

''See you around, kiddo. Don't be afraid to kick some ass. Hey, how's Elmo?''

''Not good, Tom. He's looking at his eightieth birthday. He's got some problems, but we still have dinner together three nights a week. I'd give up the shops before I'd give up those dinners. He never forgets to bring a chewie for Rosie and Harry. I love that old man.''

''I know you do, sis. Take care of him. Hey, take him to Hawaii with you. Bet he'd love that.''

''That's a great idea. Get better quick, Tom. You'll see me when you see me. Don't forget, we have a date so I can meet Lillian.''

''You won't let me forget. Get out of here,'' Tom groused. ''It's almost time for Lillian to get here.''

''I'm going, I'm going.''

* * *

Annie felt every inch a princess when she trooped up the steps of the private jet that would take her all the way to Hawaii. Rosie, Harry, and Elmo had boarded five minutes earlier. Money was a powerful aphrodisiac, she thought. At the precise moment she stepped into the plane and stewards and pilot welcomed her, she knew she could do anything she wanted to do.

She could even call Parker Grayson or better yet, take a trip up to the North Shore and say, "I was in the neighborhood." Absolutely she could do that. Of course she would do no such thing. *Then why did you buy all those designer clothes and shoes? Liar, liar, pants on fire.*

Annie buckled the two shepherds into their seats. Elmo sat in the middle while she sat across the aisle. She buckled her own seat and smiled at Elmo. "I hate to fly."

"I'm not fond of it myself. The truth is, it's safer than riding in a car. Okay, everyone, here we go! Up up and away," the old man chortled. Harry barked and Rosie joined in. Annie simply gritted her teeth.

Elmo accepted the glass of wine the steward handed him. Annie did likewise. "Please give the dogs some root beer," she said to the steward.

"There are rules. I can't serve dogs." Harry barked sharply at the steward's tone.

"There aren't any rules on this flight. I paid for four passengers. The dogs each have a seat. I explained about the dogs when I chartered this flight. I'd suggest you move your ass and get the root beer. If you don't have root beer, 7UP will do. If you don't, you won't be with us when this flight returns to Charleston. You can find your own way home from Hawaii. Or, you can get off in Dallas when we set down there. It's your call," Annie snapped.

The steward marched off. He returned with two bottles of root beer. "Didn't you forget something? These dogs are talented and incredibly protective but they do not know how to swig out of a bottle." Elmo guffawed until he choked. Harry licked at the tears trickling down the old man's face.

"This is going to be a fun trip." Annie giggled. "I had our lunch catered. You're going to love it, Elmo. Do you think you'll miss your lady friends?"

"Nope. Wouldn't even tell them where we're staying. They'd be calling all hours of the day and night. One of these days they're going to smother me. I love the attention, but sometimes it gets to be too much. Are you gonna be seeing that coffee fellow that broke your heart?"

There was no use in pretending she didn't understand what he was saying. Elmo knew her too well. "No. And he didn't break my heart. There was something off-kilter about him. To this day I can't put my finger on it. I was smitten, though."

"Then why'd you do all that shopping last week. You bought out the stores," Elmo said as he poured root beer into two plastic dishes.

"Because I'm rich, and I can shop till I drop. Everyone wants new clothes when they go on vacation. You didn't say a word when I gave you the new stuff I bought for you."

"That's different. Don't let me forget to bring back two grass skirts. Did you spend a lot of money?" Elmo asked slyly.

"A fortune. More money than I ever spent on clothes in my life. I bought a Chanel handbag, Elmo. Guess how much it cost."

"Two hundred dollars?"

"Try twenty-two hundred dollars."

"Mercy!"

"Before you can ask, I spent seven thousand bucks. I almost got sick when I tallied it up. I went crazy."

"I'd say so. Looks to me like the tranquilizers the vet gave these dogs is kicking in. What should we do?"

"Read. Or, I can have the steward put on a movie. You have to wear earphones to hear the voices. If you plug in the headset, you can hear music. If you move over here, we can play cards. Or we can take a nap."

"Let's just talk. Do you know what I heard on the news last night?"

"News?" Annie giggled.

"Yes, news but Boston news. Remember that kid that went to prison for stealing the money? He's getting out a few years early for good behavior. He's over thirty now. Imagine that. He spent the best years of his life in jail. He said something I really didn't understand. He said if the money had been recovered immediately, he wouldn't have had to serve all that time. Can that be true, Annie?"

"I don't know, Elmo. I didn't watch the news last night. When that insurance investigator was dogging all of us he never said anything like that. Maybe it's something he wants to believe. Robbery is robbery."

"What tickles me to no end is half the money being returned. When it was returned all those years ago, they said it was *fluffy*, like someone washed it in fabric softener."

"Elmo, do you believe everything you hear?"

"In this case I do. They showed the kind of money bag the bonds and money were in. When the person returned it, it filled three big garbage bags. *Fluffy* was what the reporter called it. There wasn't one fingerprint on any of the money, the bonds, or the bags."

"I guess fluffy is better than nothing. They probably found some prints and just aren't saying they did."

"Nope. Not a one. That insurance man said he personally inspected each and every bill and it took him *forever*. The insurance company got half their money back from the bank. Everyone's happy but the kid in jail.''

''You see, Elmo, that's the part that doesn't make sense. He should be happy he's getting out of jail early. I don't want to talk about it. I keep remembering how miserable that man made all of us.''

''It's okay with me, Annie. I didn't mean to upset you. I knew that old fool wouldn't get anywhere harassing us. Are you going to your fifteen-year college reunion later this month?''

''Jane asked me the same thing not too long ago. She wants to go. I've been thinking about it. Fifteen years is a long time, Elmo.''

''When you're my age, it's even longer. I'd like to see the old store again. I liked talking to the kids and hear them call me Pops. Guess it will depend on how I feel at the time. The man that bought my store promised to send me back my sign, but in thirteen years he never did. I called him and wrote a dozen letters. You don't think he's still calling the store the Richardson Pharmacy, do you?''

This was safe ground. ''Could be. I'll have our lawyer look into it. Was it part of the contract?''

''Yes, it was. When I die, I want that sign to go with me. Make a note of that, Annie.''

''Stop talking like that, Elmo. You told me that three hundred times and three hundred times I said okay. You're going to live to a hundred and ten. You know how psychic I am.''

''About as good as I am at predicting rain,'' Elmo snorted. ''I'm going to take a nap.''

Annie stared straight ahead until her eyes started to water. She thought about the strange tone she thought she'd heard in Elmo's voice. Almost as though he was trying to warn her of something. There had been moments over the years when she thought the pharmacist suspected something. But then she'd thought Jane felt the same way. All the while it was Jane Peter

Newman was homing in on. Guilty. Guilty. Guilty. Did people who got out of jail really go after vengeance? Wasn't jail supposed to rehabilitate the prisoner? Would the kid who was no longer a kid throw in his lot with the insurance investigator? To what end?

"Phooey on the lot of you," Annie muttered. "I'm off to Paradise, and I'm not going to think about any of that junk now. Maybe later. A lot later." For now she was going to close her eyes and dream about wearing the rainbow island dress Mattie had made for her years ago. Where she would wear it, she had no clue. She supposed she could wear it to sit behind the waterfall Parker had taken her to. Maybe, if she was lucky, she'd see Annie's Rainbow again. Where are you, Parker? What are you doing right this minute? Do you have a sixth sense that soon I'm going to be within shouting distance? Is there even the remotest possibility that we might run into each other? She wished now that she had called Daniel on some pretext or other and in some offhand way, casually mention that she was going to Hawaii. Why didn't I do that? Because I'm a fool, that's why.

A moment later she was sound asleep. She didn't wake until the steward tapped her shoulder lightly. "Fasten your seat belt, Miss Clark, we're about to land."

Annie walked the groggy dogs while Elmo opted to stay on the plane. They were airborne again forty minutes later. She closed her eyes in the hopes she could continue the wonderful dream she was having about Parker Grayson.

It wasn't to be; a dark-eyed young man wielding a gun, a money bag slung over his shoulder, stalked her as she tried to hide behind the waterfall where she'd spent blissful hours with Parker Grayson. Lurking on the other side of the falls was Peter Newman in a yellow-rubber raft, a gleeful expression on his face. "Gotcha!"

Annie woke with perspiration dripping down her face. Elmo

looked at her with worried eyes. "What in the name of God is wrong, Annie?"

"I just had a horrible dream. I guess it's all the excitement," Annie said as she dabbed at her face with a tissue from her purse. "Plus, I didn't eat today. Are you ready for lunch? We could watch a movie while we eat if that's okay with you. I ordered some very good wine to go with lunch."

"Then, let's do it, girl."

"You look pretty darn spiffy, young lady," Elmo said as he walked Annie to the taxi that would take her to the Grayson Coffee Company. "You will charm those Hawaiians right out of their sarongs."

Annie giggled. "They don't wear sarongs here, Elmo. I'm not even sure they wear grass skirts. The women wear colorful island gowns called muu-muus. I have one I can model for you. I'm going to get one to take home to my niece. Are you sure I look okay?"

"You look better than okay. You look like a model in that dress. Tip the hat a little. Didn't know women still wore hats," Elmo grumbled.

"Everyone wears them in the sun. It sure is hot. Don't keep the dogs out too long and make sure they have plenty of water."

"I've been baby-sitting these dogs for years. I guess I know how to take care of them. Still beats me how you got the condo management to agree to dogs," Elmo continued to grumble.

Annie rubbed her thumb and index finger together. "It's called money, Elmo. I'll call you when I'm heading back. We'll go out to dinner, walk around a little if you feel up to it, drink some wine on our terrace, hit the sack, and do some sight-seeing tomorrow. We'll rest up and head for Maui the next day. I think Maui is the prettiest island of them all. See you later."

In the taxi, Annie took great pains to smooth her dress and sit up straight, so she wouldn't be mussed and wrinkled when she showed up on Parker's doorstep. Would he be there? Would he join in the meeting? How would he look? What would he say? She'd rehearsed her responses and initiated others the night before until the wee hours of the morning. She didn't want to think about the possibility of Parker not being in the offices. He'd said he worked long hours, sometimes from five in the morning till ten at night. Who was Kiki Aellia? His assistant? A partner? An executive secretary? She didn't even know if Kiki was a man or woman, not that it mattered. She should have asked Tom for more details.

Annie stretched out her legs. The panty hose had been a mistake, but her legs were so white she felt embarrassed. Sheer Nude at least gave her a hint of color on her legs and gave the sexy, strappy sandals a little zip. The lime green linen dress was perfect for the climate. The pearl daisy pin, a gift from Elmo that first year, was pinned on her shoulder. The lime green ribbon around the band of the delicate straw hat was a perfect match. She looked professional and felt as successful as she looked.

If she'd ever felt inferior to Parker Grayson, that feeling had been wiped away. It had taken her a few years to realize her tirade against the coffee king had a lot to do with her own insecurities and feelings of inferiority as well as the other nebulous feeling that wouldn't leave her. She closed her eyes and thought about all the awards, all the accolades, all the honorary degrees, the ceremonies, and the write-ups that had been bestowed on her these past years. Being awarded Business-woman of the Year was something to be proud of. Animal rights organizations had bestowed four Golden Paw awards on her in the last four years. She had so many golden keys to cities all over the country that she'd lost count. "Well done, Annie Daisy Clark," she murmured under her breath.

"Here we are, miss," the taxi driver said, getting out of the cab to open the door for her. "It will be no problem to wait for you."

Annie shrugged down her dress and took a deep breath as she adjusted the gold-and-leather chain of the Chanel bag on her shoulder. *Please let him be here. Please, please, please.*

She was so beautiful she was almost intimidating. Almost. Annie extended her hand, "And you are . . . ?"

"Kiki Aellia. And of course you are Tom's sister, Annie. Welcome to the Grayson Coffee Company."

"Thank you."

"We have a small dining room we can use to have some coffee and sweet rolls or we can sit in my office. I've carved out thirty minutes from my schedule to see you today."

Gee whiz, a whole thirty minutes. Annie felt herself start to bristle. The hell with the dining room. She continued to bristle when she said, "I can state my business in five minutes. I certainly don't wish to intrude on your busy day. A cola would be a little more refreshing than a cup of coffee. Shall we get on with it?" Annie said in a voice that could have chilled milk.

Kiki Aellia's perfectly sculpted eyebrows shot upward. "Certainly," she said, leading the way to a beautiful office filled with native flowers. It smelled heavenly.

Annie sat down and crossed her legs. She knew the woman across from her was assessing the total cost of her clothing as well as the handbag. *Best money I ever spent in my life,* Annie thought sourly. *Where the hell is Parker?*

"Let's cut to the chase, as they say. I cannot handle an increase in coffee prices. In fact, I came here to ask you in person to shave two dollars a pound from your price."

"That's out of the question, Miss Clark. Labor prices have gone up. Kona coffee is primo. We have no other choice. Unlike the other coffee exporters, we have not raised our prices in seven years," Kiki said flatly. "Unless you want your coffee unroasted."

"If that's your final word, then there's no point in my eating into that thirty minutes you allotted me. I would like to leave you with a thought," Annie said, getting up out of the rattan chair. "If I take my business elsewhere, which I will, that means you have to peddle two hundred forty thousand pounds of coffee somewhere else. Where's the logic to that? I don't know if Tom told you or not, but we're adding something new to the Daisy Shops. We're going to start selling coffees by the pound. If our projections are on target, we would be tripling our order. So you see, the price cut is essential. Are you sure you want to risk losing ten million dollars a year? That's at fourteen dollars a pound. Roasted, of course." Annie looked at her watch. She'd used up eight minutes. She smiled sweetly. "I'm staying at the Whaler. Perhaps you'd like to think about this. I'll give you until five o'clock this afternoon. It was nice meeting you Miss Aellia. Oh, my brother said to say hello. I can see myself out. Cat got your tongue? Mr. Grayson seems to suffer from the same affliction when things get to the squeeze area. By the way, where is he?" Annie asked boldly.

"On Maui. He only comes in two or three times a week or so to check on the laboratory. I didn't know you knew my brother, Miss Clark."

Brother! "We met many years ago." *Kiki was Parker's sister.* If Parker's sister was working at the coffee company that had to mean her tirade twelve years ago had hit home. "Your brother owes me twelve thousand pounds of coffee. Feel free to mention that to him." Annie wasn't sure, but she thought she saw shades of panic in the beautiful dark eyes.

"Perhaps I can rearrange my schedule and we can discuss matters. Negotiations are always . . . interesting."

"Perhaps you shouldn't. Rearrange your schedule I mean. I don't negotiate. Heads of state negotiate. I'm just a lowly multimillion-dollar company that does business with you. That's just another way of saying we do it my way, or I take my marbles and go home.'' Annie looked at her watch. ''Oh, dear, I've taken up four more minutes of your time. Five o'clock, Miss Aellia. Not one minute later.''

''You drive a hard bargain, Miss Clark.''

''You see, that's where you're wrong. I don't bargain. Fourteen dollars a pound is a fair price. I pride myself on being fair. Thirteen would be better, but it's such an unlucky number.''

''I'll need to talk to my brother.''

''Do whatever you feel you have to do, Miss Aellia. My price is firm, and so is my deadline. One more thing. It's a small matter, but small matters sometimes influence decisions. You knew we had an appointment today. A car service here would not have gone unnoticed. I learned early on that the better you treat a customer, the better the relationship develops.''

''I'll remember that, Miss Clark.''

''So will I,'' Annie said smoothly.

Annie arrived back at the hotel to mass confusion. Hundreds of guests as well as employees were milling about chattering like magpies. She asked a young man holding a surfboard what was going on.

''Water line ruptured. All the floors are flooded. The management is going to relocate all the guests. At no cost.''

Annie stared at the mass confusion, reminded of another day, years ago, when she'd been at the wrong place at the wrong time. Her stomach started to churn. A moment later she saw two streaks of dark movement. Guests scattered as Rosie and Harry skidded to a stop, sat back on their haunches, then barked loudly for attention.

Annie tussled with them for a few minutes. ''You're scaring these people half to death. Show them what ladies and gentlemen you are." A smile on her face, Annie watched indulgently as Rosie pranced up to the guest she'd been talking to and offered her paw. Harry waited patiently until Rosie returned to do the same thing.

"Great dogs. I don't imagine they let anyone get too close to you."

"You're right, they don't. Excuse me. Elmo, over here," she said, waving the straw hat in the air.

"Guess you heard," Elmo said.

"Yes, one of the guests filled me in. Where's our stuff?"

"By the front door. They're bussing us all to another condo. We go in the next van. You got here just in time. How'd things go?"

"They didn't, Elmo. She was sitting tight. Parker wasn't there. Seems his sister more or less runs things these days. She wanted an increase, and I wanted a decrease. I gave her till five o'clock to meet my terms. I guess she doesn't have total control because she said she had to talk to her brother. Will they forward our calls?"

"They said they would. I signed for all of us."

"This new place will allow the dogs?"

"That's what they said. They're calling our names."

"I'm sorry you had to pack up all our stuff, Elmo."

"Are you kidding? The last time I saw unmentionables like that was sixty years ago, and then they had *yards* of material to them. It was my pleasure." Elmo cackled gleefully. "The dogs watched my every move. I found that interesting. It looks to me like you aren't in too good a mood, Miss Anna Daisy Clark."

"I thought *he'd* be there, Elmo. I got all gussied up, and had it out with his sister. That's a downer right there. Why do you suppose they have a laboratory? They didn't have one when I was here before. This is *not* going to spoil our vacation."

"Tomorrow's another day. He'll probably show up once we

get settled. They are not going to let ten million dollars slip through their fingers. I don't care how rich or successful they are. Maybe they need a laboratory to test the beans. Ha, I bet they're trying to make *synthetic* ones. There's nothing left today that's natural. Everything has ten ingredients in it that you can't pronounce. Why should coffee be any different?''

Annie frowned and shrugged, her thoughts far away under a sparkling waterfall. She licked at her lips as she remembered how good it felt when Parker Grayson kissed her.

CHAPTER NINE

It was three-thirty in the afternoon when Annie finally hung up her last wrinkled dress. The dresser drawers were full of what Elmo called her unmentionables. The dogs were snoozing on the balcony that overlooked the ocean.

"How about a nice frosty beer while we wait for your phone call?"

"Sounds good to me. It is beautiful here isn't it, Elmo?"

"Yes, but I don't know if I'd want to live here."

Annie accepted the beer bottle and carried it out to the balcony. She looked at her watch. "I'd say she's cutting it real close."

"She wants to make you sweat. That's business. Maybe she couldn't get hold of her brother. That's a distinct possibility, Annie."

"Maybe I should call the other condo to see if any calls came through for us."

"You did that a half hour ago. You also called downstairs. Just sit here and stare at the ocean and drink your beer."

The dogs were at the door before the knock sounded. Annie gasped, then turned white. What if it was Parker? The dogs whined their distress.

"The only way you're going to find out is if you open the door," Elmo drawled.

Annie padded barefoot to the door. She looked through the peephole. Two men. "Sit and mind your manners," she cautioned the dogs. She opened the door a crack. "Yes?"

"Miss Clark. I'm the manager, and this is my assistant manager. I'm sorry to have to tell you this, but we don't allow dogs here."

Annie's heart thumped in her chest. "If that's true, then why did you allow me to have this condo? My dogs are well trained and behave. If there's any damage, I'll be more than glad to pay for it. It isn't my fault the other condo flooded. I'm not the one who made these arrangements, they did, and you agreed. I'm not moving, and neither are my dogs."

"You don't understand; animals are not permitted," the manager said fretfully.

"What I understand that *you* don't understand is that I'm registered here now. You agreed to allow me to stay. Someone here in this facility okayed my dogs. I repeat, I am not moving. Now, what part of that don't you understand?"

"We don't allow animals."

"You already said that. You now know my position on your rule. Take it up with the Whaler condo people. If you don't like that suggestion, call the authorities. Harry, Rosie, show these nice gentlemen your teeth."

If the situation wasn't so serious, Annie would have exploded into laughter when both dogs bared their teeth. "Is that impressive or what?" she said to the jittery managers. "If I were to drop five hundred dollars here on the doorstep, will that make all this go away?"

"In the blink of an eye," the manager said smartly. The assistant manager nodded his approval.

"You wait right here." Annie was back in a minute with five crisp hundred-dollar bills. She reached out and dropped them into the hallway. "Finders keepers," she said, before she slammed the door.

"You guys did real good," she said, tickling both dogs' ears. If they had been cats, they would have purred.

"Guess you heard, huh?" Annie said, flopping down on the chaise.

"My ears didn't perk up till I heard you tell the dogs to show them their teeth. Pretty clever," Elmo said.

"Yeah, so clever it cost me five hundred bucks. What time is it?"

"Four-fifteen."

"This is too close for comfort."

"So call again if it will make you happy. My advice would be to have another beer."

"I can do that, too. Three and I dance on the table. You know that, Elmo, so stop plying me with liquor. What should we talk about?"

"What would you like to talk about?" Elmo queried.

"Why didn't you ever get married, Elmo?"

"I guess I never found the right woman. I think I was looking for someone as kind and wonderful as my mother. No one measured up. I came close a few times, but it didn't feel right so it just never happened. I did miss not having children, though. I enjoyed the kids on the campus. That's the end of that story. Why don't we talk about Mr. Parker Grayson?"

"There's not much to say. You know the story. He's too steeped in his culture and can't see beyond the end of his nose. Great kisser, though. I really liked him, and I thought he liked me. Sometimes things just aren't meant to be. Part of me wants to see him again and part of me doesn't. That's the end of that story. Now what should we talk about? What time is it?''

"It's four-twenty-five. You want to talk about the Hawaiian flowers? Hibiscus is what they call the flowers in the gardens over to the right.''

"Really. Bet you don't know the name of the state bird. It's nene. It's kind of like a goose. Wanna know the state tree? It's kukui, better known as the candlenut. Long ago it provided the Hawaiians with light, oil, relishes, and medicine.''

"You're just a wealth of information,'' Elmo said as he got up to get more beer.

"Get some root beer for the dogs, Elmo.''

Annie flipped the lid of the beer bottle and took a swig. "Boy, this is good. There's nothing like a cold beer on a hot day. What time is it, Elmo?''

"Four-thirty-five.''

"Guess what the state fish is? You spell it humuhumunu-kunukuapua.''

Elmo laughed so loud the dogs stopped slurping their root beer to stare at him. "Where'd you learn all that?''

"From the brochure on the plane. I read it word for word while you were sleeping.''

"I'm impressed,'' the old man muttered.

"You should be. Listen to this. *Ua mau ke ea o ka aina I ka pono.* That means, the life of the land is perpetuated in righteousness. They say King Kamehameha III said it when the Hawaiian flag was raised after a brief period of unauthorized usurpation of authority by a British admiral.''

"My education is now complete. Do we have any nibbles or munchies?''

"There were some corn chips and dried fruits in the welcoming basket. I'll get them for you. What time is it?''

"Four-forty-five.''

"If this phone rings one second after five, we are not answering it. Maybe I should call the Whaler again."

"If that will make you feel better, then do it."

"It's possible, Elmo, that everyone is busy over there pumping water. Maybe no one is manning the phones."

"So call. And when they answer, you'll know you shot yourself in the foot."

"You are surly, today, Elmo. Is your arthritis bothering you?"

"A little. Pretty as this place is, I don't much like it. It's too flowery. Too green. I don't like apartments. I like to go out on the porch and sit in my rocker."

"Do you want to go home, Elmo? It's okay if you do."

"I miss the shop the way I missed the drugstore when I left Boston. Would you be upset if I left? I'll take the dogs with me."

"If that's what you want, Elmo. One minute after five, I'll call the airport and schedule your flight. I can go back commercial."

"I feel like a curmudgeon leaving you."

"That's because you are a curmudgeon. I understand. Did you unpack?"

"Nope. I'm good to go. You're sure you don't mind me taking the dogs?"

"Elmo, it's okay. I just thought you would like a vacation. I don't ever remember you taking one in all the years I've known you."

"That's because I never did. Vacations don't mean much. I'm too old to waste my time sitting around. I want to be doing something. I can help Tom with the coffee bins if we're going to start selling coffee. You're going to want fancy bags. White maybe, with a daisy on them. See, I can be working on all that while you're here chasing that guy you say doesn't want to be caught."

"I never said any such thing, Elmo. What time is it?"

"Four-fifty-seven. Three minutes to go."

"What am I going to do with myself now that you're leaving? I had all these tours planned."

"You can still do them. I would have held you back. I can't walk like I used to. The dogs are happier in their own environment," Elmo said, throwing in what he knew would be the clincher.

"I can't argue with that. Guess I screwed up, huh?"

"No. No, Annie, you didn't. Sometimes you are just too kind and generous for your own good. When you get to be my age you want to be where you're the most comfortable. I like my old chair and my worn-out slippers and my big-screen TV. I like to putter in the kitchen and water my plants. I like messing up my stove knowing someone else is going to clean it. Most of all I like to sit up late at night and read all the journals and pamphlets that still come to me."

"I love you, Elmo Richardson." This time Annie didn't ask for the time. She picked up the phone she'd dragged to the balcony and dialed the number the pilot had given her. "There's been a change in plans, Captain. Mr. Richardson wants to leave as soon as possible. He's packed and ready to go. We can be at the airport in thirty minutes if that's okay with you. No, I won't be returning with you, but the dogs will, so have plenty of root beer on board and a lot of munchies for Mr. Richardson.

"We'll take a taxi," she told Elmo. "I hope we can find one that will take the dogs."

"You might have to drop some more money on the floor." Elmo cackled.

"I might at that. Maybe I'll rent a car tomorrow and explore on my own a little."

"That sounds like a good idea. I'm ready."

"Okay, guys, let's go. I think we should use the service elevator. No point in making more waves. I'll call Tom when

I get back. Be sure to check on him, Elmo. He's like you; he can't sit still. He always has to be doing something.''

Outside, a young Hawaiian boy in a red-and-white-flowered shirt approached Annie. ''Your dogs are beautiful. I always wanted a German shepherd, but my sister is allergic to dog hair. I didn't know they allowed dogs here. I'm just a valet, so maybe they don't tell me these things. You are the daisy lady, yes?''

''It was a problem. That's why they're leaving. Can you find us a cab that will agree to take the dogs? We want to go to the airport. How do you know I'm the daisy lady?''

''Miss Clark is the daisy lady, they said. It is on the bulletin board. The manager does this so we call each guest by name. I do not know what daisy lady means. If you give a generous tip, any driver will take you.''

''How does fifty dollars sound?'' Annie queried. ''I own coffee shops called Daisy Shops.''

''Thirty dollars too much. Too late,'' he said, wagging his finger playfully.

Annie handed him a ten-dollar bill as she settled the dogs in the backseat of the taxi.

''Mahalo,'' the valet shouted as he pocketed the ten dollars.

At the airport, the plane stood in readiness. Annie escorted the two dogs up the metal stairs and into the plane. ''Have a good trip, Elmo. I'll call you as soon as I know you're home safe. Take care of my dogs. I'll find you the best grass skirts the island has to offer.''

''My ladies will be mighty pleased. I don't think I'll announce my arrival right away. Some peace and quiet for me and the dogs will be nice. Are you sure you aren't upset with me, Annie?''

''I'm sure. I understand, Elmo. You guys behave yourself till I get back,'' she said, tweaking the dogs' ears. They growled good-naturedly.

The moment Elmo saw Annie on the ground walking toward the terminal he leaned back, slapped his thigh and laughed so loud the steward came running to see what was wrong. Elmo waved him off, still laughing. "We pulled it off. Now she's free to go after that guy who has been in her heart for so long. We were just excess baggage. Without us to worry about she's got all the time in the world. Now, settle in, I have a bunch of junk none of us are supposed to be eating. Licorice for you, Rosie, Pom Poms for you, Harry, and for me, cigarettes and Hershey Kisses. It's a long flight home, but I have *pounds* of treats." He laughed again. The dogs threw their heads back and howled.

"We're here, miss. Do you want the front entrance or the back entrance?"

"Take me around to the back. I think I'll sit out by the pool for a while and have one of those marvelous drinks with an umbrella in it."

Annie chose a chaise longue with a fluffy blue towel thrown over the back of it. "We're about to close the bar, miss, but I can make you one last drink," a waiter said.

"Bring me a big one with lots and lots of stuff in it. Add some cherries and don't forget the umbrella." The waiter nodded and smiled.

Annie laughed when he returned with a carved-out pineapple, filled to the brim, that required two hands to hold. A bright pink umbrella stood at attention in a mound of whipped cream. "Absolutely decadent," she giggled. "Is there a phone around here I can use?"

The waiter brought a phone with a long cord and set it on the little table next to her elbow. She tipped him generously, then charged the drink to her room.

"Good night, ma'am."

Ma'am. ''Good night.'' *Ma'am* not *miss.* Suddenly she felt a hundred years old. She didn't realize how tired she was until she took several hits from the pineapple drink. She started to relax immediately. Elmo was old. Tom was old. If she could still have babies, then she was young. *Ma'am.* She hated the way it sounded. She was a young woman in Paradise with no man in sight. *What are you doing, Parker? Do you ever think of me? Do you hate me for all those things I said to you?*

Annie looked around. It was so peaceful here. The low walkway lighting twinkled at her from the lush shrubbery. It occurred to her as she looked around to wonder if there was any crime in this peaceful setting. She shrugged when she realized she was alone in the pool area. Maybe she should go upstairs and drink in the privacy of her room. She hated to move. There was something out of sync, but she couldn't put her finger on it. ''I wish I had a lei around my neck. If I don't accomplish anything else while I'm here, I'm going to learn how to make my own.'' That's what was out of sync: The air wasn't flower-scented. She sniffed. Chlorine. Of course, they'd probably serviced the pool before closing it for the night. ''It's not fair,'' she muttered as she slurped from the pineapple.

Annie kicked her shoes off and fired up a cigarette. Alone in Paradise with a drink she couldn't pronounce and a cigarette. Even Elmo didn't want to be with her. The dogs had gone willingly. Alone. One way or another she'd always been alone.

Annie started to cry. What was it Tom always said? Life's a bitch, then you die. What a happy thought. She sobbed once, then blew her nose just as a young girl dressed in the skimpiest bathing suit Annie had ever seen and spike-heeled sandals walked past her, a bottle of Budweiser in her hand. She backed up when she heard Annie's sob.

''What's wrong? Are you okay?''

''Nothing's wrong. I'm all right. I don't know, all of a sudden

I started feeling sorry for myself because I'm all alone,'' Annie blurted.

"That won't get you anywhere. See, that was your first mistake. You should never come to a place like this alone just like you should never go on a cruise by yourself. I'm on my honeymoon. We got sooooo much money for our wedding that Joe and I decided to come here instead of going to Disney. I haven't seen a single guy since I got here two days ago. I still look 'cause it's fun. Joe looks, too. It's okay to look, but you can't touch. Stella Kaminsky,'' Stella said, swigging from the beer bottle. "Listen, honey, if you want you can pal around with me and Joe. It's not like we're on a real honeymoon you know. We lived together for five years before we decided to get married. I'll bet we could fix you up. Frizz up your hair, some darker makeup, a better-looking dress, one that says, let's get it on. You know the kind. You're kind of dressed like a den mother or something. Is that a real Chanel bag? Of course it isn't. Someday I'm going to get a real Chanel bag and sport around with it. I guess yours isn't real 'cause, if it was, why would you be staying in a dump like this?''

"Annie Clark. Is this place considered a dump?'' she asked.

"Honey, did you take a good look around in the daylight? It's downright shabby. If you want to snag a man, you need to go to some fancy place. This is okay for me and Joe because we have each other. With a little work you could probably get something going. I'm free tomorrow morning if you want me to help you. How long are you staying?''

"Ah . . . I'm leaving tomorrow,'' Annie said.

"Some guy dump you and you came here to get over it?''

"Something like that,'' Annie said in a strangled voice. "Are those breasts your own or did you have implants?'' *Oh, God, did I just say that?*

"Straight from the factory. Model number SJ264. Joe paid

for them two birthdays ago. Saucy, he calls them. I think they're perky. What do you do?''

Saucy. Perky. Uh-huh. ''I sell coffee.''

''Coffee's good. So what went wrong with the guy that dumped you?''

''He didn't like hearing the truth. The truth as I saw it. It really wasn't any of my business, but I thought I had the right to voice an opinion. I don't know if I'm sorry or not. It's getting late. Guess I'll go upstairs. It was nice meeting you, Stella.''

''Listen, I'll be out here by the pool around ten. If you need to go somewhere, I can drive you. We learned to get around in just two days. Joe and I rented a car. If you want to hang out, fine. I'll wait for fifteen minutes. Howzat?''

''That's . . . that's fine.'' Annie opened her bag and stuffed the contents into the pockets of her shorts. ''Here,'' she said. ''Consider it a wedding present.''

''Jeez, you don't have to do that.''

''Sure I do. Nice meeting you, Stella. By the way,'' she called over her shoulder, ''it's a real Chanel, not a knockoff.''

''Jeez. Thanks. Wait till I show this to Joe. These babies cost *thousands.*''

Annie smiled all the way to her room.

The first thing she did when she entered the room was check the phone's red message light. It didn't glow. ''Damn.''

Annie showered, washed her hair, mixed herself a drink from the portable bar, and carried it to the small balcony along with the phone. At one o'clock she would call Tom since he always got up at six. Elmo and the dogs were probably halfway home by now.

The minute the hands on her watch pointed out the hour, Annie placed the call to her brother. She half expected to hear a sleepy, groggy voice. Instead she heard concern when she announced herself. ''Annie, where in hell have you been all day and night? I've been calling you every fifteen minutes?''

"I guess I blew it, Tom. I came on to Miss Kiki like a pile driver. She was and is going to raise the price. I gave her an ultimatum. Who gives a good rat's ass anyway. She said she had to talk to her brother. Ask me if I care. By the way, Elmo and the dogs are headed home. He said at his age he wants to be around his stuff. The first condo had a flood, and they moved us out. Somebody I met, Stella, just told me this place is a dump, so I guess I'm going to leave tomorrow. I'll call you when I decide where I'm going. You don't need to worry about me. I'm a big girl. Elmo wants to work on the bins for the coffee we're going to sell, providing we find someone who will sell it to us. Now, tell me, why are you so worried? Why were you calling me every fifteen minutes?"

"If you'd just shut up, I'd tell you."

"By the way, how are you?"

"I'm fine. I'm really fine. I walked around the house three times today. Yesterday, I mean. Kiki Aellia has been calling here every fifteen minutes. She's been calling all over the island trying to find you."

"I don't think she tried very hard. I called the Whaler several times, and they said there were no calls for me. None were forwarded. There were no calls here at the Monarch either. Did you believe her?"

"She was certainly agitated with your deadline of five o'clock. She wanted me to intervene because she couldn't get hold of her brother. It seems his old housekeeper retired along with her husband, and now Mr. Grayson just has someone to come in and clean one day a week. Kiki says he goes fishing and snorkeling on his days off, which seem to be four days out of every week. Don't quote me on that. Maybe you should call her in the morning."

"Maybe I shouldn't, Tom. How hard could it have been for her to send someone to the Whaler or here to tell me whatever it was she wanted to tell me?"

"Listen to me, Annie. I think Kiki Aellia's situation with her brother is just like ours but in reverse. I would never make the kind of decision you asked her to make without consulting you. This is just a guess on my part, but I don't think she has the authority to make such an important decision. She'll probably lose her job, sibling or not, if you pull our business from them. It isn't her fault she couldn't reach her brother. She did call me thirty-three times. That alone shows she values our business. You're pissed, and I can't say I blame you."

"She knew I was coming here, Tom. She said, get this, she carved thirty minutes from her schedule to meet with me. Thirty whole minutes. No one picked me up. I had to take a taxi both ways, and no one gave me a lei. That really pissed me off. I hate people who are so full of themselves. If I ever get like that, slap me good."

"Give me the phone number where you're staying before we hang up. What are you going to do today?"

Annie rattled off the phone number. "When I hang up I'm going to go to bed while you eat your breakfast. Then I might meet Stella and check out this island. On the other hand, I might move to a better location. Then again, I might head for one of the other islands. Don't call me, I'll call you. Night, Tom."

"Wait a minute, Annie. What should I tell Kiki if she calls again?"

"Tell her whatever you want. I couldn't care less."

"Wise-ass."

"Takes one to know one," Annie shot back before she hung up the phone.

She picked up the phone and dialed the front desk. "This is Annie Clark in sixteen-o-four. Don't put any calls through until I tell you otherwise. By the way, were there any calls for me today? No? Thank you."

*   *   *

Parker Grayson rolled over on his side just as the first streaks of dawn crept through the louvered doors. A moment later the phone shrilled on his nightstand. Who the hell was calling him at this hour? He rolled over again to reach for the phone. He barked a greeting that would have intimidated anyone but his youngest sister Kiki.

"Slow down, Kiki. What do you mean where was I all day? I don't ask you where you go on your days off. You said you could handle things. I believed you. I still believe you. What the hell happened? Slow, Kiki, real slow. Speak in English. I'm listening. Annie Clark is here on the island. You didn't tell me she was coming. I thought we did business with Tom. She what? And you didn't call me! What do you mean she yanked her business? We have a contract. Contracts are binding. I never, ever, told you to raise the price, Kiki. That's a joint decision. Now look what you've done. She said what? I didn't think they were ready for the coffee sale. Tom said they were just in the thinking stages. Let me understand this, Kiki. You just blew ten million dollars a year because you didn't like what she said and the way she said it! I think you need to tell me what it was you said first. I know this lady. Don't leave anything out."

Parker groaned as he listened to his agitated sister. "You said you carved out thirty minutes from your schedule. What the hell schedule are you talking about? Didn't you send the van for her? For Christ's sake, you didn't even give her a lei! We always entertain our customers. I spend the whole day with Tom when he comes over here. Why would the *owner* of the Daisy Shops be any different? You should have stood on your head for her. What the hell does a Chanel handbag, whatever the hell that is, and a straw hat with a ribbon have to do with anything? Stop crying. You're supposed to be a businesswoman. No, I am not going to help you. You created this *womanly* thing, now uncreate it. I never heard of such a piss-ass way of doing business in my life. You were greedy. We do business fairly. I warned you about that in the beginning. We do not cut corners, and we do not cut deals that benefit only us. The customer is our main concern, and the Daisy Shops are half our business. You seem to have forgotten that. Papa must be spinning in his grave over this one. I'm going to hang up now, Kiki, before I *really* get mad.''

Parker swung his legs over the side of the bed, the headache he'd felt on awakening hammering inside his head. He reached for his address book, which was always within reach, and flipped the pages until he found Tom Clark's home phone number. His fingers drummed impatiently on the nightstand. ''Tom, Parker Grayson. I'm sorry to hear about your appendix. Kiki just told me. The good news is you can live without it. Listen, Tom, my hotheaded, know-it-all sister and your hot-headed sister seem to have a problem. It's some kind of woman thing neither one of us understands. Kiki kept babbling about a Chanel bag and a hat with a ribbon. Yeah, yeah, I can see how that would tick off Annie. Can't say that I blame Annie. You know that's not the way I do business. I was out and about for the past two days wining and dining some old college pals who are here visiting. I gotta tell you, we're all too old for this crap. We did a hell of a job pretending, though. Look, the deal Annie presented to my sister is okay with me. We can't cut the price two dollars, but I can go one-fifty. It's a good deal for both of us, and you know it. Of course it's roasted. I could use a little manly advice about now. How do I manage to make this right, Tom? Now why did I know you were going to tell me I'm on my own. We'll make it right. Where's Annie staying? I'll call you tomorrow. Take care of yourself.''

Parker gulped down four aspirin, showered, shaved, dressed,

and was out the door in less than twenty minutes to head for the airstrip where he kept his private plane.

After all this time, Annie had finally returned to the islands. Maybe there was a God after all.

Ninety minutes later, Parker strode into the lobby of the Monarch. At best it was tacky. He frowned. Why in the hell would Annie Clark stay in a dump like this? He found out a moment later when he asked for her room.

"Miss Clark checked out, sir."

"Do you know where she went? Did she go back to the Whaler?"

"She didn't say, sir. Perhaps one of the bellboys or the valets can tell you more."

"Yes, sir, Miss Clark drove off with one of the other guests. I know it was Miss Clark because yesterday she had two big dogs with her. She gave me a ten-dollar tip. The dogs were ferocious, big as little ponies. She was going to the airport with an elderly gentleman and the dogs. That's all I know, sir."

"Do you know the name of the other guest?"

"Yes, sir. I do."

"Well?"

The valet shuffled his feet and waited until Parker handed him a ten-dollar bill. "A honeymoon couple. Stella and Joe Kaminsky," the boy said, reading from the valet parking chart.

"When they return, will you give them this card and ask them to call me?" Another ten-dollar bill changed hands.

With nothing better to do, Parker shoved the car into gear and headed for the coffee plantation. He had a thing or two to say to his sister Kiki.

CHAPTER TEN

"This is really nice of you, Stella. I could have taken a cab, though."

"It's the least I could do after you gave me that smashing bag. How come you're leaving?" Stella said as she put the pedal to the metal. Annie's neck snapped backward. She was certain she had a whiplash when her body jolted forward.

It had been a long time since she'd talked to a girlfriend. Jane was busy with her own life now, and the few female friends she did have weren't the kind she wanted to share confidences with. This outgoing young woman with the ditzy hairdo and racy clothes had a kind heart and a warm smile. The same wonderful qualities Jane had.

"A long time ago I met this man. I thought the instant I saw him that he was the man for me. He said in turn that he felt I was his destiny."

"Wow! Joe never said anything like that to me."

Annie smiled. "Obviously he didn't need to. You're married, aren't you? You don't see a ring on my finger, do you?"

"Yeah. He's sweet. I wish you coulda met him. You'd like him, and he'd like you. He was really bowled over when I showed him that pocketbook you gave me. No one ever gave me anything that elegant."

"Joe will give you everything he can someday," Annie said.

"Yeah. He'd give me the moon if he could. You still didn't tell me what happened with that guy. You know, the *real* lowdown."

"At that time I suppose things were different. He said when his parents died they left their estate to him and him alone. Even though he had six sisters. I didn't think that was right. I still don't think that's right. I said so. He said it was the custom here. He didn't share with his sisters, either."

"That's awful," Stella said as she barreled through a yellow light.

"I asked him what he would do if we had a son and two daughters and something happened to him or me. I have my own business, so I was a little concerned. He said it would go to the son and then I asked what would happen to my daughters and he didn't have an answer. So, I told him off and left. That was years and years ago. I still do business with his company though. My brother handles it."

"Jeez, he sounds like one of those, what do you call them, Neanderthals or something like that?"

"Just out of curiosity, what would you have done, Stella?"

"Same damn thing you did. I'd just like to see Joe pull something like that on me. I don't have to worry though, neither one of our parents has much, and we'd never fight over it anyway. You still love him, huh?"

"Yes. No. I don't know. Something must have happened during those years, because his sister works for the company. She and I had a little disagreement yesterday. A rather serious one. In fact, I'm still steaming." Annie turned in her seat to face Stella, whose eyes were glued to everything but the road. "Tell me what you think of this, Stella."

When Annie finally wound down, Stella zipped to the side of the road, cutting off two other cars before she slammed on the brakes. "You own those Daisy Shops! Well, Lordy, Lordy. Me and Joe go there for cappuccino sometimes. There's one off the campus of Rutgers University. I betcha I been there three dozen times. Joe's gonna be real happy when I tell him you're gonna be selling that coffee by the pound. So what are you gonna do, Annie?"

"I don't know. With the mix-ups in the condos and all, Kiki, that's the sister, didn't call me. She did call my brother quite a few times yesterday. It seems she can't make that kind of decision without consulting her brother. There's a lot of money involved here and a lot of coffee."

"You're telling me. I don't like ultimatums."

"Neither do I. I guess I made a mistake by giving her a five o'clock deadline. She ticked me off big-time. At first I didn't know she was Parker's sister. That old devil named jealousy reared her ugly head. She was beautiful, and I immediately thought any man would be attracted to her, mainly Parker since she worked for him. I reacted."

"Don't you go feeling bad now. I probably would have done the same thing. Sounds like you got her on the run. They're both probably chasing all over this island looking for you. I bet they are, Annie. You gonna let the guy catch you? You should, but first give him a run for his money. I wish Joe was here. He'd know right off what to tell you. He's a man!" Stella said proudly.

"I just made up my mind. I'm going to Maui!"

"Good for you! You gonna stake him out or what?"

"Were you serious about frizzing up my hair?"

"Nah. That was in the dark with three Buds under my belt. Your hair's much too pretty to mess with. You're a beautiful woman, Annie Clark. You dress good, too. Someday Joe is gonna have his own garage, and he'll get me anything I want. He promised to get me a Visa card the next time an application comes in the mail.''

"Are you and Joe married to your jobs, Stella?"

"For now. They pay the rent. We're paying on a big-screen TV because Joe likes sports. He surprised me with a glue gun, a super-duper model 'cause he knows I like to make crafts while he's watching sports. They don't come any better than Joe. Takes the edge off all those cranky women I have to pamper all day long. I swear, one of these days I'm going to snatch one of them baldheaded. I like being a hairdresser most days, but there are days when it gets to you.''

"Do you mind me asking what kind of money the two of you take home every week?"

"Yeah, I do mind. That's kind of private. Why do you want to know?"

"I was going to offer you and Joe a job."

"What kind of job?"

"Running one of the Daisy Shops. We're about ready to open two very close to Princeton University. You could operate both of them. We have an excellent health plan and a very generous pension plan. You'd be able to save for your children's college educations. It's something you need to talk over with Joe, though. I'll give you my card, and you can call me with your decision. The money is very good, Stella.''

"Jeez, I almost missed that sign," Stella said as she careened past an airport van and a jeep. "Annie, I don't know anything about running a store. Neither does Joe.''

"We'll train you. Everything is premixed and prepackaged. All you have to do is read the directions. And you get to wear one of those cute little daisy uniforms.''

Stella laughed. "Why?"

"Why what?"

"Why would you do that for me and Joe?"

"Because you took the time last night to stop and ask me if I was all right. You cared enough to ask. You offered to drive me here, and you didn't even know me. I appreciate that and the advice. Besides, I like you. I think I'm a good judge of character."

"I didn't give you any advice, Annie."

"Sure you did. You as much as told me to stake him out and see what gives. I think I just might do that."

"So you're going to Maui?"

"Yep. You're sure now I shouldn't frizz my hair and get one of those dresses you suggested?"

"Nah. That's not who you are. You're a lady, Annie."

"That's probably one of the nicest things anyone's ever said to me," Annie said, with a catch in her voice.

"I bet if you give that guy a chance, he'll say all kinds of nice things to you. You gotta give him the chance, Annie."

"Here's my card, Stella. Will you call me either way? Leave a message on my machine back home. If you decide to go for it, I'll fly to New Jersey and make sure you're all set up. Thanks for the lift. See you around," Annie said, pulling her bag from the car.

"You wait right there, Annie. Listen, if I seemed uninterested or whatever . . . you know. It's just that no one ever did anything so nice for me except Joe. I didn't know how to act because I was so flabbergasted. The answer is yes. We'll do it. We'll take it. We want to do it."

"Don't you have to ask Joe?"

"Yes and no. If there's a change, I'll let you know."

"Okay. Bye, Stella. It was nice meeting you."

"Not so fast." Stella threw her skinny arms around Annie and bear-hugged her. "He's a big jerk if he lets you get away from him," she whispered.

Annie pried herself loose. "It's been a lot of years, Stella. I'll let you know how it goes."

"You don't have my phone number."

"Call my house and leave it on the answering machine. Gotta go, destiny awaits." Stella's fist shot into the air.

Annie cringed when Stella peeled away from the curb, her tires smoking.

His face murderous, Parker slammed his way out of the jeep and into the offices of the Grayson Coffee Company. The moment he saw the naked fear in his sister's eyes, his shoulders slumped. How well he remembered his own fear when he'd done something wrong and had to account to his father. He wasn't an ogre, was he? Obviously Kiki thought so.

"Let's sit down and talk this through. Maybe we can salvage the account. Tell me what happened, Kiki. Tears aren't going to help. Wipe your eyes and blow your nose. Then get me some coffee."

"Get your own coffee, Parker."

The palms of Parker's hands shot forward. "Sorry, I forgot. Women don't fetch and carry for a man anymore. It just seems to taste better when a woman hands it to you," Parker mumbled. "Sit down, Kiki, and let's hear your side of this."

"Until the day before yesterday I didn't know Tom wasn't coming. The truth is, I didn't get the message until very early yesterday morning. When I thought it was Tom coming, I didn't concern myself because you always meet him at the airport and spend the day with him. I got in late yesterday morning because I had to go to Loya's school to talk to her teacher. She's becoming a discipline problem. I'm dealing with it. Anyway, that threw me behind. I wasn't in the best of moods when I got here. My day was all mapped out. I jiggled and juggled and found thirty minutes. I thought it was going to be a cut-and-dried meeting. I was wrong.''

''Then what happened?''

''Miss Clark arrived. You know what, Parker, she looked . . . she looked like I always wanted to look. She was crisp, business-like, she was dressed beautifully, and she was carrying this gorgeous Chanel bag. Her white straw hat had a lime green streamer on it. To me she just reeked of success. She had this air about her like she was saying, I'm here, and we're going to do it my way. Or, I take my marbles and leave. She never said that, Parker, in words. It was probably my own insecurities. It was that damn Chanel bag. My son could pay his board for a full semester with the money that purse cost.''

Parker threw his hands in the air. ''I must be stupid. What in the goddamn hell does a woman's purse have to do with the price of coffee?''

Kiki burst into tears. ''I don't know, Parker. I guess it was a symbol of something I didn't have, should have, will never have. I don't know.''

''I'll buy you a damn purse just like it.''

''No. It's not the same. She bought it. She earned the right to pay thousands of dollars for a purse. Don't you get it? I know it's stupid. I would probably never spend that much on a purse, but I should have the right to if I want to. It's also time to talk about a raise.''

''You screw up a ten-million-dollar deal and you expect a raise. Nobody pays thousands of dollars for a purse. What's it look like?''

''It's just plain. It has a gold chain with leather woven through it. It has a gold clasp and is quilted. Don't buy me one, Parker. I mean that.''

''Okay, okay, what else?''

''I told her I could give her thirty minutes. From that point on, it was all downhill. I asked her if she wanted coffee and she said no but would take something cold. I never did give her the cola," Kiki said miserably.

"Let's hear it all," Parker grated.

"She told me what she was willing to pay per pound, roasted. I said no. I gave her the bit about rising costs, and she just looked right through me. Then she threw in that bit about buying the coffee to sell by the pound in her shops. I had to backpedal then by saying I had to talk to my brother. She didn't seem to know I was your sister. She looked kind of stunned for the moment. She asked where you were, and I had to say I didn't know. Then she just looked disgusted. She said she wanted my answer by five o'clock, not one minute later. I called you all day long. I sent someone to Maui to see if you'd gone fishing or something. In a way this is your fault, too, Parker. You didn't tell me you were going to Waikiki to meet your friends. I tried calling Miss Clark at the Whaler, but they said there was a problem there and she'd gone to the Monarch. I called there, and they said they never heard of her. The only thing left for me to do was call Tom, which I did. He said he'd be in touch as soon as his sister called him. I met her deadline, Parker. The screwup can't be blamed on me. Just tell me one thing, what the hell would you have done? Would you have made the decision on your own or would you have waited to talk to me?"

Parker stared at his sister. He knew his answer was very important to her. "I would have waited to talk to you. I think the two of you overreacted. Perhaps Tom and I can patch this up, and we can retain the account." *After I figure out the business with the purse,* Parker thought sourly. His gaze went to the window and the streamlined building directly in his line of vision. Very soon that building was going to make all the difference in the world to the Grayson Coffee Company.

"One of us should go to the Monarch and talk to her in person," Kiki said.

"I already did that. She checked out. I got the name of the guest who drove her away. I left a message for the woman to call me. Until we know where Annie is, there's nothing more we can do."

"Do you call her Annie, Parker?"

"Yes, Kiki, I call her Annie."

"Is she . . . Miss Clark is . . . she's the one Mattie told us about?"

Parker was on his feet. "Don't step over that line, Kiki."

"Parker, I'm sorry. If there's anything I can do . . ."

"I'll let you know. I'm going back to the Monarch to wait for the lady that drove Annie to wherever she was going. Try not to get into any trouble while I'm gone."

Kiki burst into tears.

Parker sighed. "I'm sorry, Kiki. That remark was uncalled for. Hold the fort, okay? It's not the end of the world. We'll make it come out right." Kiki nodded miserably.

It was almost noon when Parker slowed to a crawl in the circular driveway that led to the Monarch.

"Hey, mister, you need to watch where you're going. I almost hit you! I hope you carry good insurance," a shrill voice wafted toward him.

"Can't you read? The sign says ten miles an hour," Parker shot back. "You're going at least forty."

The shrill voice retaliated. "This coming from a man who's at a dead stop in the middle of a busy driveway. I-don't-think-so!"

Parker slid to the curb just as the woman with the shrill voice bounded out of her open-air jeep. He watched as a husky young man with a beard, baseball cap, and cutoff shorts embraced her. "I've been waiting, you sweet thing. Let's me and you go in the pool and do some underwater swimming." The girl's tinkling laugh made Parker smile. A head taller than the husky man, the girl wrapped her arm through his, and said, "Boy,

Joe, do I have something to tell you. I swear, in a million years, you aren't going to believe this. We were just offered the dream of a lifetime!''

Parker strode over to the valet, realizing he was never going to know what the dream of a lifetime was. He felt cheated.

''Did Miss Kaminsky return yet?''

''That's her. The tall skinny lady. She just went into the lobby. They're honeymooners,'' he said, as if that explained everything. Parker groaned as he forked over another ten-dollar bill.

In the tacky-looking lobby there was no sign of the honeymooners. ''Which way to the pool,'' he asked the desk clerk.

''Go around the corner, down the hall, and the pool door is to the left.''

Parker took a seat at one of the beach tables to wait. Twenty minutes later the newlyweds, toting beach bags and towels, set up shop two tables away. He waited until they were settled before he sauntered over to their table.

''Are you Miss Kaminsky?''

''I'm Mrs. Kaminsky. This is my husband Joe. Hey, you're the snail crawler I almost hit in the driveway. You need to learn how to drive, mister.''

Parker nodded. ''I'm sorry. I was wondering if you could tell me where you took Miss Clark. The valet said you gave her a lift someplace.''

Stella inched closer to her husky husband, who was glaring at him. ''Who wants to know?''

''I do,'' Parker said patiently.

''Who is *I*? I need a name here. For all I know you could be a pervert.''

''I've been called many things in my life, but no one has ever called me a pervert,'' Parker said tightly.

''I didn't say you *were* one. I said you could be. Who are you and why do you want to know where I took Miss Clark?''

"My name is Parker Grayson. I own a coffee plantation here on the island. I've been trying to locate Miss Clark since yesterday with no success."

"Maybe she doesn't want to be found. I need to have a little more to go on before I tell you anything. We were going swimming. We're on our honeymoon," Stella said pointedly.

"If you would just tell me what I need to know, I'll leave. What kind of purse is that?" Parker asked, eyeing the Chanel bag dangling from Stella's shoulder.

"You sure do ask a lot of questions. It's a Chanel bag," Stella said authoritatively. "Miss Clark gave it to me. Not that it's any of your business."

"Look, we're getting nowhere fast. I really need to find Annie. I love Annie Clark. We had . . . things didn't work out the way they were supposed to. It was my fault. I never had the guts to do anything about it. She's here now, and I need the chance to make things right. I need your help to do that."

"Then why didn't you say that in the first place?" Stella said.

"Because I felt like a . . . jerk."

"Yeah, I understand that," Stella said. "I took Annie to the airport. She's going to Maui."

"Maui? That's where I live."

"Yeah, I know," Stella said, leering at him.

Parker reached for Stella and kissed her soundly on the cheek. "Thanks. Thanks a lot. I'll send you free coffee for the rest of your life," he said, pumping Joe's hand vigorously.

The Kaminskys watched as Parker raced to the door. "There must be more to this coffee business than we thought," Joe mused. "You ready for our swim, sweet cheeks?"

"Ready, Joe. Boy is Annie gonna be happy. We did good, Joe. Whoever would of thought me and you would play cupid. I hope they're as happy as we are."

"Nobody is as happy as we are. So there, Stella Kaminsky."

"You're right, Joe. You're always right."

Annie walked around the spacious condo she'd rented. It was so gorgeous, it took her breath away. It was all done in soft shades of green, yellow, and off-white. In her life, she'd never trampled such a luscious white carpet. She wiggled her toes and giggled as the carpeting tickled her toes and caressed her insteps.

As she walked around, touching this, staring at that, she came eyeball-to-eyeball with four watercolors on the wall. Her eye went immediately to the signature: Jane Abbott. "Way to go, Jane," she chortled. She continued her tour of the luxury apartment. State-of-the-art kitchen, marble-and-tile bathrooms complete with telephone, king-size bed, walk-in closet, French door leading to a balcony from the bedroom and living room. Deep comfortable furniture on the balcony and the heady scent of flowers everywhere, along with a bottle of champagne chilling in an ice bucket. Compared to the Monarch, this was heaven.

Annie draped one of the fragrant leis she'd found on the bathroom vanity around her neck. With a glass of champagne, she retired to the balcony, where she settled into one of the chairs and propped her feet on the railing. She needed to map out a plan of attack. First, though, she had to call Tom.

Annie sipped at her champagne as she listened to Tom regale her with his children's antics. Someday she would have children and would love them the way Tom loved his kids and the way her parents had loved both her and Tom. Someday.

"So, where do we stand, Tom?"

"Parker called after you did. I told him what happened, and he was pissed to the teeth. It seems he was in Waikiki entertaining some college friends for two days. The sister didn't know until the last minute, she says, that you were making the trip instead of me. She was under the impression that Parker was going to entertain me. I just spoke to him a second time, about an hour ago. He said there had been some kind of problem with one of Kiki's children at school, and she was running late. Neither he nor I can figure out what your hat and pocketbook have to do with things. Guess it's one of those things only women understand. Do you know what it's all about?"

"What are you talking about, Tom?"

"Your pocketbook and your hat. Parker thinks they pissed off Kiki. Now, for whatever this is worth, he's willing to cut his price by a buck and a half, roasted, if we order our package coffee from him. He said he and Kiki talked it over and agreed. The ball's in our court, and it's your call."

"I need to think about it."

"Don't think too long or too hard, or the guy's going to have a heart attack. He wants to know where you're staying. I told him I didn't know. By the way, where are you?"

"I am in the most gorgeous, the most luxurious condo you have ever seen. There's a phone in every room, even in both bathrooms. I can sit on the balcony and see the ocean. The air is so sweet you almost feel like you're drunk. I rented a car. I'm going to explore tomorrow."

"What about business, Annie?"

"Can't I have a few days to myself, Tom? We aren't on some deadline, are we? This is my first vacation in a long time. I'd kind of like to savor it even if it's just for a few days."

Tom's voice gentled. "Take all the time you want, Annie. When you're ready to make a decision, call me. What do you want me to tell Parker if he calls?"

"Tell him anything you want but don't tell him where I am. I mean it, Tom."

"Understood."

"Are you feeling okay? Did Elmo call you?"

"About ten minutes before you did. Elmo's fine, and the

dogs are fine. He said he was going to take a nap and then work on the daisy coffee bags. End of story.''

''Tom, four of Jane's watercolors are hanging in this living room. Will you call her and tell her?''

''Sure.''

''Then I'm going to hang up and sit here and drink my champagne and read that new mystery novel I brought with me. I'll have room service send up some dinner, take a nice bubble bath, turn in, and be up at first light to explore.''

''Sounds kind of lonely to me.''

''It does, doesn't it?'' Annie said, her voice breaking. ''I'll call you tomorrow.''

Disgusted with his inability to locate Annie Clark, Parker stopped at the first restaurant he came to, where he ordered a fruit platter, a mahimahi sandwich and a cold beer. Knowing it would take at least twenty minutes, he pulled out his portable phone and placed a call to his sister advising her of the situation. Then he called Tom.

''Did you hear from Annie?''

''She called earlier this afternoon. She said she was going to vacation for a few days and didn't want to think about business.''

''I know she's on Maui because I tracked her this far. I spoke with the woman who drove her to the airport. Seems Annie gave her her pocketbook.''

''If it's the same woman she spoke to me about, Annie offered her and her husband a job. Where are you, Parker?''

''In some dive waiting for a sandwich before heading home. I'll start out tomorrow to look for her.''

''How come you never told me you were in love with my sister, Parker?'' The silence went on so long, Tom had to prod the voice on the other end of the wire.

"Business is business and pleasure is pleasure. Love's a funny thing. I don't remember saying I was in love with Annie. I never confuse the two. I didn't know if Annie had said anything to you or not. I didn't want to seem like I was trading on our business relationship. I wanted to call her a hundred times. Hell, maybe it was a thousand times. I even went to Charleston three years ago when Daniel got engaged. I went by the Daisy Shop, but an old gentleman said she was out of town for two weeks. I didn't leave my name either. What the hell am I telling you this for?"

"I'm a good listener."

"Yeah. Maybe. Listen, I gotta go. They just brought my sandwich."

"Parker."

"Yeah?"

"This is just a guess on my part, but I have a feeling Annie will find you. It's just a feeling."

"I know all about feelings. Talk to you soon."

Parker slid into the booth and stared at the sandwich and fruit platter. Neither appealed to him. He swigged from the beer bottle. He'd gotten along just fine these past years. He'd gotten past Annie's blistering tirade, made peace with his sisters, and was actually a man of leisure several days a week. Now, all of a sudden, with Annie Clark back in the islands, his whole world was upside-down again. With what he had going on in the lab, he might well turn out to be richer than Warren Buffett. Goddamn it, leave it to a woman to screw things up.

Parker slid some bills across the table.

The ride home was uneventful. The first thing he did was check his answering machine. Nine calls from Kiki. None from Annie Clark. Had he really expected one? Hell yes, he had.

Now what am I supposed to do? A voice inside his head responded sourly: *What did you do other nights for all those*

*years? You watched television, you read books, you went night
fishing. Same old same old. Why isn't it good enough for you
now? Because it isn't. If Annie Clark cancels her contract, I'm
dead in the water. I'll end up selling shells on the beach.* The
phone in the kitchen shrilled to life. He almost killed himself
in his wild scramble to get to the kitchen. "Hello!" he said
cheerfully. No point in letting the caller know he was down in
the dumps.

"Mr. Grayson?"

"Yes," Parker said, not recognizing the voice. His shoulders
slumped.

"This is Stella Kaminsky. You did give me your card. I just
wanted to know if you located Annie."

"No. She hasn't called either."

"Don't you have a phone book?"

"Of course I have a phone book."

"Then use it. Sometimes you men are so dense. Call all the
hotels on your island."

Parker slapped his forehead. Shit! He should have thought
of that himself. She was right: he was dense. Worse than dense.
He was plain stupid. "I'll do that. I just got in a few minutes
ago. I guess you haven't heard from her."

"I didn't expect to hear from her. That's not the way we
left it. She's too nice a person to be unhappy."

Parker's heart soared. "How do you know she's unhappy?"

"A woman knows these things. Good night, Mr. Grayson."

Parker let loose with a sigh that could be heard clear across
the room when he saw the list of hotels and condominiums he
had to call. By God, he'd do it even if it took him all night.

CHAPTER ELEVEN

Annie flipped through the pages of her address book, looking for the number for the Grayson Coffee Company. When she found the number she placed the call through the hotel operator. She wasn't at all surprised to hear Kiki Aellia's voice even though it was only seven o'clock in the morning. "Miss Aellia, this is Annie Clark. I'd like to meet with you today if that's possible. I'm staying at the Aston Wailea. I can either meet you at the airport or wait here for you. That's provided you're still interested in doing business with the Daisy Shops. The airport's fine with me. We can get a bite to eat, and you can take the next flight back."

Annie snapped her address book shut. Done. The biggest decision facing her now was what to wear. Business attire or casual? She finally opted for white linen shorts and a tangerine-colored blouse with matching sandals and visored cap. After all, she was a tourist. Why not look like one.

It was twenty minutes past eight when Annie walked into the airport. The first person she saw walking toward her was

Stella Kaminsky and behind her, Kiki Aellia, dressed like a New York banker. "Stella! What are you doing here?"

"Joe wanted to see this island before we leave tomorrow. Boy, is it good to see you. Is everything okay?" Stella said, giving Annie a squeezing bear hug.

Annie laughed. "Sure. Just hang on a minute. I'm meeting someone."

"Miss Aellia, it's nice to see you again. I'd like you to meet a friend of mine, Stella Kaminsky. Stella, where's your husband?"

"Men's room. Here he comes. He's all mine." Stella laughed, as she linked her arm with her husband's. Everyone shook hands.

In a million years Annie would never have matched the grinning Joe to Stella. He was a full head shorter, chubby where she was lanky. And it was obvious he was very much in love with his wife who was beaming from head to toe.

Her eyes on Kiki Aellia, Annie said, "This will only take about thirty minutes. If you wait for me, we can explore together. You didn't rent a car yet, did you?"

"We were just going to do that. We'll wait for you," Joe said.

"Jeez, this is great. What a memory, huh, hon?"

"The best." Joe grinned. He removed his baseball cap to reveal a shiny bald head. He mopped his head and slapped the cap back on. Annie winked at him.

"We won't be long," Annie said over her shoulder, as Kiki guided her to the nearest restaurant.

Seated, the two women stared at one another. "That's a lovely dress," Annie said.

"Our old housekeeper made it for me. She doesn't sew anymore. Guess I'll have to go to Hilo Hattie's from now on. I'll just have coffee and toast," she said to the waiter.

"I'll have the same."

"The coffee here is terrible," Kiki said.

She's nervous, Annie thought. "Are you uncomfortable with me, Miss Aellia?"

"You *are* the eight-hundred-pound gorilla," Kiki said quietly.

"Is that how you view me?" Annie asked.

"In a manner of speaking. I don't mean . . ."

"I know what you mean. Here's the deal. It's the same one I offered you the other day with one exception. The contract is only for six months. It's still a take-it-or-leave-it offer. Price cut of two dollars. You still roast the coffee. And, your company owes me twelve thousand pounds of coffee. You can fax the contract to our offices. For now a handshake will do it."

Kiki Aellia extended her hand across the table. "You drive a hard bargain. Do you mind me asking why the short-term contract?"

"I don't mind at all. The answer is simple. It's what I want. Perhaps it is a hard bargain. However, it's fair. Business aside, do you agree?"

"Yes. I don't know what my brother will think. We've never done short-term contracts."

"I don't know what my brother will think, either. Guess what? I don't care."

"I have to care. Parker isn't going to like the deal. His bottom line was a dollar and a half. I cannot guarantee the short-term contract. I think your brother agreed to the original deal."

Annie shrugged. "Would your brother risk losing the account altogether?"

"Would you have walked?"

"In a heartbeat," Annie said.

Kiki smiled. "I knew that. Parker didn't believe it. He still doesn't believe it. My intuition tells me he won't go with the six months. He's been trying to locate you."

Annie could feel her heart rate speed up. "Really," she drawled.

Kiki smiled. "Yes, really. Are you being evasive, elusive, or are you just playing hard to get? Woman to woman."

"All of the above."

Kiki leaned across the table. "Do you know what really makes Parker nuts?"

"Not a clue." She grinned. "Not a clue. Share."

"He hates it when a woman is right. He's come a long way, but he hasn't come all the way yet. I want to thank you on behalf of all my sisters and myself. I didn't know you were the one responsible for Parker's turnaround until Mattie told me. He chopped down the banyan tree by the front of the house. It was symbolic. He's not seeing anyone. Are you? Seeing anyone? Am I being too forward?"

"No and no. He never called or wrote. Twelve years is a long time," Annie said wistfully.

"Sometimes it takes a man forever to make a decision where the heart is concerned. They can make billion-dollar decisions in the blink of an eye, though. Parker was never the same after you left. Again, I got all this from Mattie. I probably shouldn't even be telling you this."

"I'm glad you did. I apologize for the other day."

"You must also accept my apology. My day didn't start out all that well. Then I saw you in that stunning outfit with your Chanel handbag, and something snapped in me. I always wanted to own my own company. I wanted to be a corporate giant. I guess I wanted to be like you. For a lot of years my little family had to count pennies. When I saw that Chanel bag something just happened. I think I was just tired of seeing how women had to stand behind men and take second place. Maybe I was ahead of my time. Parker's been real good about it. I made a lot of mistakes that cost the company money. All things considered, he's tolerant. If there's nothing else, I'll be heading back."

Annie stood up. She looked down at the table. Neither one of them had touched the toast or coffee. She laid some bills on the table.

"You want to know something? I gave that purse to Stella. I saw the look in your eyes when you saw it the other day. Here," she said shyly. "I bought this from a vendor outside the airport." She looped the fragrant lei around Kiki's neck. Saw the glistening tears in her eyes. "Tell your brother you're the only one in the Grayson Coffee Company that I will do business with."

"Are you sure you want me to say that?"

Annie smiled. "I'm sure. You want to know something else? Being a corporate giant isn't all that it's cracked up to be. At this moment in time, you have it all, a husband, a family, and you just clinched a deal your brother wasn't able to make. I should know, I'm a corporate giant." Both women burst out laughing.

"Do me a favor, slow down a little so my brother can catch you."

Annie laughed again. "If I went any slower, I'd be at a dead stop. Come on, I'll walk you to your gate. No hard feelings."

"None. I'm glad you gave me another chance. A man wouldn't have."

"I know that." Annie smiled. "See you around."

"Maybe sooner than you think. I'm taking my daughter to Boston in the fall. She starts college. My oldest son is finishing his first year of law school there, too. Maybe I'll stop and see you."

"Please do."

Annie stood on the tarmac and waited until the small plane took off. She waved until the plane was out of sight.

Now she was going to spend an enjoyable day with Stella and Joe Kaminsky, her new friends.

* * *

Parker felt like he was coming off a two-day drunk when he entered the Aston Wailea Resort. He strode up to the desk like a man on a mission. "I'm trying to locate a client of mine. I understand she's staying here. Anna Daisy Clark is her name. Could you ring her room, please?"

"I'm sorry, sir. Miss Clark left early this morning."

"You mean she checked out?" Parker looked at his index finger. It was red and puffy from all the dialing he'd done during the night.

"No, sir. She called down for her car and left a little before eight."

"Did she say where she was going?"

"Not to me, sir. You could try the valet."

Parker knew his eyes were wild when he searched out the valet who had brought Annie's car to the entrance. "Did she say where she was going or ask for directions?"

"No, sir, she didn't. There was a map on the front seat. Does that help?"

"Not one bit. Did she have baggage?"

"No, sir. She was dressed in shorts and wearing a baseball cap. Quite fashionable. I felt the urge to whistle, as did some of the other employees."

"What time do you go off duty?"

"Five o'clock."

"If you're on duty when Miss Clark returns, will you give her this card?"

Parker handed over a twenty-dollar bill and his business card. "Ask her to call me no matter what time she gets in. Here's another twenty. Give it to the person who takes over when you go off duty. Will you do that for me?"

"Sure."

Now what the hell was he supposed to do? Annie could be

anywhere on the island. For all he knew she could be spending the night someplace else and not returning until tomorrow. He could either sit here and cool his heels or he could go home and go to bed. The latter appealed to him, but first he had to call Kiki.

As Parker maneuvered his way through the airport parking lot, his thumb was jabbing out the office phone number. "Is anything going on, Kiki? What do you mean you just got in! It's eleven o'clock! You've been to Maui and back! Do I dare ask why? You met Annie Clark! You clinched the deal. I thought we agreed on a buck and a half. She wouldn't have walked. I *don't* know that for a fact. No one to my knowledge would pull an account that size for fifty cents. She really said Tom has no say in her decision. Don't try reading my mind, Kiki. I wasn't going to call Tom. Of course I trust you. I'm not dancing with joy. If you multiply fifty cents times a half million pounds of coffee, it adds up. No, I'm not questioning your abilities. I would have fought a little harder is what I'm trying to say. I realize I wasn't looking into her eyes. Sometimes, Kiki, you have to bluff a little. All right! Did she sign the contract? You shook hands! No, no, no, we do not do six-month contracts. You know better than to agree to something like that. You're going to fax the contract! That's pretty half-assed if you want my opinion. Men shaking hands is different."

Parker stared at the pinging phone in his hand. Kiki had hung up on him. Outrage swept through him. He punched out the numbers a second time. Kiki picked up on the third ring. Before Parker had a chance to say anything, Kiki said, "I quit! You can take this job along with my interest in the company and shove it up your royal Hawaiian ass. You louse, you didn't change at all. Shove it, Parker. I'm sending a fax to Miss Clark advising her of this latest development. You and her precious brother Tom can work it out. I'm telling you right now, you just lost yourself a customer. Don't say one more damn word.

Not one, Parker. It's none of your damn business where I'm going, but since you're so insistent on knowing my business, I'm going out to buy a Chanel handbag using the company credit card. I told you not to say anything, Parker. Furthermore, Parker, I'm calling my sisters the minute I get home. I think we just might vote you out of this company.''

Parker's jaw was grim when he listened to the pinging phone for the second time. He'd gone through this with Kiki a hundred times. His blood ran cold when he remembered the threat at the end of the conversation. That was new. So was the credit card and purse shopping.

Much to his own disgust Parker found himself dialing Tom's number in North Carolina. He broke the connection the moment he heard Tom's voice. Fifty cents a pound wasn't going to put him out of business. Suck it up. It was the six-month contract that was going to kick his ass. He needed a long-term contract with the Daisy Shops or his caffeine-free coffee beans would go down the hopper. *Make some peace with Kiki, or you're going to be working sixteen hour days again.* For all he knew they'd all hire a bus and go shopping for Chanel pocketbooks.

Parker called the office a third time. He was stunned when Kiki's assistant Mary informed him that Kiki had typed up her resignation and had taken off with the company credit card saying she would return it by mail when she was done shopping.

''Son of a bitch!''

Parker rolled over, one eye squinting at the clock. Damn, he'd slept fourteen straight hours. He needed to get up and get a move on or he was going to end up behind the proverbial eightball. As he brushed his teeth, showered, and shaved, he ran his itinerary over and over in his mind. He wasn't happy with Plan A, Plan B, or Plan C. While he was scrambling an egg the phone rang. Probably Kiki calling to apologize. Well, he knew how to be magnanimous.

"Tom, how are you?"

"Great. Feeling better each day. Listen, I'm calling to ask what the hell is going on. A fax came into the office from Kiki that's a little confusing. Actually two faxes came in. One was the contract for a six-month deal and the other was canceling the deal. So does this mean we don't have a deal? Annie called late last night and said she clinched it with Kiki on a handshake. Annie thinks we have the deal. Are you guys reneging? Annie said she won't deal with anyone but Kiki. I'd just like to know what the hell is going on."

Parker dumped the scrambled egg in the sink. Suddenly he'd lost his appetite. He eyeballed the coffeemaker, willing it to drip faster. "Kiki quit yesterday. She was pissed when I said something she didn't like. I don't know what to tell you, Tom. As far as I'm concerned we have a deal. I'm not real happy with it, but I can live with it. Grayson Coffee has never done a six-month contract. The only reason I would agree to it now is because you're an old and valued customer. There won't be another one. Remember that. There's no way in hell I'm stepping on Kiki's toes again today. I'll give you her home phone number and you can call your sister to give it to her. One of you needs to call her."

"Boy, you really don't know much about women, do you? You guys need to get your shit in one sock."

"You're right on that, Tom. As the days go by I know less and less. I did find out where Annie is staying, but I missed her. I'm going to give it another shot today, then I'm giving up. Right now I feel like giving up the coffee business for good."

"That's rather extreme, isn't it?"

"Not from where I'm standing. I'll call you later."

"I'll be here. Just for the record, Parker, I'm not calling

Kiki. The last thing in the world I would do is step on Annie's toes. She drew the line in the sand a long time ago, and I'm not crossing it. If you want some advice, and I know you didn't ask for it, I would go to my sister with my tail between my legs and apologize. Get her one of those damn pocketbooks. Gifts always help. If you're going to apologize, sound like you mean it.''

Parker hung up the phone, his head buzzing. Maybe Tom was right. Maybe the pocketbooks had something to do with this whole mess.

He hopped in his jeep for the short ride to the airport and his private plane. Forty-five minutes later he set down on the Big Island and stepped into his waiting jeep, driven by one of the workers from the coffee plantation.

''Drive me to the mall, Andy. E. Puainako at Highway Eleven. Park in front of Liberty House.''

The minute Parker stepped into the department store he knew he was out of his depth. His gaze swiveled around the store. ''Can I help you, sir?''

Relieved, Parker nodded. ''I need to buy a . . . Chanel pocket-book.''

The clerk smiled. ''Straight down and make a left. Someone will help you in leather goods.''

Parker eyed the purses on the glass shelf. Brown, black, white, beige. ''Is this all you have?'' he asked the clerk.

''Yes, sir. What were you looking for?''

''A pocketbook,'' Parker said brilliantly.

''Do you have a color preference?'' the clerk said.

Did he? Did Kiki? Probably, but since he didn't know what it was, he had to make a decision. ''I'll take them all.''

''You want them all?'' the woman gasped. ''Are you sure, sir?''

''I'm sure. Could you hurry it up?''

"I have to get the boxes and wrap them. It's going to take a while."

"I don't have a while. Can't you just put them in bags?"

"Women like the Chanel boxes, sir, and the felt bag to store the purse in. These are not Woolworth plastic bags," she said huffily.

"You can send the boxes and the bags later, can't you? I'll leave the address and pay for the delivery."

"I suppose we could do that. It's highly irregular. Your credit card, sir."

Parker thought his head was going to spin off his neck when he saw the total price, plus the tax, before he signed his name.

A shopping bag in each hand, Parker made his way to the jeep waiting for him outside the front door. When he dumped the bags unceremoniously in the backseat of the jeep, he saw the clerk wince and shudder. "Thank you, ma'am."

"Andy, take Queen Kaahumanu Highway and I'll tell you where to turn. We're going to Kiki's house. Do you by any chance know if she went to the office today?"

"No show today, boss."

Parker adjusted his Padres baseball cap until it covered his dark glasses. With his feet propped on the dash, he fired up a cigarette. He thought about his sister and how well she'd done over the past few years. She'd taken his blistering criticism without blinking, intent only on learning the business. She'd been an asset, too. The last two years he knew he could leave the business in her hands and not worry. But the big plus was he'd become close to his sisters and their families. He knew the kids now as well as their friends and all the dogs and cats. If Kiki was truly, truly angry, he could lose it all. He realized in that one heart-stopping moment that he didn't give a hoot about the business. He didn't want to lose the closeness he'd established and found so comforting. He liked going to birthday parties and graduations, liked picking up the phone to hear a childish voice say, "Hi, Uncle Parker." Because of one thoughtless remark he could well be back to square one. No family, no business, no Annie, no prize contract that he needed so desperately. He shuddered.

"Turn here, boss?"

"Yes, it's the third house on the left."

"Let me go in first, Andy, just in case Kiki starts throwing things. Give me five minutes and bring up the bags. Okay?"

"Okay, boss."

Parker walked up a neatly trimmed brick path to the front door. There was always a fresh plumeria wreath hanging on the front door. His other sisters had wreaths on their front doors, too, the same way his mother had them. Like mother, like daughters. He rang the bell.

Kiki opened the door, still in her robe. "What do you want, Parker? Oh, I get it, you came for the credit card. Wait here, and I'll get it." Parker stepped back when his sister slammed the door in his face. He opened it boldly.

"I didn't come for the damn card. I came to say I'm sorry." He motioned for Andy to bring the bags into the house.

"You're too late, Parker. Get out of my house. I don't want you here. Here's your card. You know what you can do with it, don't you?"

"Look, Kiki, I'm sorry. Old sayings, old habits die hard. I told you it wasn't going to be easy. I told you I'd slip and for you to bring me up short. I can accept criticism, and I can accept you telling me off. I don't want you to quit. You're doing a hell of a job. Customers like you. That thing about Tom and the handshake came out of left field. What can I do besides say I'm sorry."

"I could accept that if you were sincere. Sometimes, Parker, you just mouth words and don't know what you're agreeing to. You agree because you think it's what I want to hear. If you don't understand it, what's the point?"

"I want you to come back."

"Why? So you can get the Daisy Shop contract? I canceled it."

"I know. I don't care about that, Kiki. I care about us, the family. Annie Clark can buy her coffee wherever she wants. I brought something for you. I didn't know what color to get, so I bought them all. They're going to deliver the boxes and some kind of bags. The clerk said women want the boxes and the bags, and I didn't want to wait for them. Why would you want empty boxes and bags?" he asked fretfully.

"How many . . . You bought them all! Parker, this is ridiculous."

"I know. It's my point, Kiki. You and the others are worth more to me than these silly pocketbooks. I hate it when we squabble. I hate it when you're right, and I'm wrong. If you want, Kiki, I'll turn over my share of the business to you and the others. I won't interfere. Not the lab, though," he said as an afterthought.

"The coffee business is your life, Parker. What in the world would you do?"

"I don't know. Maybe a tour guide. Sell shells on the beach."

"You need to take these handbags back to the store."

"Oh, no. That woman thought I was nuts as it is."

"You are nuts, Parker. I love you anyway. By the way, I didn't use the credit card. Even though you pissed me off big-time."

"I know, and I'm sorry. Okay, I have to get back to Maui. I still haven't located Annie Clark. I know where she's staying, but I can't hook up with her. Is it settled, then, you go back to work tomorrow?"

"Yes, Parker. I'm not calling Miss Clark, though. That's something you're going to have to take care of." She smiled and stepped closer to her brother. "I hope you find her, Parker. The island isn't that big. Camp out by her front door. Sooner or later she has to come in or go out. If she calls me, I'll let you know. Thanks for the handbags.''

Kiki put her arms around him. ''See, the world didn't come crashing down on us. It's okay to admit you're wrong as long as you try to make it right.''

''You sounded like Mom just then, Kiki.''

''That's one of the nicest things you ever said to me, Parker. You aren't tough and narrow-minded like Pop was.''

Parker laughed. ''Now that's one of the nicest things you've ever said to me. I'll call you, Kiki.''

''Make sure you do.''

Exhausted, Annie crawled into bed. She knew if she closed her eyes she would go to sleep instantly. She wondered if she had the energy to return Tom's calls and Elmo's calls. She also had to decide what to do about the note she'd found on her door along with Parker's six phone calls. It was Elmo's three calls that worried her. Maybe her dogs were sick. She looked at the clock. Elmo was always an early riser, getting up at five, puttering around for an hour or so before opening his store at seven. A man of habit. She placed her call.

''Knew it would be you, Annie. Listen to me, girl. I have some news. As you know I still get my periodicals and the local newspaper as well as the campus paper. Most times I let them pile up, then read them when I can't sleep. It seems in January the guy that was in prison was released. He'd been in a halfway house for a year. They released him early for good behavior and all that garbage. It seems he has aligned himself with Peter Newman, the insurance investigator. They never closed the case, Annie. I didn't know that. Did you?''

Annie's heart fluttered in her chest. Of course she knew that. They couldn't close the case until all the money was returned. Something she was going to do as soon as she returned home.

She was wide-awake now. "If they couldn't find any proof in thirteen years, what do they hope to gain now?" How calm her voice was. She shivered under the light blanket.

"The insurance investigator had rules and regulations he had to abide by. He backed off when we all called the company and said he was harassing us. The boy, he's a man now, doesn't have those rules and regulations. I just think it's strange that he would sidle up to Newman. Don't you, Annie?"

"It doesn't make sense, Elmo."

"When I tell you this, it will make sense. I got a letter today, mailed from the town where the money was returned."

Annie's heart stopped beating for a second. "What kind of letter, Elmo?"

"You know the kind where the words are cut out of newspapers? It said, I KNOW WHAT YOU DID AND I'M GOING TO PROVE IT! I went by your house to see if you got one, and sure enough you did. I called Jane, and she got one, too. It isn't over, Annie."

"All the letters in the world aren't going to change things, Elmo. Save yours and mine. Don't go to the police, though. Let's see what develops. How are the coffee bags coming along?"

"Shiny apple green bags with a daisy appliqué on the front and back. Very stylish-looking. I got the rough draft of it today, but the colors aren't true. Jane's well but worried now. I told her to stop, that I would do the worrying for all of us. I called Tom, and he's doing really well. He's walking almost a mile a day. He's definitely on the mend. Dogs are fine. Harry had the splats. That's under control. Rosie wants macaroni and cheese all the time. I tried giving her some of that Kraft stuff, but she walked away from it. Forget the dog food. They'll starve before they eat that stuff. Can't say that I blame them. It looks like rabbit poop to me."

"I love you, Elmo."

"Did you see that guy yet?" Elmo asked slyly.

"No, not yet. Maybe tomorrow."

"What are you waiting for, Annie?"

"I don't know, Elmo. Maybe I'm scared he won't ... be interested in me anymore. I was pretty nasty to him the last time I saw him. This isn't what you think it is. I have reservations about him. It's like he's this fancy-wrapped present in glossy paper with a shimmering gold bow. I don't know what's inside that box. My gut is telling me to go slow, to tread lightly, and to carry a big stick."

"I guess it all makes sense in an Annie Clark kind of way. I can't believe I'm hearing this from you. Did you hear about that new invention that's out now?"

Elmo loved gadgets. "No. What is it this time?"

"It's called the telephone," the pharmacist cackled gleefully. "You pick it up, you dial a number, and you get to hear a voice."

"Maybe I'll do that tomorrow."

"You aren't getting any younger, you know. Annie, I'm worried about that Newman fellow."

She was worried, too, but she wasn't going to admit it. "He's just spinning his wheels. Make yourself some breakfast and forget about it. I'm going to go to bed now and dream about covering my naked body with plumeria petals. Talk to you in a day or so, Elmo."

But the moment she hung up the phone, she started to shake and couldn't stop.

At six o'clock the following morning, Annie took the elevator to the garage level and drove her car out to the road. She'd asked for directions to Parker Grayson's house and the best way to get to the waterfalls the night before. She looked down now at the squiggly red lines on the map. A piece of cake.

The sun was high in the sky when Annie parked her car, kicked off her sandals, and made her way to the path that led to the falls. She was wearing the island dress Mattie had made her so long ago. She was going to sit in the carved-out rock and do nothing but stare at the shimmering falls. When she had her fill of the beauty and a few rainbows under her belt, maybe, just maybe, she'd make her way to Parker's house and knock on his front door. Maybemaybemaybe.

Parker Grayson stormed out of the Aston Wailea. Once again he'd missed Annie Clark, and it was only 6:45 A.M. "I just goddamn well give up. I'm going fishing. I'm going to get an egg sandwich and some bait and fish all day," he muttered as he floored the gas pedal.

An hour later, the smelly bait in the back of his jeep was making him gag. The prospect of sitting in the hot sun fishing no longer held any appeal for him. Maybe he'd go to the rock behind the falls and sit. It was as good an idea as any that he'd had of late.

He parked the jeep in the quarry stone parking lot, entered the house, changed his clothes, slung a towel over his shoulders, and headed for the falls on foot.

The sun was high now. He'd never seen a rainbow *behind* the falls before. He wondered if it was an omen of some kind. He splashed his way over to the side and ran between the walls of dripping water. He stared at her, his gaze unbelieving, his heart thundering in his chest.

"What took you so long?" Annie drawled.

CHAPTER TWELVE

Parker was too stunned to do more than stare at the woman clad in a rainbow-colored dress. His hands started to shake, the towel dropping to the ground. It was soaked in minutes. He needed to say something meaningful, something brilliant. "Sometimes I'm a little slow." He winced at his sparkling repartee.

"Sit down," Annie said, patting the stone seat next to her. "How have you been, Parker?"

"Sometimes good, sometimes not so good. I wanted to call you a hundred times, maybe two hundred times. I'm sorry I didn't." He was getting more sparkling by the minute. At least he wasn't grunting.

"I was wrong to say the things I said. Your life was none of my business. I'm sorry for that. The truth is, I'm embarrassed," Annie said.

"No, you were right. Old traditions die hard. I thought I was doing what my parents wanted me to do. I tried to make it right. It took me a little while. I wanted to call you and tell you how it all went, but you were so vehement that day. I guess I thought you'd say something like, you know, too much, too little, too late. Kiki says it's never too late if you mean what you say. Thanks to you, I have a family again. You could have called me to tell me how you were or just to talk business, Annie. I spent hours, days, weeks, and months waiting for the phone to ring.''

''I wanted to call you. I picked up the phone a hundred times, maybe two hundred.'' Annie smiled. ''I guess I didn't want to hear you tell me to mind my own business.''

''We lost a lot of years, Anna Daisy Clark.''

''I know that, Parker Grayson.''

''I thought there was a rainbow behind the waterfalls when I first got here. I've done everything in the world to find you with the exception of calling out the National Guard. Today I finally gave up and came here to lick my wounds.''

Her hand was suddenly in his. It felt cool and soft. He inched closer. ''I fell in love with you that day, Annie.''

''I fell in love with you, too, Parker.'' *At least I think I did.*

''Does that mean we are *in* love, Annie?''

''I can only speak for myself. I am.'' *Liar, liar, liar.*

''Me too. What should we do about it?''

''You think about it, Parker, while I go for a swim.''

Parker watched as the rainbow-colored island dress slithered to the ground. A second later, two pieces of lace sailed backward, and then she was gone, through the falls and down into the sparkling blue pool.

''My mother didn't raise any fools,'' Parker muttered as his bathing trunks fell on top of the rainbow dress. He executed a perfect dive, slicing through the water and then rising to the top like a phoenix, his body glistening with diamondlike droplets of water.

''Great dive! I just jumped,'' Annie said, treading water.

''As children we spent most of our days diving from the

rock. You should see my sister Teke dive. She's good enough to be an Olympic champion. I was the worst compared to them.''

''A pity she never got the chance to do that,'' Annie said.

''You're driving home a point, eh? You're right, though. Teke's son is following in her footsteps. He's a great surfer, too. He's one of the top three to surf the Banzai Pipeline. He wants to be a dentist.''

Annie laughed, then did a perfect jackknife, diving down into the crystal waters and coming up behind him. She reached for his head and pushed him under. They frolicked then like children until they were both exhausted.

''I think it's time to get out. Even my toenails are puckered,'' Annie said. She had a bad moment when she realized she was stark naked. Being naked in the water was different from being naked and climbing up on a ledge with your butt in the air. ''You go first,'' she said magnanimously.

Parker laughed. ''I'm a gentleman, first, last, and always. After you.''

Annie grimaced. ''Then turn around!''

''Not in this lifetime. After you,'' Parker said, waving his arm gallantly.

''I need a boost.''

Parker cupped his hands for Annie to step into. She did and then gave one kick that sent him flying backward into the pool. She scrambled upward, and by the time Parker made his way to the stone chair, she was dressed in the rainbow island dress. ''Nice buns,'' she giggled. ''Turn around!''

''Cold water does . . . It isn't always . . . just you never mind, Annie Clark,'' Parker said hoarsely.

''What should we do now? Shouldn't we be having adrenaline rushes and fast-beating hearts?'' Annie continued to giggle.

His bathing trunks secure, Parker reached for her hand and yanked her off the stone chair.

"Wherever are you taking me, Parker Grayson?" Annie asked coyly as she was dragged alongside Parker, her feet barely touching the ground.

"To my lair, that's where."

On the last bounce before they arrived at the house, Annie managed, breathlessly, to ask, "Are you going to ravage and plunder me?"

"Yeah, twelve years' worth."

The kitchen screen door banged shut, and she was suddenly being kissed like she'd never been kissed in her life. "When your teeth start to rattle, let me know," Parker said as he came up for air.

"They're rattling."

Annie felt herself being slung over Parker's shoulder for a bouncing ride down the long hallway to his bedroom, where he dumped her unceremoniously on his bed. "Get ready," he said, dropping his bathing trunks.

"What . . . what happened to foreplay?" Annie squawked.

"That was foreplay back at the falls. This is *it!*"

"Well, I like . . ."

"God, you talk more than my sisters do. What do you like?" She told him. "Of course if you can't . . ."

"I guarantee that I can."

"Or my money back?" Annie said breathlessly.

"My guarantees are foolproof."

"Prove it!"

A long time later, Parker managed to croak, "Do you want your money back?"

"God, no. Tell me something. Can you do *that* again?"

Parker laughed. "Maybe in about three days. How about you?"

"At least three days."

"At least we're on the same wavelength. I thought this day would never come."

"I thought the same thing, Parker."

"I want to marry you," Parker said.

Annie leaned up on one elbow. She was tempted to say, but we hardly know each other. Instead she said, "I accept." *Fool, fool, fool,* her mind shrieked.

"You do! When?"

"Whenever you want. I've had twelve years to think about this. I can be ready in six months." *Annie Clark, you are out of your ever-loving mind. You don't love this man. Why are you doing this? Just so you can belong to someone. Uh-huh, all the wrong reasons.*

"Six months is perfect. I have a harvest to get ready. Shall we have the wedding here in the islands?"

"I'd like that very much."

"That means winter of next year, right?"

"Right. That kind of makes it eight months, though," Annie said. "I have new stores to open, and I need to prepare for the selling end of the coffee. How does February of next year sound?"

"It sounds like a very long time. I can wait. Now, what about that six-month contract. I can't live with that, Annie."

"I can come back and forth and you can come to Charleston or we can meet halfway. We won't be apart much. I think I can handle it. Can you? What do you mean, you can't live with it. It is what it is. I'm not changing my mind, Parker."

"You have to change your mind. If we're getting married, we have to make decisions together. If you can handle the separation, then I can handle it. Will it be possible for us to live here on the island, Annie? I have to be honest with you. I don't think I could survive anywhere else. Those years away at school proved that to me. I'm an island boy through and through. If you want to live on the mainland, I'm willing to give it a try.''

Annie felt like she'd been hit in the gut. Deal with it now or later? Later would work. She needed to think. ''I would love to live here part of the year. I'm not giving up my business, Parker. Or my dogs. The contract stands, too.''

''I would never ask you to do that. You aren't going to be working seven days a week, are you? I love dogs. But we have to change the contract.''

''No, the contract stays. Maybe two or three days a week. I have very capable people working for me. Tom can handle it just the way Kiki handles the coffee business. This is the best of all worlds if you meet me halfway. My business is mine, Parker, and yours is yours.''

''Maybe we could coax Mattie out of retirement, and, along with my sisters, they can teach you about the islands. If you want to learn, that is. No, no, Annie, it doesn't work that way. We have to *merge*.''

''I want to learn everything there is where you're concerned. I want to know the man I'm marrying inside and outside. Up one side and down the other. But there won't be a merger.''

''There has to be a merger. Our attorneys can work it out. I guess that means no secrets if you want to know everything about me. That's okay, I don't have any secrets. As they say, my life is an open book. Much the way yours is. You don't harbor any deep, dark secrets do you, Annie?''

Annie felt her heart skip a beat. ''Me!'' She needed to back up here and straighten out the merger business right now.

''I have a few pet peeves or hates, whichever you prefer. One, I can't stand a liar. Two, I hate broccoli. Three, I don't like short hair on a woman. Will you let yours grow?''

Annie felt like her blood was freezing in her veins. ''No. I like short hair. No merger and no extended contract. Why are you being so persistent about this? You're making me very uncomfortable, Parker."

"Then I guess I'm going to learn to love short hair. You won't ever serve me broccoli, will you?" he said lightly. "I'm being persistent," he said teasingly, "because I want us tied together. A union is a union. What's mine is yours, and what's yours is mine. Fifty-fifty."

She had to get out of there right now. Leave it alone and work it out later. Leave, you foolish girl. "I'll think about it."

"Promise you'll never lie to me?"

Annie squirmed in the big bed. Her heart pounded in her chest. "I promise," she said weakly.

"What about your pet peeves and hates?"

Annie shook her head, not trusting herself to speak.

"None?"

"I'm willing to accept you just the way you are," she croaked. "Why can't you accept me the way I am? Why do we have to make promises? Why is that unity thing so important to you?"

"It's a quirk of mine. Do you have a problem with it?"

"People make promises in good faith and sometimes things go awry and a promise gets broken. One or the other party then gets upset. Tom and I used to do that, and invariably there were hard feelings. I'm one of those people who remembers things like that. So, to answer your question, yes, I have trouble with promises. I'm also having a great deal of trouble with your merger plans. I almost think you asked me to marry you for my business."

"Okay, I just canceled them out," Parker said airily.

"That's good, Parker," Annie said, feigning sleep. *He's lying.*

Annie lay quietly, her mind racing as she listened to Parker's steady, even breathing. What would he do if he ever found out she was a criminal? He'd dump her so fast her head would spin. Maybe this was all a big mistake. Maybe she needed to leave and forget about this man once and for all. If things were heating up back on the mainland, she needed to be able to cope with it. God in heaven, what if Parker was visiting and the insurance investigator showed up at her door? How would she ever explain that away? *Maybe I'm just not meant to be happy. Maybe this is my punishment for taking that money in the first place. If I'm stupid enough to agree to his little merger, and I get caught, that leaves him in control. Maybe he knows.*

Annie looked around the room she would share with the man next to her if she did go through with the marriage. She thought she could be happy here in this land filled with sunshine and beautiful flowers—on a part-time basis. Could she love this man next to her into eternity? Even though her biological clock was ticking, she could still bear children. A son for Parker to carry on the Grayson family name and a daughter for both of them to love and cherish. A family. Her family. But it didn't feel right. Something was wrong. She just didn't know what it was.

Assuming she wanted all these wonderful dreams, could they be ripped away with one slip of the tongue? Should she confess now to certain things? Not necessarily confess, but inform Parker of the insurance investigator. No, better to keep things quiet where that matter was concerned and hope for the best. She'd been more than clear on the merger business. Did she deserve or even want this little bit of happiness? Was this all one big giant mistake on her part?

Her thoughts tortured, Annie waited for sleep to drive them away.

Annie's eyes filled with tears as Parker slipped a lei around her neck. It was so fragrant it made her dizzy. "I'll miss you," she said in a choked voice. "This has been the nicest two weeks of my life."

"And mine. I'll see you in two weeks. You can show me Charleston, and if you like, we can fly to New York and see a Broadway show."

In spite of herself, Annie laughed. "You hate New York."

"I know, but you like Broadway. I might learn to like it with you at my side."

"There's about as much a chance of that as me starting to like poi."

"Is everything okay between you and Kiki now?" Parker asked.

"Yes."

"Annie, did you really say you would only do business with Kiki?"

"Yes. I said that, and I meant it. Just like I meant it when I said the contract is only for six months and there will be no merger."

"You really would have walked?"

"I told you, Parker, in a heartbeat."

"Absolutely amazing. Kiki is walking around like a peacock."

"A female peacock, right? Deservedly so. She did what you weren't able to do. I wouldn't have signed with you, Parker. I would not mix business with pleasure. We are clear on that, aren't we?" Annie had to turn away at the look she saw in Parker's eyes.

"Painfully so. I don't want you to go."

"I don't want to go, either, but I have to. Two weeks isn't that long. Remember there are telephones, and they work from here and from Charleston."

"You're the last one to board. Go on now before I slam this gate closed myself. Call me."

Annie's smile was weary. "I will."

*   *   *

They were all waiting outside the airport for Annie: Elmo, Tom, the two dogs, and Jane. They shouted, ''Welcome home!'' Rosie and Harry strained at their leashes.

''Wow! I don't think I ever had a greeting like this. I'm glad to be back. I missed all of you. Jane, it's so good to see you. Is something going on I should know about?''

''We'll talk at home. I cooked dinner,'' Elmo said. ''At your house. I knew you'd want to be among your own things. It's good to have you home.''

Annie bit down on her lower lip. Elmo didn't look right. How was it possible for a person to change so much in just two short weeks? Was he ill? Whatever it was, she knew she would have to wait until they were all ensconced in her kitchen with plates of food in front of them. Elmo did love family dinners with good conversation. Her own news would have to wait.

While everyone jabbered in the car about everything and nothing, Annie tussled with the dogs, trying hard not to notice the worry on Jane's face.

Thirty minutes later, Tom announced their arrival. ''I swear, Annie, this is the prettiest house on the battery. I can't remember ever being this hungry.''

Annie laughed. ''I guess that means you're feeling a lot better.''

''I never felt better. I'll take your bags upstairs.''

''Wash up, everyone. Dinner is warming. Table's been set. I fed the dogs before we left for the airport,'' Elmo said.

''What *is* this?'' Annie asked as she peered into the chafing dish.

''It's an oriental dish with a peanut butter base,'' Elmo said. ''It took a long time to make. When something takes a long time to prepare, you know it's going to be good. Eat hearty. I made enough for an army.''

"I'm not eating anything until I know what's going on here. I'm glad you're here, Jane, but I have to wonder why, when you haven't been near this town in eight years. And you, Tom, what brought you here today of all days? Somebody say something," Annie said.

"I'm scared, Annie. I never told my husband about that crazy episode in our lives. I don't like getting weird phone calls with heavy breathing in the middle of the night. I'm afraid when the doorbell rings. That letter was downright scary. I have a daughter I worry about as well as a husband. He's never going to understand my being stalked like this. I didn't do anything, and I'm scared out of my wits. I came here so the three of us could put our heads together and come up with a way to stop all this. I brought the letter that was sent to me. I hate to even touch it. I put it in one of those plastic bags just so I wouldn't have to handle it. Oh, this is good, Elmo," Jane said, tasting a forkful of Chinese noodles.

"The same things that have been happening to Jane have been happening to me. I assume if you had been here, Annie, you would have gotten the same heavy-breathing telephone calls. I, too, find myself getting apprehensive when the doorbell rings. The doctors tell me my heart is finally going to give out on me, and no, there is nothing that can be done. That said, we aren't going to discuss it again. Do we understand, ladies and gentlemen?''

Annie's eyes filled. She didn't have to look at Jane to know she was teary-eyed as well. She nodded miserably.

Tom just stared at the old man. "I know of a specialist . . .''

"Been there, done that. Not another word," Elmo said forcefully. Tom clamped his lips tight.

Harry whined softly at Annie's feet. Rosie swiped at him with one paw.

''Now tell us your news, Annie,'' Elmo said, helping himself to the concoction in the chafing dish.

Annie cleared her throat. ''We have a great six-month deal with Grayson Coffee. That's the good news. The bad news is, Parker asked me to marry him. We set the date for February. I . . . I said yes. Parker wants a merger. I said no. He did not like a six-month contract, but he had to swallow that one. I want you to be my matron of honor, Jane, and Elmo, I want you to give me away.''

''I'd be honored, Annie. However, February is a long way away. I have to be realistic according to my doctor. He said . . . maybe as little as six months.''

''Six months!'' the others said in unison.

Elmo held up his hand. ''I don't care to discuss this matter. Give or take a few months on either side, possibly longer. It's the way it is. Let's move on here.''

''I'll talk to Parker. I'm not getting married unless you give me away. That's the way that is, Elmo. So there. I said yes in the heat of the moment. I'm not sure I want to get married at all. I'm terribly confused right now.''

The old man cackled. ''What's the sense in waiting if you love one another?''

Annie choked up. ''Business. Details. A wedding dress. Stupid stuff. Parker has a harvest to get in. Prenuptial agreements. They take *forever.*''

''You work on that, young woman. We need to put our heads together where this insurance fellow is concerned. Jane told me the alumni association moved back your reunion to September of this year. If you plan to go to it, you could arrange a meeting with the insurance company. Or, you could do it now if you want, since Jane is here.''

''I can't stay, Elmo. School is out, and my daughter's dance classes begin next week. I don't have the free time I used to have. I'm also behind in my commissioned paintings, plus I teach a class two nights a week. If I budget my time, I should be clear by September. I really want to go to the reunion.''

Annie felt sick to her stomach. Later, when she was alone, she would think about all of this. For Elmo's sake, it was easier to agree. ''Okay,'' she said. ''Why did they move back the reunion date?''

''The questionnaire they sent out asked which month was preferable, and they picked this September. I guess June is a busy month for everyone. I find it hard to believe fifteen years have gone by since we got our bachelor degrees. I screwed that up, didn't I, Annie?'' Jane asked fretfully.

''Not at all. If you want to go, then I'm going, too.''

''Then it's settled,'' Tom said. ''Let's work out a plan for what you're going to say and which insurance executive you're going to say it to. That case should have been written off the books by now. The statute of limitations should have passed by now.''

Elmo twirled his fork around the Chinese noodles on his plate. ''It's the boy. He's a man now. He's bitter and angry about serving all that time in prison for something he claims he didn't do. His family has a lot of money.''

''A jury thought there was enough evidence to convict him,'' Annie said coldly. ''Why is he hounding *us*?''

''*Allegedly* hounding us. We don't know who's sending the letters and making the phone calls,'' Elmo said.

Jane shivered. ''Twelve years in prison makes for a lot of hatred, especially if the guy is as innocent as he says he is. Do we know for a pure fact that Newman eliminated everyone but us?''

''He said it. He's being very careful because we could sue him for libel and slander,'' Elmo said.

''I repeat, a jury listened to the evidence and said the evidence was sufficient to convict him. We weren't even *in* Boston when he went to trial. This is just too far-fetched,'' Annie said.

"We'll deal with it in the morning. It was a great dinner, Elmo."

"If it was so great, why aren't you eating?" the retired pharmacist asked sourly.

"I guess I kind of lost my appetite. It is tasty, though. I'll eat it for lunch tomorrow."

"You always say that, then you throw it away," Elmo grumbled as he started to clear the table.

"That's my job. You sit, Elmo, since you cooked," Tom said.

Annie shrugged and lit a cigarette. Jane followed suit. "Want some wine or beer?" Annie asked.

"I'd like a double shot of bourbon straight up," Jane said.

"I think I'll join you," Annie said.

Elmo was off his chair in a minute. "I'll get the bourbon."

"Elmo, did you bring one of the coffee bags? I can't wait to see it."

"Got it right here. Tom said they look classy."

"Oh, I like this," Annie said. "What do you think, Jane? Your artist's opinion."

"It has a good feel to it. Just the right weight paper. I'm partial to apple green no matter what. The daisy is perfect. I like the idea that it's raised, kind of puffed. Tom's right, these are classy bags. Did you order matching takeout bags?"

"Yes, but lighter-weight paper. Tom and I kicked it around for two days and decided to go with lettering and just a spray of daisies on the lower corner."

"I'm glad you didn't go with those plastic bags with the holes for handles. This is quality. Did you get a good deal?" Annie asked.

"Yes, he did," Tom said. "The raffia handles were Elmo's idea. They're secure. Two pounds of coffee can be heavy. Assuming someone buys two pounds at a time. It was cheaper to get the bigger bag as opposed to two bags for two pounds."

"You guys did good," Annie said fingering both the shopping bag and the coffee bag. She wished she could feel more excitement. Another time, another place, and she would have been ecstatic over these latest ornaments to her business.

"By the way, Annie, Stella and her husband are going to take to the business like ducks to water. She's learning to use a computer. Another week or so and she'll master it. That was a very wise move on your part. You might want to think of managerial positions for them at some point," Tom said.

Annie nodded. Right now, all she wanted was to be alone with the dogs.

"That does it. I'm going to drive Elmo home. I know you must be tired, Annie, so I'll say good night. We have all day tomorrow to talk about things."

"I am tired. Thanks, Tom."

Annie walked to the door with her brother and Elmo. She hugged the old man. "We need to talk, Elmo," she whispered.

"No, Annie, we don't. Let it rest. I mean that."

Annie's throat closed up tight. She nodded.

"It was a damn good dinner, too," Elmo grunted.

"I swear I'll eat it for lunch. Maybe breakfast. I swear, Elmo," Annie said, a desperate look on her face.

"Annie, look at me. I'm okay with this. I've lived my life, and it was a good life. I have no regrets. If it's my time, then it's my time."

Annie nodded again as she chewed the inside of her cheek. She knew by morning her mouth would be raw. She managed a raspy, "Good night."

Back in the kitchen, Annie looked at Jane's glassy eyes and then at the bourbon bottle. Suddenly she was seeing someone she didn't know. "Spit it out, Jane. We've been friends too long for me not to know when something is wrong."

"Every damn thing in the world is wrong. I think my husband is cheating on me. No, that's wrong. I *know* he's cheating on me. I hired a baby-sitter one night and followed him. She's nineteen if she's a day. She's gorgeous with a drop-dead figure. She drives a racy red MG convertible. She comes from a rich family. Her father owns the company Bob works for. He walks around with this sappy look on his face. He leaves early in the morning and comes home after midnight. He has no interest whatsoever in our daughter. She was having problems in school. He doesn't attend any of the events. It's like I'm a widow.''

"Why didn't you tell me this before? How long has it been going on?'' Annie demanded.

"Almost two years.''

"And you're just telling me *now!*''

"I'm so ashamed. I don't even know why I feel like that. I'm not good enough, not pretty enough, not rich enough. It's me. What's lacking in me? I was a damn good wife. I'm a good mother. I have a career. We certainly don't want for any material things. It has to be me.''

"Stop that right now. It's not you, it's Bob. Did you try talking to him? Confront him. If it's true, then boot his ass out the door. Why are you making yourself miserable by pretending you don't know?''

"I told you, Annie, it's that shame thing. I thought about going for counseling, but what good is it if I just go? And the other thing that's bumming me out is''—she paused and took a deep slug of bourbon—''I finally decided that . . . it's Elmo who took the money.''

"What?'' The single word burst out of Annie's mouth like a gunshot.

"You heard me. I think he had the money, then got scared and sent it back. When you're old like Elmo you do crazy things like that and then your guilty conscience takes over. It's the only thing that makes sense. Just sit there and think about it, Annie. Elmo has all this money. He sure as hell didn't get it from that rinky-dink little drugstore. So where did he get the money to buy that big house down here? He has a new car every year and an investment portfolio. I think he used the money to earn interest in different banks. He made a windfall, then gave it back.''

''That's the craziest thing I ever heard come out of your mouth, Jane. Do you see this bottle? You drank half of it. It's one-hundred-proof bourbon. You are drunk. If you weren't drunk, you wouldn't be saying these things. Elmo would never in a million years take something that didn't belong to him. Furthermore, I used to do his books once a month if you remember. Yes, he had an investment portfolio, but it was small. He'd buy five shares of something, sometimes three shares. At the most it was seventy thousand dollars. He gave away half of what he earned, and you damn well knew it just the way I knew it. He sold his business for one hundred and fifty thousand dollars. He paid one hundred and twenty-five for his house here. He leases his car every year. So what if he likes a new car every year. At his age he deserves everything life has to offer. He worked damn hard all his life, and he was good to us, Jane. How can you believe or say such a thing about him? I also pay him for any work he does for the Daisy Shops. He had a private pension plan he set up, and he collects social security. I'd like an apology right now, Jane.''

''Shut up, Annie. You always wear me down. I can't help what I believe. I told you nothing else makes sense.''

''You're the one who doesn't make any sense, Jane. It's not Elmo at all. You're just looking for something to vent on instead of talking things out with your husband. It is possible to save your marriage if you work at it. Two years is just too damn long to carry something like that around with you.''

''What if he leaves me? What if he doesn't want us anymore?''

''What am I missing here? Are you saying you are willing to stay in a marriage where you know your husband is being unfaithful just for the sake of being married? That's sick. No wonder Daisy has problems. Kids pick up on stuff like that and don't know how to handle it. You should talk to Tom. He's been through all that. I wouldn't mention that stuff about Elmo to him because he'll take your head off.''

Jane sniffed. ''You always have all the right answers, don't you? Just because you're this big tycoon now you think you can still tell me what to do. You got it all, didn't you, the business, the money, the power, Woman of the Year, and now you snag this rich coffee king. Anna Daisy Clark, the queen of everything.''

Annie felt hot tears prick her eyelids. ''I worked my ass off, Jane. Sometimes getting by on two or three hours' sleep a night. I offered you a full partnership. You turned it down. You wanted to get married and move to California to do your own thing. I gave you one of the shops. You said you only wanted one. I did what you wanted. I told you to get a lawyer, and you said no. We pay you some megabucks every year. We do all the work and you just sit there and collect the money. Where the hell is the money, Jane?''

Jane burst into tears. ''Bob took it to invest. Nothing worked out. At least he said it didn't. We used to stand by the mailbox to wait for the next check.''

''All of it's gone!''

''Every penny,'' Jane sobbed.

''What about the taxes and all that stuff?''

Jane cried harder. ''I don't know. Bob handles all that. He's a CPA. I just sign the forms when he hands them to me. A lot of mail has been coming lately from the IRS. Bob just puts it in his briefcase. I don't know what it's all about.''

''That's stupid, Jane. You don't ever screw around with the IRS.''

''There you go again! You know everything! Keep your nose

out of my business. For all I know you're the one who took the money, because I sure as hell didn't take it. Did you take the money, Annie?''

Here it was, right in her face, the question she'd been dreading ever since that fateful day back in Boston.

CHAPTER
THIRTEEN

Annie grappled with her emotions, hoping they didn't show on her face. "I don't think I care to dignify that question with an answer, Jane."

Jane's face crumpled. "I'm sorry, Annie. I didn't mean to say that. Really, I didn't. I didn't mean to say it about Elmo, either. It must be coming up to that time of the month to make me say things like that."

Annie reached for the bourbon bottle with shaky hands. She shook her head when Jane held out her glass. "This is for me. You already have a snootful. It's time to put you to bed. In the morning we'll talk about what we're going to do for you. I'll take you back into the business. I'm willing to share everything I have with you. Except for Parker. On second thought, maybe you can have him, too. I'd love to get to know my godchild better. You can stay here in the house. If, and that's a big if, I marry Parker, I'm going to be living in Hawaii part of the time. I can get you up on your feet, Jane, but you have to meet me halfway.'' She gulped at the stinging bourbon, her eyes watering.

Jane's head bobbed up and down. ''She isn't really nineteen. The bimbo. She's twenty-nine. She's pregnant, too, Annie.''

''We'll handle it tomorrow when the sun is shining. Come on, Jane, let's go to bed.''

''You're a good friend, Annie.''

''So are you.''

''What are we going to do about Elmo?''

''Nothing. That's the way he wants it. We'll be here for him the way he was always there for us.''

''See, you always have the right answer.''

''You just think I do. This is your room. Crawl into bed, and I'll check on you later. Do you want one of the dogs to stay with you?''

''No. I'm okay. Thanks anyway. Night, Annie.''

''Night, Jane. Tomorrow's another day.''

''Annie?''

''Yes.''

''Did you mean what you said about helping me?''

''Of course. What kind of friend would I be otherwise?''

''You're the best,'' Jane said. A moment later Annie heard her snoring lightly.

In her room with the door closed, Annie sat down on the bed next to her dogs. ''I don't know what to do,'' she said miserably. ''I can help Jane. I can be strong and tough where Elmo is concerned. At least I think I can. It's Parker that worries me. I don't know if I really and truly love him. I also have to send that money back if Jane moves into this house. That dumb, stupid thing I did years ago is going to haunt me for the rest of my life. If I confess now, Parker will never forgive me because he hates deception and secrets. If I thought for one second that Jane truly believed Elmo took the money, I'd fess up. She doesn't believe it. She was just letting off steam. I thought she had a really good marriage. I don't know what to do, guys.''

Rosie wiggled closer, trying to nudge Harry out of the way. Both shepherds pawed her arms and licked at her face. "It's okay. I'm just kind of out of it. The trip was long, Elmo's sick, Jane's in a funk, and then there's that other stuff staring at me. C'mere, you guys," Annie said, rolling over to stretch out on the bed, the huge dogs trying to stretch out alongside her. She played with them until she was tired. "Okay, let's go for our last walk outside. No leashes. We stay in the courtyard, then it's bedtime for all of us. Let's go!"

They were twin streaks of black lightning the moment Annie opened her bedroom door. Panting and breathless, they waited at the kitchen door for their mistress to open it.

The air was clear and dark, the heavens star-spangled. A faint light from the second-floor landing shone downward, illuminating Tom sitting on one of the wooden benches under the old angel oak.

Tom held out a Budweiser to his sister. "This is nice out here, Annie. Do you spend much time here in the garden?"

"Sometimes. It doesn't feel like home for some reason. The house is big and beautiful, this garden with the tree is magnificent. I think I like it better than the house. I don't know what it is. It's simply a place, and I find that sad."

"Maybe it's because you don't have anyone to share it with. You've been alone a long time, Annie. Now that you and Parker are together I'm so happy for you I could just bust. Is there anything you want to talk about?"

Annie could think of a hundred things. She shook her head. "Well, maybe one thing, Tom." She told him about Jane.

"That rotten SOB."

"Yeah, he's that all right. I told Jane she could come back and work for the company. I'm willing to share. She could help you, Tom. With Elmo . . . it might work,'' she finished lamely.

"Look, sis, I know that Elmo's condition came out of left field to you as well as it did to me. I've come to depend on him and his good sense. No one can replace him. We both know that. This is just my opinion, and you can chop me off at the knees if you want, but I don't think you should just *give* anything to Jane. If she works for it, fine. If she has to work for her money, she might not be so quick to squander it next time. It was how I learned, thanks to you.''

"We'll work it out in the morning. Jane's too proud to take. She'll want to work.''

"Tell me about Parker, Annie. Share a little. You looked so happy, so sparkly when you got off the plane. Now you look like you've been through the grinder.''

"Jet lag, no sleep, different water, it takes its toll. I think I'm happy. No, that's not true. I feel very confused where Parker is concerned. It's like he's got everything all mapped out. All these plans. It's almost as though . . . he knew this was going to happen. I don't know if I want to live on an island no matter how beautiful it is. Parker says we should look into decaf coffees. I don't think we can handle anything else, do you, Tom?''

"I'll run it by Elmo tomorrow. He loves it when we ask for advice. Listen, Annie, I didn't want to say anything in front of the others, but something happened a few days ago. Mona called me. I have no idea how she found me. I didn't ask, and she didn't say. She didn't even ask about the kids. Do you believe that?''

"Sure I believe that. Did she want more money?''

"No. She said some guy named Newman came to her house and started asking her a lot of questions. Personal questions. Like why did we get divorced. Why did she give up the kids. She told him it was none of his business. At least that's what she said she said. I believed her. She said he hinted that he knew what her bank balance was. If nothing else, Mona can smell trouble. She claims she just stared him down, and he finally left. She thought I should know. I sent her ten thousand dollars in cash through Federal Express. I know only a stupid person would do something like that. So I'm stupid and I did it. She got it just fine. Money talks, Annie, and money can buy silence. I went with the latter because I don't know where you got the money you gave me to buy off Mona, and I don't want to know. The businesses are cash cows, we all know that. If you ever get audited, you're going to have to be able to explain the missing hundred grand. *If* that jerk Newman manages to tap into Mona's old bank records, it could happen. She said she only deposited small amounts at a time. She's not stupid. Right now she's kind of scared, and she isn't sure why that is. What I'm trying to tell you is, she won't give up anything.''

Annie's heart thumped in her chest. It was coming apart, closing in on her. How long would it take for the noose to fall down around her neck? She swigged from the long-necked beer bottle, hoping she presented a picture of nonchalance. ''I guess we'll worry about that when the time comes. I'm out on my feet, Tom. We can talk tomorrow. How long are you staying?''

''I'm heading home in the morning.''

''I might go to California with Jane to help her if she needs me. Do you think it will be okay to leave the dogs with Elmo?''

''He'd have a fit if you don't. It's business as usual where he's concerned. Don't let him see you cave in, Annie.''

''I'll try, Tom. God, what will we do without him?''

''I honest to God don't know, Annie. If Jane comes back, it might all work. Say good night, Gracie,'' he said fondly.

''Okay. Good night, Gracie.''

Annie laughed all the way up the steps to the second floor, the shepherds bounding along ahead of her.

She stopped to peek in at Jane, who was sleeping soundly. She turned off the light and closed the door.

It was all going to work out. She had to believe that.

"Like they really get ice water in hell," she muttered.

"It's a pretty house, Jane. I like your flower beds. They remind me of a rainbow," Annie said as she stared at the sprawling ranch-style house with its multipaned windows.

"Daisy likes to weed the garden, then she picks me a bouquet. She hasn't done that for a long time now. I can't wait for you to see your godchild. She's gotten taller and seems to be all legs, and she has these wonderful, big dark eyes. She's too thin, though. Smart as a whip, her teachers say. Lately, her grades have gone down alarmingly. We might as well get to it, Annie."

"Are you sure you're ready for this? It doesn't have to be today."

"Yes, it has to be today. I need your backbone. Having you here with me gives me the courage to do what I should have done two years ago. I just didn't have the guts."

"Then let's pack up your stuff."

"Kind of like that last day in Boston. Boy, we were hyped that day. We had the rest of our lives in front of us. Those checks from Elmo made all the difference in the world back then. God, I wish I could turn back the clock, Annie."

"You can't unring the bell. What are you going to do about the house?"

"Nothing. There's no equity left. Bob took it all out. Let him worry about it. I just want Daisy's and my things. It shouldn't take us long. There isn't that much."

There isn't that much. Annie wondered what that meant exactly. She found out soon enough: Jane's wardrobe was skimpy, her art supplies just as skimpy. Daisy's toys were old, battered, and worn. There was no sign of Barbie gear, a bicycle or scooter, or any of the things most little girls had. Her clothes were worn, mended, and faded.

"Jane, why didn't you tell me? You must know I would have helped you. I need to know why you lived like this."

"You were so successful. I didn't want you to know. Shame is a terrible thing, Annie. How could I have been so wrong about Bob?"

"You were in love. That's as good an explanation as any I can come up with. I want to be sure that you're sure you don't want to try the counseling route."

"Look at me, Annie. I lied to you. I did go. It didn't help. If anything, it just made me more miserable. I feel like I betrayed our friendship."

"I kind of feel that way, too, but I think we can fix it. When are you going to tell Bob you're leaving?"

"I wasn't going to tell him. Old habits die real hard, Annie. I was just going to take the easy way out and leave with Daisy. When he comes home, he'll figure it out. If anything, he'll probably be relieved."

"What's wrong with face-to-face? If you don't face him down, this is going to hang over you for the rest of your life. If you and your daughter are going to start over, you need to do it with a clean slate. Call him up and ask him to come home. Wait till we're done packing, and the stuff is in the car. We'll pick up Daisy from the sitter's when we leave."

"I don't know if I can do that, Annie. I'll break out into a sweat, my voice will crack, and he'll know I'm everything he says I am."

Annie's voice turned to steel. "And what does he say you are, Jane?"

"It doesn't matter, Annie. This is the end of the road. I'll do it."

"Then we call all the utility companies to turn everything

off and tell them to take your name off each one. I'm glad we stopped at the bank first and did the same thing. I'm also glad your Daisy Shop is back in my name. He won't have a claim to it. I know all about this stuff from Tom. He went through it with Mona. She called him and didn't even ask about the kids.''

''Some people just aren't parent material, Annie. I found that out the hard way.''

''It's just so hard to believe parents can turn their backs on their own flesh and blood.''

''Shhhh. This is Jane Granger. Can I speak to my husband please? I don't really care if he's in a meeting or not, Miriam. Both of us know that isn't true, so just put me through. I wouldn't be calling if it wasn't important.''

''Good,'' Annie whispered.

''Bob, I need you to come home after work. I don't want to hear you have to work late. I gave up believing all those lies a long time ago. Fine, if you don't want to come home then I guess you aren't interested in the fact that Annie sold my Daisy Shop out from under me. Oh, you will be home. Make it early. Four-thirty is good for me.''

''I thought you said you didn't have any guts.'' Annie smiled.

''Only when you're around. Let's finish up, so I can call the utility companies. Bob hates it when there's no air conditioning.''

''Do you know what he does or where he goes?''

''There's been a string of women. This last one is the daughter of his boss. It's not a large company that he works for, but it is successful. If Bob had been a good husband, we could have had a good life. Daisy's future would be secure, and I wouldn't have to worry about paying bills and dodging creditors.''

''What did he do with the money, Jane?''

''He likes expensive suits and custom-made shoes. He leases

a Porsche. He has a boat. He has two Rolex watches. He goes on trips. He has a passion for Las Vegas. I couldn't go along because Daisy was in school. He never asked me, though. I think he married me because he believed I was going to be a famous artist someday. I sell, but I'm not famous. You should have seen his face when he found out about the Daisy Shop. It's called high living. I really did love him, Annie, but that love died a long time ago. I wasn't smart enough to get out. I guess part of me kept hoping it would get better. Instead, it got worse. Daisy is going to need some counseling."

"We'll take care of all that. I guess this is the last of it. Anything else you want to take?"

"That's it. I'll call the utility companies and tell them to turn everything off by five."

"Sounds good to me. Let's have something cold to drink and make a plan for Daisy. How about a good summer camp? Tom's daughter is a camp counselor summers at a really good one. It will give you time to get on your feet. She'll be happy with other kids, and in the fall, when it's time for school, you can be all settled in."

"No stress, no strain. It sounds like heaven."

Annie forced a laugh she didn't feel. "No, the stress is going to come when it's time to go shopping. Charleston has some beautiful stores, or we could spin up to Atlanta and shop there. We're going to start you off right."

"How can I thank you, Annie?"

"Thank you is good enough. You're my friend, Jane. We always said we'd be friends forever and ever. I meant it when I made the promise. I thought you did, too."

"Annie, I wanted to call you so many times. They say pride is the deadliest sin of all."

"That's in the past. This is a new day. Make your calls, and I'll fix us some ice tea if you tell me where everything is."

Jane pointed as she dialed.

At three-thirty, Bob Granger roared up the driveway and parked his silver Porsche under the carport. His roar was as loud as his sports car when he stormed into the kitchen. "What the hell is going on?" he demanded.

"I just wanted to get your attention," Jane said in a trembling voice.

"Well, you got it. What's going on? I was in a meeting with a client, Jane. I told you not to call me at work."

"I guess that's because you don't want me to know you're never there. I don't care, Bob. I'm leaving."

"You called me home to tell me you're leaving. Where are you going? I hope you're taking the kid with you. I'm not doing that baby-sitter shit. When will you be back?"

"Daisy is going with me. I'm not coming back. I'm leaving you. I'm filing for divorce."

"What the hell's gotten into you?"

"What part of what I just said don't you understand, Bob?"

"The part about why your friend is here and all of a sudden you're getting a divorce. I always thought there was something fishy about the relationship between the two of you."

Annie's insides turned to Jell-O. She saw Jane raise her arm, heard the slap she rendered high on her husband's cheek and the tirade that followed. Her stomach started to quiver at the ugly words being uttered.

"Stupid, ugly bitch! Who the hell would want you? Look at you. You're nothing but skin and bones. I can see through you, for Christ's sake. That hair of yours is like a wild mop and your face is bony and long and those freckles are not the least bit attractive. You sound like a horse when you laugh, and I'm ashamed to be seen with you. The kid looks just like you. Go. Who gives a shit. We'll divide everything evenly."

Annie was off the chair like a bullet. She pushed Jane out of the way. She jabbed her index finger in the middle of Bob's neck. "You miserable, stinking bastard! You say one more word about my friend, and I'll lay you out cold right here in this kitchen. You get nothing but this house and whatever bills you've run up. Jane signed over the Daisy Shop to me, so you can forget that. It's time now for your wife to live like the queen she is, and your daughter—my godchild—will be a princess. You, you son of a bitch, are the ugly frog in your custom-made Armani suit. Read my lips, Mr. Granger. You fuck with me, and it will be the last thing you ever do. Don't sneer, don't snarl, don't try to bluff me with indignation because I'm capable of wiping up the floor with you. Oh, by the way, you can have this house and that car in the driveway, you know the one, the junk pile Jane drives. She'll be driving a Mercedes from now on. You can keep your leased vehicle. Jane doesn't want it. We will be asking for those two Rolex watches for Daisy. Child support is going to come high.''

"Get the hell out of my house," Granger sneered.

"It will be my pleasure to leave this house," Annie snarled in return.

Annie had to prod Jane to get her to move. "They were just ugly words, Jane. That's all they were. Ugly people say ugly things. It's behind you now. Don't let what he said blind you. You are just the opposite of everything he said. Except for that wild bush of hair. Come hell or high water, you're getting it cut. That's my only stipulation to this whole deal."

Jane smiled. "I never, in all the years I've known you, heard you talk like that. He was afraid of you. I didn't think he was afraid of anything. I usually tie it back. You're right, it needs to be cut. I'm okay. Thanks for standing up for me back there. I just froze. Bob never talked to me like that before. I guess that's how he felt all along. God, how could I have been so blind?''

"Your eyes are wide-open now. Let's get this show on the road. We have to pick up Daisy Jane Granger. I'd give some thought to taking back my maiden name if I were you. I like the way Daisy Jane Abbott sounds.''

''I do, too. Thanks for being my friend, Annie.''

''Thank you for being mine, too, Jane.''

Annie walked through the big house, aware of the silence. She looked down at Rosie and Harry, who were always at her side. ''We have a child in the house. I would think there would be noise. Maybe Daisy and her mother went out.'' Harry stopped in his tracks and whimpered as he nudged his mistresses's leg, inching her toward the kitchen and the door that led to the garden. ''Okay, you want out. Let's go.''

She saw her then, a bundle of arms and legs curled up in the wooden chair under the umbrella tree. She'd been crying, but her eyes were dry now. Clutched in her hands was a tired and worn stuffed dog that had seen far too many washings. A plate of cookies and a glass of milk stood untouched on the table next to her.

''Hi, kiddo. Where's your mom?'' Annie asked cheerfully.

''She's taking a shower. She wants us to look nice when we go shopping.''

''Are you excited about going shopping? I know this great store that has the prettiest bicycles and the fastest scooters. They have a magnificent Barbie house in the window. Did I tell you Rosie knows how to play checkers? Harry is learning to play, too.''

The little girl with the big brown eyes looked skeptical. ''Really and truly, Aunt Annie?''

''Really and truly, Daisy. I taught Rosie, and Harry watched. You see, before you and your mom came here to live, I was all alone. Sometimes I wanted to play checkers, and the dogs were the only ones around, so Uncle Elmo and I taught them how to play. Rosie cheats.''

Daisy smiled, then she giggled. It was a delightful sound to Annie's ears.

"Does your dog have a name?"

"Elizabeth. Will they let me take Elizabeth to camp? Can I come home if I don't like it?"

"Of course you can take Elizabeth with you. I can see she's your loyal and trusted friend. You can come home if you don't like camp. I think you're going to love it. You'll make all kinds of new friends. You'll get to meet my niece Mandy. She's going to look out for you. You get your own pony to ride every day. You'll learn how to play tennis. Mandy is going to give you swimming lessons. The campfires are wonderful. You'll toast marshmallows, roast weenies, and tell ghost stories. You have to promise to write at least once a week."

"Is my daddy going to come here?"

"No, Daisy, he isn't going to come here."

"Truly truly?"

"I'm sorry, Daisy."

"I don't want him to come here. I don't like it when he makes Mommy cry. Elizabeth doesn't like it either."

"You don't have to worry about that anymore. You and your mommy are going to live here from now on. Your daddy is going to live in California. That's three thousand miles away. You can bring all your friends here to play in the garden. I called a friend of mine who said he can build you a playhouse in the garden. You are going to have so much fun you won't want to go to sleep at night. I saw your mommy laughing last night. She's happy to be here. I hope you're happy, too. I think I hear her now. Guess that means we better get moving. I have to warn you, I love to shop!"

"Oh, Aunt Annie, you are so funny." The little girl giggled.

"I don't think anyone ever called me funny before."

"You girls ready?" Jane called from the kitchen doorway.

"We're ready, aren't we, Daisy?"

Both women watched as Daisy handed her worn, stuffed animal to Rosie. "Watch Elizabeth for me till I get back." Harry woofed softly.

"I think Elizabeth is in safe hands, Daisy. Rosie will guard Elizabeth, and Harry will guard them both. Are we ready, ladies?"

"We're ready, Aunt Annie." Daisy giggled.

"Just five days, Annie, and I can see a difference in my child. I'm so grateful to you," Jane whispered.

It was four o'clock when the weary shoppers returned home. Annie made ice tea while Daisy demonstrated all her new toys and clothes to her captive audience of three: Elizabeth, Rosie, and Harry. She generously handed out treats to the panting dogs, whose tails swished furiously in delight.

"I think we had a good day, Jane. Daisy seems happy. You look great with your new haircut. I'm off tomorrow for New Jersey, so you guys are going to have the house to yourself. Elmo will be here with the dogs, but I'd appreciate it if you kind of watch over Elmo without him knowing you're watching."

"For you, Annie, anything. Is there anything you want me to tell your niece when she arrives to pick up Daisy?"

"Nope. Tell her I love her and to take good care of my godchild. Are you going to be okay alone?"

"Annie, I've been alone so much these past years it doesn't matter. I'm comfortable with my own company. This will give me some quality time with Elmo."

"Then I think we're all set. Since you agreed to cook dinner, I think I'll go upstairs and call Parker. I want to change my shoes and clothes."

"Take all the time you want. Thanks, Annie."

"Pooh. It was nothing."

Annie looked at her watch as she settled herself in a comfortable chair that allowed for a view of the water. It was nine-thirty in Hawaii. She dialed and waited.

"It's Annie, Parker. I've been thinking of you all day. I have so much to tell you. Oh, I'm sorry. Go ahead, talk to your nephew. Call me back later. I'll be here all evening."

It was nice that Parker's nephew called from college. She knew Parker liked to be asked for his advice and always went out of his way for his nieces and nephews. Maybe it was better that Parker would be calling later.

With nothing better to do with her time, Annie called Kiki Aellia's private number. She smiled at the upbeat tone when her soon-to-be-sister-in-law answered.

"It's Annie, Kiki. I just called to say hello. How's everything?"

"At this point in time, things couldn't be better. Who knows what tomorrow will bring. How are things with you?"

"Pretty good, all things considered. My friend Jane and her little girl, who is my godchild, are staying with me. Parker is going to call later tonight. He was on the phone with one of his nephews when I called. Tomorrow I go to New Jersey. By the time I get back, Parker will be here. I think we might be moving up our wedding date to September."

"Why is that? It's good, but is there a reason?"

Annie told her about Elmo.

"I am so sorry, Annie. If there is anything I can do, call on me."

"The wedding may have to be here. I don't know if Elmo will be up to the long plane ride."

"Then we will bring the islands to you, Annie. It can be done. If this happens, let me know, and my sisters and I will arrange things for you. It will be our pleasure."

"That's very kind of you, Kiki. I appreciate it. I guess I'll say good-bye for now."

"Thank you for calling, Annie."

It was nice being friends with Kiki. She'd never had a sister, and now she was going to have a big wonderful family with lots of sisters. Life couldn't be better. Or could it?

Annie was aware suddenly of how dark her room had become. She looked out across the water as a storm roiled inward. One of Charleston's famous thunderstorms was about to shatter the quiet. She gathered up her ice tea glass and ran to the stairs. Before long there would be thunder and lightning. Rosie was petrified of storms, and Harry always ran and hid under the staircase leading to the second floor.

Annie felt like a mother as she herded Daisy and the two dogs into the house.

It was a wonderful feeling.

CHAPTER
FOURTEEN

Annie looked down at her watch, amazed that it was five minutes to midnight. She and Parker had been talking for over two hours about everything and nothing. She smiled to herself as she listened to Parker regale her with some of his childhood antics. She yawned elaborately as she realized she was tired of hearing his voice. It was all me, and I did this and I did that and then I did something else.

"Are you going to go to sleep, Parker? It's almost time for you to get up."

"I'm so wide-awake there's no point in trying to sleep. See, that's what talking to you does to me. I'd rather talk to you than sleep. I'm counting the days till you get back from New Jersey. I'll be there in Charleston the moment you get home. I miss you, Annie. I didn't think it was possible to miss someone as much as I miss you."

"I feel the same way. You understand about Elmo then? Kiki said she would bring the islands to Charleston if we decide to get married here. I'm not sure I know what that means."

"Well, if Kiki said it, then she means it. The whole family will be there, nieces and nephews. Aunts, uncles, cousins. Can you handle it?"

"Of course. My garden is wonderful. The house is spacious. The kitchen is huge. It won't be a problem."

"If you like, we can have a traditional Hawaiian wedding later on. I like the idea of marrying you twice," Parker said jubilantly.

Annie winced. She wasn't sure she wanted to get married once, let alone twice.

"That's exactly what we'll do," Parker said sprightly. "The family is big, Annie."

"My family is very small. Speaking of family, how is your nephew doing?"

"Right now, Ben isn't doing so good. It seems one of his law professors assigned each student a police case to solve. By that I mean a case that's still on the books. I think he said it was over thirteen years old. The professor divided the youngsters into teams, and Ben and a fellow student named Andreas were assigned a case that took place in Boston back when you were just leaving for South Carolina. That's if my memory is correct. You never said anything about a bank robbery to me, did you, Annie?"

"No, I don't think so. If it's the case I'm thinking of, it happened the day before graduation, then Jane and I left right after graduation the following day."

"Well, Ben has himself in a tizzy over this. Wanted my advice as to how to go about it."

Annie felt like she had a scoop of peanut butter in her mouth. She tried clearing her throat, but it felt so dry she gulped at the warm ice tea on the little table next to her chair. She finally managed to say, "What . . . what's he going to do?"

"That's just it. He doesn't know what to do. Andreas is a French student, and his English isn't that good. He wants to do the paperwork and the files and have Ben do all the legwork. Ben says it's fair. He just doesn't know where to start. I told him to go to the police and get the report, then the library for all the articles that were written, and from there I would imagine he should go to the insurance company. What's your opinion?''

Annie mumbled something, and a moment later couldn't remember what it was she'd said. "I hear Daisy, Parker. I want to get to her before the dogs start to bark and wake Jane. I'll call you tomorrow.''

"I love you, and don't you ever forget it.''

Annie broke the connection and replaced the phone. It took both her hands to hold on to the receiver. She felt so faint she had to put her head between her legs. *Is this pure coincidence or something else? Now what am I supposed to do? Run? Hide? Call off my marriage to Parker? Should I tell Jane and Elmo? Maybe Jane, but not Elmo. Elmo has enough on his plate right now. God, what should I do? How can one person be so happy one minute and then so miserable the next?*

Shaking from head to toe, Annie crept from her room and down the steps to the kitchen, the dogs trotting alongside her. Her whole body felt like it was on fire as she made her way to the garden. She needed to think, but her brain felt numb. Maybe what she was feeling was the first step in a nervous breakdown. *God in heaven, what will happen to everything if I'm reduced to a blithering idiot? How will Tom cope? Jane is in a fragile state, as is Daisy, and Elmo is . . . is ill. I can't tell any of them. I can't ask any of them for help. There isn't one other person in the whole world I can talk to.*

Perhaps I should consult a lawyer or a shrink. They are bound by confidentiality oaths. Going it alone is tough. Damn it, I gave half the money back plus interest. I'll pack up the rest and drop it off on my way to New Jersey tomorrow. I've tried to lead a good life. So I made one mistake. I've paid for it dearly every day of my life.

Annie cried then because there was nothing else for her to do.

At four o'clock in the morning, Annie climbed the stairs to her room, her back ramrod stiff, her eyes dry and miserable. She was like a robot as she pulled out the chair nestled underneath the cherry wood secretary. From one of the drawers she withdrew letterhead stationery and a pen. She took a deep breath as she started to compose her letter.

Dear Parker,

    I don't know quite how to say this, Parker, other than to just come out and say it. I can't marry you. I realized after talking to you this evening that I can't give up my business and relocate to your beautiful island. I guess I am a career woman after all. A selfish career woman who doesn't want to share the fruits of her labor. I must think of Elmo and Jane and do what I can for them. I'm sorry if this causes you pain. Please explain to your family. I also want to assure you that my decision to call off our marriage will not affect our business relationship during the next few months.

                                    Annie

Annie folded the letter and slipped it into a matching envelope. The envelope then went into a Federal Express envelope. She filled in the air bill, marked it for next-day delivery. She'd drop it off in the special drop box at the bank when she left in the morning.

The next two hours were spent getting the rest of the money ready for delivery to whichever bank she came in contact with first. At one point she became so confused with the interest she owed, she simply dumped in two packets of money from her safe. Money that she swished and dipped into the back of the toilet tank filled with Clorox. She tiptoed down the steps and loaded the bags into the cargo area of her all-terrain vehicle.

With nothing else to do, she packed her bags and carried them down to the car and put them in the backseat. She was drinking coffee when Elmo arrived at six o'clock. The dogs circled him, waiting for the treats he always carried in his pockets.

"You're up early this morning, Annie. You look kind of peaked," Elmo said as he opened the door to the garden. The dogs barreled outside. "You've been crying, haven't you?"

"So what if I have, Elmo? Where does it say that I can't cry? Why do I always have to be the tough one? I have feelings, and I hurt just like everyone else."

Elmo poured himself coffee. "Feeling sorry for ourselves this morning, are we?"

"So what, Elmo? So what?"

"Does this have anything to do with Jane and little Daisy?"

"No, of course not."

"Are you stewing and fretting about me? If you are, I won't tolerate it, Annie."

"No, Elmo, it has nothing to do with you."

"Did you have a fight with Tom?"

"No, Elmo, I did not fight with Tom."

"See, now we're getting somewhere. That leaves Parker Grayson."

"I'm calling off the wedding. I'm not getting married. I decided I don't want to live in Hawaii. I'm a career woman. I'm not giving up my business. I busted my ass, Elmo, and I'm not going to sit back and clip coupons."

"Do you mind me asking what brought this to a head?"

Annie leaped up from her chair and started to pace the kitchen. "You know what, Elmo, it's that damn bank robbery that's been hanging over our heads for thirteen years. Wait till you hear this. Just wait till I tell you what Parker told me tonight. Well, last night, you know what I mean.''

''I'm listening, Annie.''

''So, that's what happened,'' Annie said fifteen minutes later. ''See, you don't know Parker like I know him. He hates lies and deceit. I didn't exactly lie, but by not telling him about being under suspicion, I was deceitful. He made a point to ask about secrets, and I didn't say anything. It was baggage, Elmo. I didn't . . . You know what, I'm glad I didn't tell him, or they'd be hounding him now the way they're hounding Tom's ex-wife. It plain out sucks, Elmo. So, I decided to call it off. Then there's the merger stuff. No way. I mean, that's simply out of the question. I'm not going to spend the rest of my life worrying about what if he finds out, what if, what if. This is the best way.''

''Don't you think you might be shortchanging the fellow? How do you know how he would react? If you explain the circumstances, I'm sure he'd understand. I feel duty-bound to tell you this is a dumb, stupid thing you're doing.''

''Give it up, Elmo. Don't you see, if I say anything now, Parker will be convinced his nephew's doing the legwork on the case scared me. It's all screwed up in my head. This way is best. Don't interfere, Elmo. I will never forgive you if you say even one word to Parker. This is my personal problem, and I'm handling it the best way I know how.

''Now, are you sure you don't mind taking care of the dogs? If I leave now, I can make the interstate before rush-hour traffic.''

''I can handle the dogs, Annie. I think I will stay here, though. I need to work with Harry to perfect his checker game. He bit Rosie's tail the other day when he caught her cheating. I swear, Annie, that's a true story.''

''I know, Elmo. Harry's real smart. You need to stop giving

them so many treats. Harry gets the splats. I didn't hear you give me your word where Parker is concerned.''

''You have my word, Annie. What about Jane and Tom?''

''Not a word.''

''Why'd you pick me to spill the beans to about you and Grayson, Annie?''

''Because, Elmo, you're like my father. If I had a father or a mother, I would have talked to them. Take charge, Elmo.''

The frail old man hugged Annie. ''Don't worry about a thing. We'll all be here when you get back. By the way, when are you coming back?''

''Not for a long time, Elmo. I'm going to do the circuit in the car. I'll just go from one place to the next. I'll check in. It won't be necessary to tell anyone where I am. Okay?''

''Okay, Annie.''

''Then I guess I'm outta here,'' Annie said in a choked voice.

''Guess so.'' Elmo waved airily as he poured more coffee into his cup.

The moment Elmo heard the engine of Annie's car start up, the phone was in his hand. ''Tom, there's a problem here. Sit down, and I'll tell you.''

''You broke your word to Annie! She's never going to forgive you, Elmo,'' Tom said when the old man wound down.

''She's only going to find out if you blab, Tom. We need to put our heads together and figure out what to do. Your sister isn't thinking clearly. This is way too serious for us to ignore. Now, you need to skedaddle down here so we can make a plan. Miss Daisy is leaving for camp today with your daughter, so you just hitch a ride with Mandy. Yes, of course I'm going to tell Jane. She's a part of it just like Annie and me. We need to go on the *attack!*''

* * *

Parker ripped at the red-and-blue Federal Express envelope. Annie must be sending him some of the pictures she took at the waterfall. He was going to frame all of them, one for every room in the house, so no matter where he was, she would be in his line of vision. He felt like a young teenager as he ripped at the envelope, all the while realizing it wasn't heavy enough to hold snapshots.

He read the letter, once, twice, then a third time with disbelieving eyes. His fingers flew over the keypad on the telephone. A strange voice said, "Hello."

"This is Parker Grayson. I'd like to speak to Annie please."

"I'm sorry, Mr. Grayson, Annie isn't here. She left yesterday to make her rounds of the different Daisy Shops. She does that on an ongoing basis. No, she didn't tell me which stores she was going to first. I'm Jane Abbott, Annie's friend. Yes, it is nice to finally talk with you. I wish I could help you. If she checks in, I'll give her your message."

There was no doubt in Parker's mind that Jane Abbott would give Annie the message. There was also no doubt in his mind that Annie wouldn't return his call. He sat down with a thump. Now what the hell was he supposed to do? He'd heard of men being left at the altar and had always wondered why something like that happened. Didn't people know when they were in love? Didn't they realize how precious love was? He needed to think, but his head felt clogged up. Damn, what was this going to do to his real coffee without the caffeine? Maybe a drink would help. Maybe several drinks would help. Maybe a whole lot of drinks would do a whole lot of good. He poured generously into a squat tumbler and took it neat. His throat burned, and his eyes watered.

While he slurped at the next glass, he ran the two-hour-long conversation he'd had with Annie over and over in his mind. They'd said so many things, all of them loving and wonderful. A frown built between his brows. He realized he'd done most of the talking, and Annie had listened. Why was that? And then, according to the letter just hours later, she'd had a change of heart. Why? Was he the only one who said loving, wonderful words? He tried to remember what she had said. He couldn't remember a thing. His glass full to the brim, he guzzled it as if it were mango juice.

Parker wondered if he was drunk. He peered at the contents of the bottle then and *knew* he was drunk. He drained it. So what if he was drunk? No one cared. He didn't even have a housekeeper who could drag him to bed and cover him up. He needed to call somebody to find out why his love had dumped him so unceremoniously. Kiki might know. Tom might know. He had a right to know. Every damn right in the world. Damn it, now he was going to have to close down the laboratory.

Parker yanked at the drawer in his desk for his address book. He wondered why he didn't know his love's brother's phone number by heart. Maybe he needed to put on his glasses. It took him ten minutes to realize he didn't wear glasses, reading or otherwise. "Shit!" he said succinctly. His arm reached out to the small bar set against the wall. He snagged a fresh bottle of scotch just as Tom's voice came over the wire.

"I need to know why your sister dumped me, Tom, my good buddy. Don't give me any of that bullshit that you don't know. Everything was fine one minute, then not fine. I got a fucking Dear John letter by Federal Express. What do you have to say to that, Tom, my good buddy? Your sister doesn't want me but she wants my fucking coffee. Didja hear that, Tom, my good buddy. It don't work that way. If I'm not good enough for your sister, then neither is my coffee. You got that, Tom, my good buddy? Why aren't you saying something, Tom?"

"I was waiting for you to stop talking. I don't know what it's all about, Parker. You know I never interfere with my sister's decisions. She has a mind of her own. I thought everything was roses for you two. Look, if you want to cancel the contract, that's your decision. It has five months to run before we renew. Right now I think you're three sheets to the wind. I suggest you sleep it off and call me so we can talk intelligently.''

"Are you telling me you don't think I'm intelligent? Did your sister tell you to say that?''

"No, Parker, she didn't. She's on the road as we speak. I don't know anything about any of this. Sleep it off and call me back. You're drunk, Parker.''

"You'd be drunk, too, if someone left you standing at the altar with some shifty explanation that doesn't make sense. Never mind, I'm going swimming.''

"Parker, wait, don't do that. I don't think you're in any condition to go swimming. Parker, are you listening to me?''

"Why should I listen to you? You don't say anything. I'm sorry I bothered you. I won't call again. Tell your sister to have a good life.''

"Parker, wait . . .''

Parker staggered out of the house and down the path that would take him to the waterfalls. He fell twice but never lost his grip on the scotch bottle in his hand. Halfway to the falls he sat down on a rock to admire a perfect rainbow high in the sky. "That's Annie's Rainbow,'' he said, taking a long pull from the bottle in his hand. He squinted to see how far he was from the falls. He lurched forward, looking over his shoulder every other minute to see if the rainbow was still in the sky. He knew that when it disappeared, there would be another one. Annie said she loved rainbows. She loved rainbows, but she didn't love him.

He was panting and perspiring profusely as he made the way up the incline that led to the chair behind the falls. When he looked down he noticed he'd lost one of his sandals. He kicked the other one off and laughed as it sailed through the air. That little feat certainly called for a drink. Maybe two. Feat. Feet. He laughed uproariously.

By the time he reached the thick shelf behind the falls that led to the stone chair, he was seeing double. *Maybe Tom was right, I am drunk. I deserve to be drunk. Maybe Tom was right about taking a nap, too. Hell no. I've come this far and I'm going to get to the chair if it kills me.* The chair where he and Annie had sat professing their love for one another.

Precariously, step by step, Parker teetered this way, then that way, his arms swinging outward for balance. Then he was in the chair behind the waterfall. Directly in his line of vision was the most gorgeous rainbow he'd ever seen. "I'll drink to that," he muttered. "To Rainbow Falls! To this stone chair! To my coffee beans! To . . . Shit to everything!" He gurgled from the bottle, his eyes crossing as the liquor seared his throat.

A long time later, in his drunken stupor, Parker heard his name being called over and over. Then he saw them, his sisters, Lela, Teke, Cassie, Mahala, Jana, and Kiki.

"Parker, are you in the chair?"

"Yeah. I'm not moving either. Are you going swimming?"

"No, we came to take you home."

"My six sisters came to take me home," Parker singsonged. "Why is that? How did you know I was here? It doesn't matter. I'm staying here all day. All night, too."

"Then so are we. This is stupid, Parker. You're so drunk I bet you can't even stand up," Kiki said.

"That's true. That's why I'm sitting here, and that's why I'm not going home with you."

"It's going to be pretty crowded in here," Lela said, walking through the falls, her sisters behind her.

"Only two people are supposed to be here at a time. That's what the legend says," Parker singsonged again.

"So we're screwing up the legend," Kiki said. "Listen, girls, I have an idea. If two of us hold on to him, we can jump in and make sure he comes to the top. We'll never get him off the ledge. What do you think?"

"I think no more coffee to the Daisy Shops. She wants my coffee, but she doesn't want me. Do you hear me, Kiki? She isn't going to renew the contract."

Kiki nodded. To her sisters she said, "Can we do it?"

"Sure, you take one arm and I'll take the other," Mahala said.

Kiki reached down to grasp her brother under the arm while her sister took the other arm. "That's it, upsy daisy."

"Do not say that to me," Parker snarled drunkenly.

"Shut up, Parker, and jump!"

Kiki swung one leg backward to kick her brother in the bend of his knees. They sailed through the air and hit the water at the same moment.

"Let's do that again," Parker said as his head bobbed above the water.

"Shut up, Parker. This is a three-hundred-dollar suit I'm wearing. Now it's ruined."

"Did you ruin your Chanel purse, too?"

The sisters burst out laughing as they dragged their brother to the edge of the pool.

"I don't think I ever saw Parker drunk," Jana said.

"He's just a social drinker," Mahala said.

"What the hell happened?" Lela asked.

"Annie Clark dumped him. Via Federal Express," Kiki volunteered.

"Stop talking about me like I'm not here," Parker said.

"Your body is here, but your mind is pickled. One of us is going to stand you under the shower, and the rest of us are going to make you coffee. How much whiskey did you drink?"

"A lot."

"What's a lot?" someone asked.

"How much was in the bottle at the chair?" Parker asked craftily.

Kiki shrugged helplessly. "I didn't look."

"Well, there you go. How do you expect me to know if you don't know?"

"Just shut up, Parker, and get in the bathroom. Can you take your clothes off or should we help you?"

"You sounded just like Mama. I can do it. I said I can do it. Where's my shoes? Oops, that's right, I lost them."

"Parker, it isn't the end of the world," Kiki said.

"For me it is. I don't understand it. I'll have to close down the laboratory if she doesn't renew the contract."

"When you're sober we'll talk about it. Maybe we can help."

"Okay, Kiki. I'll buy you a new outfit."

"I don't want a new outfit, Parker. I just want to help you. When you're sober you'll realize what a scary thing that was for all of us. You literally could have killed yourself."

Parker sighed as he stepped into the shower, clothes and all.

Annie stared at her room-service tray, debating if she wanted to eat the soggy french fries or not. She still couldn't figure out why she'd ordered the greasy food to begin with. She was a salad and broiled chicken person, not a burger and fries person. The wine was tasteless and felt like it had been watered down.

There was nothing on television, no in-room movies, and she'd forgotten to bring books with her. It was only eight-thirty. The night loomed ahead of her. She supposed she could take a shower and wash her hair and use up thirty or so minutes. Then what would she do? She wanted to cry so badly she bit down on her lower lip. Crying never solved anything. All crying did was give you a headache and red eyes.

Was she overreacting to Parker's announcement about his nephew? It wasn't the end of the world. What was it her father always said when they were children and things went wrong? Ah yes, we need to be thankful we have a roof over our heads, food on the table, and our health. For some reason, back then, those words had sounded important to her childish mind. Now they were just words even though they were true. She had all those things plus much more. She had her brother, two nephews and a niece she adored, two wonderful friends, and a godchild she loved dearly. And the money from the bank robbery—every penny of it, plus interest—was paid back, as of yesterday.

Annie was on her way to the bathroom when a knock sounded on her door. She frowned as she stood on her toes to look through the little glass hole. "Stella!" She couldn't open the door fast enough. "What are you doing here?"

"I don't know what I'm doing here. I had this feeling. Joe says he thinks I'm psychic sometimes. He could be right. I tune in to people. When I saw you this morning you looked like you did that night in Hawaii. I don't like it when my fairy godmother is miserable, and I know you're miserable. Why else would you pick this dump to stay in? You probably just stopped at the nearest hotel and hoped for the best. Right?"

"More or less." Annie grinned.

"I don't know the area very well yet, but I do know where they have good pizza and the beer is cold. They have other stuff, too, if you don't like pizza. Joe is home with a stomachache. He ate six eclairs and a meatball sub. I don't feel the least bit sorry for him. Besides, it was his idea for me to come here. I would have come anyway, it just makes it more official when a married couple agrees," Stella said breathlessly.

"Okay."

"So are you going to tell me what's wrong? I swear to you, Annie, I will never tell a soul, not even Joe. I'd like to help you if there's anything I can do. We owe you so much. I still can't believe you picked us of all the people in the world, to come here and take over the Daisy Shops. Joe just loves it, and the best part is the college kids love him. Joe just loves to shoot the breeze. He's one of those guys who can talk about anything to anybody. I swear, I don't know how that happened. He's just so smart. I'm just average. He should have gone to college, but his parents wanted him in that damn garage. I'm ready if you are. Do you think I talk too much?''

"No. I like listening to you. Sometimes I don't think I talk enough. Conversation is an art form, I guess. I never mastered it.''

The two women made small talk until they arrived at Dominic's in Avenel. When they were seated with frosty beer bottles in front of them, Stella said, "Now tell me what's wrong? Did something happen to that guy in Hawaii? He was one cool dude, Annie.''

"He asked me to marry him. I said yes.''

"Well, we need to drink a toast to that!'' Stella said, clinking her beer bottle against the one in Annie's hand.

"I sent him a Federal Express letter breaking it off two days ago.''

Stella waved away the waitress and set her beer bottle down carefully. "What am I missing here?''

"A long story.''

"I have all night. Before I forget, I want to tell you Joe went to the library here at Rutgers and read up on everything that was ever printed about you. We kind of view you as our own personal guardian angel the way you came out of the blue and did all this good stuff for us. We think it's just great that you were voted Businesswoman of the Year three times. You do all that good stuff for people no one knows about. Somebody had to do some heavy digging to come up with all those words they wrote about you. That must make you feel really good. It was easier after reading all that to understand why you helped me and Joe. You're a really good person, Annie. So I guess you had your reasons for whatever you felt you had to do with your fella. Want to tell me that long story? It will never go any further than right here.''

Annie felt a lump start to form in her throat. She could feel hot tears prick her eyelids. "I do need to talk to someone, Stella. If you ever tell a soul what I'm about to tell you, you could ruin my life. We need to be clear on this from the git-go."

Stella squirmed in her chair, her eyes wide and curious. "We're clear on it, Annie. Talk."

Annie talked. And talked. "Now do you understand why I can't marry Parker?"

"I understand why you *think* you can't marry Parker. If he loves you, it won't make any difference. What came before isn't important, Annie. That was your other life before you met him, and, to tell you the truth, that life is none of his damn business. As for that other. . . *episode*, that's over too. You paid it all back. Where the hell is Bonnie Doone, North Carolina? So you kept it a little longer than you should have. I can't say I wouldn't have done the same thing. It's so easy to Monday morning quarterback as Joe says. Listen to me, you aren't thinking of doing something foolish like *confessing*, are you? Please tell me the answer is no."

"I have been thinking about it, Stella. The problem is, I don't have the guts to do it. I just have this feeling the net is about to drop around me. It might be better if I turn myself in and take my punishment. This has hung over me for too many years. I think about it every single day of my life. It's the only wrong thing I've ever done in my entire life. To this day, I don't know why I kept that money. To answer your question, Bonnie Doone is H-fourteen on the map. I drove there and left the rest of the money. It was out of my way. Maybe they'll tie it to me, and maybe they won't. I did it at night. I'm not sure, but I think I put a lot of extra money in the bags. I put a lot of Clorox and fabric softener in the water behind the toilet. That was kind of clever, don't you think? I couldn't risk doing the washing-machine thing again."

"I need to think about this, Annie. I don't want you going off half-cocked and doing something you'll regret."

"What would you do, Stella?"

"I sure as hell wouldn't volunteer anything. I think I'd wait for them to catch up with me, and I don't see that happening. The case is closed, you paid back all of the money. The guy that got out of jail is just bitter and angry. A jury convicted him. He's probably lying about not being involved. If his father was as rich as you say he was at the time, the kid would have had the best defense going. So, what went wrong that a jury didn't buy into it? As for that insurance guy, *pffft,* he's history, too. He probably has a black mark on his personnel file and wants it erased. In the end the bank paid back the insurance money. Nobody is out anything."

"Except me. I'm out of all my emotions. I just want it to be over. What are they going to do to me if I confess?"

"Toss you in the slammer for starters. Now, how's that going to look?"

"Stella, it's wearing me down. My shoulders feel like I'm carrying the weight of the world on them. So I get some jail time, I take my lumps, and when I get out, Elmo will be gone, Jane and Daisy will have a jailbird for a friend, and I'll go off to some mountain retreat to live out my days. It's not pretty, is it?"

"God, no. Annie, you have a lot of money. I assume you must have some of the best lawyers money can buy. Oh, all right, let's order, Annie. I'll have the ravioli and another beer for each of us," Stella said to the waiter who had finally come to take their order.

"I'll have the same."

"Annie, I know I'm not in your league, but Joe said information is power. I believe that. Take all the harassing you've gone through, take the facts as you see them, and go to your lawyers and, remember, do not confess. Tell those fine legal minds to file suit against the insurance company and the investigator for harassment and discrimination. Always throw in discrimination. That makes everyone sit up and take notice. Then what you should do is call up Parker and tell him what you've done. Don't give him a chance to say a word until you finish. Then you hang up. You put the ball in his court so he's either going to dribble or do whatever those basketball players do. There's no proof anywhere of anything. That's what you can't get through your head.'' Stella grinned. ''Jeez, Annie, you pulled off the perfect crime.''

Annie burst into laughter. ''I never thought of it quite like that. I guess I did.''

''So, are you going to do what I suggested?'' Stella asked, waving a breadstick under Annie's nose.

''Yes. Yes, I am. I will call the attorneys first thing in the morning.''

''Attagirl. I love it when a woman kicks ass. So does Joe.''

Annie burst into laughter a second time. ''I'm not sure about Parker, though.''

''You're going for broke here, Annie. You don't have a thing to lose, and you have everything to gain. The love of a man who might someday be almost as good as my Joe. That man does love me. He'd suck my toes if I asked him to do it.''

Annie's face registered amazement. ''No kidding.''

''That's a mark of true love,'' Stella said. ''You need clean feet,'' she added.

Annie laughed so hard she almost fell off the chair. People at the neighboring tables stared at the two women. Annie just laughed harder.

Three beers later, Stella grasped Annie's arm to lead her from the restaurant. ''We shouldn't be driving in this condition,'' Annie said.

''You are absolutely right, Annie. I called Joe from the rest room. He's coming to pick us up. I'll get my car tomorrow.

Ah, there he is, stomachache and all. Our chariot awaits, madam,'' Stella said, bowing so low her husband had to catch her with his outstretched arm.

Annie started to laugh, doubling over. ''We have a snootful, Joe.''

''I see that. Pile in, ladies.''

''See, I told you he was a prince,'' Stella said as she landed in the front seat, her arms and legs at awkward angles.

Annie started to laugh all over again. She couldn't remember ever having such a fun evening. Her heart felt lighter, her shoulders straighter, and the world hadn't come to an end with her confession to a person she'd known less than a month.

Maybe somebody really was watching over her.

CHAPTER FIFTEEN

Peter Newman's apartment was small, shabby, and cluttered. A man's apartment, he was fond of saying. He looked around at his comfortable clutter, his gaze going to the young man standing in the doorway. A look of revulsion settled on his face. "What do you want this time, Mr. Pearson?"

"I want what I've always wanted. To be exonerated. I didn't rob that bank, and I want those years I spent in prison back. Do you know what happens to guys like me in prison?"

"We've been over this a dozen times, Mr. Pearson. A jury found you guilty, and there's no way I can change their decision. If your daddy's money didn't work for you, I have to assume you're guilty. Personally, I don't care one way or the other what happened to you in prison. You play, you pay. I'm not a cop. I'm an insurance investigator. I'm going to retire in six months, and I don't want anything to interfere with that retirement. When you first came to me for help I said I would allow you to look at the files. I've done that. My firm, and that includes myself, and the bank, have closed our files. My company has been repaid. The bank got their money back. Plus a little extra. You did your time. It's time to get on with your life. I can be of no further help to you. It's been thirteen years, Mr. Pearson.''

"I know how long it's been, Mr. Newman. I counted the hours and the days for all those years. Someone has to pay for that. I was not a party to that robbery. What can I do to make you understand that?''

"Nothing. Tell me, what will harassing those three people get you?''

"They know something. At least one of them does. I want that person to live what I lived all those years.''

"It ain't gonna happen, Mr. Pearson. The file is closed. That's the end of it.''

"It's the end of it when I say it's the end. Not one minute before. Who's going to give me back the best years of my life? You said yourself you believed one of those three was the guilty party. I can do what you couldn't do. You'd be surprised at the stuff I learned while I was incarcerated.''

"Believing and proving something are two different things. I have my orders. I closed the files. It's over. I don't want you to come here again. And in case you're thinking of ransacking my apartment, let me tell you, there are no files or notes here. I was asked to turn everything over to my superiors, which I did. Let's look at the best-case scenario. Supposing one of the three admits to taking the money. How in the hell is that going to prove you weren't one of the bank robbers? None of the three were anywhere near the bank that day. They have it all on film. Their alibis are airtight. You're swimming upstream.''

"If the money had been turned over that same day, I would have gotten a lesser sentence. I might have been allowed to plea-bargain. Oh, no, they sit on the fucking money, use it for their own purposes, then get an attack of conscience and return it. Meanwhile my ass is fried, and I go down for the count. Goddamn it, I didn't rob the fucking bank!''

"A jury of your peers says you did. What is it you want from me?"

"I want you to tell me everything you know about your Three Musketeers. I want to know what makes that old coot tick. What's that string bean got going for her? And the rich one. There's something there, I can smell it."

"They are what they are. Mr. Richardson is a bona fide pharmacist who retired at an appropriate age. He had no family. Miss Clark and Miss Abbott are like his children. He retired to the South shortly after they did, and he helps them with their business. I scoured Miss Clark's records, and they're as squeaky clean as Elmo Richardson's. Miss Abbott is married to a bounder who spends her money like water. She's clean, too. That's all I can tell you. Just tell me what it is you think you can do at this stage of the game?"

"My father has given me a large sum of money to try and prove my innocence. He's the only one in the whole world who believes in me. I'm going to use that money to try and get the person who took that money."

"And then what are you going to do? Kill them? Try to ruin them? Get it through your head—it's over. Look, Andy, put it behind you and get on with your life. Use the money your father gave you for a new start. You can't live in the past. You are so full of hate you aren't thinking straight. If anything happens to any of those people, the police are going to come after you. You're the first person they're going to come after. You have a record now. The Clark woman is rich, and she undoubtedly has the best legal counsel money can buy. She won't hesitate to turn her legal eagles loose on you. Now, don't slam the door when you leave."

The young man's face turned ugly. "Would it interest you to know that for the past month, at any given moment of the day or night, I can tell you exactly where those three people are and exactly what they're doing?" Newman shook his head, then watched Pearson square his shoulders, watched him ball his hands into tight fists. He sucked in his breath as he did his best to stare down the felon standing in front of him. He was forced to look away out of fear of what he was seeing in Andrew Pearson's eyes. For the first time in his life, he felt truly afraid. He was so limp with relief when he heard the door close behind Pearson that he collapsed onto the nearest chair.

When he felt strong enough to stand on his own two feet, Newman got up, fortified himself with a stiff drink, and picked up the phone. His first call was to Anna Clark. He wasn't the least surprised when Elmo Richardson answered the phone. He identified himself, and said, "Mr. Richardson, I'm calling to warn you about something I have no control over. I want you to listen to me very carefully, then I want you to relay this message to Miss Clark and Miss Abbott. If you think it will be better for me to call the two ladies, I will be happy to do so. I just happen to think it will sit better coming from you. What I'm about to tell you in regard to the case can be verified by the bank and by Boston Insurance. I believe you have the phone number. The bank and Boston Insurance have signed off on the case. The feds never sign off. It will just remain an open file and get shoved somewhere in some deep, dark file room. What you need to be aware of is Andrew Pearson and his hatred. He just left here. I believe the man is teetering on the edge. He's full of hatred and vengeance, and he plans to go after the three of you. He wants to get even for being sent to prison. He still maintains his innocence. It seems his father has given him a great deal of money to go out and try to find the real truth. Whatever that may be. He says he knows what the three of you are doing every minute of the day or night. I want you to know I did my best to discourage him. I also want you to know that the man frightened me. I don't frighten easily, Mr. Richardson."

"Why are you telling me all this, Mr. Newman? You've

hounded the three of us for years. Why should I believe anything you say now? What brought on this particular attack of conscience?"

"I was doing my job, Mr. Richardson. I did what I was told to do. Do you think I liked hounding you? I didn't. It was my job. I'm good at my job, and that's why I'm able to take early retirement. I plan to spend the rest of my days fishing and hunting. I throw the fish back, and if I see an animal, I shoot in the air so it runs away. I'm not a violent person. Andrew Pearson is a violent person. I know obsession when I see it. He's very clever. Those types of people usually are. I just wanted to warn you. I can't stress how important it is to go to the police. I probably don't have any right to ask this, but has anything happened? Have there been threats or unexplained things that are making you nervous?"

Elmo explained about Tom's ex-wife, the letters, and fear for Annie, who was on the road. "He's using your name, Mr. Newman. Tom's wife said the man who came to see her said his name was Peter Newman."

"It wasn't me. I told you, Boston closed the case. If I were you, I'd urge Miss Clark to return home as soon as possible. There's nothing else I can do, Mr. Richardson."

"You still think one of us did it, don't you, Mr. Newman?"

"Yes, Mr. Richardson, that's what I think. It's a moot point now. The case is closed. Like I said, I was just doing my job."

"I guess I appreciate the warning on behalf of the girls. Speaking for myself, go to hell, Newman."

Elmo could hear the insurance investigator chuckle as he hung up the phone. He thought the sound ominous.

Annie looked around the hotel room and realized she was sick to death of traveling, eating in restaurants, sleeping in strange beds. Right now she was so tired she knew if she leaned up against the wall she'd fall asleep. Obviously, it was time to go home. If she had one wish, it would be to fall into a deep, dreamless sleep that would last for twenty-four hours. She tossed her bag onto the bed. Why was it motels always had orange-flowered bedspreads and matching drapes?

As Annie uncapped a bottle of ice tea she noticed the red light blinking on the phone next to the bed. Answer it now or later? She looked at the watch Tom had given her. A super-duper job, he said, that gave the date, the time, doubled as a compass, which continent she was on, time in different countries, and if she could figure out how to adjust it, tell her if she was at sea level or not. August 26. Time was 4:45. The only people who knew she was here were Elmo, Tom, and Jane. God, had she really been traveling for eight weeks? Unless the super-duper Swiss watch was wrong, that's exactly how long she'd been on the road. She really had to be home by the weekend because it was Daisy's birthday, and her special present was due to arrive at ten in the morning the day after tomorrow. She wanted to be in attendance to see the little girl's face.

The phone rang just as she took the last swig from the ice tea bottle. Her tone was less than cordial when she barked a tired, "Hello."

"Annie, it's Elmo. Are you okay?"

"I think so. Why do you ask?"

Elmo told her about his conversation with Peter Newman. "You need to come home, Annie."

"I was just thinking that myself, Elmo. I'll leave first thing in the morning. I want to be home for Daisy's birthday. I heard sleep-away camp was a roaring success. How are the dogs? Are you just saying they miss me because you think I want to hear that or they really do miss me? Tell me, Elmo, did you believe Newman?"

"Yes, I did. He sounded worried. Maybe scared would be a better choice of words. The dogs do miss you, Annie. They sleep on your bed with your pillows. They run right up there as soon as we come in the house. I want you to be real careful driving home. It's a long stretch. If you get tired, stop and rest."

"I will, Elmo. How are you feeling?"

"I have good days and bad days. There was a sense of urgency in Newman's voice, Annie."

"If the case is closed, and we knew that when we tried to file suit six weeks ago, then he's out of our hair. When I get back, we'll file another police report and tell them what Newman said to you. It pays to stay on top of stuff like that. Any mail?"

"No mail from Hawaii if that's what you mean. There's a ton of other stuff here."

"Any calls?"

"None from Hawaii if that's what you mean. A list of calls to be returned is as long as my arm. Nothing pressing.

"Annie, you need to be extremely careful. I didn't like what Newman said about the Pearson man saying he knew what the three of us were doing every minute of the day. That means he has someone watching us or he's following one of us. I want you to call me when you start out and call along the way, every few hours. Jane and I will stay close to home until you get here. I don't think we need to worry about Tom, he's out of the loop. All that stuff with Mona was just to make us crazy. It worked for a little while."

"All right, Elmo. I'll see you late tomorrow night."

Annie popped the lid of a Diet Pepsi. She paced as she drank the diet drink. She was off the hook as far as the bank and the insurance company went. All she had to contend with now, according to Peter Newman, was a deranged young man bent on vengeance. She shivered in the air-conditioned room. Maybe she shouldn't wait until tomorrow morning to leave. Since she hadn't unpacked, she could settle her bill and get five hours worth of driving in before she called it a day. If she drank coffee along the way, she might even be able to do six or seven hours.

Twenty minutes later she was on I-81 heading south, where she would pick up I-70, then I-270, which would take her to the Beltway and I-95 and home. By leaving now she would miss the Washington, DC rush-hour traffic.

It was ten minutes past eleven when Annie crossed the state line into North Carolina. She cursed under her breath when she whizzed past the Roanoke Rapids exit. Now she had to drive another fifteen or so miles to the next turnoff. It all just went to prove she was beyond tired. She was exhausted, and on top of that it was starting to rain. She hated driving in the rain, hated the double headlights reflected on the asphalt road, hated the fact that she had to drive defensively on the busy interstate, where eighteen-wheelers and speed demons were kings of the road. She eased up on the gas pedal as she turned on the windshield wipers. She could feel the tension start to build between her shoulder blades as she leaned closer to the steering wheel for better visibility. Her eyes went to the rearview mirror. She wondered if it was her imagination that a pair of headlights behind her had stayed with her since Richmond. When she first became aware of the lights, she'd sped up and then slowed down to see what the car behind her would do. The driver had followed suit. As near as she could tell, the same car was still with her.

''Damn!'' She needed bright lights and human beings, not this endless stretch of highway with torrential rain. She drove steadily, staying in the right lane, praying for her first glimpse of the overhanging green-and-white sign indicating a turnoff. It was raining harder, a strong wind whipping up. A thunderbolt of sound almost ruptured her eardrums as a jagged streak of lightning ripped across the sky. A late-summer storm. She

certainly knew about daily summer storms living in South
Carolina—storms that could last fifteen minutes or two hours.

Annie wanted to sing her relief when she saw the overhead
sign directly ahead, swinging in the wild wind. She slowed the
car, eyes peeled to the right for the turnoff one mile down the
road. She risked a glance in her rearview mirror to see what
the car behind her was doing. The glimmering lights looked
like they were slowing, too. The relief she'd felt at the sight
of the sign turned to anxiety. If she did get off the exit, where
would it take her? Would there be a motel or restaurant? Was
it just a gas station or truck stop that served food? For all she
knew it might just be a rest stop with a bathroom facility,
vending machines, and dog runs for weary travelers with children and pets. There was no way she would get out of her car
if it was a rest stop, no matter how well lighted it was.

She would have missed the turnoff again if it hadn't been
for a vicious streak of lightning that lit up the sky. She reduced
her speed to fifteen miles an hour as she rounded the curve
that would take her to a secondary road. It was black as tar as
she crept along, the headlights six or seven car lengths behind
her. Maybe the driver was as tired as she was. Maybe the driver
had missed the Roanoke Rapids turnoff the way she had. Maybe
he or she just wanted to get out of the storm like she did. She
switched on her high beams, hoping to see the sign she knew
would be at the end of the exit road. The driving rain made it
impossible to see the sign. Her options were to go left or right.
Which way? She opted for right and turned on her signal light.
The car behind her followed suit. Perhaps he was depending
on her taillights to guide him. Her neck muscles felt so rigid
she could barely turn her head to either side. All about her
was darkness, with no other vehicular traffic. The shimmering
headlights behind her followed as she shifted the 4-by-4 into
first gear to crawl down the dark, steep, curvy road.

Fifteen minutes later, Annie knew she was in trouble when

there was still no sign of any other kind of traffic or habitation. She risked a glance at her gas gauge. Almost on E. That was why she'd wanted to get off at the Roanoke Rapids exit. Once the gas gauge light came on, she had five gallons left. With seventeen miles to the gallon, conceivably she could drive eighty-five miles to get to a gas station, if she was lucky enough to find one open at this hour of the night. Where in the hell was she? She wished now she'd called Elmo to tell him she was leaving. "Always after the fact, Annie," she muttered as she strained to see through the driving rain. Where was her cell phone? Had she put it in her purse or her carryall bag? And where was the gun Elmo and Tom insisted she carry with her? In the carry bag, along with the cell phone in the cargo area of the 4-by-4. A lot of good either one of them would do her now. Even if she did have the cell phone and gun, she knew they would be worthless to her. Never in a million years could she shoot someone. She'd only gotten the Glock to shut both men up. The cell phone would be worthless out here in nowhere land.

The headlights of the vehicle behind her were still shimmering in her rearview mirror. She'd never been this tired, this wired up in her whole life. Who was the person behind her? Friend or foe? Elmo's ominous words rang in her ears.

What if I die out here? Who would find me? More to the point, when would I be found? Don't think about things like that. Think about all the dreams you had. Think about the relief you felt when you finally sent the rest of the money to the bank.

The warning light for the gas gauge flashed on, once, twice, then remained steady. Eighty-five miles to go. Possibly she could drive an hour and a half if she were going sixty miles an hour. She had no idea how long the gas would last the way she was crawling along.

Overhead, thunder rolled like an angry bongo player bent on destroying his drums. Lightning danced across the sky. She saw trees and fields and deep ditches along the side of the road and nothing else.

The lights behind her remained steady. If she wanted to, she could put the utility truck she was driving to the test. The video she'd watched with such intensity said it could do *anything,* including going up steep mountains, going down steep mountains, fording rivers and gorges, driving faster than a pack of wolves. If the person following her, and she knew now that was exactly what was happening, thought she knew what she was doing and where she was going, she could make a turn to the right or left, go down and up the ditch, and hope and pray to God she didn't hit a tree on the upswing. She needed another bolt of lightning to show her the way clear. If the person following her was driving a regular car, even if it had four-wheel drive, he'd never be able to cross the ditch. Did she dare risk it? What if she got stuck? What if she didn't shift quick enough? The video said that would *never* happen. If this vehicle's makers said it could prevail on the frozen tundra, the African jungles, and the Sahara Desert, then it should be able to cross a North Carolina *ditch. Go for it, Annie.*

Annie continued to drive, waiting for lightning to light the sky. Thunder rolled overhead, but the lightning was slow in coming. That must mean the storm was moving north. Or maybe it was east. She wished she could look at the watch on her wrist. The lights behind her seemed closer. Annie's throat closed up tight. She felt an adrenaline rush as a bolt of lightning finally zipped across the sky. She didn't think twice as she cut the wheel to the left, floored the gas pedal, and took off. She was jolted forward, but kept her foot to the pedal. The Rover strained, bucked, shot backward, then forward, clearing the ditch. "Way to go, Annie!" she shouted at the top of her lungs. An open field lay directly in her line of vision. The twin set of headlights didn't seem to be moving. That had to mean the driver was stuck in the ditch, or he'd stopped in time to avoid going nose down.

Now, if she could just figure out where she was, she would be okay. When she turned on the overhead light to look at her watch, the compass part of the Swiss mechanism told her she was going southwest. Before she searched out her map she needed to crawl into the back for her carryall bag. If nothing else, the cell phone and the gun would give her a false sense of security. She felt another adrenaline surge as she stuck the Glock into the waistband of her jeans. The cell phone went into her denim shirt pocket. Sooner or later she'd be in range and she'd be able to call Elmo and Jane on the cell phone.

The car's headlights were still faintly visible. That had to mean her lights were visible as well. Would the driver of the car realize she was at a standstill or was he incensed that he was stuck in a ditch? There wasn't *that* much distance between them. Possibly a half mile at the most. She needed to move and she needed to move *now*.

Annie shifted gears and knew instantly her back wheels were mired in mud. Lots and lots of mud. She must be in some kind of cow pasture, and of course there was mud. She climbed from the car, the flashlight from the console in her hand. If there was ever a time to throw a hissy fit, this was it. There was no way she could hope to get the Rover out of the mud. Only a tow truck with a top grade winch was going to get this truck out. She looked down at her feet and saw only mud. She struggled to pull her right foot out and heard a loud *glop*. She lifted her other foot out of the mud and heard the same sound. Damn. She was going to need *wings* to get out of this mess. There was nothing behind her but total blackness and driving rain. She squinted, trying to see if the car's headlights were still on. She simply couldn't tell.

Move, move, move, her mind shrieked. *Get out of this mud and get out now. Move, girl!*

Moving in the ankle-deep mud was the single most torturous thing she'd ever done in her life. Where were her guts and willpower? In the fucking mud, that's where. The wind whipped at her face and hair, doing its best to send her backward, but her tenacious hold in the thick mud prevented it. Rain lashed at her from the front and back. She was moving, but only by instinct. She couldn't keep her eyes open and needed both arms for balance so she didn't fly forward into the gloppy mud. This was not where she should be with all the lightning playing across the sky. She needed cover. Even a fool knew lightning loved open fields. Acres and acres of endless fields. Where were the damn trees she'd seen earlier? Left or right? For one brief second the entire field turned light as day. Trees to the left. Not many but some. Maybe they would lead to other denser wooded areas. She turned, but her feet remained mired in the mud, forcing her forward. Before she knew what was happening, she was facedown in the mud. She started to curse, using every unmentionable word she'd ever heard until her mouth filled with mud.

Annie struggled to get to her feet as rain slammed at her from all sides. It was impossible, and she knew it. Better to crawl on all fours and hope for the best. Somewhere along the way she'd lost her shoes. She moved as fast as she could then when she heard a sound she couldn't identify. Would a man be able to make better time in the mud? Would his height and weight help him move faster than she was able to do? She crab-walked as fast as she could, her heart beating like a trip-hammer. Where was he? How close was he? Did he know she'd veered off to the left? Was he dumb enough to head across the field with the lightning ripping across the sky? Did he even care?

Annie started to cry when she realized how little headway she was making. She was so tired, and she ached with the strain of moving through the thick mud. She stopped, falling forward again. *Please, God, help me. Please give me the strength to get up and move. Please.*

She heard it again, the same strange noise she'd heard before. This time the sound seemed to be coming from the trees, the same trees she was trying to reach. Maybe the person chasing her had seen the same trees and gotten there ahead of her. Well, she still had the gun tucked into her jeans. She knew now she was capable of using it if she had to. Tom and Elmo were right. Faced with a do-or-die situation and the gun was the only way she'd walk away safe, she'd use it. If she got the chance, she could always aim for the person's kneecaps. She wondered if the barrel was full of mud and, if so, would it fire? She'd probably kill herself in the bargain. She shook her head to shake off some of the thick mud that was filling her ears and nose.

Leapfrog, Annie. Do it. Do it now, a voice inside her head warned. Annie obeyed, then she was out of the mud and on soaking-wet pine needles.

Exhausted, she rolled over and let the rain beat down on her. For one wild, crazy moment she thought someone was *licking* her face. She must be delirious. She rolled over again and suddenly felt a solid weight on her back. Frightened out of her wits, she tried to make her tongue work. "Who are you? What do you want? I don't have any money. I'm half-dead. Leave me alone," she pleaded as she tried to work her hand down to her waistband for the Glock.

"Woof!"

Annie rolled over, struggled to sit up. She couldn't see the animal, but she could feel his breath on her face. "Oh, God, oh, God! Come here, you dear sweet thing. Let me touch you. God, you're real. You're really real. Please, God, don't let this be a wild dog."

The dog woofed again, louder this time.

"Same to you, fella. I need some help here."

More barking.

"Yeah, okay," Annie said as she sensed the dog moving in the darkness. She was on her feet and moving, too. Obviously that was what the dog wanted. Maybe he would lead her some-place safe. Maybe to the owner of all these fields. "I'm coming, I'm coming."

Annie fell four times during the long trek. All four times the dog turned to wait, licking her face, barking in her ear until she thought her head would explode. Each time she got up and staggered after the dog. She wished she knew what he looked like. Maybe the dog was a she. Female dogs were very protec-tive. But then so were male dogs.

"Woof!"

"Lights!" Annie said hoarsely. "Listen, dog, I can't make it. You're going to have to go and get someone. Your master. Your mistress. When I fell the last time I think I did something to my knee. This is as far as I can go. The rest is up to you." Annie lurched drunkenly, then fell. The dog, uncertain, whined softly. "Go get help. Please, dog, go get help," Annie whim-pered.

She felt the dog move, knowing he'd recognized the urgency in her voice. Then there was nothing but blackness.

She felt herself being picked up, felt the rain beating on her face and body. Her knee felt like it was on fire. She knew she was safe because she could hear the dog whining and whimpering. Or were the sounds coming from her? She didn't know, and she didn't care. She was safe. That was all she cared about.

"Good boy, Jake. I can take it from here," the giant said.

"You smell good. Is that your dog?"

The chuckle she heard was deep and rich. "Jake is my dog.

He's the one who found you. A nice porterhouse steak would be appreciated when you're feeling better.''

"You got it. He's got it. Whatever." And then the blackness overcame her again.

"I guess my scent overpowered her again, Jake. She's a bit of a mess right now. I guess we should just take her to the shower and let the water do the rest. What do you think, boy?''

The golden Labrador nudged his master's knee.

"She said I smelled good.'' His chuckle was just as rich and deep as the first time. "We'll talk about your disobedience later on, Jake. You know the drill: you go out, you do your business, and you come in and we go to bed. That's the rule. You break the rule and you get no Oreos. You got that?''

"Woof, woof.''

"I'm going to ignore the rule this time because obviously you picked up on this young lady's distress. Wonder what she looks like under all this mud.''

In the kitchen under the blinding fluorescent lighting, Clay Mitchell stared down at the woman in his arms. "Okay, Jake, lead the way to the guest bathroom.'' The Lab bounded up the kitchen stairway and down the hall, his master directly behind him.

The bathroom was blue-and-white tile, the shower stall, overly large with a corner seat. Clay had never known the true purpose of the seat. There was one in his own shower, too, but he'd never used it. He sat Annie down carefully, nudging her to wakefulness. She tried to open her eyes, but the thick mud on her lashes made them close again.

"Stay with me, young lady. I'm going to turn on the shower. I think it might be better to wash off the mud first and then you can shower up and wash your hair.''

"You smell good,'' Annie said. "My brother smells like you. At first I thought Tom had found me. I did something to my knee. I don't know if I can stand.''

"That's why this seat is in here. I'll adjust the showerhead, and the spray will do the rest. Here, I'll help you with your jacket." Annie was like a rag doll as her benefactor pulled and tugged at the denim jacket. A hissing sound escaped his lips when he saw the gun in the waistband of her jeans. Annie reached for it and set it on the tile seat next to her.

Clay tossed the muddy jacket into the corner of the shower. He adjusted the showerhead, then closed the door. He heard her voice as he moved about the bathroom. "I'm not a criminal. This gun is for my personal safety. Someone was chasing me."

"Sounds plausible," Clay said to Jake, who was up on the bed, trying to turn down the covers. When he succeeded in pulling the blanket from under the pillows, he sat up on his haunches.

"Yeah, yeah. You do good work, Jake. Who in the hell would be chasing someone like her through our fields during one of the worst storms of the year?" He walked over to the window and sat down on the seat. As a kid, this had been his room. He'd sat here trying to figure out the secrets of the universe, and this was where he sat to wait for Santa when he was little. From this same seat he'd wished on the first star so many times he'd lost count. And this was where he'd come when he was punished and confined to his room. Light-years ago. The gun was serious-looking. A Glock, if he wasn't mistaken.

"I need some scissors!"

Jake bounded off the bed and barreled to the bathroom.

"What for?" Clay shouted.

"My knee is too swollen to pull the jeans down. I can't get all the mud off. I could use some help here."

Help. She wanted him to help her take off her clothes. A decade ago he would have shouted, "I'm your man." That was before Ann Marie and her death. Now he was nervous and jittery at the thought of seeing a naked woman in his bathroom.

"I don't have any scissors. At least I don't think I do. Will a pocketknife do?"

"I guess so. Listen, I've been trying, but I can't get my clothes off. You have to help me."

"Listen, I think if you just . . ."

"Are you telling me you won't help me?"

"I'm not saying that. Look, if you don't care, then I don't care. Most women who *drop in* like you do wouldn't want someone seeing their naked body."

"Right now, mister . . . what is your name anyway? I don't give a damn if you see my naked body or not. I don't care if your dog sees my naked body. Can we get this show on the road? My knee is killing me."

"I'm Clay Mitchell. Okay, *let's do it.*"

Annie clenched her teeth as Clay's knife ripped through the wet denim. She squealed her relief when the denim broke free of her swollen knee. "Okay, help me with my shirt," she said, standing up and hobbling about on one foot. "My name is Annie Clark. I like your dog."

"Just because he saved your life don't go getting any ideas. He's mine." Everything else in his life had been ripped away from him. Nobody was taking his dog.

"All I said was I liked your dog. Does this gun scare you? What's your problem?"

"I don't have a problem and, no, your gun doesn't scare me." Perfectly proportioned. Just like Ann Marie. Blond hair. Ann Marie had dark hair. This woman had blue eyes like the bluebells Ann Marie had planted. Ann Marie had green eyes. He wanted to say something smart, something totally outrageous about her lacy underwear. Years ago, before Ann Marie, he wouldn't have had a problem coming up with the right words. He would have been able to make this young woman laugh with his remark. These days he was a stick-in-the-mud, a recluse, a man without a life. She was staring at him, waiting.

"That underwear doesn't leave much to the imagination," he blurted.

That's just what the girls at Victoria's Secret had said. "I think I can handle the rest. Do you have a robe or something I can borrow?"

"I'll hang it on the door. In the meantime I'll get you an ice pack for your knee." As an afterthought he said, "Do you want something to eat?"

"I think I'm too tired to chew, Mr. Mitchell. I would like something to drink, though. Do you have an extra toothbrush, and I'm going to need a phone."

"I think I can handle all that. At the Mitchell farm we aim to please." He wondered if the bedraggled woman would pick up on his sarcasm. It occurred to him, as he walked down the steps, to wonder why his heart was beating so fast. And why he was sweating. And why his dog was still upstairs when he was always at his side. Trust a woman to foul things up and knock everything out of sync.

When Clay marched up the steps forty minutes later with a tray holding a new toothbrush, his portable phone, a tray of double Oreo cookies, and an ice pack, he saw Annie curled up on the bed, nuzzling Jake, who was loving every minute of it.

She sure wasn't beautiful. He wasn't even sure if she was pretty. Her skin was shiny and looked like she'd taken at least two layers of it off when she scrubbed up. The gun was on the pillow next to her. The gun made everything different.

Annie slapped the ice bag on her knee and yelped. "How close is the nearest doctor? Is there anyone who can pull my truck out of the mud? You forgot the aspirin."

"Gee, did I? Do you suppose I forgot them because you didn't ask for them?"

"Could be," Annie said, biting into one of the Oreos. She handed one to Jake.

"Your master is a bit testy. I have two big dogs like you.

They like Fig Newtons. Thanks for bringing me here, big guy. You know what they say, when you save a person's life you are responsible for them from that day on.''

''That's a myth,'' Clay snapped.

''The Chinese don't think so,'' Annie said, licking off the frosting between the cookie's layers. Jake eyed them hungrily. Annie handed them over. ''I have two German shepherds. This is a beautiful dog. I bet you love him to death.''

''Yeah, I do. Now, do you mind telling me what the hell you were doing in my field at this time of night with a gun in your pants?''

''I told you. Someone was chasing me. How was I supposed to know your field was a sea of mud? I didn't know what his intentions were. I was plain-out scared because no one knew where I was. I wasn't supposed to leave until tomorrow, but I left earlier and didn't call. Then the storm came up, I took the wrong turnoff, and I was low on gas. That's the story.''

''Why was someone chasing you?''

Annie sniffed. ''Like I know! Why do perverts do the things they do? I'm assuming you're going to let me stay here tonight. I'll be more than glad to pay you for all the trouble I've been. I just love this dog,'' she said sleepily. A minute later she was sound asleep.

Clay picked up the tray. ''You stay here, Jake. Come and get me if things change.''

The Lab raised his head just long enough to stare for a second at his master. He woofed softly before he lowered his head to nuzzle Annie's leg.

Clay closed the door halfway. He made his way downstairs to take up his position in front of the television. He knew for a fact there wasn't much on the boob tube at three in the morning. One long arm reached out to the portable bar behind his chair. He popped a Corona and leaned back.

Every night for three long years he'd sat in this chair staring at nothing. Three long years since the knock sounded on his door and the sheriff told him straight out that Ann Marie was dead. Some damn drunk had run her off the road and her car turned over and exploded. Three very long years.

Jake had just been a pup then, but he knew Ann Marie wasn't coming back. He'd cried and whimpered right along with him for all those long nights. Tonight the big Lab had been friskier than he'd seen him since puppyhood.

Why the big gun? Who in the hell is Annie Clark?

CHAPTER SIXTEEN

At the first sign of approaching dawn, Clay was off his chair to make his way to the back door. Time to check out Annie Clark's story. A battered Dodge Dakota with close to 200,000 miles on its odometer waited next to a rotting barn. He loved this old vehicle that had once belonged to his brother Bobby. Retired now and living in Key Biscayne, Florida, Bobby and his wife drove a pearl white Cadillac. Bobby had been a star player for the Celtics back then, and he'd just been a young kid learning the game. In most ways his own star had outshone Bobby's when he played with the Lakers. He'd invested almost all of the money he'd earned playing in the NBA. Those investments plus his pension enabled him to live a life of luxury if he chose. Luxury had never been a top priority with him, so he'd chosen to come back here to the farm when he quit the FBI. Retirement at the age of forty-four wasn't at all what he thought it would be. All he did these days was a little gardening, a little cooking, a lot of reading, and a lot of hiking with his dog.

The engine of the battered truck turned over on the first try. He headed out to the main road, where he turned left. All night long he'd tried to figure out just where Annie Clark left the road to cross his fields. Five miles down the road he spotted a dark blue Chevrolet Cavalier nose down in the ditch on the left side of the road. He pulled over to the narrow shoulder. So the lady with the gun was telling the truth. He pushed his Lakers cap back on his head as he stared at the car. No license plate. He didn't know why or how he knew, but he was certain there would be no fingerprints anywhere in this particular car. He hopped the ditch to stare across the field. In the distance he could see a mud-caked all-terrain vehicle, its back end low in the soft mud. Obviously he needed to call Omar's Towing Service, and the sheriff as well, if Annie Clark gave the okay. For some reason she didn't seem the type to want strangers knowing her business. Satisfied that her story checked out, Clay climbed into his truck and headed back to the farm.

Jake was waiting for him on the back steps. He tussled with him for a few moments before entering the house. "So, how's our guest? Guess it's time for coffee. The lady had meat on her bones, so I'd say that warrants breakfast. Bet you could go for some bacon and eggs. Come on, boy, kitchen duty calls, but first I think we need to check on our guest."

Jake raced up the back staircase and stood panting outside the door of Annie's room. She was awake, propped up on the pillows.

"How's your knee?"

"It's not as swollen as it was last night. It throbs. Can I trouble you for some more aspirin?"

"Have you been up yet?"

"I can't put any weight on it if that's what you mean. I can hop around on my right foot, though. Enough to let your dog out and get back up here. If you can get someone to pull my truck out of the mud, I think I can make it back home."

"That probably isn't a good idea. I'm going to call Henry Masterson. He's our local doctor, and he makes house calls. However, he doesn't like to be called before seven-thirty. It's just that now. I'll get you some clothes and help you downstairs."

"I don't know how to thank you, Mr. Mitchell."

"My name is Clay. Mr. Mitchell was my father. Are you hungry?"

"I'm starving. Anything will be fine. I hate to keep troubling you."

"I'm afraid I'm not a very good host. I don't get much company way out here in the country."

"Why is that, Mr . . . Clay?"

"People gave up on me a while back. Okay, here's some shorts and a shirt. If you wait here, I think I know where there are some scissors. I'll call the doctor and be back up to help you down the steps." He returned moments later with a pair of orange-handled scissors.

"Sounds good," Annie said, eyeing the clothes Clay laid on the bed. Women's clothes. They looked like they would fit, too. She wondered whom they belonged to. She asked.

"They used to belong to my wife," Clay said curtly.

"Oh," was all Annie could think of to say.

"She was killed by a drunk driver three years ago. How do you like your eggs?"

"Over easy. I'll take three. Do you make hash browns? If you do, I like onions and peppers in mine."

"That's how they serve them at Millie's Café in town. She doesn't charge extra for the grease, either."

Annie laughed. "Guess that means we aren't having hash browns."

Jake threw his head back and howled.

"Now you've done it. He won't be happy unless I make the whole nine yards. This dog is smart. He eats what I eat. Boy, does he like Boston cream pie. Minus the chocolate. Chocolate isn't good for dogs.''

"I know. Mine eat people food, too. The vet has a fit. They're healthy and happy, and that's all I care about. Oreos are chocolate, Clay.''

"Yeah, I know. He only gets them once in a while. He's kind of partial to Pecan Sandies. I'll make the call and be back.''

"You know what, Jake,'' Annie whispered to the dog. "He's a curmudgeon but kind of nice. It's hard when you lose someone you love. I guess you miss her, too, don't you, big guy?'' Jake whimpered. "I wish you could talk. I owe you my life. I guess you kind of know that, don't you?'' Jake whimpered again.

"So what do you think?'' Jake continued to whimper. "Ah, I get it. Her scent is still in these clothes, eh? Okay, we can fix that right away.'' Annie pulled off the shorts and shirt and slipped back into Clay's robe. "Howzat?''

"Woof.''

"Gotcha,'' Annie said, tickling the big dog behind the ears.

"Didn't the clothes fit?'' Clay said from the doorway.

"Actually they did, but Jake didn't seem to want me to wear them. I guess maybe your wife's scent is still in them. It's okay. If you get someone to pull out my car, I have things in the cargo area. I'll just stay in the robe if you don't mind.''

"The doctor is on the way, and so is Omar. He's going to tow your truck here. An hour at the most. By the way, as soon as it got light out, I drove down the road to see if I could spot your truck. There's a Chevy stuck in the ditch, nose down. No license plate. Door was locked. The sheriff will have to decide what to do about it.''

Annie nodded. "It smells good. I think frying onions and peppers smell better than perfume. Guess you're making hash browns, huh?''

"Jake likes them. You like them. I like them. So, I said to

myself, what the hell, I had everything in the fridge, so we're having hash browns.''

''I hear a car.''

''It's probably Henry. He likes hash browns, too.''

Thirty minutes later, Annie stared at the old doctor in dismay. ''You want me to stay off my leg for forty-eight hours? Can't you bandage up my knee? I have to get home, I really do. I'll keep ice on it.''

''The answer's no. You stay off that leg.''

''What if I find someone willing to drive my truck to Charleston? I could stay in the back with my leg up.''

''That would be okay. Sorry, Clay, I can't stay for breakfast. Leroy Adams broke his collarbone yesterday, and I need to check on him. Mind me now, Missy Clark.''

When the screen door slammed behind the doctor, Annie asked, ''Do you know anyone I could hire to drive me home?''

''No. I'll do it.''

''Oh, no, I can't expect you to do that. How will you get home?''

''Don't you know someone who could drive me back?''

Annie burst out laughing. ''I might know someone. Are you sure you don't mind?''

''I'm a little tired of watching the grass grow. I haven't been to Charleston in a long time. Might do Jake and me some good to get out and about.''

''Any other time, I wouldn't care but it's my goddaughter's birthday tomorrow, and I have to go to the airport to pick up her gift.''

''It must be pretty special.''

''It is.'' Annie told him Jane and Daisy's story.

''What a bastard! For sure I'll drive you. You really think this little Teacup Yorkie is going to do the trick where the little girl is concerned, huh?''

''You bet I do. Animals are the best cure for physical and

mental problems that I know of. Look at you and Jake. What would you have done without him? Rosie and Harry got me through some bad times. Daisy needs someone to love. Someone to love her unconditionally. The pup will be just for her, and it's only going to weigh around five pounds. It will be her own special bundle of love. Child and dog. What could be better? When she gets home from school, he'll be waiting for her. He'll sleep at the foot of her bed if he's not on her pillow. I want it to work for that little girl. I want her to have happy memories. The ones concerning her father are not happy at all. Most likely those memories will fade in time, but they'll always be there in the background. The dog will make it easier to bear. She did well at camp for the most part, but she isn't over the hump.''

''You're absolutely right. I'll drive you.'' Clay's voice said he wasn't taking no for an answer. ''You know, if you eat all that, you won't have to worry about moving. You won't be able to stand up, much less move.''

''I eat like this all the time. I have a great metabolism. Tell me about you, Clay. Do you farm here? What do you grow?''

''Weeds. I retired here. I played basketball in college and was good enough to be drafted by the Lakers. When rheumatoid arthritis cut my career short, I joined the FBI. I may have been the oldest rookie agent in the Bureau. When I got tired of chasing the bad guys, I came back to the farm because my wife wanted to live here. She died six months after we got here. She had this grand plan to raise melons. She had a green thumb. We were going to have a few chickens, a milk cow, and two horses. Both of us liked to ride. We had it all planned out. Winters we were both going to teach at Chapel Hill. Spring and summers would be spent here at the farm. It just never got off the ground the way most dreams do. I made megadollars and invested wisely. Was an All-Star six years running. Money still comes in from all the endorsements I did back then. The first year and a half is pretty much a blur. My snoot was in the bottle most of the time. Jake took care of me. He really did. Henry stopped by once or twice a week and brought food his wife cooked. I can't remember if I ate it or not. Then one day, Jake got sick. That woke me up in a hell of a hurry. That's the end of my story. What's yours? I'd really like to know why someone who looks like you packs a serious gun like a Glock. I would have thought a twenty-two would be more to your liking. Remember, I was a Special Agent. I know about stuff like that.''

Annie felt her heart rate accelerate. Just her luck to meet up with an FBI agent. ''I told you, I spend a lot of time on the road. My brother and Elmo made me get the gun. I know how to shoot. I'm not sure if I could kill anyone or not. I know the rule is if you pull out a gun you better be prepared to shoot. I'd probably aim for the kneecap.''

''What do you do that you're on the road?''

''I check on my stores. Make sure everything is running smoothly. I like to stay personal and up close with my employees.''

''What kind of stores?''

''Coffee shops. I have one in Chapel Hill. They're called Daisy Shops.''

''Jesus, you're kidding! Ann Marie loved that place. We went to Chapel Hill before we moved here to set things up. In one week's time I don't think I ever ate so many tuna sandwiches and brownies or drank so much coffee. You own those, huh?''

''Yeah. We're going to start franchising them. Elmo is working on it, and so is my brother. My friend Jane is back in the fold, too. We're also going to start selling coffee by the pound.''

''Who's Elmo?''

''He's a wonderful friend who's been like a father to Jane

and me. He's also very sick right now,'' Annie said with a catch in her voice.

"I read about you in the Sunday papers a few times. I thought you looked vaguely familiar. You were voted Businesswoman of the Year a few years running, weren't you?'' Annie nodded. "Ann Marie thought it was wonderful the way you started up your business on a shoestring. I think you would have liked her.''

"I'm sure I would have.''

"There's more, isn't there?'' Clay asked.

"More what?''

"More than you're telling me.''

"No, that's pretty much it. Unless you mean about my personal life. I was more or less engaged to be engaged and maybe married. It didn't work out. Not that it's any of your business.''

"Why didn't it work out?''

"Are you writing a book or something? My personal life is no one's business.''

"Are you hiding something? Are you ashamed of something? It's a simple question. Most people would ask it out of concern for you, which is what I just did.''

"I met this man a long time ago. I more or less fell in love but he had a different culture than mine. He owns the coffee company that supplies most of my coffee. His parents left the whole kit and caboodle to him, and his sisters were out in the cold. I stuck my nose into his business and told him what I thought of that idea. At the time I don't think he appreciated it. I didn't see him again for a long time. Then in June I went to Hawaii to renew our contract and to order more coffee. His sister was at the helm. Kind of. Flash forward. We met again, and it was like old times. But he still has ideas and beliefs I do not share. My opinion is whatever came before is not important. He seems to think it is. I called it off. Well, first, I moved up the wedding date from February of next year to

September, next month, because I wanted Elmo to give me away. He's on borrowed time. Then I changed my mind and wrote to tell him so. He called Jane once, she passed on his message, and I haven't heard from him since.''

"And your feelings are . . .''

"Numb. What's your feeling on the past?''

"I say let sleeping dogs lie. Resurrecting something always manages to hurt someone. Why is it people think they need to know every stinking little detail about the other person? Life starts when you meet. Life is what two people make it. The past is prologue. I guess you're bumming, huh?''

"I'm over the worst of it. I'm just going to be an old maid. What are you going to do?''

"Exist.''

"That's a bummer, too.''

"I could coach if I wanted to.''

"Maybe you just aren't ready to take that step yet. Three years is a long time, and yet in other respects it isn't long at all. When the time is right, you'll do something.''

"That sounds like something Ann Marie would say. Sometimes I can't remember what she looked like. Other times I can *feel* her. What would you do if I leaned across this table and kissed you?''

"I'd probably slap you. Why would you want to kiss me?''

"To see if I'm as dead as I feel. You're pretty. I even kind of like you. My dog likes you. You have a brain. We can talk intelligently.''

"Okay, go ahead.''

At best it was a brotherly kiss.

"Well?''

"The earth didn't move. My brother Tom kisses me like that. You need to put some gusto into it.''

"Oh, yeah.''

"Yeah. You smell good, though.''

"Yeah?"

"Oh, yeah. I'm a lady that likes things to smell good. Especially a man. Do you like perfume?"

"I like perfume. Flowery stuff. Soft music. I'm kind of sentimental. At least I was. I don't know what I am these days."

"Me too," Annie said. "Want to try again?" She wondered where the laughter in her voice was coming from.

"Well, hey, sure." He leaned across the table.

Annie closed her eyes. They snapped open almost immediately. "Whoa."

"You said gusto." Clay laughed. "So, did the earth move?"

"Nah. I think you just need more practice. Don't get any ideas about me being your guinea pig."

"Didn't it move even a little bit? A tremor?"

"Nope!"

Jake let loose with a sudden earsplitting bark.

"Guess that means Omar is here with your truck. You're sure you want to leave? You're welcome to stay as long as you like. One of the sofas in the den opens to a bed. You could sleep down here, so you don't have to climb the steps."

"No, I have to get back. Daisy is what's important right now."

"Let me settle up with Omar. He always carries extra gas with him, so I'll have him fill your tank. You said you need your bag, right?"

"If it isn't too much trouble. My wallet's in my purse. Just take the money out to pay him."

"Omar sends bills. He likes to keep his wife busy. She handles the business end of things. You never throw Omar a curve."

"Okay. Guess you have to clean up. It was a great breakfast. Thanks."

"My pleasure. I could just throw the dishes and stuff away. If I did that, we could leave as soon as you get dressed."

"Go for it!" Annie giggled. "I always wanted to do that. It's so ... decadent. Can you imagine just eating and then throwing everything away, even the pots and pans?"

"That's why they make paper plates and plastic forks and knives."

"Yeah, I know, but it isn't the same thing."

"I guess that's called a quirk of your nature."

"Admit it, Clay, wouldn't you like to do the same thing?" Annie teased. "Wow, look at my truck!"

"Isn't that one of those pricey ATVs whose advertisements say it can do anything?"

"You mean like going over the frozen tundra, handling the jungles of Africa and the Sahara Desert, not to mention scaling high mountains and carrying a whole zoo of animals? Yep, that's the one. It doesn't do mud."

"I'd demand my money back."

"I'm thinking about it."

Annie finished her coffee and wished she had another cup. She looked down at her knee. It was as big as a melon. She swallowed three more aspirin from the bottle on the table with the last swig of coffee.

"Okay, here's your bill and here's your bag. Your purse wasn't in the car. Don't go thinking Omar took it. He's a deacon in the church. I think it's safe to say the guy chasing you last night took it. Did you have anything important in it?"

"Yes, I did. Do you have a cell phone we can take with us?"

"Sure. I keep one in the truck for emergencies."

"Good, I'll call Elmo and Jane, and they can notify everyone. They'll have to get the locks changed on the house. I had spare keys in my wallet. Is there a bathroom down here?"

"Off the hallway."

Annie hopped to the bathroom. Clay handed her the bag. She emerged five minutes later in a yellow sundress properly spritzed with sinful-smelling perfume.

"Okay, we're done here," Clay said, tossing the two fry pans into the trash bag. "Can you make it to the truck on your own?"

"Sure, but you'll have to adjust the seats."

"Just let me take this trash out. I'll get some pillows to elevate your leg and an ice pack. I just have to get Jake's blanket and lock up. Is it okay for him to sit in the front with me? He knows how to buckle up."

"Absolutely. Will you bring my bag?"

Annie climbed into the truck. She had a bad moment when she realized whoever had chased her the night before had sat in this vehicle, touching and going through her things and stealing her purse. "Bastard," she muttered.

"I'm going to need at least a five-minute lesson to learn all this fancy-dancy stuff. You need to buy American."

"I'm thinking about it."

"You think a lot, don't you?" Clay teased.

"Keeps your mind sharp. Everybody *thinks.*"

"Settle back and enjoy the ride, Miss Clark. Would you care for some music or would you like me to expound on the vagaries of the world?"

"Music please. But after I call home," Annie said sweetly.

"I think you were fibbing about the earth not moving."

"No, I wasn't fibbing."

"In my heyday I was known as Shake, Rattle, and Roll Mitchell," Clay snorted.

"What year was that?"

"None of your business. I'm not sharing anything else with you, Annie Clark."

"Okay."

He was nice. She liked him. For a little while she'd forgotten about Parker Grayson.

It was a great welcoming home party. Even her brother was standing on the porch along with Elmo, Jane, and Daisy. Rosie and Harry stood next to Daisy.

Clay fit right in from the moment he carried her up the front steps to the house. Everyone shook hands and thanked him for taking such good care of her. She watched as the dogs checked each other out. Rosie circled Clay several times, while Harry untied his shoelaces. Jake stood back, his eyes going from Rosie to Harry and back to Clay. Satisfied that nothing was going to happen to his master, Jake entered the house.

Everyone immediately started fussing over Annie. Jane insisted she stretch out on the sofa. Tom brought her a glass of frosty ice tea. Daisy brought two of her storybooks for her to read and then turned on the television, handing her the remote control. Elmo, his breathing raspy and harsh, sat down on the love seat opposite Annie.

Annie wanted to cry at the drawn look on his face. He just wasn't going to give up. When his breathing was under control, he spoke. "The locks were changed an hour ago. All the credit-card companies were notified. We had the bank flag all your accounts and new account numbers will be issued tomorrow. Jane notified DMV. When you're up to it, you'll have to go there personally to get your license reissued. Same thing for your car registration. All you have to do now is stay off your feet and let your knee mend."

"Tomorrow is my birthday party, Aunt Annie. Mommy is letting me help bake the cake. Tessie and Junior are coming to the party. Mommy said it was okay."

"Of course it's okay." Tessie and Junior were twins who lived three doors away.

"Let me give you the grand tour, Clay," Tom said.

When the two men were safely out of earshot, Annie said, "You look like you want to tell me something, Elmo. How are you feeling?"

"I'm feeling better than I look. Each day it's getting harder and harder. I'm not giving up. You were right, there is something I wanted to tell you. Mr. Grayson called yesterday. He's here. Not here in Charleston but in Boston. He said his nephew needed his help. He asked when you would be back, and I said I didn't know. Tom said he's called him several times. He didn't give up any information either. That's a real nice fellow that brought you home, Annie."

"Elmo, you only talked to him for five minutes. How can you tell if he's nice or not?"

"It's in the eyes. I saw the way he treats his dog. Yours, too. He took care of you, didn't he? Drove you all the way here because of Daisy's party tomorrow. That to me means the man is a real nice fellow."

"He is nice, Elmo. So is his dog. I'm going to let him take the Rover back and at some point Jane and I will drive up and get it. He used to play for the Lakers. His wife died three years ago. I don't think he's over it yet."

"He's over it. He just feels guilty about getting on with his life. Real nice fellow."

"You said that already, Elmo," Annie said tartly.

"Sometimes, Annie, you don't see what's right in front of your eyes. Sometimes you need a little nudge and even that doesn't work and I have to give you a shove."

"Elmo, are you trying to match us up?"

"Why would I be doing something like that? You're mooning over that Hawaiian fellow. What would be the point?"

"I'm not mooning over anyone, Elmo. Parker and I are at opposite ends of the spectrum. I've had a lot of time to think, Elmo, and I came to realize Parker is not the man for me. We are too opposite in our thinking. Oh, it might work for a while, but eventually the marriage would erode. He wants me to give up too much, and I want him to give up too much. Neither party should have to give up anything. I care a great deal for him, but I'm not in love with him. I know that now.''

"Well, thank the Lord for small favors.''

"Are you telling me you never approved of Parker, Elmo?''

"I'm not saying that at all. I just plain out didn't like the man.''

"Elmo, for God's sake, you never met him.''

"What's that got to do with anything? I talked to him hundreds of times. Tom told me things. You told me things. Jane told me things. I just didn't like the man. And you know what else, Annie? The man didn't like me. I had the sense that he has no patience with old people. I wouldn't have said a word if you hadn't said something first.''

"You should have said something earlier, Elmo.''

"I thought I did when I came back from Hawaii with the dogs. You were in love. At least you said you were.''

"I think I was in love with the word *love*. I wanted someone of my own. I thought Parker was that special person who would light up my life. Maybe he is that person, and I'm simply too dumb to see it. Any news from our friends in Boston?''

"Not a word. Tom, Jane, and I had this idea to go on the attack. It fell flat. We don't have criminal minds. By the way, did you file a police report about last night?''

"No, Elmo, I didn't. I didn't see anyone. A car was behind me. There's no law against that. I managed to scale the ditch. He didn't. He, whoever he is, would say he lost his bearings in the heavy rain. You couldn't see an inch in front of you. I depended on the lightning, and don't think for one minute that I don't know someone up there was watching over me. Clay said there were no license plates on the car and that it was locked. Yeah, my purse is gone. How do I prove he, whoever he is, took it? The police will tell me if I was stupid enough to leave it, I deserve whatever I get. That's the way it is, Elmo. I don't want you worrying about me.''

''Fine, I won't worry about you,'' the old man snapped. ''What's for dinner?''

''I have no clue. What'd you get Daisy for her birthday?''

''A big red wagon. She'll be able to pull that dog you're getting her around in it. Kids love doing that. Annie, I saw my lawyer last week. I didn't say anything to Jane about this, but I want you to know. I'm leaving everything I have in trust for Daisy. I want her to have a fine start when she finishes college. You aren't upset, are you?''

''Not one little bit. That's so kind of you, Elmo. Jane won't be upset either. She'll be as grateful as I am. Daisy's a sweet little girl.''

''She's a whiz at checkers, I can tell you that. She's starting to come around. She's got a long way to go, but she'll make it.''

''More tea, Annie?'' Jane asked as she sailed into the room.

''Sure,'' Annie said, holding out her glass.

''Nice guy, Annie. Real nice.''

''Don't you start now. He drove me home is all. His dog is the one who found me. He helped me; that's all there is to it.''

''I saw the way he looked at you. He's interested.''

''I don't believe the two of you. He lives in North Carolina. I live in South Carolina.''

''It's closer than Hawaii,'' Jane said.

''I suppose you're going to tell me you don't like Parker, either.''

''If you love Parker, then I love Parker. Speaking for myself, no, I did not like the man. I didn't like his attitude on the phone. I never met him, so that's probably not a fair assessment. I never would . . .''

"Have said a word unless I brought it up. Does that mean Tom doesn't like him either?"

"As a business associate I think he likes him just fine. Personally, I don't think he does. You need to clarify that with him.

"He's sure chatting up a storm with Mr. Mitchell in the garden. They're drinking beer and talking basketball. Man's man. You know, guy stuff. None of that flower necklace stuff," Jane said.

Annie wasn't touching that one. "What's for dinner?"

"Last of the summer corn. Big garden salad. I went to the market earlier and everything was so gorgeous I bought a little of everything. Chicken on the grill. Ice-cold beer for us grown-ups and lemonade for Daisy. Chicken and rice for the dogs. It's cooking as we speak. Mr. Mitchell is staying, isn't he?"

"For today. I thought I'd let him drive the Rover back and then, when my knee is better, you and I can drive up and get it if that's all right with you."

"Sure. Name the day. Did you decide on the reunion, Annie?"

"Yes. I'll go if you want to."

"Are you sure that's wise, ladies?" Elmo asked.

"Wise or not, we're going," Annie said. "And when I'm there, I'm going to light a fire under someone. I'm going to put a stop to this once and for all. I will not live in fear, nor will either one of you."

"What about Parker and his nephew?" Elmo asked.

"I'm going to take care of that, too. What happened to me in North Carolina was the last straw."

"I guess that means you're going to finally kick some ass, huh, Annie?"

"That's exactly what it means."

CHAPTER
SEVENTEEN

Annie woke from a terrible dream, her body drenched in sweat, the light summer blanket she'd covered herself with wrapped around her neck. She leaned back into the soft, down pillows trying to figure out if it was the dream or something else that woke her. The dogs were quiet. Late-summer heat lightning could be seen through the Charleston blinds on the front window, but there was no rolling thunder. Where were the dogs? Probably sleeping with Daisy behind closed doors. Jake was probably upstairs with Clay with his door closed. Elmo was sleeping in the small bedroom off the center hallway. His door was probably closed, too. Jane and Tom were on the second floor at the end of the hall. Undoubtedly their doors were also closed. So what was it that woke her? She grunted when she realized her knee was throbbing.

Jane had left a bottle of aspirin and a glass of ice tea, now warm, on the end table next to the sofa in case she woke and was thirsty. Annie tossed the lightweight blanket to the side, grasped the arm of the sofa, and got up, wincing painfully and being careful not to put any weight on her injured leg. She hopped her way through the dining room and down the hall to the kitchen in the dark, only to find Elmo standing in the open doorway to his room, a strange look on his face.

"What's wrong?" she hissed.

"Don't know. I thought I heard something. Sit down, Annie. I'll get you whatever you want. Stay off that leg."

"Why are we whispering? I don't think there's anything out there, Elmo The dogs would be barking their heads off."

"The dogs are upstairs at the front end of the house. Jane bought some gadget that plays soothing sounds for Daisy so she can fall asleep. It plays all night long. It's one of those hypnotic, restful things. The dogs are probably zonked along with Daisy. I heard something," he insisted.

"Maybe we should call Tom to check outside. I can buzz him on the intercom. We have a child in the house, Elmo."

"It could be anything, Annie. Kids going by, kids throwing stuff over the gate. A raccoon on the roof. It just so happens we both heard something. It doesn't have to mean it's related to . . . that other matter. We're both being silly to worry."

"After my experience in North Carolina, I'm ready to believe anything. You did say that Mr. Newman volunteered the information that the man said he knows all our movements twenty-four hours a day. What am I supposed to think? I'm not going to be able to go back to sleep. Would you like some coffee, Elmo?"

"Coffee would be good right now."

"Regular or decaf?"

"Regular."

"Elmo, there's something I want to talk to you about. Remember how I told you there was something about Parker that bothered me? I didn't exactly say that, but I always had the feeling something was going on somewhere that I should be aware of. That's the best way I can explain it."

"So."

"I read this article about real coffee without the caffeine while I was in the hotel. It seems that certain scientists have learned how to create coffee plants that are missing the caffeine gene. They did some tests on the leaves of their decaf coffee plants and they show only one percent of the caffeine in regular plants. The breakthrough came with the discovery of a gene necessary for production of caffeine by the plant. This was all done at the University of Hawaii. It seems that they can now knock out the gene in certain pieces of coffee plant tissue and regenerate the tissue into new plants. What that means, Elmo, is this. Caffeine knockout means you can produce decaf coffee without putting the beans through the extraction process, which reduces flavor.

"Elmo, this is going to be big business. The commodity market for coffee is a twenty-four-billion-dollar-a-year business. Possibly more. In case you don't know this, it's second only to oil. According to the article I read, it's going to take two years to produce the beans. I think Parker has been doing this all along, and that's why he's turned the everyday part of the coffee business over to Kiki. I never understood why a coffee company had to have a laboratory. I think he's marking genes in coffee plants that involve flavor and yield. If he can do that, it will enhance his coffee flavors, reduce bitterness, and increase the number of beans produced per plant."

"What does all that mean to us, Annie?"

"If Parker is ahead of the pack, he can win big. Right now he needs my contract and my money to finance this new venture, at which point his price to me will double and I'm dead in the water and the Daisy Shops go under. Now I know why they were so insistent on a long-term contract. I am so glad I had that niggling feeling I was being squeezed. I only signed on for six months. Tom thought I was out of my mind. Parker almost stood on his head to try and convince me to extend it.

It wasn't sitting right even then, but I wasn't able to put it all together until a few days ago. Parker sure as hell knew how to play the game, though. Right now he's counting on the fact that we pay on delivery, unlike some firms who take as long as ninety and some times one hundred twenty days to pay up. Scientists are expensive. Laboratories cost a fortune to maintain. I almost fell for it, too. Do you think I'm crazy, Elmo?''

"About as crazy as I am," Elmo snorted. "So now what?"

"I don't know. We let the contract run its course. It has three months to go. I'm going to talk to Tom in the morning. We need to get ready for Plan B.''

"Do you still love him, Annie?"

"I thought I did. I allowed myself to paint this rosy picture in my mind. You know, life after the Daisy Shops. A family. I always knew there was a shadow in the picture. I'm not faultless here. We both played the game. Unfortunately, I didn't know the rules. The thing that really got me, Elmo, was this. I couldn't get that business with his sisters out of my head. Parker has no respect for women. Oh, he says he does, but he doesn't. When you think you're in love you only see what you want to see. My little affair was a moment in time. Everyone has moments like that. It's a memory.''

"And here I thought you called it all off for other reasons. Reasons we don't need to discuss.''

"That was part of it, Elmo. Fear does strange things to a person. It also opens your eyes to what's around you. Fear for your well-being and your life make you so aware of things it is almost impossible to miss all those things you ignored along the way. Does that make sense?''

Elmo nodded and looked at his watch. "It's four-thirty. Everything seems quiet. I guess our nerves got the best of us.''

"Seems that way.''

"Want to play some checkers or some gin rummy?''

"Checkers," Annie said.

"I'll get the board."

"I'm going to use the bathroom. What are we playing for?"

"Money, what else?" Elmo cackled as he headed down the hall to his room.

Two minutes later, just as Annie opened the bathroom door, an explosion rocked the back end of the house. Annie fell backward, reaching for the towel bar and swinging wildly on one foot so she wouldn't fall. "Elmo!" she screamed at the top of her lungs.

"What the hell was that?" Elmo shouted as he tottered to Annie, his arms outstretched.

"My God! Call the police, the fire department! Are you okay, Elmo?"

"Scared the bejesus out of me, but I'm okay. Where's the phone?"

Annie hopped over to the bottom of the steps. "Everyone get down here! Tom! Jane! Clay! Hurry! There was an explosion in the kitchen. We need to get outside. Hurry! Hurry!" Annie screamed to be heard over the crackling flames in the kitchen.

Five minutes later they were all clustered together on the sidewalk in front of the house as the fire engine and police cars raced to a screeching halt, the ambulance directly behind the police cars.

Everyone started talking at once, the dogs barking and howling as the sirens continued to wail.

"Oh, Annie, your beautiful house is ruined. Thank God you're okay. Thank God, we're all okay," Jane dithered as she crushed Daisy to her chest.

"I don't care about the house. If Elmo hadn't decided he wanted to play checkers and if I hadn't gone to the bathroom, we'd both be *dead* now."

Clay Mitchell stared at the firemen and the police as they raced inside the house. "What the hell is going on here, Tom? Do you have gas in the house?"

''No. Everything is electric,'' Tom said as he clenched his teeth and balled his hands into tight fists.

Clay thought about the gun Annie kept near her at all times and the mess she'd been in a little more than twenty-four hours ago. Common sense told him he should take his dog and beat feet. Instead he planted his feet more firmly on the concrete. He'd never run out on a friend in his life. He'd never been one to run from trouble, either. His adrenaline started to boil when he saw the fear on everyone's face, especially the little girl. ''Easy, Jake. Stay,'' he said calmly to the jittery dog.

An hour later, the investigating police officer offered to drive all of them to Elmo's house with a strict warning not to return to the house until it was safe to do so.

''How long will that be?'' Annie demanded.

''It could be days. It could be weeks,'' the officer said. Annie groaned.

''Did my birthday cake blow up?'' Daisy whimpered.

''I think so,'' Jane said. ''We'll bake another one at Elmo's house.''

Annie climbed into the police car and sat down next to Elmo. ''We were all in the house. The three of us, Elmo. You know what this means, don't you?''

''I'm afraid so, Annie. I don't know if Jane's figured it out yet, though.''

''We aren't going to be safe anywhere. If the only way to get that man off our backs is a confession, then I'm going to the police and cross my fingers and confess. There was a child in the house. Doesn't he care? Clay Mitchell has nothing to do with this. He's an innocent party and he could have been killed and so could Tom. The bastard wants us or one of us three. I'm going to do it, Elmo. I can't take this anymore.''

''You're not going to do any such thing. The police will handle this. Listen to me, Annie. I'm speaking now to you like a father. I want your word.''

Annie clamped her lips shut. She unlocked them a moment later. "Don't tell me what to do, Elmo. I'm all grown-up now."

"Mind me now, Missy Clark. You will do nothing. That's an order. You are not going to do any talking to anyone today or any other day. That's the end of it."

It was easier to agree than it was to argue with Elmo. She'd never yet won an argument where he was concerned.

Once the group was settled in Elmo's spacious kitchen, it was agreed, through eye contact, that there would be no discussion of what happened while Daisy was within earshot. Jane and Tom bustled about the kitchen preparing breakfast while Elmo showered. Daisy romped through the house with the three dogs, returning every few minutes to make sure those she loved were safe and secure. Annie sat across the table from Clay.

"For whatever it's worth, I'm sorry."

"Hey, I've never been blown out of bed before. It was an experience. Sometime when things are dull, I'd like to know what's going on. Maybe I can help," Clay said.

"If you like, you can drive the Rover back and Jane and I will pick it up at some point. I don't mean to insult you, but I would like to pay you for your time."

"It's okay. Thank you is good. So, do you want me to drive you to the airport to pick up that special present?"

"Good Lord, I almost forgot. I need to be there by ten. We can keep the you know what in the garage until the party. I wonder if the wagon Elmo bought and left in the garden was ruined. Guess we have to stop and get a new one. Toys Я Us isn't far from the airport. That's if you don't mind."

"I don't have anything better to do. I haven't had this much excitement since the playoffs years ago. You people do lead exciting lives."

"I'm probably the most boring person in the world, Clay. This is one of those little blips that happens to everyone once in their lives."

"Some blip."

Jane turned away from the stove. "Are we still going to the reunion next week, Annie?"

"Damn straight we're going. I've been thinking, Jane. I think I'll charter a plane so Elmo can go with us. I know he's just itching to see his old drugstore. I was going to ask him today. You're still planning on going, right?"

"I'm taking Daisy with me."

"Sure."

"She could stay with me. I could have Mandy drive down and pick her up and bring her back Sunday night," Tom said.

Jane's voice was sharp when she said, "No, Daisy stays with me."

"It's not a problem," Annie said. "However, there are two schools of thought on that, Jane. Daisy might be better off with Tom."

"No," Jane said adamantly. "She belongs with me. She stays with me. We go together."

Clay wondered if the tall thin woman was talking in some kind of code only Annie understood.

"Okay, it's settled then. I'll call and make the reservations this afternoon. By the way, what time is the party? I hope the drugstore hasn't changed that much. Elmo will be upset if the new owner turned it into one of those shiny chrome, glass, and overlighted stores that stays open twenty-four hours a day."

"The party is dinner. I'll have to drive down to the battery to pick up the twins this afternoon. The kids can have their party outside in the yard. It'll last an hour, and that will be that. Who knows, maybe the twins' parents won't want them coming here. Everyone knows about the explosion. Parents are funny about stuff like that. I hope Elmo is up to the trip, Annie. He's getting more frail by the day."

"He loved September when all the kids returned to school. I think it was his favorite time of year. This might . . . this might be his last chance to . . . you know, see the place where he spent most of his life. It will be his decision, Jane.''

With Daisy at the table, the talk was centered on her birthday, birthday wishes, and a possible pony at some point in the future.

Clay pitched in and helped with the cleanup while Annie got dressed for the ride to the airport.

''I have to bring Jake, Annie. He wigs out if he's left behind.''

''It's not a problem. The pup might find it comforting. God, I hope Daisy likes this present. An animal is such a responsibility. Maybe she's too young.''

''I think you're worrying needlessly. She was real good with Jake and your own dogs. When she has one of her own to smother with love it will make all the difference. Do you want to talk about what went on earlier?''

''Not really but I guess I owe you some kind of explanation. Something happened a long time ago. Jane and I were getting our master's at Boston University . . .''

Ten minutes later, she finished her story. ''They never found the money.''

''I remember hearing about that. You're right, it was a long time ago.''

''Then a year or so later, maybe it was two,'' Annie said vaguely, ''the money was returned. Half of it. Not too long ago, the rest was returned. Plus interest. That wasn't the end of it, though. Newman kept after the three of us. Just recently the kid, well, he's a man now, got out of prison. Newman called to warn us that the bank robber was, for want of a better word, after us. The guy seems to think if the money had been returned, he would have gotten a lighter jail term. He boasted that he knows what the three of us do, twenty-four hours a day. I think it was him following me the other night, and I sure as hell think it was him early this morning. Who would want to blow up my house? Who doesn't care about the lives of innocent people? No one I know, that's for sure. That's where it all is right now.''

"Is the case closed?''

"It's been closed. The insurance company and the bank signed off on it. To my knowledge, no one lost a penny.''

"That's some story.''

"Story, my foot. Try living it. Turn left here and just stop by the Delta door. I can manage, and don't lecture me. This is something I want to do. The stewardess that's bringing him said she'd meet me at the baggage area.''

"You shouldn't be walking, Annie.''

"I'm not. I'm hopping.''

Clay reached for a cigarette from the console, his eyes on the wide double doors. He saw her stop for a moment to peer into the little canvas bag. A smile brighter than the September sunshine spread across her face. In that one brief second he wished with all his heart that the earth had moved when he kissed her.

"Oooh, oooh, wait till you see this little guy. Is he precious or what? Oh, look, he loves me. Kisses, kisses. You poor little thing. All that way in that little bag. Want to hold him? Just for a minute. We don't want him bonding with either one of us. He's Daisy's pup. He's so warm and soft. Look at those eyes. Oh, he's shaking. I have to cuddle him. Doncha just love him? I want one of these,'' Annie babbled.

"I never saw such a tiny dog. How much does he weigh? He's a fur ball. What do you think, Jake?''

Jake leaned over the seat to sniff the little creature. Then he started to lick the puppy's head and his paws.

"Guess he likes him,'' Annie said. "He weighs about two pounds now and will probably go to five. Just right for a little girl. I already got him a bright red leash and collar with his name on it. It's Charlemagne. Charlie for short. Oh, look, he came with his own toy and blanket. We're going to have to wash them first, and there's a letter from my friend Cher. I guess it's for Daisy so we shouldn't read it. Oh, he's asleep. Okay, we can go now. When we get to Toys Я Us you are going to have to go in and get the wagon. Try and get one that's put together unless you want to do it. Well, maybe Tom will do it but he's not good at stuff like that. He taught me how to hot-wire a car.''

''What!''

''Yeah. I learned all kinds of things from him and his friends. Man they could swear up a storm. They were always getting into trouble. I was a model of decorum.''

Clay laughed. ''Tell me where to turn.''

''Right at the next light. Will Jake stay with me?''

''Sure. He knows I'll be back. He can tell the difference between being left behind and being left in a car while I get something in the store. I told you he was smart. What are you going to do now, Annie?''

''I don't know. Move to Australia. Europe. Like Scarlett said, I'll think about it tomorrow. Right now Elmo and Daisy are my top priorities.''

''Listen, Annie, what happened tonight . . . early this morning, is not funny. People could have been killed. I can call some of my old friends from the Bureau. Not active agents, people like me who left. They know how this stuff works. You have the resources so use them to put this guy away, so he's out of your hair once and for all.''

''I'll think about it.''

''What's to think about for God's sake? Either you do something or you don't. Let me help.''

''Why do you want to help me? Just tell me that.''

''Selfish reasons. I like you. My dog likes you. Doing something constructive for a change will help me get back among the living. Who knows, you might want to give me another chance to see if I can make the earth move for you.''

"I'll let you know, Mr. Shake, Rattle, and Roll." Annie laughed. "Okay, turn right here. There's the store, and here's the money for the wagon."

"Since Daisy invited me to the party, I need to get a gift, too. What do little girls like?"

"One of those pink Barbie race cars you pedal. It should fit in the back with the wagon. Jake can sit up here with me and Charlie."

"Stay, Jake. I'm coming back," Clay said. "See, I told you he understands."

"Go already," Annie said.

Annie leaned her head back against the headrest and closed her eyes. Fear ran rampant throughout her body. Her heart started to pound inside her chest. She'd missed death by mere seconds, as had Elmo. Dear God, what was she supposed to do now? Tears burned her eyelids and rolled down her cheeks. Jake whined softly. "I wish I knew what to do, Jake. I'd confess in a minute if I thought it would help. I wish I'd done it years ago. Too much too little too late." The pup opened one eye and closed it.

Jake scrambled into the cargo area just as Clay arrived with a stock boy, a wagon, and a bright pink Barbie race car.

"Wow!" Annie said. "It didn't look that big when I saw it in the store the first time. Will it fit?"

"Sure will. Are we ready to go home now?"

"I'm ready. Thanks for doing this, Clay."

"It was my pleasure. Jake is having himself a good time. I guess chasing rabbits gets boring after a while. He's a people dog. What shall we talk about now? How about the skinny on that boyfriend you dumped."

"How about the skinny on Ann Marie," Annie said sharply.

"What do you want to know?"

"Everything."

"I thought you said whatever came before didn't count," Clay said.

"Oh. Well then, tell me about your career as a hoop star. Did you like the roar of the crowds, the adoration, the big paychecks?"

"All of the above. Next topic."

"Your farm."

"Five hundred acres. Been in the family for hundreds of years. I lease the fields to other farmers. My brother doesn't want any part of it. No other family."

"Oh."

"Next."

"Are you going to stay there forever?"

"Someday I might stick a pin in a map and head in that direction. For now it serves a purpose."

"Oh."

"Next."

"Would you be interested in learning the coffee business?"

"I might. What do you have in mind?"

"No one is ever going to be able to take Elmo's place. We're going to need some extra help. Tom is on overload. Jane can do just so much. Daisy needs her mother. I'm not going to be renewing my coffee contract, so we need to find a new supplier. Are you willing to travel?"

"I might be. What do you have in mind?"

"Right now my head is too clogged up to think straight. I'll talk to Tom and see what he has to say. We have real good health benefits. That's important today. Really important. Three weeks vacation. Good pension plan. All the coffee you can drink. Not to mention tuna and brownies. It's an attractive package. We really don't have a corporate office. We should. It doesn't work for me. You could work out of North Carolina. Tom lives there, too. Do you think we should have a corporate office?"

"My theory is this. If it ain't broke, don't fix it."

"My thought exactly."

"What are you going to do, Annie? You can't pretend it didn't happen. What if there's a next time?"

"You don't have to try and scare me. I'm already scared. I have to think it through. I have to consult with Tom and the others. Tonight after the party when Daisy's in bed, we'll talk. You're staying the night, aren't you?"

"Am I invited?"

"I thought Daisy invited you. I heard you promise."

"I thought I needed a grown-up invite. Okay, okay, I'm staying. I'll leave in the morning. Was that a bona fide job offer?"

"Yes, it was."

"Then I accept."

"You do! That's great, Clay."

"Woof."

Annie giggled as she nuzzled the little ball of fur next to her neck. How sweet he smelled. How soft and warm.

"Are we ready?" Daisy whispered.

"We're ready. Now remember, you have to make your wish, then blow out every candle. You can't tell anyone what that wish is. I'm going to turn out the light. We'll sing 'Happy Birthday' and then you blow out the candles. After the cake you get to open your presents."

Jane turned out the light. Everyone sang with gusto, the dogs howling right along with the off-key singing.

"Blow, honey!"

"Yay!" everyone said as they clapped hands. Jane turned on the light. "Can Jake have cake, Clay?"

"Absolutely. I'll have a big piece."

"Can I save mine for later, Mommy? Can I open my presents while the big people eat their cake?"

"I don't see why not," Elmo said. "You go ahead and start to open the ones with all the pretty wrappings and ribbons. I'll fetch mine and Annie's presents from the garage."

"I'll help," Clay said, jumping to his feet.

"I like that guy," Jane hissed.

"I do, too," Tom said.

"All right, all right. Yes, he's nice. Yes, he's very nice. I offered him a job today. He accepted, but we have to work out the details."

Daisy squealed as she opened each package. Storybooks, games, puzzles, a new book bag, hair ribbons, and a scarlet-satin purse with a crisp ten-dollar bill inside. Annie smiled when the child looped the long gold chain around her neck and sashayed around the kitchen to show off the vibrant purse.

"It's just what I wanted, Aunt Annie. Thank you."

"Well we have a few more presents for you that Elmo and Clay are bringing in for you. Okay, are you ready?"

"I'm ready. I can't wait! What is it? Oh, a red wagon! I always wanted a red wagon, Uncle Elmo. Thank you so much," she said, throwing her arms around the old man. "You're the best," she whispered.

"This is from Clay," Annie said.

"Oh, Mommy, look at this! My very own car. Thank you, Mr. Clay. You too, Jake," she said impishly.

"One more, little lady," Annie said, handing over the green canvas bag. "Careful now."

"It's alive! It's a dog! Is it for me, Aunt Annie?"

"I think so. There's a letter inside the bag. I think it's probably for you."

"Read it, Mommy. Read it to me," Daisy said as she cuddled

Charlie next to her cheek. ''Oh, is he really and truly all mine?''
Annie nodded as Jane read the letter.

GOLDENRAY
CHER HILDEBRAND

Dear Daisy,
   This little guy is a Yorkshire Terrier. He is very special and looking for a very special little girl of his own, which is why he is coming to you. I understand that you are very special and have a lot of love to offer him. He needs you and I know you will take good care of him & love him as he loves you. You will be his sunshine.

                     Yours truly,

                  Cher Hildebrand

                  Cher Hildebrand

''Daisy's going to be busy for the rest of the evening. Why don't we all have a beer out on the patio,'' Elmo said.

''We need to talk,'' Tom said.

''I can go upstairs,'' Clay volunteered.

''No. You can stay. Clay told me about an idea he had on the way home from the airport,'' Annie said. ''I'd like you all to hear it.''

''Then let's get comfortable,'' Tom said.

''Let's hear your ideas, son,'' Elmo said.

CHAPTER EIGHTEEN

Parker Grayson tossed his lab coat into a corner. He stared for a long moment at his nephew. Once he'd been this young. Once he'd been full of spit and vinegar like the young man standing in front of him. The only difference was, this boy loved living on the mainland and going to school. He'd hated it. He wondered if he'd ever been idealistic. "Let's talk in my office, Ben."

"How's it all going, Uncle Parker?"

"Slow. You know us island people. The world thinks we do nothing but bask in warm trade winds making leis for tourists. If there's one thing I've learned, it's that you can't rush science. Were close, though. So, are you ready to go back to law school? How did the summer project go?"

"I've been ready for weeks now. I love autumn, with the changing of the leaves and the smell of burning leaves. I like the football games and all the holidays. It's so different. I know you said you hated all that. I guess I don't understand why."

"It was another time. I'm an island boy. I guess I'll always be an island boy. I thought you were going to spend the summer here. Instead you blow in and blow out like the summer winds. When do you leave?''

"Tomorrow. I just came to say good-bye.''

"Your mother insisted, is that it?'' Parker grinned.

"Something like that. I would have done it over the phone. Lately it doesn't seem like I have enough hours in the day. This case kicked my butt. It kicked all our butts. We have to wrap it up by next week. All we have is speculation, and each one of us has a different idea. How do you defend something that can't be proven?''

"The law is not my forte, Ben.'' He was a handsome young man, Parker thought. Bright, intelligent, dedicated to learning the law and motivated beyond belief. He wondered where he'd come by all those traits. "Do you want to run it by me for my opinion?''

"Yes and no. I have to get back home to pack up. If I miss my flight, I'm up a tree as the saying goes.''

"I have an idea. Why don't I fly you to school. I can take a few days off here. We can talk through the flight.''

"I'm meeting up with my partner in LA. We planned to fly back together. Will it be a problem?''

"Not at all. So, you didn't solve the case, eh?''

"We did and we didn't. As I said, we each have a different opinion. I think mine is right on the money, but then Andreas thinks his is, too. I'm the prosecution, Andreas is the defense. I think I can make a good case. The real reason I came here, Uncle Parker, is to warn you. I talked about it to Mom, and she said she didn't think you knew about it. She said she thought you needed to know.''

"Maybe you better explain what you're talking about,'' Parker said.

"It's about Miss Clark and her friends. The lady who owns

all those Daisy Shops. The same Miss Clark you were going to marry."

Parker's face set into hard lines. "Let me make sure I understand this. The case your professor assigned you, a criminal case of some sort, has to do with Annie Clark? I think you need to explain that to me, Ben."

"I didn't know she was the lady you were engaged to until after the fact. When I finally realized it, I tried to switch up with some of the other guys, but they were already into their cases and didn't want to trade. I didn't say anything because everything I knew at that point was circumstantial, and I didn't want to open cans of worms for the family. Things like this tend to backfire and cause all kinds of problems. Like I said, it was all circumstantial."

"Just spit it out, Ben, and let me be the judge. What is it you think she did?"

The words ricocheted out of the young man's mouth like bullets from a machine gun. Parker listened, his eyes popping and his jaw dropping. His brain whirled. Now he had the answer as to why Annie had broken off their relationship. For two months he'd played and replayed their two-hour conversation over and over in his mind. Now it all made sense.

"Annie Clark is an honorable person, Ben. She didn't rob any bank. I'd stake my life on that."

"You weren't listening, Uncle Parker. I never said Miss Clark robbed the bank. I came to the same conclusion the insurance investigator came to, and I can't prove it any more than he could prove it. The case is closed. Miss Clark committed the perfect crime in my opinion. And she got away with it. Where the law is concerned, opinions and theories don't work. Only hard, provable facts count. I'm going to zero out because I can't prove anything."

Parker felt his stomach start to churn. "Is that how she started her business, with the bank's money?"

"No. I have every profile ever written about her. She's just who she says she is. She started the business on the proverbial shoestring. There is no money trail. There's nothing. The same thing goes for the pharmacist, Elmo Richardson, and Miss Clark's very good friend, Jane Abbott."

"Then why do you say Annie is the guilty party?"

"Because all the evidence points to the three of them, her in particular. All the other suspects were eliminated. There are literally *pounds* of reports. I went through all of them; so did my partner. It's either Clark or Abbott. Miss Clark was, as the police say, on the scene. Jane Abbott was in the apartment, and there's no one to vouch for her. Mr. Richardson was in his store. And, his car windows were closed and his car locked. The Abbott and Clark cars were open and unlocked. There were eleven or twelve other cars with open windows but they weren't anywhere near where the robber could have tossed the money bag. The Abbott and Clark cars were right there, in the first row of parking spaces. Andreas and I did dry runs for a whole day. First I'd run with the money bag and toss it, then he would do the same thing. Each time it landed in the Clark car. Peter Newman did the same thing while he was investigating the case. He was convinced it was the Clark car."

"If it was such a perfect crime and if Annie Clark did find the money, why in the hell did she give it back?"

"Guilty conscience. Everything I've ever read about the lady says she's squeaky-clean and a straight arrow. Fear maybe. The Abbott woman and the pharmacist are above reproach. Abbott's husband is a scoundrel. They have zip when it comes to money. He lives beyond his means. She appears to be quite frugal, and there's a child involved."

Parker digested the information. "A half million dollars is not that much money, Ben. Annie Clark has megamillions."

"Back then she had zip and she was working sixteen and eighteen hour days. A half million dollars was the pot of gold at the end of the rainbow for someone like Annie Clark, who worked her way through school carrying a full load. My guess was she found it and panicked.''

"I don't believe any of this. Annie is a fair, tough-minded businesswoman. She's not a thief. All right, let's head out. I need to pack a bag. Meet me at the airport in say, three hours.''

"You're upset, aren't you?''

"You could say that. Did you talk to Annie at all?''

"No. I planned on doing that in Boston. Andreas tells me her class reunion is scheduled for next week. He got a copy of the acceptance list, and her name and Jane Abbott's are on it. It's my last shot. Andreas is going to take Abbott, and I've got Clark.''

"If I asked you to let this go, would you do it, Ben?''

Ben stared at his uncle for a long time before he replied. "No.''

"What about the pharmacist?''

"We've crossed him off our list.''

"You shouldn't have done that.''

"In my opinion, it was the right thing to do. He's old and in failing health. His bank records show nothing but regular deposits and a history of hard work. The last report we had on Mr. Richardson is that he is terminally ill. Neither Andreas nor I want to be a party to anything that might ruin his last days. Besides, we're convinced he had nothing to do with it.''

Parker closed the door behind him. It was all making more and more sense by the minute. Annie's deep, dark secret. The way her face had gone alabaster white when he'd said the rainbow was Annie's rainbow. Pot of gold at the end of the rainbow. Damn, what the hell was this going to do to his business? The six-month contract had only three months to run. Would Annie renew? Would he be forced to shut down the lab? What could two law students do that the police and a monster insurance company couldn't do? Rake up old skeletons? To what end? The case was closed. He wondered then if he was capable of blackmail. How far would he go to pursue the work he'd started in the lab? How important were the caffeine-free coffee beans to the world? Damn important. No one in their right mind would pass up billions of dollars down the line. Christ, he was so close. Another six to eight months and he was sure he'd have the decaf coffee beans. So close. All he needed was money—Annie Clark's on-time money payments. With only three months remaining on the present contract, he could lose everything if he didn't get her to renew.

Parker watched his nephew drive down the hill before he climbed into his own jeep. He needed to pack a bag, needed to issue a few orders, and, by God, he needed to do some heavy-duty thinking. If he called Annie, would she talk to him? Probably not. Maybe he should call Tom. He really needed to know which way the Daisy Shops were going to go at the end of the six months. He was still smarting over the fact that he hadn't been able to charm Annie into a three-year contract. Marrying her was the only option left, and now that was swinging in the wind. He'd been so sure, so confident of a happy ending, he'd gone ahead and given the sisters control over the business. Kiki had threatened once to bring things to a boil. She might still do it, and where in the hell would that leave him? Without a coffee bean to his name.

He thought about Annie then because he often thought of her these past weeks. He could have been happy married to her. He would have made a good husband and father. There had been no doubt in his mind that the moment children arrived on the scene, Annie would turn her end of the business over to him, content to raise her family and do all the things wives and mothers do. How could he have been so wrong about so many things? Was it even remotely possible that she had seen through his charade? Did he give off bad vibes along the way? He knew his lovemaking had been more than satisfactory.

Things hadn't chilled until she started questioning him on the laboratory and what it was he was testing. Then after what he now referred to as the infamous two-hour phone call, where he'd told her about Ben and his casework, things became downright bone-chilling.

Maybe he could turn things around. Maybe he could convince her he didn't care about her past. Maybe if he called her and warned her, she'd take it as a sign that he really did love her. And he supposed he did, in his own way. His gut told him when Annie Clark made a decision, she stuck with it and she didn't look back.

So then, if he knew that, why the hell had he offered to fly his nephew and his friend to Boston?

Was it because he was a man and his ego was bruised and bloody and all because of a woman?

Parker pressed the pedal to the metal. Business always came first. He was simply taking care of business. Everything else would fall into place.

"I hate leaving with things hanging in the air," Annie grumbled to Jane, who was calmly sipping coffee at the kitchen table.

"It's only been a week, Annie. You know the authorities never work quickly. Why would you want to go back to a house that isn't structurally sound?"

"I don't. That's not the point. The point is, they must have every investigator in the state working on this, and not one of them has told us a thing. It was probably something very sophisticated and outside the realm of what they normally deal with. Once the house is repaired, I'm never going to live in it again. Hopefully some fool will buy it from me. I feel so violated. I felt the same way when I realized some person sat in my car and pawed through my stuff and ended up stealing my purse.''

''How's your leg this morning?''

''Each day it's better as long as I don't stand on it for long periods of time.''

''Have you heard from Clay Mitchell, Annie?''

''I sent a box of T-bone steaks for Jake. He called to say they were tasty. Guess that means he ate one of them. He said the car was gone from the ditch and it was a rental. The name on the lease was Stephen Lake. Lake reported it stolen that very night. No fingerprints. No nothing inside the car other than hairs and fibers that belonged to Stephen Lake. Another dead end. They aren't going to find out anything from the debris on my house, either. We're dealing with one clever man. A man who has no intention of getting caught.

''You know, Jane, I think it's real nice that you're bringing Daisy. I think she's going to like seeing where we lived and worked and went to school. Maybe someday she'll want to go to college in Boston. Like mother, like daughter. She can walk Charlie all over the grounds.''

Jane hooted with laughter. ''That dog's feet haven't touched the floor in a week. He sleeps right next to her on her pillow. He perches on the edge of the tub while she's taking a bath. He cries all day while she's in school. I carry him in a knapsack. He knows the minute her feet touch the sidewalk out front. You did good, Annie. I need to thank you for that. The change in Daisy is so wonderful. She's a happy little girl again.''

''When I was that age I would have killed for a pet like Charlie. I had goldfish.''

Jane's voice dropped to a low whisper. ''Are we doing the right thing by taking Elmo, Annie? He's so frail.''

''I hope so. I asked him last night if he was sure he wanted to make the trip, and his response was, 'Try going without me.' Then he got real feisty and wanted to know if we were objecting to pushing his wheelchair. He said he wanted a motorized one. I said okay. You know when he gets testy like that it doesn't pay to argue. He doesn't have long, Jane. We have to prepare ourselves.''

''You can't prepare for something like that. You think you can, but it doesn't work. When it happens, it slams right into you. Either you deal with it, or you don't. I fall apart in a crisis, you know that.''

''I'm no better.''

''Tell me, how do you really feel about Clay Mitchell? Isn't it time we talked about Parker?''

''I like Clay's dog. I think Clay's a nice person. I offered him a job. He said he would let me know. He said yes at first, but he didn't mean it. He's got a lot of personal baggage he has to deal with. I told him I didn't want him or his old FBI friends helping us with our problems. I think he got kind of miffed about that. When we get back from Boston we'll drive to North Carolina to pick up my truck if that's okay with you. I might even take Rosie and Harry and let them run to their heart's content. I bet Jake can show them all kinds of rabbit warrens. They're city dogs, though.''

''Parker?''

''Parker is someone I used to know. I was one of many who thought they fell in love in the islands. I understand it's a common occurrence. Sometimes reality has to slap you in the face. It was a mistake, and I'll live with it.''

''Kind of like the one I made.''

''You were in love back then, Jane.''

''No, I wasn't, Annie. I was afraid. I wanted to get away from you and Elmo. I have no guts. You know that. It's all in the past. From where I'm standing, the future looks pretty damn good. By the way, I found a little house yesterday in Summerville. It's close to the school, and Daisy can walk. It's got a fenced yard and everything. It's just twenty minutes from

Charleston. I think I'm going to take it. I want your opinion first, though.''

Annie leaned across the table. ''Jane, don't rush into anything. Listen, I don't know if I should be telling you this or not, so keep it to yourself, okay?''

''Sure.''

''Elmo is leaving his entire estate in trust for Daisy. That means this house, too. It's perfect for you and Daisy. It's got a pool, the grounds are fenced, and the gardens are great. Daisy loves it here. Don't do anything rash just yet.''

Jane burst into tears.

''Shhh, here comes Elmo. Right on time. The car service should be arriving any minute now. You better get Daisy and Charlie. With you and Daisy on each side of him, he can handle the ramp. I can handle the bags.''

In the car, sitting next to Elmo, Annie felt her heart start to flutter. She risked a glance at the old man. His color was bad, and he seemed to be having difficulty breathing. ''We don't *have* to go to this reunion. If you aren't feeling well, Elmo . . .''

''I'm feeling just fine, and, yes, we do have to go to this reunion. I don't like it when plans switch up. I have myself psyched to see the old store. I'm going. I'm a little winded, that's all. I have all my medication. That's the end of it, ladies.''

''Do you want to hold Charlie, Uncle Elmo?'' Daisy asked.

''I'd love to hold the little guy. He isn't going to poop on my new suit, is he?''

''Oh, Uncle Elmo, you are so funny. Charlie only poops on the paper or the grass. He knows how to behave.''

''I knew that. I was just testing you, Daisy,'' Elmo wheezed.

''I wonder if what's his name, from the campus police, is still working? Remember how he used to have a crush on you, Jane?'' Annie giggled.

''What I remember is him calling *you* on the phone.'' Jane giggled.

"Yes, but to talk about you. He's probably married by now with six kids," Annie retorted. Out of the corner of her eye, she watched Elmo nod off. She reached for the little dog and handed him over to Daisy.

"Is this really an adventure, Mommy?" Daisy asked.

"You bet it is, honey."

"Oh, boy, Charlie, we're going on a real live adventure, on a real airplane!"

Jane rolled her eyes. Annie clenched her teeth. Adventures sometimes had a way of turning into disasters.

"Okay, Jake, we did our walk. We went grocery shopping. We did our laundry. I cleaned the bathroom. I read the paper from front to back. There's nothing left to do. There's nothing on the tube, and I refuse to watch soap operas. I feel like I should be doing something, but I don't know what that something is. What in the hell did we do before you dragged Annie Clark into our lives? This is all your fault, Jake."

Clay's tone of voice was so new to the Lab he slunk across the room on his belly. "C'mere, I didn't mean it in a bad way." The dog bounded over to Clay and hopped on his lap, all 130 pounds of him.

"She offered me a job. Kind of. I have to make a decision about that. I like old Tom and her two roommates. The old guy is okay. Jane's a real mother, and the kid is okay, too. Ya know, Jake, they're a family. We're kind of lacking if you know what I mean. You know what they're doing right now? They're getting ready to go to Boston. We could do that, too, if we wanted to. I've chartered planes before. I can certainly afford it. You could sit in first-class with me. Hell, it's all first-class when you charter a plane.

"Two women, one kid, and a dying old man. What kind of odds are those for someone who means to harm them? Not good. What'ya think, Jake? All it takes is a phone call. I could be packed in five minutes. It will just take you a second to get that raggedy-ass blanket and squeak toy you drag with you everywhere. So, say something!''

Jake bounded off Clay's lap and ran for his blanket and toy. ''Okay, let's do it!''

''It occurs to me, Jake,'' Clay said on the drive to the airport, ''that maybe we are overstepping our bounds here. Maybe I should call Tom Clark and tell him what we're doing. Yeah, yeah, that's what I'm gonna do. If he nixes the idea, we can cancel the flight.''

Jake stirred himself long enough to lick at his master's hand as he punched out a series of numbers.

''Tom, this is Clay Mitchell. Listen, I had this cockamamie idea that I would charter a plane and go to Boston. There's something about two women, a kid, and a dying old man that bothers me if something goes awry. I don't know what good I'll be, but at least I can . . . you know, be visible.

''Why? Well, I got tired of talking to my dog. Is it okay with you, then? Hey, I can have the pilot stop and pick you up at your airport if you want to come along. Yeah, yeah, I did get the idea that your sister doesn't like anyone sticking their nose in her business. My concern is the old man and the kid. Well, yeah, sure, I like your sister. What's not to like? She sent my dog twelve T-bone steaks. Okay, then, Jake and I are going to Boston. While I'm airborne I'm going to try and figure out what I did for the past three years. Sure, I'll let you know. This is going to sound kind of sophomoric, but did Annie say anything about me? You know, any little thing. So tell me already. She said *that!* Are you putting me on? No kidding! Well, thanks, Tom. Nah, I haven't decided if I want to work for a woman or not. They get their panties in a wad over every little thing. She really said that, huh? Okay, I'll give it some serious thought. Wait a damn minute. Are you saying if I buy into the Daisy Shops, I would have an equal voice? Is that what you're saying? Uh-huh. I'll keep that in mind. I'll call and let you know how things are going. Sure. Nice talking to you, too.

"You are never going to believe this, Jake. Never in a million years. Hot damn! This is almost as good as coming straight from the horse's mouth. Listen to this, Jake. Miss Annie Clark told her brother Tom Clark that the earth *did* move when I kissed her!"

Jake threw his big head backward and howled until Clay swatted him. "So, Mr. Shake, Rattle, and Roll hasn't lost his touch after all. Damn! I feel like howling myself, Jake."

Parker Grayson set his private plane down smooth as silk. "You guys go ahead. I'll meet up with you for dinner. I need about an hour here and I have some phone calls to make. I'm going to rent a car. Just give me directions to the hotel. Tell me again where the reunion is being held." Parker scribbled in a small notebook. "I'll meet up with you later."

An hour later, all the flight details taken care of, Parker headed for the car that would drop him off at the main terminal. He spent another hour calling all the hotels in the city to find out where Annie was registered. He finally struck paydirt when he called the Four Seasons. He debated a full minute before he made a reservation for himself, then asked to be put through to Annie's room. He was told his party hadn't checked in as yet. Parker left a message. "I'm registered here at the hotel. Please call me."

Parker used up another forty minutes filling out the forms for a rental car. With a map on the front seat, he exited the airport, realizing how much he truly hated city life. There would never be a time in his life when he would appreciate the genteel streets lined with elegant brick town houses. There was no way in the world he would or could accept the public greens and the gardens, not when he came from an island so lush with greenery and brilliant flowers it took your breath away. What did he care if the savvy spin doctors touted the city as America's mother city. The colonial steeples and expressways that raced around the buildings for people to recall the scrimshaw era had absolutely no interest for him. He flat out hated it.

What was it Ben had said, or was it his friend Andreas who said there was nothing better than Boston fish cakes and yesterday's baked beans. He'd gone on to say boiled or nouvelle-fangled wood-grilled lobster with wild seasonings was to die for. He knew if he did eat it, he would probably die. Not one word had been mentioned about pineapple, mangos, or any of the luscious foods found in Hawaii. What had really stung was the way his nephew had agreed with Andreas. Damn, his nephew had turned into a Bostonian.

What in the hell am I doing here anyway? Am I such a miserable human being that I have to get in Annie's face and let her know I know her dirty little secret as my way of punishing her for rejecting me as a person? Is her coffee contract that important to my business? Yes to all of the above.

Is this what I've come to? he wondered.

The bright red Mustang convertible made Clay's eyeballs stand at attention. "We can handle this, Jake," he said, settling himself behind the wheel. "Buckle up, buddy, we're gonna roll. Four Seasons here we come. They're going to do a double take when they see you, Jake. They said small dogs were acceptable. The word small means different things to different people, so behave yourself. I don't think we're going to have a problem since my brother was such an icon when he played with the Celtics. If all else fails, I'm going to tell them I'm Larry Bird's brother. That should get us some first-class accom-

modations, buddy. Babe Ruth used to hang out here. Then they
went and traded him to the damn Yankees. I used to come here
all the time, Jake. It's a great city. I got some of the best lobster
I've ever eaten right here in this town. I took this girl I was
dating at the time to a Harvard-Yale game. I thought I was in
love. That day proved I wasn't. Someday I'll bring you here
to see the Bruins and how they rule the ice. I'm telling you,
this is a great city. It's amazing that Annie went to college
here.

"She's sure going to be surprised when she sees us. Especially you. Me, I'm just the guy that made the earth move.
Christ, Jake, I feel like some damn teenager. I really like that
woman. You know what else, there's more to this than her
coming here for a college reunion. She's coming back to the
scene of the crime hoping to draw that crazy guy out in the
open. That's what this is all about. Trust me. Great little car,
huh?

"Did I always talk to you like this, Jake? Weren't there any
people in our lives these past few years? Guess not. Damn, I
wish you'd hold up your end of the conversation."

Clay drove aimlessly, up one street and down another until
he made his way to the Four Seasons. He'd stayed here many
times before he retired to the farm. He wondered if any of the
old staff would remember him. He didn't have long to wait to
find out. The moment he pulled to the curb, the doorman stepped
back and then forward, a huge smile on his face.

"Mr. Mitchell, nice to see you again. It's been a long time.
How's your brother?"

"Living in the land of sunshine and playing golf every day.
This is Jake, Carl. Do you think I'll have a problem? When I
made the reservation they said they accepted small dogs. I left
the Great Dane at home knowing he wouldn't qualify."

"Why don't I check you in and you take Jake up in the
freight elevator. I know for a fact you're on the fifteenth floor.

I'll send one of the boys up with the key. They've been talking about you all day, ever since your reservation came in over the wire. That means you're preregistered.''

"Thanks, Carl. By the way, would you happen to know if some friends of mine checked in yet? Two young ladies, a little girl with a tiny dog, and a frail old man."

"Several hours ago. The ladies went out, and the gentleman is still in his room."

"Would you do me a favor, Carl? Tell the desk clerk to leave a message for Miss Clark. Mr. Richardson might be sleeping, and I don't want to wake him. Just say I'm here and to call my room."

Clay slipped the doorman a twenty-dollar bill. He was in good hands now.

"Let's go, Jake. We walk down to the dog run, then we're going upstairs for a nice cold beer."

CHAPTER NINETEEN

Annie helped Elmo into the king-size bed. He looked so awful, so frail, so sick she wanted to cry. "It's time for your pills, Elmo."

"I'm not taking any more pills, Annie. That's it. I'm going to take a nap, then I'm going to get up and have a double scotch on the rocks. I know you have things to do, so go out and do them. I'm all right. It's not my time yet. I'd know it if it was. I never lied to you, girl."

He looked incredibly tired and weary. Annie smoothed the sparse hair back from his forehead with gentle hands. "I know that, Elmo. I shouldn't be more than an hour, two at the most. Jane said she'd stay here with you."

"That's not necessary. I'm going to sleep. You young people came here to do things, so go out now and do them. I'm just fine. Plus, I know how to press the zero on the telephone if I need help."

Annie kissed his wrinkled cheek. Sometimes life just wasn't

fair. In a perfect world, good people like Elmo Richardson would live forever.

In the sitting room she met Jane's worried gaze. "He wants us to go out and do whatever we came here to do. He refused to take any more medication. There's no way I was going to try and talk him into it. He'll sleep for a while. You and Daisy have plans and . . . I have a few of my own. How about if we meet up, in let's say, three hours. I told Elmo I'd be back in two hours. I'm giving myself an extra hour. I think he'll sleep for a good three or four hours. The room's cool and I closed the drapes. No one is going to call, so the phone won't wake him. On second thought, I'll call down and tell the desk not to put any calls through. Tom might try to call, though, so I'll call him when I get a chance. I'll rent us a car. Is all this okay with you, Jane?"

"It's fine. Daisy and I are going to walk. If we get tired, we'll hail a cab. Don't give either of us another thought. You go ahead. I want to change my shoes."

In the lobby, Annie whizzed by the front desk, then backed up. "Young man, I'm in room fifteen-oh-two. Do not put any calls through until further notice." A second later she rounded the corner, credit card in hand. "I need a full-size car. I called earlier. The reservation is under Anna Clark." Annie blinked in surprise when a set of keys slid across the counter. She did like advance check-in.

"Third car in the second row. Gas tank is full. Return it the same way. There's a road map on the visor. Sign here." Annie signed her name in two places and initialed it in three other places.

"You're good to go, ma'am."

Ma'am. Suddenly the one word made her feel as old as Elmo.

The moment the engine turned over in the silver gray Pontiac, Annie rolled down the windows. She inched her way out of the crowded lot, turned right on Arlington Street and then made a left onto Commonwealth Avenue and followed it all the way to University Road.

Boston University loomed ahead of her. She felt a pang of sweetness as she stared at the university. She drove around until she came to a sign that said, VISITOR PARKING. What was she doing here? Sooner or later, criminals always returned to the scene of their crimes. Obviously this was her sooner as well as her later. She couldn't help but wonder who was watching her. She could feel unseen eyes boring into her back. Out in the open like this, she was a living, breathing, moving target. She couldn't worry about that now. She had things to do. Somewhere in the vast campus library she was sure she could find what she was looking for. If not here, then the archives at the local newspaper. Maybe all she needed to do was ask someone where Andrew Pearson's father lived. Notoriety made the local citizenry aware of people's addresses. If that failed, there was always the green stuff called money.

Forty-five minutes later, Annie settled herself behind the wheel of the rental car. She was two hundred dollars poorer, but she had Clyde Pearson's home address, his telephone number as well as directions to his Boston home. She also had the address and phone number of the boy who had been killed after the robbery, just in case she decided to pay the family a visit.

"Time to get this show on the road," Annie mumbled as she shoved the key into the ignition. She looked down at the map on the seat next to her and then at the directions in her hand. Beacon Hill. Well, she knew where that was. She drove, uncertain of what she was going to do when she finally faced down Andrew Pearson's father.

It was a beautiful street, tree-lined, each house more magnificent than the next. She thought she could smell the old money behind the iron gates leading up to the beautiful houses. She slowed until she found the house number she wanted painted on the curb. She pulled into the short driveway and waited for the speaker system sticking out of the ground to activate. "I'm here to see Mr. Pearson," Annie said when a garbled voice asked what she wanted.

"What is your name?"

"Anna Clark. I'm a . . . friend of Andrew's," she lied. She waited a moment to see if there would be further conversation. When the system remained silent, she climbed back into the car. Almost immediately, the ornate gates began to open. Annie drove through in a burst of speed, praying the person controlling the huge gates didn't have a change of heart.

Up close, the house didn't look quite as nice as it did from the street. The windows needed to be cleaned, as did the copper gutters. The steps and banisters needed fresh paint. One windowsill was almost rotted through. *So much for old, moldy, musty money,* Annie thought as she rang the doorbell.

A plump, apple-cheeked woman with a hearty topknot smiled a welcome when she opened the door. "Come in, Miss Clark. Mr. Pearson is expecting you."

"He is? I just got here a few hours ago. Is it possible you have me mixed up with someone else?"

"I don't think so. Mr. Pearson said you would come someday." The woman's voice turned fretful. "I wish you had come sooner. Mr. Pearson is not well. Some days he does not remember from one minute to the next. I called upstairs to tell his nurse you were here. Go right up; it's the first door on the right. Can I bring you some tea or coffee?"

"No thank you." Why would Clyde Pearson be expecting her?

Annie climbed the magnificent mahogany staircase, marveling at the stained-glass window on the landing. Everything was clean and polished and smelled faintly of lemon. There wasn't a speck of dust to be seen anywhere. The hall at the top of the steps was wide and monstrously long with what she supposed were Pearson ancestors in gilt frames and little tables underneath that held books and silver-framed photographs. She knocked tentatively.

"Come in, Miss Clark," a nurse said cheerfully. "Mr. Pearson is waiting for you."

Annie took a deep breath. Nothing in the world could have prepared her for the sight of Clyde Pearson. Elmo looked robust compared to this bony caricature of a man.

"Mr. Pearson, I'm Anna Clark. I've come to talk to you about your son Andrew. Do you know where he is, and if you do know, will you tell me?"

The skeleton in his nest of pillows held up a bony claw of a hand. He waved it back and forth.

"That means he doesn't know where Andrew is. That young man skulks around here from time to time. He steals from his father and thinks we don't know. Mr. Pearson disowned him after the bank robbery."

"I'm sorry. I didn't know that. It was my understanding that Mr. Pearson believed in Andrew's innocence and gave him money to find the person responsible for keeping the robbery money even though the money was returned later on."

The clawlike hands waved furiously. "No, Miss Clark, that is not true. Young Andrew came here once in the middle of the night and cleaned out his father's safe. He's forged his name to checks. According to the household help, Andrew was always a troubled child. Of course that was before my time. The boy's pranks became more serious the older he got. The bank robbery was the last straw for Mr. Pearson. That's when he disowned Andrew. A week later, Mr. Pearson suffered a stroke. He was seventy-five percent recovered with extensive therapy. Then when Andrew was released, the poor dear suffered another stroke."

"I can't prove this," Annie said, "but I think Andrew tried to kill me one night and then threw some kind of bomb into my house. No one saw him. There was a child in the house and a very old sick man. If we hadn't left the kitchen when we did, we would be dead. I don't know what to do. I thought if I came here and you told me where he was, I could try to talk to him. It wasn't my fault he was sent to prison.''

The bony arms and hands flopped up and down in a frenzy of motion. ''Mr. Pearson understands what you're saying. He can't speak. He's upset for you. We spoke of this many times while he was mending from his first stroke. My name is Selma Daniels, Miss Clark. Mr. Pearson had me type up a letter for you to give the police should you ever come here. Andrew doesn't know about the letter. As I said, Andrew came here several times and boasted about what he was going to do. He's waiting for his father to die, thinking he will inherit, but Mr. Pearson changed his will years ago. Everyone in this house is as afraid of Andrew as you are. Security guards patrol the property with guard dogs. The police can't do anything because he hasn't made any threats against his father. This is still his legal address. Unfortunately, it is not illegal to wait for one's parent to die. Sad as that may sound.''

''If he doesn't stay here, where does he stay?''

''We don't know, Miss Clark. All we can do is give you the letter and some other reports that might be beneficial to you. Mr. Pearson calls them affidavits. Go to the police with what we give you.''

''Do you know any of Andrew's friends?''

''Those old friends want nothing to do with Andrew these days. I'm afraid the friends he has today aren't the kind of people you would want to talk to.''

''I have to do something. I can't just sit around waiting for him to kill me or my friends. I came here to Boston to my reunion hoping to draw him out. I thought maybe the newspapers would do another story on him. My next question is, if Andrew was as troubled as you say, why wasn't he given help?''

"Mercy, child, the boy was in one psychiatric facility after the other. There is a list of psychiatrists as long as your arm in the Rolodex. Andrew had every psychiatric test there was. He was so smart, he could anticipate the questions and give the right answers, then gloat about it. I guess he just wore Mr. Pearson down. It became easier to look the other way because he was afraid of the young man. This is all detailed in the report we drew up for you."

"Why me? Why did Andrew single me out?"

"He convinced himself you had the money, and had you turned it in, he would have gotten a lesser sentence or he could have plea-bargained and gotten community service. It isn't true, but he thinks it is. It is indicative of his mental state to blame everyone else. If you wait here, I'll get the report."

"He probably knows I'm here. I think he's watching me and my friends. What will you say if he comes here after I leave?"

"We'll say whatever you want us to say."

"Tell him to call me at the Four Seasons. I'll meet him wherever he wants. Of course, if he's afraid of a face-to-face confrontation, tell him I understand the coward's way out. I appreciate you talking to me. I'm very sorry, Mr. Pearson."

Garbled sounds came from the man's scrawny throat. Annie looked questioningly at the nurse. "I think he's trying to tell you to be careful." Annie nodded.

At a loss as to what to say or do, Annie paced the sickroom. She was not unaware of the priceless oriental rugs and the antiques that filled the room. Where would they all go when Mr. Pearson died? Would being cut out of his father's will push Andrew over the edge? In her opinion, he was already over the edge.

The nurse returned with a legal-size manila envelope. It was so fat, a rubber band was needed to close it. Annie stuffed it into her carryall and zipped it closed.

As she descended the steps she realized how fearful she

really was and what she was up against. Knowing it and doing something about it were two different things.

Annie looked at her watch. She'd been gone from the hotel for two and a half hours. Time to get back. Time to get Elmo dressed so she could take him to his old pharmacy. She hoped the old dear was up to the trip.

Back at the hotel, Annie turned the rental car over to the valet. She smiled wearily as the doorman held the door for her. She felt tired, sad, and vulnerable. All she wanted to do was lie down and go to sleep and pretend this particular time in her life was all a bad dream. She wished, the way she'd wished a thousand times over, that she could turn the clock back and be that eager young woman living in the cramped little apartment with Jane.

"Annie!"

"Parker! What are you doing here?" This wasn't a bad dream—it was a damn nightmare. Surely she was going to wake up any minute now, in her own bed. She squeezed her eyes shut, then opened them. Parker was still standing in front of her.

"I flew my nephew here, the one I told you about. Annie, Annie, why didn't you tell me about that little episode in your life? I thought we agreed to be open and honest with each other. According to Ben, it's a closed case and will probably never be solved. I couldn't figure out what made you do such a turnaround. It finally dawned on me that it was when I mentioned Ben and his project that you called everything off. I think you owed me more than a Fed Ex letter, Annie. I thought we were in love. We mapped out our lives for years to come."

"The middle of a hotel lobby is not the place to discuss this, Parker. It was more than that, and we both know it. Yes, Jane, Elmo, and I were under suspicion after the bank robbery. To this day we are under suspicion. It was a harrowing experience being hounded like that. It wasn't something I felt comfortable talking about. It also wasn't any of your business. Just like what you were and probably still are doing in that laboratory of yours. Would you like to expound on that? By the way, the police, the bank, and the insurance company closed the case. The money was returned. I really have to go, Parker. Elmo and Jane are waiting for me.''

''Can we have dinner this evening, Annie? I'd like you to meet my nephew Ben. He needs to hear your side of the case before he turns in his report to his professor.''

Annie stared bug-eyed at the handsome man she'd promised to marry. Did she just hear what she thought she'd heard? She struggled to feel something. She'd made love to this man, lain in his arms, promised him there would be a future for the two of them. Now she could barely stand the sight of him. What did that say for her? ''I don't think so, Parker. Just about every hour of my time here is accounted for. Why don't I call you when I get back home?'' How inane. She might as well have said, let's do lunch sometime in the next decade.

''I think you owe me more than a Fed Ex Dear John letter, Annie. My nephew and his partner are going to your class reunion tomorrow, so why don't I tag along. Surely we can find ten minutes to talk. I'm not giving up, Annie, I want you to know that.''

A chill ran up and down Annie's spine. ''Why would your nephew be going to my class reunion?''

''He wants to meet you and Jane. This project is very important to him. He's convinced you are the one who took the money.''

''Really! Read my lips, Parker. I'm up to here with theories and suppositions where that robbery is concerned. Your nephew had better not show up. He had also better not plan on causing any kind of a ruckus. Are we clear on that?''

''Then have dinner with me and meet him.''

''Not in this lifetime, Parker.'' Annie fired off her last zinger as she turned to walk away from him. "The Daisy Shops will not be renewing our contract with the Grayson Coffee Company. Sit on that one, Parker, and do a full spin."

Annie beelined for the elevator, whose door swished open. She was shaking so badly she could hardly press the button for the fifteenth floor. She wondered if Parker had the gall to stand and watch the overhead numbers of the elevator to see which floor she got off at. She started pressing numbers and got off on the eighth floor to take the stairs to the fifteenth. She didn't need Parker Grayson knocking on her door. If he slipped someone money, would they give up the information? Of course they would. The answer to that was she would move over to the Ritz Carlton but not check out of the Four Seasons until it was time to leave for home.

Annie was winded and breathless when she opened the door to her suite. She wondered if her expression betrayed what she was feeling. She had her answer a moment later when Elmo, who was sipping his double scotch, and Jane both said, "What's the matter?"

"You look funny, Aunt Annie. Did you run up the stairs?"

"Actually, Daisy, I did run up seven flights. I needed the exercise. Would you get me a soda from the fridge, honey?"

"We're going to be leaving soon, Daisy. Go into the bathroom and clean up. Put on that pretty pink dress we just bought, okay? Make sure you pick the right ribbon for your ponytail."

"Do you need to do grown-up talk, Mommy?"

"Uh-huh. I'll call you when it's time to go."

"I'll have another double scotch, Jane. I haven't felt this good in weeks." Jane rolled her eyes but did as the old man asked. "What happened, Annie?"

Annie explained her visit to Andrew Pearson's father and what she'd learned. "His nurse gave me this," Annie said, tossing the packet to Jane. "Then when I got to the lobby, guess who I ran into! Parker Grayson. He flew his nephew here, and the nephew is going to our reunion. He figures I was the one who found the money. He and another law student were assigned unsolved crimes, and this kid just happened to get the one that involved us. Parker wanted to take me to dinner so I could meet him. I said no. I also told him I wasn't renewing our coffee contract.''

"Good going, Annie," Elmo said, smacking his lips.

"Does that mean we aren't going to the reunion?" Jane asked.

"That's what it means. In addition, we are moving out of here. Call the Ritz Carlton and make us a reservation for like now. We can go down in the freight elevator with our baggage. We aren't checking out of here, though, until we're ready to leave.''

"Very clever, Annie," Elmo said. "More ice, Jane."

"I feel like everyone in the whole world is watching us."

"They probably are," Elmo said. "If you aren't going to get gussied up to go to your reunion, why do we need to take our bags? Jane came in loaded down with shopping bags. Just put what we need in them. Someone might see us leave and think we're checking out without paying our bill.''

"I guaranteed our stay with a credit card, Elmo. I know, I know, money talks. I found that out today at the university. We could simply leave here, check in at the Ritz, and buy what we need in the shops. I've worn the same clothes for three days in a row before, so it won't be the first time. Personally, I don't care if I miss the reunion or not. How about you, Jane?''

"Couldn't care less. This is more important. Are you okay with the Parker thing, Annie? If you're having second thoughts, I can take Elmo to the drugstore.''

"I'm okay with it. I had a couple of bad minutes, but that was it. I'm glad I did what I did when I did it. Just think, it could be hitting me in the face now out of the blue. No way are you going to the drugstore without me. You do the shopping bags, and I'll call the Ritz. You guys go down in the freight elevator and take the car to the Ritz and check in. I'll go down to the lobby and take a cab and we'll meet up at the drugstore. I'll give you a forty-minute head start. Do you think we're being melodramatic?''

''Maybe,'' Elmo growled. ''It's better to be safe than sorry. Do you want us to take this envelope or are you going to take it?''

''You take it, Elmo. We have to decide what we're going to do with it. Are you sure you're okay? You're not tired?''

''Annie, I had a three-hour nap. The scotch is coursing through my bloodstream. I feel fine. I should have stopped taking those damn pills months ago.''

Who was she to argue with a pharmacist who practiced pharmacology for forty-five years and stayed on top of the profession to this day. She nodded bleakly.

Charlie poked his head out of Daisy's canvas bag and woofed softly. ''Shhh,'' Daisy said. ''Oh, oh, look, here comes Jake.'' The Yorkie wiggled and wiggled until he had his little body free of the loose flap on the canvas bag. A second later he was romping down the hall, Daisy in hot pursuit.

''Clay, what are you doing here? Whatever it is, I don't care. I'm just so glad to see you,'' Jane babbled. She threw her arms around the ex-basketball player and hugged him.

''Now, that's what I call a real warm welcome. Where's Annie?'' Clay asked, looking around. ''How are you, Mr. Richardson?''

''I've been better. Today started out to be a good day. Why are you here?'' he asked more bluntly than Jane had.

''I got worried about all of you, so I chartered a plane. Women aren't the only ones who have intuition or go by gut instincts. Jake seemed to think it was a good idea. I left a message, didn't you get it? Where's Annie?''

Elmo stared up at the tall man with the honest concerned eyes. There was no debate, no indecision. He told him what had happened. ''Annie is waiting for us at the drugstore. We were going to check in and go through these papers before we meet up with her. She's giving us a forty-minute head start.''

''Then let me put the top up on the car I rented. If someone is watching you, they have your car tagged. It might be a little tight with Jake, but I think we can all fit in. We can ditch the wheelchair, and I can carry you if you have no objections. I can pull my car right up to the side entrance. You guys hop in and we're off. How's that sound? We can pick up another rental at the Ritz. I'll call in a reservation from the car, or I can drive you to the drugstore if you tell me where it is.''

Jane almost fainted with relief. Elmo sighed. Daisy giggled as Charlie and Jake romped outside the elevator. ''I'm worried about Annie, Clay.''

''I can see that. Annie is no fool. She can take care of herself.''

''Parker Grayson is here. She ran into him in the lobby.'' Jane recited Annie's story on the ride down in the elevator.

Clay winced. He didn't know what to say, so he remained quiet. He'd come prepared for anything and everything. The anything and everything didn't include an ex-fiancé.

''All of you wait here. Jake, come with me. Daisy, put your pup back in the bag. We don't want to call attention to ourselves,'' Clay said gently, a twinkle in his eye.

''God, Elmo, suddenly I feel so much better,'' Jane said.

''I'm going to need the chair,'' Elmo said. ''All of a sudden, I'm not feeling so good.''

''It's the excitement, Elmo,'' Jane said, concern written all over her face. ''We'll stuff the chair in the trunk and have Clay park in the campus lot. I'll push you from there. How's that? We have to believe those watching eyes can't be everywhere.''

Jane motioned for Clay to pop the trunk, then helped Elmo to his feet. ''I'll fold it up. We have to take the chair, Clay. It won't be a problem, though. I know where we can park so the car won't be recognized.''

''I called the Ritz. There's a black Lincoln waiting for us. More room. Do you want to pick it up now or wait till we see Annie at the drugstore?''

''Elmo, what do you think?''

''Let's go to the drugstore,'' Elmo wheezed. Alarm registered in Jane's eyes as the color left Elmo's face. The moment Elmo and her daughter were settled, Jane hopped into the front seat with Jake. Daisy was holding Elmo's hand and babbling ninety miles to the minute. Clay kept one eye on the road and one on the rearview mirror to check on his passenger in the back.

Fifteen minutes later, Daisy let out a whoop. ''There's Aunt Annie. See, she's standing in the doorway.'' Clay swerved and made a U-turn in the middle of the road.

''I would have missed her, Daisy,'' Clay said, pulling to the curb.

''I thought we were going to park in the lot and push Elmo here.''

Clay looked in the rearview mirror. Jane turned and blinked. ''Too late now, we're here.''

Annie saw Jane's wild red hair; then she saw Jake. ''Clay!''

''Yeah, it's me. Hope you're glad to see me and my dog.''

''Well, yes, I am, but what are you doing here?''

''You and your little band of followers made such an impression on me I got worried about you. The plain damn truth is, I got sick and tired of talking to Jake. You got me out of my shell, so you need to take responsibility for this.'' Clay's voice dropped several octaves. ''One very sick old man, a woman with a kid who has a pup under her arm and another woman who packs a gun and romps through mud fields ... Well, wouldn't you have been worried? What would you have done if you were in my place?''

''Annie, Elmo's color is gone, and he's not breathing right. Hold the door so we can get the chair inside. Thank God the store didn't change, at least on the outside. Were you inside?''

Annie's throat closed tight when she saw Clay lift Elmo into the waiting wheelchair. ''Look, Elmo, they made a new sign. It's just like your old one.''

''The owner left your old sign for you. The pharmacist is holding it for you. Guess they figured it worked, huh?'' Annie said, her eyes filling with tears. Her throat muscles relaxed. ''It smells the same, Elmo. Sniff. Smell the Chantilly and the Max Factor powder. They just made fresh coffee. It smells heavenly. I feel like I stepped back in time. The toothpaste is in the same place, so are the antacids. The licorice sticks are still by the register. The only difference is the bubble-gum balls are bigger and cost a quarter now instead of a nickel. This is Andy Jan, the pharmacist. He's worked here since you sold the store to the Havermeyers. He loves it here.''

''It is my pleasure to meet you, sir,'' Andy said. ''Miss Clark has told me all about you. Is there anything I can do for you other than to hand over your old sign?''

''No. I just wanted to see the old place one more time. Do you serve tuna sandwiches?'' Elmo gasped as he struggled to speak.

''Only on Friday. Egg salad with a slice of tomato on whole wheat is our big seller.''

''Fancy that.''

''Would you like to come behind the counter, sir?'' Elmo nodded.

''I was about to fill a prescription for Amoxicillin. Would you like to do it?''

''I would like that very much,'' Elmo managed to say.

Annie's hand flew to her mouth to stifle a cry. Jane turned away, tears rolling down her cheeks. Daisy counted the boxes of Jujubes on the candy counter. Clay jammed his hands into his pockets, deciding he must be allergic to something in the store. Why else would his eyes be burning like this?

They stared at one another as they waited for the pharmacist to wheel Elmo to the front of the store. When they heard his running feet they met him halfway down the aisle. "I called an ambulance. It should be here any second. He finished the prescription and collapsed. I'm so sorry."

Annie patted the young man's arm. "That was a kind, wonderful thing you did for Elmo. Knowing he was coming here is what kept him going. We're all grateful."

"Mr. Richardson asked for two aspirin. I gave them to him. Sometimes it helps a little. Ah, the ambulance is here. Hurry, hurry," he called to the paramedics.

Annie and Jane watched helplessly as Elmo's frail body was placed on the gurney and wheeled to the ambulance. One and all noticed the weathered sign clutched to his chest. "I'll go with him," Annie said.

"We'll be right behind you," Clay said.

Jake held the paramedics at bay, all one hundred and thirty pounds of him. He growled menacingly, his fangs bared. Daisy raced up to him. "It's okay, Jake, Uncle Elmo isn't feeling good. They're going to make him better. That's a good boy, Jake."

"Jesus," one of the paramedics said, "I wouldn't want to meet up with that dog in a dark alley."

"Jake doesn't go in dark alleys, mister. He goes on the grass. Don't you, Jake?"

"Get in the car, Jake. In the backseat with Daisy and Charlie. Do you know the way, Jane? They're going to use the siren, and I can't run red lights."

"I know the way," Jane blubbered. "I'm glad it happened

here. I didn't want it to happen at all, but this is the best place. He got to fill one last prescription. For Elmo, it didn't get any better than that. He wouldn't take any more medication. He just flat out refused. I think he knew this was going to happen just the way it did. Today he insisted on drinking scotch. He had two doubles. I didn't want to give it to him, but I could never refuse Elmo anything. Do you think that did it, Clay?''

"No. It's his time, Jane. Not many people get to do that one thing they love doing best in the whole world before it's time to go. From what I know, Mr. Richardson had a good life. He has wonderful friends he loves and who love him. He was a lucky man.''

"Annie and I are the lucky ones. We were all the family Elmo had.''

"He might come out of this,'' Clay said, his eyes on the careening ambulance ahead of him.

"No, not this time,'' Jane said sadly. "Annie's going to fall apart. You don't have any idea how much she loved that old man. I'm so glad you're here.''

"Me too,'' Clay said quietly.

CHAPTER TWENTY

"Who are all those people trooping in and out of Elmo's room?" Annie asked. "I thought only family could visit patients in Intensive Care. Where's Clay?"

"Annie, please sit down," Jane said. "You're making me nervous. This is as hard on me as it is on you. I don't know who those people are. Clay is outside with Daisy and the dogs. As you know, they don't let dogs in hospitals. They'll let us see him when it's time. Why don't you go outside and check on things. I'll wait here. If anything happens, I'll call you."

"Do you want some coffee?"

"Coffee has been running in my veins for the past few hours. It's lucky Elmo's old doctor is still practicing. Elmo felt good about that. We could be here for a very long time. How do you feel about me telling Clay to take Daisy and Charlie back to his hotel room. It has to be the Four Seasons, because the Ritz doesn't allow animals. We were pushing our luck with Charlie in his little bag. I think Clay can handle anything that might come up. I'm not saying anything will. And there's Jake.

Nobody in his right mind would tangle with that animal. Did you see how he acted when they were wheeling Elmo to the ambulance?''

Annie smiled at her friend. ''You know what, Jane? I think I'd trust that man with my life. I know I've only known him a short while. Sometimes that's all it takes. And, he really did make the earth move. No one has ever been able to do that to me. I also love that dog of his. Don't go getting any ideas, Jane. I hate it when you try to play matchmaker.''

''Hey, he didn't make the earth move for me. That has to count for something.''

Annie smiled. ''I wish Tom would get here.''

''He'll get here in time, Annie. Go on now, get something to eat while you're downstairs. By the way, you look awful.''

''Guess what, Jane. You look like I feel. We're cranky, you know that, don't you? I didn't think it would happen here. For some crazy reason, I thought Elmo would . . . You know, go in his sleep. You know how he likes to orchestrate everything.''

''Annie, stop torturing yourself. We got him back here in time. He got to fill a prescription. He got to see that his old store where he spent most of his life didn't change. He got his sign, and he's still hanging on to it. They couldn't pry his fingers loose. Dr. Quinlan said it was okay, germs and all. We did our best. Elmo says you never look back.''

Annie ran from the room.

It was a beautiful autumn day with just the right amount of sunshine. It wasn't hot, and it wasn't cold. Elmo's kind of day. She blinked away her tears.

Clay, Daisy, and the dogs came to her in a wild rush. She wanted to throw herself into Clay Mitchell's arms more than she ever wanted to do anything in her life. She held back and didn't know why. ''Did I thank you for coming, Clay? Twice now you've come to my rescue. I'm grateful. I have a favor to ask of you. We don't know how . . . what I mean is we might be here for a while. Would you mind taking Daisy back to the hotel? There's no point in your hanging around outside the hospital. You said yourself that you can't leave Jake anywhere, that he has to be with you at all times.''

''You don't think you'll need me here?''

''You know what, Clay? I don't know. Tom is on his way. He should be here soon. We need to make sure Daisy is safe. Jane trusts you to take care of her daughter. That's quite an endorsement.''

Clay could feel his chest puff out. ''Consider it done. Will you call me if you need me?''

''Absolutely.''

''Are you sure the earth didn't move, Annie Clark?''

''Nah. Steady as a rock. If you play your cards right, I might give you a second crack at it.''

Clay laughed. ''Do I have to worry about that coffee guy?''

''Nope.''

''If that job offer is still open, I'll take it.''

''Consider it yours then. What made you decide to take me up on the offer?''

''You're nice people. I like that old man, I really do. Jane's great. I like the way she practices motherhood. Your brother is an okay guy, and you're kind of nice yourself. Did I miss anything?''

''You're kind of nice yourself, Clay Mitchell. I love your dog. I gotta get back inside. Jane or I will call you to keep you posted.'' She hugged Daisy and tickled Charlie under the chin. Then Annie dropped to her haunches. ''Listen to me, big guy,'' she said to Jake. ''You saved my life, so that means you're responsible for me. Take care of things, okay?''

''Woof.''

''That's it?'' Clay asked. ''Nothing for me?''

''Winsomeness doesn't become you.'' Annie smiled in spite of herself. ''I want to make sure my feet are firmly planted on the ground when you make your next try at making the earth move.''

''I'm beginning to think I lost my touch.''

''Maybe we'll never know,'' Annie said, tweaking his cheek.

''What about that coffee guy? Did he make the earth move?''

Annie surprised herself by laughing aloud. ''He did string a mean lei,'' she called over her shoulder as she tripped her way to the front entrance of the hospital.

Her heart skipped a beat when she stared down the long hallway that led to the elevator. For one heart stopping moment she thought she saw Peter Newman. Right stance, right profile, wrong man. She was just on edge.

Annie backed up and entered the coffee shop. It smelled almost as good as Elmo's old drugstore. She ordered soft drinks and two sticky buns to go.

Jane was crying into a wad of tissues when she entered the waiting room. ''Did something happen? What's wrong?'' Annie demanded.

''Nothing's changed. Elmo's doctor came out to talk to me. It was only for a minute, then he was paged in emergency. He's as old as Elmo, and he's still practicing medicine and taking care of patients. It doesn't seem fair.''

''He's not as old as Elmo, Jane. What did he say?''

''He said Elmo made a lot of strange requests and they were working on them. His minister is on the way. You know doctors never commit to times or anything like that. He left me with the impression the end is a matter of *hours.*''

''Can we go in?''

''Not yet. There are a lot of people in there. I don't know if they're all for Elmo or the man in the next unit. Dr. Quinlan said the nurse would let us know when we can go in. Sticky buns, Annie?''

''There wasn't much to choose from. I think I just bought them to have something to do. If you don't want them, toss them in the trash. Clay took Daisy back to the hotel. He's going to take us up on the job offer. He said we were nice people."

"We are nice people," Jane said smartly.

"I hope Elmo isn't in any pain. Do you think he is, Jane?"

"No, I don't think so. The doctor said he was resting comfortably. He slips in and out of consciousness. That's usually the way it works in books and movies. I don't want to cry anymore, but I can't help myself. Who *are* those people?"

"Who cares?" Annie muttered.

Annie heard her before she saw her, the white oxfords squeaking on the polished floor, the rustle of her starched uniform. For some reason she thought nurses today wore soft nylon and tennislike shoes. Then she looked up. This nurse was from the old school and still wore her starched cap. That had to mean Elmo was in good hands. She heard Dr. Quinlan's name over the loudspeaker.

"Come with me. Quickly, ladies."

Annie ran, Jane right behind her.

Annie pulled up short when she entered the room. Damn it, who were these men? She voiced her question in a snarling voice. "Who are you? What do you want? What are you doing in here? Visiting in ICU is just for family members. Get out of here *now!*"

"Annie, Jane, I invited them here," Elmo whispered in a barely audible voice. "I want you to listen and to be quiet."

Annie bit down on her lower lip as her right hand reached for Jane's left hand. She could feel her body start to shake. She listened, her face full of horror. She felt rather than saw Jane's knees start to buckle. She grabbed for her. This wasn't happening.

"This isn't true! Elmo isn't the one who found the money. It was me!" Annie shouted. "Elmo, take that back."

"Miss, Mr. Richardson gave us his statement thirty minutes

ago. His doctor was here as a witness. It's been signed and witnessed. I'm Police Chief Tobias.''

''You just tear that statement right up. Elmo Richardson never did a wrong thing in his life. I'm the one you want. Not him,'' Annie snarled. ''Why won't you listen to me?''

''No, it's not Annie. It wasn't Elmo either. It was me,'' Jane said in a strong, forceful voice. ''You tear that confession up right now. I'm confessing.''

''Mr. Richardson said you would say what you both just said. We have no other choice but to go by his confession. He's provided every single detail.'' With that said, the small army of men left the crowded ICU room.

Annie threw herself on the bed, tears flooding her eyes and rolling down her cheeks. ''Elmo, do you know what you've just done! You can't do this. Take it back. Please. I can't let you do this,'' she pleaded. She felt his hand on her head and felt him beckoning her closer. She had to strain to hear his words.

''Let it alone, Annie. Go on with your life. You'll all be safe now. Don't you see, it was all I could do for you and Jane. I promised the two of you I would always take care of you.''

''How did you *know*, Elmo?'' Annie whispered.

''I always knew. You changed after that day. You were never the same. You gave it all back. I knew you would. Everyone is satisfied, so you have to let it go. I want your promise, Annie.''

''No, Elmo. I did it. I'll pay the price. I wanted to do it a thousand times. I simply didn't have the guts. I refuse to let the world believe you're a criminal. Do you hear me, Elmo. I refuse!''

''Your promise, Annie. That's all I ask.''

And because she could deny him nothing, she gave her promise in a tearful voice.

"It's not right, Elmo, that I go off scot-free and your memory is tainted."

"You aren't off scot-free, girl. Carrying the secret forever is your punishment. In the end, I'm the one who is getting off scot-free."

"Does Jane know, too?"

Annie had to wait so long for his response she panicked, and shouted, "Elmo! Elmo!"

"Yes. We both knew."

And then he was gone, his hand going limp in Annie's hard grasp. "Jane!"

"I'm right here, Annie."

"He's gone."

"I know."

"You both knew I took that money and never said a word."

"Whatever are you talking about, Annie?"

"You know damn well what I'm talking about."

"No, I don't, Annie. When I make a promise, especially to a dying man, I keep that promise." Jane bent over to kiss Elmo's sunken cheek. "I'll wait outside if you want a few minutes alone. What happened in this room, stays in this room, Annie. Forever and ever."

"Go with the angels, Elmo," Annie whispered tearfully.

Outside in the crisp late-afternoon sunshine, Annie turned to Jane, and said, "No one in their right mind will believe Elmo Richardson did what he confessed to. Do you hear me, Jane, no one will believe it."

"What do we do now?"

"Go back to the hotel. Daisy's waiting for you. I'll go back inside and make all the arrangements. Don't worry about me."

"Annie."

"Yes."

"I'm so very sorry."

"I am too, Jane."

It was almost dark when Annie walked out of the hospital to hail a cab. She felt numb and disoriented. Life would go on. Elmo said it would. Even if she took out full-page ads in every newspaper across the country professing her guilt, no one would believe her. Elmo had taken care of all that the way he'd taken care of everything since the first day she'd met him. The grief she felt was so total, so all-consuming, she couldn't cry. She climbed into the waiting taxi in a daze. Where was she going? To the Four Seasons or the Ritz Carlton. ''The Four Seasons,'' she mumbled.

Parker Grayson set his drink down on one of the shiny tables when he spotted Annie Clark walk through the door. ''Hold up, Annie.''

''What is it, Parker? I don't have anything to say to you. I'm really very tired right now. Wait, there is one thing. Tune in to the eleven o'clock news. I guess your nephew missed the boat. Sorry about that.''

''Annie, we need to talk. I can't let it end like this.''

''You don't have any other choice, Parker. When something is over, it's over. I'll send you a Christmas card. Excuse me.''

Parker reached for her arm and started to pull her backward.

Annie saw the golden streak out of the corner of her eye and then 130 pounds of yellow Labrador slammed Parker Grayson to the floor of the lobby. A smile tugged at the corner of her mouth as Jake raised one huge paw and daintily placed it in the middle of Parker's neck.

''That's his best trick,'' Clay said, coming up to stand next to Annie.

''Awwk,'' Parker grunted.

''And a good trick it is. Jake can keep this up forever. He's got discipline. It's your call, Annie.''

"Make nice, Jake," Clay whispered to the dog.

Jake's massive head lowered until he was eyeball-to-eyeball with Parker. Then he licked his face from top to bottom.

"That's his only other trick. He can keep that up all day, too. Your call, Annie."

"In case you haven't noticed, we've drawn a crowd."

"Well, in that case we need to do something." Clay snapped his fingers. Jake reared back and removed his paw from Parker's neck. Parker scrambled to his feet, his face brick red. He backed away toward the elevator, his eyes spewing sparks.

"Is that the end of that?"

"Yes," Annie said. "Listen, Clay, there's something I have to tell you."

"Whatever came before doesn't matter, Annie."

"It matters to me. I can't lie anymore. Do you have any idea of how I feel?"

"Probably pretty shitty if I'm any judge. You have to take it one day at a time. Just don't put your snoot in a bottle like I did."

"Elmo made a deathbed confession and saved my skin. I don't know how to handle that. I told those men I was the one who did it. They wouldn't listen to me. Then Jane swore she did it. I think they thought we were a comedy team. Elmo took my crime to the grave with him. You knew I did it, too, didn't you?"

"I more or less suspected. This is how I look at it, Annie. Your good outweighs your bad. You aren't home free. You'll carry your guilt for the rest of your life. I guess Elmo, wise man that he was, saw that as a more fitting punishment. You have the rest of your life to make up for that one mistake. I'd like to help you."

"Mr. Shake, Rattle, and Roll himself?"

"Yeah."

"It's a deal."

The door to the freight elevator swished open. Jake's big paw pressed the number *15*. "Daisy taught him that trick. They must have ridden this elevator one hundred times while I sat here on the floor. You see, you forgot to give us a key."

"Oh."

"Yeah, oh. How about I take you three ladies out to dinner?"

"What about Jake and Charlie?" Annie asked.

"I didn't say a linen tablecloth place. I was thinking more along the line of Burger King."

"I'm your girl," Annie quipped.

"Annie?"

"I went through that packet of papers. Tom and I took them to the police station. Tom has some news for you, too."

"What is it?"

"Tom called the Charleston police, and they said Andrew Pearson checked a book out of one of the branch libraries on the art of bomb making. They issued an APB for his arrest. I think everything is finally going to be okay. We'll know more tonight on the news. Are you okay, Annie?"

"No. But I will be. I'm going to need some time. Elmo will be cremated tomorrow. I'll take his ashes home with me. Someday, when I have a permanent home and a family of my own, I'll decide what to do with his ashes. With Jane's approval, of course."

Clay nodded. "Speaking of time. That's all Jake and I have these days."

"Elmo believed a wake should be a party. I could never figure that out. He really hated it when he would see one of us cry. He made me swear after he passed over, as he put it, we'd do a wild jig or something that passed for a jig. We actually promised. Do you believe that. I wish I could figure out the way his mind worked."

"Don't try, Annie."

"I'm really glad you came here, Clay. I mean that."

"I know you do. That's why I'm staying."

"I guess that's it," Jane said, turning off the television set. "I thought they'd make a big deal out of Elmo's confession. If something more exciting had happened in town, they probably wouldn't have mentioned it at all. I bet they bury it on page nine in the paper tomorrow. Andrew Pearson got more airtime than Elmo, and the guy's a shit. Well, I'm off to bed."

"Me too," Tom said, yawning elaborately. "By the way, Clay, Jake's sound asleep in Daisy's room, with Charlie right alongside him."

"No kidding," Clay said just as elaborately.

"You know what I'm thinking?" Clay said when everyone's door closed.

"I know exactly what you're thinking, Mr. Mitchell. There's this great suite of rooms at the Ritz Carlton that are sitting empty right now. How am I doing so far? And we have our choice of at least four vehicles to make the trip to said hotel. That is assuming we want to make the trip over there. What's your feeling on that, Mister Shake, Rattle, and Roll?"

"I made that up," Clay grimaced.

"No!"

"Yeah, I did. I never made the earth move for anyone, either. I made that up, too."

"No!"

"Yeah."

"Then what do you have going for you?"

"I make pretty good pancakes. My dog loves me. Little kids like me. I'm solid and dependable. I almost have a job. I love unconditionally. I try never to do the wrong thing. I do get poison ivy every year, though. I'm a real mess for about two weeks until it clears up."

"A girl would be a fool to pass you up."

"Yeah. Yeah, that's my thinking, too. So do you want to go over to the Ritz or what? We could do a jig over there."

"You just uttered the magic word, Clay Mitchell. Race you to the door!" Annie grinned.

For a taste of another
delicious novel by
Fern Michaels,
turn the page . . .

CHAPTER ONE

Kristine Kelly propped her chin on her elbow to better observe her husband's slick, naked body. She felt a second burst of passion but knew she had to squelch it. Instead, she stared boldly at Logan's hard, wet body, aware that he was staring just as boldly at her. How was it, she wondered, that after twenty years of making love to the same man, she could feel exactly the same as she had felt on her wedding night? She was about to voice the question aloud when Logan said, "Was it as good for you as it was for me?" She squirmed closer, savoring the slickness of their two bodies meshed together. Was it her imagination or did Logan's words sound practiced, rehearsed, even flat? Where was the light teasing banter that was always present after one of their marathon lovemaking sessions? Why wasn't Logan lighting a cigarette the way he usually did? A cigarette they both puffed on. According to Logan, a cigarette was the ultimate conclusion to a satisfying session of lovemaking. She didn't know if she agreed or not. If the choice was hers, she would opt for serious pillow talk and a second round of lovemaking. The cigarette was always better the second time around. She waited.

"Well?"

"Of course," she said, offering up her standard response. "I feel like crying," she blurted.

"Are you going to cave in on me now, Kris? We've been over this a hundred times. You said you were okay with it. The kids said they were okay with it. Thirty days is not an eternity. You've been a model military wife, so don't go all wimpy on me now and screw it up. We've always gone by the book. It is not the end of the world. When you return to the States you will be so busy you won't have time to miss me. You need to register the kids for school, get the farmhouse ready, buy a car, get ready for the holidays. It's the way it is, Kris. What *is* your problem?"

Kristine picked up on the impatience in her husband's voice. So it wasn't her imagination after all. Logan was annoyed with her, and he wasn't bothering to hide his feelings. She felt the urge to cry again and didn't know why. No matter what she said or how she said it, her voice was going to be defensive-sounding. She struggled for a light tone. "I guess it has something to do with your long career coming to such an abrupt end. Twenty years is a long time, Logan. I think we handled it well. Like you said, we went by the book and never complained. We were a family of good little soldiers. I wish for your sake that you could have gone all the way and made general because I know it's what you wanted. I have to take issue with the medical board. Why does having just one kidney prevent you from getting promoted and staying in for thirty years? You never faltered, you did your job, you went by the book, and we all played by the rules. It's not fair. I know it's bothering you because it's bothering me. I don't like it when you pretend, Logan."

"I don't want to talk about it, Kris. It is what it is. I'll muster

out in two weeks and two weeks later you'll see me driving
up the road. Make sure you have a big, four-layer chocolate
cake and a very large pan of your lasagne waiting for me. Two
bottles of wine. Good stuff now. One for you and one for me.
After that, if we're still standing, we'll make love all night
long. How do you feel about that?''

"It sounds wonderful, Logan. I wish I could turn off my
emotions the way you can, but I can't. The truth is, I'm going
to miss you terribly because you're going to be half a world
away. Figure it out, Logan, how many miles is it from Leesburg,
Virginia, to Bremen, Germany?''

This time the impatience in her husband's voice was more
noticeable. "The mileage isn't important. I'll call and write.
I've never let you down, so where are these negative feelings
coming from? Are you telling me now that you aren't capable
of taking the kids back to the States and getting the house
ready? I've always admired the fact that you were your own
person. There isn't anything you can't do if you set your mind
to it. It's just thirty days! We've been separated before, and
you never acted like this. I need to know what it is, specifically,
that's bothering you.''

Kristine looked her husband in the eye. He was almost snarling now, and she hated it when he got like this. "It's the end
of a chapter for us. The end of our lives in the military. The
kids don't know anything else. Nor do I. I guess being a civilian
again scares me. I try not to think about it, but most times I
lose the battle. It's all going to be so *new*. The kids are scared,
too, even though they've been managing to bluff their way
through the days these past few weeks. Furthermore, I just
don't understand why we can't stay and go home together.
Why do we need to go first and you follow thirty days later?
We should be here with you when you walk out those doors
for the last time. I put in my twenty years, too, Logan.''

"Kris, we settled this months ago. Our belongings are en

route. Major Tattersol is ready to move in here the moment
we move out. You said you could handle this.'' Logan swung
his legs over the side of the bed and stomped to the bathroom.
''You do realize you just ruined what was supposed to be a
perfect evening, don't you?'' Logan shot over his shoulder
before he slammed the door shut. Kristine cringed when she
heard the lock snick into place.

Kristine buried her face in the pillow. *Damn, I can't do
anything right. Perfect evening, my foot. What is wrong with
saying how I feel? Doesn't he understand how much I love
him, how much I'm going to miss him? Thirty days could be
an eternity when one has to cope with three teenagers who
have a hate on for everything in the world, including their
parents. Shit!* She hadn't even mentioned their finances. Her
eyes filled. *I'm sick and tired of being a good little soldier. I
never wanted to be a soldier. All I ever wanted was to be a
good wife and a good mother.* She moved then to curl into the
fetal position, at the same time noticing the two rolls of extra
flesh that moved upward to press against her breasts. She yanked
at the sheet as she wiped at her tears with the hem of the
pillowcase. The evening was not going the way she had planned.
In four short hours she would be herding the children out the
door to a waiting car for the ride to the airport. She needed to
do something, but had no idea what it was.

Kristine squeezed her eyes shut as she ran the scene over in
her mind. The kids would be cranky, mouthy, and hateful
because they were leaving their friends, enduring the long plane
ride home, and taking up residence in a place they could barely
remember. The worst thing of all for the three of them was the
prospect of starting over in a new school. She'd spent whole
days trying to reassure her children things would be wonderful
if they would just open up to the move. Nothing had worked,
probably because they sensed her own anxieties and fears,
something a good soldier should never reveal.

Kristine jerked upright when the bathroom door opened. She stared at her husband, who was fully dressed. "Where . . . where are you going at this time of night, Logan?" she whispered. She hated the sound of fear in her voice.

"I'm going to take a walk. I need some fresh air. Look, Kris, I'm sorry. I guess I'm just as *antsy* as you are. Believe it or not, this whole thing is just as traumatic for me as it is for you."

"I love you," Kris whispered again.

"I know, Kris, I know. I won't be long. Why don't you try and get some sleep?"

"Is that what the book says, sleep? How can I sleep, Logan? Something is wrong here. I can sense it. It's not my imagination."

"Yes, Kris, it is your imagination. This separation is just a little rocky bump. We've had rocky bumps before. Thirty days is just thirty days. I expected more from you, Kris."

Kristine sighed. She was about to throw off the sheet and swing her legs over the side of the bed until she remembered the two rolls of fat. "Go for your walk. When you get back, I'll make some coffee."

Logan blew his wife a kiss before he left the house. Kristine's heart fluttered in her chest when she heard the front door close.

She headed for the shower, her shoulders shaking with unhappiness. Under the tepid spray she allowed her mind to conjure up the early days of her marriage to Logan Kelly. They were so happy when they said their vows and walked under the crossed swords at West Point. The twins came first, then Tyler came along shortly afterward. Logan had been delirious with joy just the way she had been. It was wonderful living all over the world. Her children spoke four languages, as she did, thanks to their multifaceted education. She was one of the rare wives who loved life in the military, but she didn't love the stupid rule book Logan insisted they live by. He could recite chapter and verse at the drop of a hat. She also knew the book by heart, which was all the more reason to hate it, and her children hated it even more than she did. Logan lived by it, page by page, word by word. Would he discard it when he got back to the States or would they continue to live by it? Logan's rationale would be that the book had served them well for twenty years and to tamper with it in the private sector would be sacrilegious.

As Kris stepped from the shower, towel in hand, her thoughts stayed with her. She wrapped her body in one of the few remaining towels, then dabbed at eyes that were now red-rimmed. Early on, Logan had sworn he would make general, go all the way, maybe even become a five-star. They'd played a game in those early years about the things they would do, how they would act when the fifth star was pinned on his shoulder. How sad for Logan that it could never come to pass. He had said he accepted being felled by a rare kidney disease in his seventeenth year in the military, knowing he would get passed over because his medical condition would be a blight on his record. He'd slapped her once, shouting to be left alone when she'd tried to console him. She needed to give him space now to come to terms with what Logan considered betrayal on the army's part in giving him a medical discharge, something he fought against and lost. He had a right to be bitter, but he didn't have the right to take his bitterness out on her. She'd wanted tonight to be perfect so that Logan would remember their last night and look forward to the time when they'd all be together again back in the States. Now it was all spoiled. Here she was taking a shower in the middle of the night while her husband was out walking alone. She crossed her fingers and offered up a little prayer that Logan's attitude wasn't a harbinger of things to come.

Thirty minutes later, Kristine was in the kitchen, fully dressed and making coffee. She looked in dismay at the small amount of coffee left in the can. Logan liked his coffee black and strong, the way most of his colleagues liked it. There was barely enough left to make two full cups, and at best it was going to be weak. She'd cleaned out everything from the ancient refrigerator because Logan was going to stay at the barracks until it was time for him to leave. The new tenants would move in the moment their belongings were unloaded from the truck. The army did not sit around sucking its thumb when it came to the comfort of one of its officers.

When the coffee finished perking, Kris poured a small amount into a cup, leaving the rest for her husband. She sipped at the coffee, her eyes on the blackness outside the kitchen window. She shouldn't be sitting here alone. Her husband should be with her, holding her hand, telling her things would be okay. The kids hadn't wanted to stay home with her either, preferring to spend their last night with their friends. She'd begged them to stay home with her and Logan, but the three of them had kicked up a fuss. In the end she'd given in rather than stare at their miserable faces all evening. She looked at the clock. Ten minutes past four. Tom Zepack would drive them. Logan would say his good-byes at the door because he had to report for duty at six o'clock. And she still didn't have the bankbooks from Virginia. Logan had said everything was in the glove compartment of the car.

Her coffee finished, Kris meandered out to the car parked at the side of the house. She withdrew the small packet with her name on it, carrying it back to the house. Relieved that she hadn't forgotten, she slipped the envelope into her purse. She wished she knew more about their finances, but Logan had always handled them. It would be nice, though, to know how much her husband's pension would be once they were home. She knew they would be more than comfortable, thanks to the check that came every month from her parents' estate. Logan was going to do some consulting work, and she'd given serious thought to starting up her parents' business again. She could breed the world-class dogs her parents had bred for decades prior to their deaths. She was actually excited about working at her own business. With the monthly check from her parents' estate, Logan's pension, and whatever she was able to bring in, the kids would be able to go to the best colleges in the country.

Life was going to be wonderful, she told herself, once they settled in and adjusted to farm life in Leesburg, Virginia. They could renew old friendships, join clubs, get involved in community affairs. When the twins went off to college next year, and Tyler the following year, they would have the house to themselves and a twenty-four-hour-a-day marriage, the way it had been before the kids came along. Yes, life would be good, very good, provided that Logan threw away the damn rule book. She poured another inch of coffee into her cup. It tasted like colored water. Logan would surely have something to say about it.

She heard her children before she saw them as they bounded into the house, snapping and snarling at one another. It was obvious to Kris they hadn't slept.

Tom Zepack held the door for Logan, a frown on his face. Even from this distance, Kris could smell liquor on her husband's breath. For some strange reason it elated her, proving, she thought, that this parting was just as hard on him as it was on her. She smiled. She would be upbeat if it killed her. No tears, no clutching, no sobbing. Maybe she should just pat him on the cheek and say something flippant like, "I'll see you when I see you. Let's go, kids." Could she do that? Never in a million years. She could try, though.

"Time to go!" Tom Zepack said.

"Do you have everything, Kris?" Logan asked.

"Yes. You know me. I was packed two weeks ago. We're ready."

The kids barreled out to the car, Tom Zepack on their trail.

Kristine sucked in her breath. "I made some coffee, Logan. It's on the weak side because there wasn't enough left. I guess I cut it too close. Rinse the pot and throw it away or leave it for the new officer and his wife. Remember to take the wet towels with you."

"Yeah, sure. Ah, listen, Kris, I'm sorry. I acted like a real ass earlier."

"It's okay, Logan. We're all upset. We all knew this day was coming. Even though we thought we were prepared, we weren't. I guess I better get going. Tom is such a slow, careful driver. I don't want to miss the plane. Take care of yourself. Call me so I can meet you at the airport when you have your flight information."

"Kris?"

"Yes."

"We had a good life, didn't we?"

"The best. We've been happy. We have three wonderful kids. This move is hard on them because they know it's the last one. As Macala said, from here on in everything *counts.*"

"You sound strange, Kris. You aren't going . . ."

"No, I'm not going to make a scene. Take care of yourself, and hopefully we'll all be together for Christmas. I know just where I'm going to put the tree, too. I do love you, Logan. I just want you to know I will always love you."

Logan nodded. "I feel the same way, Kris. Don't make this any harder than it is. Go on, Tom's waiting."

Go on, Tom's waiting. That was all she was going to get? "See you," she said in a choked voice.

"Bye, Dad," the kids shouted from the car.

"Bye," he shouted in return.

Kris climbed into the car, tears streaming down her cheeks. If nothing else, she had at least waited until her back was turned before she allowed the tears to flow. She looked out of the car window, expecting to see Logan outlined in the open doorway. The door was shut. She couldn't even wave good-bye.

"Relax, Mom, thirty days will go by just like this," Macala said, snapping her fingers.

"Thirty whole days without that damn book," Mike, her twin, said happily.

"I like the book. It's how things get done. Everyone needs structure in their life," sixteen-year-old Tyler said, slouching down in the corner of the car.

"That's a crock, and you know it," Mike said. "That stupid book stinks. You're just a suck-up. Get over it. The book is history."

"Hear! Hear!" his twin said.

Kris continued to cry.

Chaplain Tom Zepack stared at the road in front of him, wondering what lay in store for the Kelly family once they returned to the States. With God's help they would all survive and lead happy productive lives. He was almost sure of it.

"This is it! It looks . . . shabby, Mom. Do we *really* have to live here?"

Kristine took a deep breath. "It does look shabby, Cala, but you have to remember that no one has lived here for over twenty-two years. This dreary, rainy day isn't helping either. By this time next year your dad and I will have it all fixed up. Paint works wonders." It was hard to believe this strangled-sounding voice was coming from her own mouth.

"I don't think a bucket of paint is going to do it, Ma," Mike said. "Did that banker guy get someone to clean it up? Is there any furniture? Did our stuff get here? Are we going to be sleeping on beds that are full of dust? Jeez, why can't we stay in town. This place is in the middle of *nowhere*. Do we have a telephone?"

"Of course there's a telephone. Mr. Dunwoodie said everything was hooked up and turned on. It's going to be okay. We're always jittery when we move to a new place. It was a beautiful estate when I was little. It can be that way again."

"Ma, that was back in the Dark Ages. Look at it! Forget the way it looked *back then*. Are you seeing what we're seeing? Half the shutters are gone. The porch is sagging. Jeez, I bet it isn't safe; and take a gander at those steps—they're lopsided, too. It will cost a fortune to fix this baby up. Do you and Dad have a fortune?"

Did they? She had no clue. Logan had handled their finances from the day they got married.

"I think it's safe to say we have enough to get by. Repairs won't be done all at one time. We'll work on it. Now come on, let's exit this brand-new station wagon and open our front door. We're home. My old home, our home now. All those other places we lived were just buildings where your dad and I paid rent. This is home, like it or not."

"Add my name to the list of people who don't like it," Cala snapped. "God, I will never bring anyone here. That's assuming I meet some farmer who is interested in me, which is so laughable it's beyond belief."

"I second that," Mike said as he hefted his bags from the backseat to dump them on the ground.

"Did Dad know what this dump looked like when he decided to ship us here?" Tyler demanded.

Kristine dropped her overnight bag on the ground. "Listen to me. I'm only going to say this one more time. This is our new home. No, Tyler, your father hasn't seen this house in fifteen years. Time takes its toll on everything and everyone. We have no other options. The farm your father grew up on is probably in worse shape than this one. Instead of fighting me every step of the way, help me. The four of us can make a beginning. I know that if your father was standing here, none of you would have opened your mouth. Why are you taking this out on me? I'm trying to do the best I can.''

"What page is that on in your book?" Cala snarled.

"Page sixty-two, and watch your mouth, young lady. End of discussion. Now move your asses and get in the house.''

"Wow!" young Tyler said as he walked around the spacious rooms. "Was I ever here, Mom?"

"You were just a toddler when we came back here the last time. You were too little to remember. Cala and Mike spent the whole time sliding down the banister. It's a wonderful old house. All the beams and wainscoting are original, as are the wooden pegs they used for nails back in those days. The floors are solid oak. They could stand to be refinished at some point. The people Mr. Dunwoodie hired to clean everything up did a good job. It's more than livable.''

"It's freezing in here," Cala grumbled.

"Guess that means you kids have to go outside to the wood-shed and bring in some wood. Mr. Dunwoodie said he had two cords of cherry wood delivered. In the meantime I'll turn up the thermostat and hope it works. Take your gear upstairs, pick out a bedroom, and put on an extra sweater. This house was always drafty, and heat rises," Kristine said, pointing to the high ceilings. "I want to check out the kitchen to make sure the stove and water pump work.''

"Are you saying we have to *pump* water too?" There was such disgust on Mike's face, Kristine cringed.

"If you want water, that's exactly what you do," Kristine said, her patience wearing thin. She wondered what her children would say and do when they saw the archaic contraption that heated the water in the upstairs bathroom.

Kristine was priming the pump in the kitchen when she heard her daughter's screech. "One bathroom! There's only one bathroom up here! What am I supposed to do? There's no vanity either. What the hell is this . . . thing?"

Kristine knuckled her burning eyes. She would not cry. She absolutely would not cry. "You should be here, Logan. We should be doing this together. They wouldn't be acting this way if you were here," she muttered under her breath as a steady stream of rusty water shot from the pump spout. She continued to pump water because it was something to do. She didn't want to think about what Cala would say when she washed her hair for the first time in the hard well water. She wished she could lie down and go to sleep and not wake up until Logan walked through the door.

"It's sleeting out, Mom. The temperature is dropping," Tyler said, coming up behind her. "How much wood do you want us to bring in? I counted ten fireplaces in this house. Which ones do you want to light?"

"I guess you better light the ones in the bedrooms and the one here in the kitchen and the one in the living room. The heater doesn't seem to be working. The propane tank could be empty. I'll look into it tomorrow. I don't think we'll freeze. My mother had wonderful quilts and down comforters on all the beds. A lot of wood, Tyler. There's a wood carrier in the shed that holds a lot of wood. Off the top of my head I'd say you need four loads. Bring it to the kitchen door. If the three of you work at it, you should be able to drag it up the kitchen staircase. My father used to do it on his own, so I think you three robust children should be able to handle it. It's called, work, Tyler."

"There's no television set, Mom."

"So there isn't. I guess you'll just have to miss the tube for one day until our belongings get here tomorrow. Read a book."

"This is like one of those houses you see in horror movies," Mike said as he slammed through the kitchen door behind Tyler. "What do you mean there's no television set?"

Kristine clenched her teeth so hard she thought her jaw would crack when she opened the refrigerator. Eggs, a can of coffee, bread, butter, jam, bacon, juice, and milk. "This certainly takes the guesswork out of what to cook for dinner," she muttered. *Tomorrow things will be better,* she thought.

Since the preparation time for dinner would be ten minutes or so, Kristine gathered up her baggage to carry upstairs. She shivered as she walked through the old house, drafts swirling about her legs. She took a minute to marvel at the old furniture, antiques really, and the fact that everything was in such good condition. Her own comfortable, worn furniture wasn't going to fit in anywhere in this barn of a house. Still, she would have to spread it out for the children's sake and gradually get rid of it. There was a lot to be said for antiques.

Cala swept by her on her way down the stairs. "I can't believe you're making me carry in firewood. That's a man's job."

Kristine turned. "Cala?"

"Yeah."

"Don't say yeah. I need to know why the three of you are so . . . belligerent today. Why are you fighting me over every little thing? We belong in the United States. We're citizens of this country. This is where we belong. Daddy's tour is over, and this is what we decided to do. I grant you it's an adjustment, but if we all pull together, we can make it work. In September you and Mike will be going off to college, so what's the big deal. It's nine months out of your life."

"Daddy said it was your idea to come back here. He said since you never squawked about moving all over the world every couple of years, it was your turn now. Daddy didn't care. He would have been happy staying in Germany. We didn't want to come back here. You're the one who wanted this move."

"Of course I wanted it. Your father did, too. He was upset, Cala, about being passed over. He had no other choice. What kind of work would he have done over there? Nothing that paid any kind of money, that's for certain. I would never renounce my citizenship to live in a foreign country. There's too much unrest in Europe. I wanted us to be safe on our own soil.''

"Skip it, Mom. We're here, so what difference does it make. Don't think I'm joining one of those farmer 4-H clubs, either. I'm not going to have one thing in common with anyone around here. I know it, and so do Tyler and Mike. Right now Mike and I could go right into our second year of college. Tyler could be a freshman. Instead, we're going to be going to some rinky-dink high school where we have to take classes we took two years ago. It's not fair. There's no stimulation in doing something like that. You didn't think about that, did you?''

"No, I didn't. I will now, though. Perhaps something can be worked out. I've been away so long I don't know what the requirements or procedures are these days. Tomorrow when I take you to school I'll find out. In the meantime, will you cut me some slack and help your brothers.''

"Sure, Mom. When I finish doing that, do you want me to plow the south forty?'' Cala shot over her shoulder as she continued to stomp down the steps.

Kristine made her way to her old bedroom at the end of the long hallway. Her hand trembled as she turned the flowered white-ceramic knob. She found it amazing that everything was as she remembered it. The double four-poster was polished, as were the two oak dressers. Years ago there had been dresser scarves on them, along with all the junk young girls needed or thought they needed. The cushions on the old Boston rocker were faded but fluffed up by one of the cleaning crew who had gone through the house. The windows sparkled behind the Venetian blinds. She wondered what had happened to the Priscilla curtains her mother favored for the dormer windows. Rotted, she supposed. The seat cushion on the window seat matched the one on the old rocker. It, too, was faded but fluffed up. Old toys that were probably antiques by now marched across the white shelving that covered all four walls. How strange that her mother had kept things the way Kristine left them when she went off to college. She wondered if her mother ever came into this room when she was at school just to sit in the rocker and remember happy days when she was little. Reminiscing about past birthday parties, Christmases, and, of course, all those times when she was sick in bed with a cold.

Kristine sat down on the rocker, amazed that the dry old wood didn't squeak on the shiny hardwood floor. She'd had a big old tiger cat named Solomon back then who sat on the rocker or on the window seat to wait for her to come home from school. He'd died when she was in her second year of college. Logan had never understood why she had to rush home because a stupid cat died. That was probably the only time in her life when she'd stood up to Logan and told him she didn't give a good rat's ass if he understood or not. She'd done nothing but cry for a solid week. Her first experience with death. She was back at school less than two weeks when she was summoned home a second time. Nothing in the world could have prepared her for the deaths of her parents. According to Dunwoodie, her parents' banker and trusted advisor, the barn had caught fire and her parents had rushed in to save the dogs and been overcome with smoke.

She hadn't gone back to school that semester. Instead she'd sat in her rocker for months trying to figure out where her life was going. Logan had been so supportive during that awful time. It was Logan who put the dust covers on all the furniture, Logan who did all the things necessary to closing up a house, Logan who locked the door for the last time, and Logan who drove her away and held her hand when she looked back over her shoulder, tears streaming down her cheeks.

They'd come back to Virginia fifteen years ago when Logan's elderly father passed away. Even then she was barely able to open the door and walk through her old home. Logan held her hand that time, too, while she struggled with the key.

Kristine rubbed at the tears in her eyes. It was all so long ago. Another time, another life.

As she unpacked her bag, Kristine wondered if living here with her family would be as good as the life they had led in all the foreign countries they'd lived in.

Logan's picture was the first thing that came out of her bag. She set it on the night table next to a small onyx clock that no longer told time. It would be the first thing she saw when she opened her eyes in the morning and the last thing she saw before she closed her eyes at night. "I wish you were here, Logan," she whispered. "We should be here together." She was jolted to awareness when she heard a loud thump and squabbling coming from the hallway.

"Now look what you did. I'm not picking it up. You were supposed to hold up your end, Tyler. God, I hate it when you act like a *priss.*"

"Stuff it, Cala. I'm soaking wet, and I'm freezing. Mike should be on the bottom and I should be on the top with you."

"Guess what, you jerk, we're cold and wet, too. We still have three more loads to go, so get moving."

"Do it yourself. I'll make my own fire with my own wood. I'm sick and tired of getting dumped on by the two of you. I don't give a shit if you're twins or not. So there."

"That's enough," Kris shouted from the hallway. "The quicker you get those fires going, the sooner you'll be warm. You won't be able to take a hot bath because there's no propane."

"Are you saying there's no *shower?* I hate taking a bath because you just sit in your own dirty water. I hate this stinking place. I really hate it!" Cala said tearfully.

"That's exactly what I'm saying. Now, get moving, and

someone has to clean up all the splinters from the steps. I'll start dinner.''

''I'm not hungry,'' Mike muttered.

''Me either,'' Tyler grumbled.

''What could there possibly be to eat in this dump?'' Cala said, blowing her nose.

Kristine threw her hands in the air. ''Fine, don't eat. Starve. I've had it with the three of you.'' She stared at the phone that suddenly pealed to life. A phone call! She picked up the receiver to hear her husband's cheerful voice.

''Logan! Oh, Logan, it's so good to hear from you. Is everything okay?''

''More to the point, is everything okay with you?''

''No. The kids hate it. There's no heat. They're giving me such a hard time. I guess we're all just tired. The house is fine inside. It's clean and there's some food. Tomorrow I'll get the propane. It's sleeting out, and this house is drafty. At least the phone is working. I picked up our new station wagon.'' Kristine lowered her voice to a hushed whisper so the children wouldn't hear her. ''This is the right thing, isn't it, Logan. Moving here, I mean.''

''Kristine, what's going on?''

''It's the kids. They're mouthy, disrespectful, and they hate it. Maybe it's first-day jitters and tomorrow will be the first day of school in what they refer to as a rinky-dink farm school. Look. You didn't call me to hear me complain. Do you miss us?''

''Of course I miss you. That's why I called. Did the furniture get there?''

''Dunwoodie said it would arrive tomorrow afternoon. Do you think I should call a plumber to install a shower? No one likes to take a bath.''

''Sure. Make sure it's all done before I get there. I hate a messy bathroom." Logan chuckled. "Make sure you position my chair just right."

"Yes, sir, Colonel Kelly, sir."

"I'll say good-bye then. I'll try to call again next week. Take care of things, Kris. Love you, old girl. Let me talk to the kids now."

Kristine crooked her finger at her oldest son. "Your father wants to talk to you."

"Ah shit," she heard Mike mutter. Cala sat down on the top step, her eyes murderous. Tyler leaned against the wall, shivering.

Kristine stepped over the fallen logs on the steps as she made her way to the kitchen. Her shoulders straightened imperceptibly as she slid strips of bacon into an old cast-iron skillet. Suddenly she felt better than she had in weeks. Logan would straighten the kids out in two seconds. Her husband loved her, but then she'd known that. Still, it was nice to hear the words occasionally. Now if she could just get the kids back on track, maybe things would fall into place.

What seemed like a long time later she heard movement behind her. She turned to see her three bedraggled-looking children. She smiled. "Dinner's almost ready. Change your clothes. By the time you get down here the kitchen will be warm and toasty."

"We're sorry, Mom," the three of them said in unison.

They were just mouthing words. Their eyes said they weren't sorry at all. "Me too. Hurry now before you catch cold."

"I'm starved," Mike said.

"I could eat a horse," Tyler said.

"I'll settle for three eggs, four pieces of toast, and six slices of bacon," Cala said.

"Coming right up," Kristine said cheerfully as she struck a match to light the logs in the cavernous kitchen fireplace.

More by Best-selling Author
Fern Michaels

__About Face   0-8217-7020-9 $7.99US/$10.99CAN

__Kentucky Sunrise   0-8217-7462-X $7.99US/$10.99CAN

__Kentucky Rich   0-8217-7234-1 $7.99US/$10.99CAN

__Kentucky Heat   0-8217-7368-2 $7.99US/$10.99CAN

__Plain Jane   0-8217-6927-8 $7.99US/$10.99CAN

__Wish List   0-8217-7363-1 $7.50US/$10.50CAN

__Yesterday   0-8217-6785-2 $7.50US/$10.50CAN

__The Guest List   0-8217-6657-0 $7.50US/$10.50CAN

__Finders Keepers   0-8217-7364-X $7.50US/$10.50CAN

__Annie's Rainbow   0-8217-7366-6 $7.50US/$10.50CAN

__Dear Emily   0-8217-7316-X $7.50US/$10.50CAN

__Sara's Song   0-8217-7480-8 $7.50US/$10.50CAN

__Celebration   0-8217-7434-4 $7.50US/$10.50CAN

__Vegas Heat   0-8217-7207-4 $7.50US/$10.50CAN

__Vegas Rich   0-8217-7206-6 $7.50US/$10.50CAN

__Vegas Sunrise   0-8217-7208-2 $7.50US/$10.50CAN

__What You Wish For   0-8217-6828-X $7.99US/$10.99CAN

__Charming Lily   0-8217-7019-5 $7.99US/$10.99CAN

Available Wherever Books Are Sold!

Visit our website at **www.kensingtonbooks.com.**

Put a Little Romance in Your Life With
Joan Hohl

__Another Spring   0-8217-7155-8   **$6.99US/$8.99CAN**
Elizabeth is the perfect wife and mother. Until she is widowed. Jake takes
his pleasures where he likes—and to hell with tomorrow. Then he takes
Elizabeth to bed . . .

__Something Special   0-8217-6725-9   **$5.99US/$7.50CAN**
Nobody spins a love story like best-selling author Joan Hohl. Now, she
presents three stories, filled with the passion and unforgettable characters
that are her trademark . . .

__Compromises   0-8217-7154-X   **$6.99US/$8.99CAN**
Now that Frisco's father has jeopardized the family business, it is up to
her to prevent the takeover bid of Lucas MacCanna. But Lucas wants
more than the business, he wants Frisco.

__Ever After   0-8217-7203-1   **$6.99US/$8.99CAN**
Cyndi Swoyer never expected her prince to arrive . . . in a late-model
Buick! Now suddenly Bennett Ganster has driven into her small town to
make her an offer no woman could refuse.

__Never Say Never   0-8217-6379-2   **$5.99US/$7.99CAN**
When Samantha Denning's father died leaving a will stipulating that she
marry within five months or lose everything, she decides Morgan Wade
is the ideal candidate for groom. It was supposed to be business . . . until
Morgan made their marriage personal . . .

__Silver Thunder   0-=8217-7201-5   **$6.99US/$8.99CAN**
Jessica Randall managed her family's Wyoming ranch. She was a woman
who defied traditional roles . . . until a handsome cowboy rode into her
life. Duncan Frazer belonged to no one. But then he was Jessica . . . and
wanted her with all his heart and soul.

Discover the Thrill of
Romance With

Kat Martin

__Hot Rain
0-8217-6935-9 $6.99US/$8.99CAN

Allie Parker is in the wrong place—at the worst possible time . . . Her
only ally is mysterious Jake Dawson, who warns her that she must play
the role of his reluctant bedmate . . . if she wants to stay alive. Now, as
Alice places her trust—and herself—in the hands of a total stranger, she
wonders if this desperate gamble will be her last . . .

__The Secret
0-8217-6798-4 $6.99US/$8.99CAN

Kat Rollins moved to Montana looking to change her life, not find
another man like Chance McLain, with a sexy smile of empty heart.
Chance can't ignore the desire he feels for her—or the suspicion that
somebody wants her to leave Lost Peak . . .

__The Dream
0-8217-6568-X $6.99US/$8.50CAN

Genny Austin is convinced that her nightmares are visions of another
life she lived long ago. Jack Brennan is having nightmares, too, but his
are real. In the shadows of dreams lurks a terrible truth, and only by
unlocking the past will Genny be free to love at last. . .

__Silent Rose
0-8217-6281-8 $6.99US/$8.50CAN

When best-selling author Devon James checks into a bed-and-breakfast
in Connecticut, she only hopes to put the spark back into her
relationship with her fiancé. But what she experiences at the Stafford
Inn changes her life forever . . .

Available Wherever Books Are Sold!

Visit our website at **www.kensingtonbooks.com**.